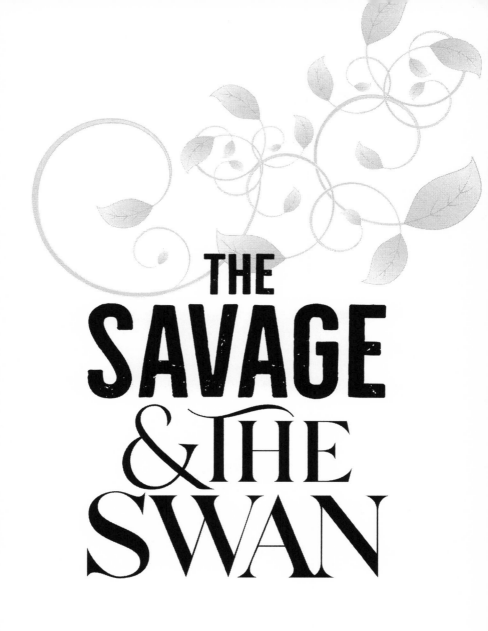

# THE
# SAVAGE
# &THE
# SWAN

# ELLA FIELDS

**Editor:** Jenny Sims, Editing4Indies
**Formatting:** Stacey Blake, Champagne Book Design
**Cover design:** Sarah Hansen, Okay Creations

For those who love with a ferocity that reinstalls
faith and burns through armor.

# ONE

**M**Y HAND FELL AWAY FROM THE DOOR I'D BEEN ABOUT TO open to bid my parents good night.

"The human prince?" my mother cried. "To hand her to him, *to them*, is not only a betrayal to our daughter but it is an insult to everything we've built while suffering their presence in these lands."

"You think me unaware of that?" my father boomed. Frozen, I waited, withering on the spot as his voice softened. "We have no other choice, Nikaya. It's this or await the map of the stars to unfold, and we both know what *he* will do to her, to any of us, should he be given the opportunity."

My mother gave no response, and I could picture her serene face mottled with concern, ruby cheeks twisting with her worrisome thoughts.

"They will take her, this I know, and although she might not care for the prince, nor he for her, she will be safe."

"Safe?" My mother half laughed. "They may fear us and do our bidding, but make no mistake, Althon, they mock us all the same," she seethed, her voice uncharacteristically cold. "They will be anything but pleasant to her."

Water welled in my eyes, my hand shaking as I lifted it to open the door. My father's next words stopped me. "Better for her to be uncomfortable than to be tortured or to meet her end before she can produce an heir like Joon. This grants protection and therefore time for Opal to ensure the Gracewood line continues."

I turned away at that and raced downstairs to the empty kitchens below, my nightgown fluttering behind me, catching the gathering wind as I exploded through the door and into the rear gardens. Uncollected fruit and leaves splattered and crunched, but I didn't stop.

The sky deepened with darkness as I forced my feet to carry me faster through the ankle-deep grass. As I tried to outrace my thundering heart.

The swish of the blades, the lavender fields, the stars overhead, and the spray of dirt beneath my bare feet were the only witnesses to my escape.

I ran for the shelter of the pitch-black woods—to the path through them I'd memorized by heart as a child long before the attacks and bloodshed began—and I didn't stop until I'd reached the mouth of the low-lying cave.

There, I crawled through, rising to my full height as the tunnel grew deeper while yawning slowly down toward the cliffside of the ravine. The dead tree, hollowed out and nearly as wide as the castle towers, blocked the exit. I walked through it, desperate to escape the damp dirt and feel the breeze and starlight upon my wet cheeks once more.

A branch, gnarled and blanketed in moss, tucked against the inner belly of the tree, awaited my soiled feet. Up they climbed until my head breached the hole, and I could grip the knots on either side of it to haul myself up to sit aside the opening.

For precious moments, I just breathed, the bark warm and rough against my legs, my feet dangling high over the water that trailed beneath the tree. It danced its way between the two lands, turning the numerous bends as it gradually headed out to sea.

The moon's reflection wrinkled and warped, the stars winking within the ripples and gurgling bubbles. This tree hadn't always been here, though it'd been here far longer than I had. Long ago, two gigantic bridges kept Nodoya and its mystical kingdoms of Sinshell and Vordane joined—its people united.

They said we were once a whole. Though something told me that wasn't precisely true, else there would never have been such a divide. A crack was all we needed to create a chasm. And a chasm would only grow and deepen over time.

Staring down into the ravine widened from war and hatred, the rotted remains of wood and stone from decimated ships and a long-ago bridge, I cursed and brushed my hand beneath my nose, willing my eyes to dry. I'd known since I was a youngling that I'd be forced to marry and likely before I was ready, but I had never dared to think it would turn out like this.

That most suitors would be dead—and the only one who remained was human.

It wasn't that I hated the idea of marrying a human. Quite the opposite. Prince Bron was handsome. He carried himself with an air of nonchalance that struggled to veil his arrogance. He was lean and tall with deep brown hair struck through with streaks of gold from his many days spent outdoors hunting and training in the sun. The few times I'd seen him, he was wearing a smile that never failed to make the heart stall a beat.

I'd spent countless hours afterward trying to capture the way that smile touched his dark eyes on my pad of parchment, never quite satisfied I'd gotten it right. He'd seldom even looked my way. Though when he had, his lips had lowered and flattened, eyes assessing.

To him, I was nothing but a faerie—just another creature who could not be hunted.

If history was anything to go by, many of us did stupid things out of fear, so I wouldn't allow myself to fall into wishful thinking. To believe that, should we wed, he would be happy about it.

And although I thought him handsome and charismatic, my mother was right. I would live in perpetual discomfort at best and in fear for my life or injury at worst.

"And here I'd thought I had this rotted-out corpse of a tree all to myself."

Startled, I scrambled back over the last remaining crossing that linked the lands of Nodoya and nearly fell, my nails scoring into the bark. Never, not once, had I encountered another soul in my hiding place.

The hooded figure slipped a broadsword inside a sheath at his back and crept closer along the rocky cliffside with alarming agility.

I should've moved. I should've demanded he go back the way he came. Though something whispered that either would be futile.

He was not of gold blood, nor was he human. His scent of smoke and cedar washed over me, into me, raising every tiny hair on my body. "You cannot be here."

"Says whom?" he asked with a tilt of his head that exposed pieces of white-blond hair. His voice was lemon and chocolate—decadent and bitter, rich and low.

"Says me," I declared, thankful my words did not shake.

"Ah." He then dropped with eye-widening speed and accuracy onto the fallen tree, the hole—my only exit—between us. "And who might you be?"

I was too stiff to be offended, every part of me locked and preparing to flee. "You know very well who I am."

Removing the hood of his cloak, he slowly lifted his eyes to mine. "We are a realm divided, Princess, so do not expect us all to recognize you." My heart raced, my mind skipping over avenues of escape. All the while, his dawn blue eyes tracked over my face. "I've no interest in hurting you."

I blinked. "You're crimson. I can scent it…" My eyes slid over his tunic and cloak, both a midnight black fringed with red. "As well as see it, so if you don't mind—"

"Why are your eyes wet?" Gazing at my cheeks, he murmured, "You've been crying, oh sunshiny one." I made to slip back inside the hole, but his next words halted me. "I wouldn't do that just yet if I were you."

He'd barely finished speaking when footsteps, howling hounds, and snarling shifters carried over the breeze, the water below. "You're on patrol."

"They'll move along soon."

Confusion twisted my features. He watched with an amused glint in his eyes.

"You're a guard," I said, eyeing the hilts of the two blades visible over his shoulders. "A warrior. Why not alert them to my presence?" Stupid words to say, but if he were going to hand me over to the blood king, the king of wolves, he'd have made his move by now.

"Call me curious," he said in a tone that sounded more bored than intrigued. "It has been a while since I've seen a gold one up close, a daughter of the sun, and royalty at that."

A collection of growls grew nearer, followed by laughter as his murderous friends called to one another.

The male next to me wasn't just any male. He was a crimson—blood Fae—which meant I couldn't trust a word he said. It was because of them that our people were now divided. Violent, bloodthirsty, and corrupt—mayhem was a song in their veins, and it'd made enemies of Nodoya's royal factions long before my two and twenty years.

One kingdom was life—creation and peace. The other death—power and violence.

We of the sun had fought and lost many battles against the crimson's invading armies these past several years, and though it had been relatively quiet for a couple of moons, I wasn't naïve enough to believe they wouldn't attack again.

No one was certain of what they hoped to gain besides death and destruction and—due to the demise of the blood Fae's previous king and queen—revenge. The decimation of the harbingers of light—my family and my people.

The ravine below made it harder for them to surprise us, but it never stopped them. Our ranks grew thin, and they knew we could no longer patrol and protect as we once did.

They'd been the ones to destroy the First and Old Bridge, but they continuously brought their own contraptions for those who couldn't make the leap or fly across.

A loaded minute passed with my breath growing hotter. Then another. The patrol began to move on.

"Shouldn't you be going with them?"

The guard shrugged. "They won't come looking for me if that's what you're worried about."

Many things currently worried me—his presence, so heavy the air seemed to slow into an oil that slathered my pebbled skin, being the biggest concern.

As if he could sense that, his plush lips curved slightly. "You didn't answer my question." Noting my frown, he said, "You were crying. Why?"

That last word was clipped, a command more than a question, and I would've balked at his audacity if I didn't know better. We were alone, and though I could hold my own to a certain degree, he was a trained killer wearing weapons.

The only weapon I carried laid inside me. For the most part, it was as useless as many of the gifts bestowed upon the light carriers. Healing, mending, growing, creation—we were but wisps compared to the dark's descendants. Their abilities were vast, and I knew only some. I'd only heard tales of their might.

Tales that made me wonder how we'd survived all this time and what in the stars had ever possessed my grandfather to go up against the late rulers of the blood kingdom—to war with Vordane.

The male stared down at the water, so very still. I wasn't sure why I answered, but the words left my mouth before I could think much of them. "I hear I am to marry."

If it were possible, the stranger seemed to still even more, his entire frame, large and imposing, shunning the starlight that attempted to reach his blond hair. Clearing his throat, he kept his attention fixed on the traveling water below. "That is what princesses do, do they not?" His tone was colder, frosted. "So it seems pointless to whine about it."

If I hadn't been offended before, I was now.

I released a rough laugh as I curled my legs up over the tree to leave. My feet hit the inside of the trunk when I heard him say, "Wait."

I didn't. I'd been a fool to even spend time in his company. Guard, foot soldier, beast warrior—whatever he might be—it didn't take away from the fact that he was the enemy, and I should consider myself lucky that I still breathed.

A yelp tore from me when he appeared before me. I stepped back, my heart galloping. "What...?"

"There's another hole," he said by way of explanation. Before I could look up to see where it was, he took my hand, calluses rubbing over my skin as he pulled me through the fallen tree's innards and back inside the cave.

"Release me," I snapped, tugging my hand free.

He didn't apologize for his poor decorum. He merely smirked as he turned to walk backward, half shielded in shadow. "The human prince, I presume?"

It took me a moment to realize what he meant, and I felt my stomach ice. "That's really none of your—"

"Makes sense," he murmured. "Your lot are growing that desperate." He stopped, and I almost walked right into him. "Tell me, sunshine, do you know how to fight?"

Incredulous, I gaped at the overconfidence of this male. "Sunshine?"

His smile tilted higher into one cheek, revealing a dimple and darkening his commanding eyes. "Answer the question."

"Answer mine."

"That wasn't a question."

I half rolled my eyes. "I believe it was, and you know it was."

He blew out a petulant sigh. "Are you always this difficult? And stupid?" My eyes widened, but before I could retaliate, he raised a large hand, waving flippantly at me. "Did you not hear me say daughter of the sun?"

My cheeks flushed, the burn creeping down my neck. I was grateful he couldn't see.

His rough chuckle said otherwise, but I was too distracted by the sound to care. It slid over my skin to seep inside it, slipping underneath to warm my blood. Tearing myself away from the feeling, I lifted my shoulders and chin. "I'm sure you're aware that you're insulting royalty."

"Insulting?" he purred, unsheathing a sword from his back in one swift movement. "Why, you're lucky that's all I'm doing, *Princess.*" He hissed the title, his blade absorbing the precious little light from behind us.

Fear clouded, weighing every limb as I stepped back. "You wouldn't dare."

Pursing his lips, the crimson looked from his blade, which hung limp at his side, to me. I didn't let that fool me into thinking he couldn't strike before I could protest.

I was as hard to kill as he was, but all he needed to do was slide that sword into my skull. If it contained iron, then my heart, or he could carve the organ from my chest and reduce it to dust.

None of it sounded very appealing to me.

"If you hadn't so rudely interrupted me, then you'd know I do not intend to kill you..." The way he made those soft words linger suggested he would not harm me right now. "Insults, sunshiny one, are going to be the least of your concerns if you are indeed to marry the human prince."

He spoke true, so I said nothing, trying to gauge if I could move past him and somehow outrun him. I was royalty, and though my powers were not as great as those who hailed from Vordane, I was faster than most—especially a lowly guard who'd taken it upon himself to go rogue for the evening.

As though he could guess at my thoughts, his eyes flashed. A dare. A male who wanted to chase. Since some of the blood Fae and all of those in the king's military were shifters, that did not surprise me. Though I'd heard enough horrific tales of what his ilk did to females they chased down to reconsider.

*Careful,* a whispering voice seemed to croon. *Careful now.*

He tossed his sword to his other hand, eyes never leaving me. "Where's your weapon?"

"I'll have you know—"

He raised a brow.

I bristled, loathing to admit, "I... I don't carry one."

Thick golden brows furrowed. "You truly wish for me to believe you'd leave the safety of your nest to tempt the shadows beyond without being prepared?"

I swallowed, unable to look at him, and shifted on my bare feet.

He drank me in then. I could feel it, his cool gaze chilling my blood as he no doubt studied my soiled gown and feet, and pieced the puzzle together. "You fled in a rush."

"I did."

"Fool," he spat as though I were a child in need of scolding.

I had no idea who this mongrel was, but he'd lingered long enough for me to detect and confirm the scent of a wolf. I was about to call him as such when he threw his sword at me. "But you do know how to fight, don't you, sunshine?"

I caught it, the leather pommel warm from his touch. "Of course, I do."

He unsheathed his other sword, this one shorter. His gaze cooled a fraction, lips lifting once more. "For your miserable life?"

"You're disgustingly rude."

"But am I wrong?"

I scowled. "My life is not..." I stopped and drew in a lungful of breath, not wanting to go there. My life was anything but miserable, but I wasn't about to admit to him that it wasn't anywhere close to what I'd hoped it would one day be. That would be selfish given the many people, villages, and towns we'd lost. Though I hadn't created a dream firm enough to seek even before the attacks had begun, I had hoped for something. Something more. "Yes."

His sword twirled in the air before he caught it with a flourish that ended with his booted feet braced apart. "Show me."

"I do not need to show you anything—" Air sliced from my throat as his blade lunged for my hand, and I dived out of the way, tripping over the long skirt of my nightgown. Wincing, I blinked up at the dirt, rock, and tree-root-packed ceiling of the cave. "I'll have your head—*argh*," I screamed and rolled, strands of my long golden hair embedded in the dirt beneath the stranger's sword.

Breathing hard, I gaped at its owner, who glared down at me with his arms crossed. "I see. You wish to die."

"I do not," I spat, hurrying to my feet.

Stepping forward, he drew uncomfortably close, close enough for me to see tiny flecks of black within his deep blue eyes and the vast length of his golden lashes that framed them. "They will have their way with you. Mark my words, Princess, and then you will be discarded." Every word was pushed from between perfect white teeth, the canines on either side sharper than any I'd seen before, and my neck cricked back farther as he loomed over me. "Treaty or no, the human kingdom tolerates our lot at best, and would rather see you burn than married to their precious bratty prince."

Lifting the hacked strands of my hair, he watched them regrow in his palm, but I didn't remove my eyes from him. From the rigid, harsh cut of his square jaw peppered with days' old stubble. His nose, strong and straight, twitched as his nostrils flared and he stepped back.

As if I could finally breathe again, I swallowed gulping lungfuls of damp, earthen air.

I'd never been that close to a blood Fae before—I'd never even spent time in the same proximity as one. The closest I'd come was hearing their bellowing howls and cries from our dungeon if they'd been captured spying or sneaking too close to the castle.

Even before the attacks had begun, there had been nothing but silence since the first war. Nothing but a deep, brewing tension for years and years as the two lands became separated by more than growing water.

And so I'd never known, hadn't even heard that being as close as this stranger and I had just been, could extinguish breath and rational thought.

"He'll take you," he murmured now. "Of that, I am sure, but for what purpose? He'll never mate with you, never be allowed to keep you, so"—he turned—"I guess we wait and see."

Flustered and shaken, I ignored the warning lurking beneath his last words. "I need to go," I said, trembling as I spied the sword I'd dropped. "They'll soon come looking for me."

"Do you always do as you're told?" A caressing taunt but he didn't stop at one. "Do you always coast along the waves of this rotten life, hoping for better instead of taking action?"

Rage unfurled from somewhere deep inside me, unexpected but not alarming enough to halt my tongue. "Stop it. You have no idea what you're even saying."

"Oh, but I do," he said, brushing his thumb beneath his plump lower lip. "And I fight with everything I am, everything I am not, for all that I am." His gaze grew lupine, both bright and dark, as it slid over me. "Are you a tool or a weapon, sunshine?" My mouth dried, and he barked, "Become a weapon no one can wield. *Pick up the sword.*"

Tears welled but not from fear. No, they came from someplace I'd rather not visit, but thankfully, I did not have to. I allowed it enough freedom to bend down and rip at my nightgown, the material now sitting just above my knees as I rose with the sword.

The crimson guard didn't look at my legs. He didn't take his attention from my face as I braced my feet apart, inhaled deeply through my nose, and nodded.

I danced around his first strike, and when he turned, our swords met with a resounding clash, my shoulder barking from his strength.

Sweeping back, I advanced when he did and ducked beneath his arm. He laughed and then struck with so much force, I had to jump, and our blades met in the air, the downswing of mine saving my hand.

"Better," he said, standing back.

I swiped sweat from my brow, knowing he'd been holding back—not knowing why but appreciating it all the same.

In circles and leaps, we parried, blood trickling from my arm and leg. The cuts weren't deep, I could tell, but they were enough to fuel the fire this stranger had stoked to life.

And with noises leaving me that I hadn't known myself capable of, I lunged over and over.

He met me blow for blow, and I knew I would never best him, but I didn't care. It wasn't about that, and I refused to let it stop me from trying and failing and trying again.

"The moon leaves," he said when we separated once more, his face free of perspiration while mine dripped. "And so must you."

In clumps and heaves, my breath left me, lifting and lowering my chest, and finally, the crimson dared a glimpse at my body. His lips slackened, and he seemed to shake himself free of whatever thoughts had taken his mind.

He turned and headed back inside the hollowed tree.

"Your sword," I called out.

"Keep it," he returned without looking back. "We will meet again." And then he was nothing but shadow eaten by darkness.

I was halfway home, the sun smearing the dark mountains beyond the castle in the distance, when I realized I hadn't gotten his name.

# TWO

"**O**PAL," MY MOTHER CALLED UP THE STAIRS OF MY TOWER the following morning. "Stars above, what is wrong with you?" she asked, opening the door to my chambers. "It's almost noon."

Groaning, I gathered the blankets higher over my body, certain the cuts and nicks I'd garnered overnight had healed but not wanting to risk her seeing in case they hadn't. "I had trouble sleeping."

Not a lie. When I'd gotten home after I'd hidden the crimson guard's sword beneath an old carriage wheel in the fields beyond the castle grounds, I'd stared at the whorl bedecked ceiling in a trance, half wondering if I'd dreamed of meeting him.

Until I remembered what I'd overheard beforehand and the reason I'd fled to my rarely visited safe place of solitude. I wasn't sure of much these days, but I was sure it was no longer safe, and that I would likely return regardless.

Mother pulled the thick lace drapes apart, the breeze sailing in to bid us hello. She smiled, always pleased by this, but that smile fell when she laid eyes on me. "You're filthy."

*Shit.* Perhaps that guard was right, and I was nothing but stupid. For I hadn't even thought to check my reflection in the mirror above my dressing table before falling into bed. "I forgot to bathe yester-day," I murmured.

After staring at me for moments I feared would unthread the truth, Sinshell's queen tutted, muttering to herself as she sang out the door for Linka to come draw me a bath. Returning, her features, though only finely lined considering she was nearing two hundred years of age, creased deeply. "Hurry. Your father and I await you for lunch."

My stomach hollowed. Both fear and hunger. "I need to tend to the south gardens."

"You need to do no such thing," she scolded with warmth. "Make haste, the food wastes."

I refrained from rolling my eyes at her overused words and threw off the bedding when she'd left.

Linka arrived as I was undressing, a pixie who held mild elemental abilities, and got straight to work on filling the deep tub in the adjoining chamber. A gasp pulled my spine taut, and I turned before the dressing table to find her fingers, so pale they were a soft pink, flutter to her mouth. "Opal, what in the stars happened to you?"

Shifting slightly, I spied what she saw in the mirror above the perfume I'd crafted and bottled myself, various combs, my tiara, rouge, the half-read books, and inwardly cringed. "Oh." I thought quickly, hoping it was enough. "I had a late training session yesterday."

"Your father is not usually so..." Linka tried and failed to find the right words, and she was right.

"He was in a mood, I guess," I mumbled, then sped past her into the bathing room.

Caramel and vanilla wafted from the warm depths of the tub, and I climbed in. Feeling stiffer than I'd thought I'd be, I was thankful for the salted ginger Linka had tossed in to aid in faster healing.

"I thought your father was busy meeting with his generals yesterday afternoon."

*Stars shun me.* I knew that lilt to her deep voice, the spark in her vivid cerulean eyes. She'd sniffed out my lie, something I too often forgot pixies were adept at doing, and now she wouldn't quit.

I could trust her. We'd known one another since I was a young-ling of seven years and she was growing into her womanhood and entering service to the Gracewood castle. But if it came down to it, I was painfully aware that trust would only extend so far if she feared I was in danger.

"I ran into a soldier in the fields beyond the castle," I murmured, tugging the washcloth from her outstretched hand and dunking it into the water.

"Your fallen tree, you mean. The remaining crossover." Her brow was raised when I looked up, annoyed I'd told her of the crossover in my excitement after finding it some years ago in my youth. "Now is not the time for riddles, Opal. You've bruises on your hips and el-bows, scratches that have yet to heal, too."

I hadn't realized the crimson male's sword had hit me so hard and frowned into the cloth as I scrubbed my face. *Not his sword*, I re-membered, but the times I'd fallen while dodging it.

"Fine," I huffed, scrubbing my arms. "I expressed my concern over not having enough practice of late, and he decided to humor me."

"Who is this soldier? Elhn?" She meant my father's favored cap-tain, who'd often trained me when he was unavailable while growing through my maturing years. It just so happened that Father was too often unavailable.

That was until I'd had a slight tantrum one afternoon and had al-most done something unforgivable. Elhn had thought me unwell, but Father had known otherwise. And nowadays, he said my skills were enough that I could wait until he was free.

The crimson wolf would most certainly disagree.

I might not know as much as I wished I did, but I did know one thing. Father had agreed to train me himself because he'd do what-ever it took to keep my secrets hidden. It would do no good for word of my gifts to spread, evoke fear, and place a target upon my back, nor would they help save this dying realm.

"No," I said in a tone curt enough to suggest I would say no more.

Sighing, Linka mercifully let it go, her next words carrying a different type of wariness. "Look, I'm not sure if you've heard, but I don't want you blindsided…"

"I know," I said, dunking the cloth. "About Prince Bron."

Linka quit fussing with the shelves behind me that housed oils, salts, combs, and cloths, coming away with a large one of the latter for me to dry myself with. "You know they wish to see you two marry."

"I overheard them discussing it, yes," I said and finished cleaning myself.

Silence trickled with the water as I wrung the cloth and hung it over the rim of the tub before stepping out. Linka wrapped me, tucking the edges of the cloth under my arm as she met my eyes, hers reaching my chin. "I think I now understand why you trained when you've no need to."

Indeed, it had been some winters since I'd last taken up a sword with my father. He could say he had more pressing matters to tend to with Vordane's forces stealing into our kingdom in small groups to assassinate nobility and high-ranking officials, and the continuous ambushes upon the Royal Cove. Though the latter dwelled in Errin, the human kingdom, we all needed use of it for trade due to the narrow entrances and cliffs surrounding the rest of the northeastern lands of Nodoya.

A weakness of which the blood king was aware.

"A game," my father had concluded a few months ago in a meeting with his war council. "He plays with us. We are the mice, and he is the feral cat, weakening us while he readies himself for a killing blow."

I'd listened outside the doors, my heart in my throat and the roses I'd plucked from the gardens to melt and bottle crushed in my trembling hand.

Helpless. As their sole heir, my brother dying before I was born alongside my grandparents in the battle of falling bridges, I wasn't locked away, but I was given little freedom to help in this seemingly endless war.

And that guard last night, the enemy who could and perhaps should have slaughtered me, had given me a stale reminder of that.

I could be a weapon. I could help. Instead, they wished for me to be a tool.

"It's for your own protection," my father ground out from the head of the table as he chewed his venison, his fingers curling into a fist over the giant slab of wood. "Not only that but you will carry on our bloodline. With their protection, you can make haste in ensuring that happens. Send the babe across the seas to the other realms, I care not. But mark my words, Opal." His voice lowered. "He will come for us, and it's time we're more proactive instead of denying this fact. It is clear now that we cannot defeat him. No one can. When he says it's our time…" He spread his hands, not bothering to finish a sentence that didn't need completing.

The crimson guard had said the same.

*Mark my words.*

A babe. Across the sea. Every emotionless word out of his mouth pushed my panic higher, my fork nearly bending in my hand. "I cannot mate with a human."

"Of course, you won't," my mother said from beside me. "Should they agree to the betrothal, Elhn will accompany you to Castle Errin as your personal guard. He will see to that duty himself."

*Duty.*

Dizziness swamped me. It didn't matter that I didn't want this or that I wasn't ready for any of it. I couldn't so much as fathom a time when I would be. They knew that. My parents were well aware of the fact that I was younger than many of our kind would deem appropriate to create another life.

But that was my role, *my duty*, and I carried no delusions. My existence, my father's detachment, my mother's stern worry, my inability to create a life outside of this castle—my purpose was clear to everyone. Most of all me.

I was loved, and I knew that, but I was alone. A princess but a replacement for a much-loved prince. A way to carry our family name forward into an uncertain future. Nothing more.

A tool.

I didn't dare look over at Elhn, who I knew was standing in the doorway, hands behind his back, heavy gaze upon me. Older than my mother by at least a decade, he was handsome if not a bit cold, but he was also mated. To ask this of him… "And what if they don't agree?"

My mother gave my father a look that said she'd asked that very same question. "They will," my father said, then nothing else as he finished his wine.

The dark unspooled slowly as though time did not wish for me to leave the safety of our moonstone fortress and race through the kitchens and fields in search of the hidden sword.

Regardless, two nights later, I waited until the occupants of the castle were slumbering, and that was exactly what I did.

He was already there, and I wasn't sure why I was both relieved and jittery at seeing his shadowed form seated upon the last link between our lands.

His voice was crisp and toneless as though saying something at all annoyed him. "I came last eve, but you never did."

My palm nearly slipped as I hauled myself through the hole to take a seat on the other side of it, just as we'd done the other night. "Doesn't your king need you?" The question might have been more dry than I'd intended, but surely, he had to know what a monster his ruler was if he hadn't yet sought to take me to him or harm me.

Acknowledging that perhaps not all crimson creatures were heartless killers who wanted us dead wasn't something I was comfortable with doing just yet, but I'd often wondered if that were indeed the case.

If perhaps there were some—just enough to turn the tide of this war.

The guard said nothing. When I settled over the moss-blanketed wood, my furred boots dangling mere feet from his own, which were pointed, knee-high, and black leather, I looked over to find him grinning down at a small dagger in his hands. "He is likely too busy with one of his many lovers to care about my whereabouts." Plunging the dagger into the tree, tearing a hole in the skirt of my nightgown, he said, "I trust you can use one?"

"I can," I said, though I hadn't as much training with one as I'd had with a sword. Staring down at the dark hilt, etched and crusted with worn rubies, I shook my head. "Why did you come back?"

"Honest answer?"

"Always," I said, tired of being kept in the dark until it was too late.

"You intrigue me, sunshine. Just a little." He made to rise and jump down through the hole but paused and lowered when I looked behind him to the muddy wall of the cliff. "What is it?"

"How'd you get here?"

"A secret," he said, and I knew he was smiling by the darker cadence of his voice before I allowed myself to look at him. "Tell me yours, and I'll tell you mine."

Unsure why when I was only staring into his glittering blue eyes, I felt my cheeks heat. "Keep that secret, but tell me your name."

His head tilted, the action entirely too lupine, and purred, "We're nowhere near getting to know one another in that sense." Jumping down through the hole, he continued, knowing I'd hear. "Fear not, I'll let you know when it's almost time so you can shout it to the stars."

My cheeks burned hotter, and I was thankful he could not see. "Shameless," I muttered, plucking the dagger free and following him down through the tree and into the cave.

His eyes widened when I stripped out of my nightgown and tossed it to the dirt near the entrance of the tree. I held my lips between my teeth, glancing down at my leather training pants and long thermal. "I thought it best to wear more appropriate clothing."

The crimson male blinked, clearing his throat as he turned away and muttered something under his breath I didn't catch over the sound of another dagger being unsheathed from his boot. "You returned my sword."

"Of course." I twisted the dagger in my hand, studying the fine art in the leather hilt that wound between the rubies. Vines, maybe, or they'd once been before aging beneath his iron-clad grip from overuse...

The dagger fell to the dirt.

The crimson watched me with raised brows. "Butter on your fingers, Princess?"

"H-how many of my people have you killed with... with *that?*"

The words were too soft for such ugliness. "More than you can dream. Now pick it up."

I didn't, couldn't. I stared at it, remembering the screams I'd heard from miles away, the vicious roars, the pounding of horse hooves carrying my father and his soldiers to their aid, but too late.

Too late, the village decimated, flames giving ash to the night sky...

"Opal," the enemy barked, snapping me from my trance. He was before me, so close yet I hadn't seen him move. I'd been too lost to the nightmare, just one of many that he and his people had given to us. "Pick up your weapon."

I had to leave. Clarity swept in far too late. I had no reason to linger in this place that once belonged only to me with this intruder. With an enemy who wouldn't hesitate to capture or kill me if ordered to.

*Shit.* Of course. That could be exactly what he was waiting for... an opportune time to catch me unawares and maybe even steal me for his king to use as bait against my parents.

"Opal," the crimson said when I walked around him, heading for the small mouth of the cave that'd brought me to him.

This odd male was wrong. I wasn't just stupid. I was an idiot starbent on ignoring the obvious—we were all headed straight for certain doom. My father had been right to make his plans, as ludicrous and unfair as they seemed. With our people being plucked off, village by village, city by city, and our land butchered beneath their dying bodies, it was no longer a matter of *if* the king would come for us but *when.*

About to break into a run, I nearly tripped over a boulder when he said, "Fang."

Stilling, I slowly turned back to find him standing there, cloaked in night in the center of the passageway, tucked away from the moonlight's reach.

"My name. They call me Fang."

A peace offering.

A plea to stay. I should have ignored it, but I knew even without knowing anything of this Fang at all that such a seemingly normal thing was rare for him.

"Fang," I repeated, tasting it, unsure what to make of it. "You…" My stomach heaved, the chicken dumpling stew we'd eaten for dinner roiling and rising as I drifted back toward him. My voice rasped, choking on the question. "You've murdered us, Fang, and for what?"

"Because we can," he said as simply as the rising of the sun and retrieved the blade he'd handed me. Waiting until I'd drawn closer, until I'd entered the wider opening we'd found this strange truce in, he took my hand and pulled me to him. His scent followed as he pressed the hilt into my palm, his fingers cool against mine but nowhere near as cold as his gaze. "And we won't stop, we won't falter, we won't tire. So fucking stab me."

It was as if he'd known precisely what to say to make that bone-deep fear morph into a blistering rage.

I struck, almost falling flat on my face as he lunged to the side, laughing. "Hone that anger, make it yours, not mine." He lurched forward, and I gasped, my blade taking the sudden impact of his right before my chest. Breathing through his nostrils, he grinned, then turned us. His front at my back, strong arms caged me, threatening and warm at the same time. "Reel it in, sunshine," he said, throaty and low as I struggled to no avail. "That fiery rage is a mighty powerful weapon, but only if you reel it in, use it, and do not allow it the chance to use you."

My breathing steadied all the while my heart skipped too many beats. That scent, cedar and smoke, clouded my mind.

The hand swallowing mine, calloused and huge, readjusted my

grip on the dagger. "Close combat," he murmured as if wanting to explain why his body had molded to my back, "on the ground, cornered, unwanted confrontation, whatever it may be, you cannot hesitate." His breath washed over my ear and cheek, stirring the fine hairs from my braid. "You stab instantly." Spinning me, he drew my hand toward my chest, dangerously close to my breast, and pushed toward my armpit. "If they're armored, find the gaps and use them."

Nodding, I followed his movements when his hand fell away, and then we started again.

With each lunge, every thrust, and the dance of my feet, Prince Bron, my father's plans, the distant howls and the trill of night birds, the fact that my enemy was teaching me how to survive people just like him—all of it flowed to the dark edges of my mind. There was only this strange male named Fang, his grunted half-laughs, the odd curse, the sharp agility that constantly caught me off guard, the harsh tempo of my heartbeat, and the sweat that misted my entire body.

When the baying of creatures, wolves and otherwise, across the ravine only grew in volume, I faltered, narrowly dodging his blade as it skimmed the arm of my thermal, wool fluttering to the dirt.

With a smirk curving into his cheek, feverish eyes a wild blue, and his blond hair standing in every direction, Fang swept into a deep bow, then took his leave.

He didn't say goodbye. He left with the moon and never looked back.

Dawn gathered light and bathed the dark with smoky gold.

Fires raged in the east across the river, destroying one of the last northern towns before the woods that bordered the cliffs.

On horseback and on foot, the survivors, few as they were, arrived with their meager belongings and children in tow. Saddlebags and baskets swayed over the ash-dusted beasts, plumes of heavy breath blowing before them in great huffs.

Faces, blackened with soot, shining with sweat and tears, stared blankly at me as they passed, herded behind the city walls.

I wasn't permitted to head to where many would need my help. *There are others*, Mother would say, *enough that you do not need to endanger yourself.*

Helpless, all I could do was stand there and await the worst of the injured to arrive. Then I could be of assistance. Then I could feel useful. Then some of this sorrow that carved away at flesh and bone would find another outlet—another purpose.

Once they'd all been shown to the city hall, where they'd stay with other families who had yet to find new housing or leave the city in search of wide-open forests, farms, and fields, I stared at the morning sky as the rising sun gathered what remained of their burning homes and swallowed it within its golden fist.

I gathered more feverfew and golden root in the fields beyond the castle, the sun now a sinking ember behind the looming pines that guarded the darkening woods.

Many people had arrived and then perished, and many were healing but forever scarred.

Setting my wares inside the basket, I lowered to the wildflower-strewn earth, gazing toward those woods with a question I'd asked myself but wouldn't dare say aloud. Not for fear of reprimand but for fear of the answer.

Without even asking, I knew nothing would make him stop. The blood king and his vengeance-sworn armies would pillage and plunder, and it seemed they wouldn't tire until every last creature of Sinshell was dead.

What it must be like to live with a hatred so deep, so untouchable, so incurable... I didn't want to know.

I would never pity him, of that I was sure. Not when wagons were still ambling over the horizon outside the city, carting the dead to their final resting places by the cliffs.

Staring over my shoulder, I watched them in the distance. The castle at their backs seemed to watch on, its luminous stone dull with dismay.

When I looked back to the forest before me, I found a pair of staring eyes.

The fawn wobbled as it dared to breach the canopy of greenery, large eyes blinking, absorbing, and finally settling upon my face. With an excited waggle of its backside, it bounded over the grass and promptly fell on its fresh legs.

A watery laugh shocked me, and sniffling, I rose to my feet, heading over to help her rise.

Before I could reach the bumbling babe, an arrow whizzed by, and the deer slumped into the grass.

Whirling, I glared at Deandra. "She was just a baby."

The soldier loped past me, the thick dark braids that kept her hair from her face bouncing against crusted armor. Bending, she retrieved her arrow. Blood still covered her brown cheeks and forehead from the battle across the river. If you could call it a battle. Few of the blood king's regiment had remained when our soldiers arrived, their task in terror and murder already achieved.

Deandra shot me a grin. "A delicacy, Princess."

Horror gripped me so swift, I had to look away when she tossed the deer around her plated shoulders.

She laughed. "We ought to get you involved in the real action and create a hardened barrier for that soft heart of yours."

I had no words for that. There was only that nagging guilt, and it clamored and clawed with the reminder that I wasn't doing enough. None of us would ever be able to do enough. "What are you doing out here?"

Deandra waded back through the thick grass, and I collected my basket, following as she said, "I was told to find you. We have a guest."

# THREE

**T**HE PRINCE HAD ARRIVED ON HIS OWN.

His parents, Prince Bron had said, were not well pleased by the idea of a marriage between our two kingdoms, but upon receiving my father's letter, he'd found himself curious.

Curious enough to have a large chunk of his army escort him here before having them disperse throughout our city and the fields and woods beyond, it would seem.

Rattled by nerves but resolved after the day's bloodshed to do whatever necessary, I'd hidden in the antechamber of the great hall to listen to their stilted greetings and small talk until my mother sang my name, summoning me.

I'd expected disdain, disinterest at the very least. I hadn't expected the prince to have grown more handsome than the last time I'd seen him three years ago. His rich brown hair curled around his hairline, whispered over a sharp chin, his eyes aglow beneath thick brows.

Full lips parted, those soil-dark eyes flicking over me once, then again with a slowness that seemed deliberate. He inclined his head. "Princess, how lovely you have grown."

I'd matured years ago, but I didn't bother reminding him of that. He'd been too busy tending to his female companions to notice a faerie princess within his midst.

Now, walking alongside him in the gardens, listening to him regale me with tales of their tense journey here and the delightful bakers in Tulane who'd offered him the most scrumptious scones he'd ever tasted, I half wondered if he was even aware that we'd met before.

"You'd best not eat them in future." I finally formed words, though they were quiet. "Or anything else from strangers in Sinshell."

His feet, clad in gleaming brown boots that matched his eyes, slowed as we rounded the fourth circle of greenery and color. The shrubbery climbed higher here, the castle courtyard at our backs and only the rooms in the towers visible.

"I'd thought food spells and faerie poisons to be nothing but grotesque bedtime stories."

I contained a snort of laughter. "There is nothing grotesque about it," I said, stopping before a cluster of roses and brushing my fingers over a small bud. "Your scones back in Errin will now taste of soot is all."

"Right," he clipped. "And what of other meals?" He shifted, the warmth of him nearing my arm. "Surely, I can eat something without worry of it ruining me for all else."

The way he'd said those words, uttered the last few with a lower, deeper cadence, drew my eyes his way. "We will likely feed you a meal you cannot find in your kingdom."

"Indeed," Bron rumbled in a way that pulled at my brows. His gaze drifted from my face to my hand, my fingers cupping and encouraging the unfurling rose. His lips parted, then closed as he swallowed. "God, you truly are a faerie princess."

I raised a brow, making to leave when he grasped my hand. His touch was gentle and warm as he pulled me close. He was tall for a human, but Fae, especially nobility, were taller than most any humans, so our noses were nearly perfectly aligned when his fingers rose, awaiting my permission.

Curious, I lifted my lips into an agreeing smile. They broke open with a ragged breath when his fingers shifted my hair behind my ear.

Gentle and almost reverent, they traced the arch, the near point that, if not for anything else, made it so plainly obvious we were different.

"Soft," he whispered, as if to himself, while furrowing his brows. "You wear no jewels in your ears."

"I used to but too often forgot, and we heal fast." My voice was breathy, and I swallowed when his finger slipped over the small lobe to trail down my neck, nearing the fine silk strap of my heavy apricot gown. "Bron," I said, more of a warning, but for whom, I didn't know as my stomach filled with tickling moths.

Seeming to catch himself, he removed his touch, smiling as though he'd been caught stealing a treat and he wasn't sorry. "You are beautiful."

"As are you," I said, to which he released a shocked laugh. "What are you doing here, Prince?"

A brow rose, and he took one step back, tiny gold flecks in his eyes exploding under the sun. "Your father wrote us, as you already know."

"You cannot mean to marry me." Unable to meet his burning gaze, I fastened my eyes on his velvet bronze tunic and cloak. "We both know that."

He was silent for long moments, lashes dipping as he turned on one foot and peered around the garden. We weren't alone, but I didn't bother telling him. Turning back, he pursed his lips, studying me, and a rip sounded when he dared to take a step closer.

It was quiet enough that I didn't think he'd even heard it, but with my hearing, I did, and I used the distraction to prolong whatever excuse he'd been about to give me. "Your cloak," I said, forlorn and lowering, reaching for the hem. Gazing at my roses, I hissed, "I apologize. They're usually much better behaved."

"The flowers?" he asked, puzzled.

I hummed, rubbing my fingers over and along the broken velvet and stitching. The tear was too ragged, stubborn. It didn't work. With a sigh, I rose and suggested, "Leave it with me, and I'll mend it after dinner."

Bron removed the cloak and gathered the heavy material, but

before he could place it in my outstretched hands, he leaned forward, his lips brushing my cheek. "Kind *and* beautiful."

I watched him leave, my cheeks warm, one more so than the other, the wind kicking leaves around his fast steps. He'd left to avoid answering me, and I was too distracted by the softness of his full mouth upon my skin to care.

Over dinner, news arrived that some of the prince's men had been attacked in the Spring Forest.

Up until that point, it'd been a quiet, tense affair. My father studiously ignored my mother's warning looks whenever he'd spoken of a marriage contract, not needing to hint at the reasons but doing so all the same.

I'd sat and stared at my full plate of roasted bear and spiced turnips, pushing some of the meat into the puddle of white cream upon its side.

The prince hadn't eaten either, though he did drink the wine.

Fool, I'd thought, being that I'd warned him of the food, and he'd not thought it would extend to drink as well. Our wines were crafted the same way most wines were, but with a faerie's hand. The passion for their task and their lifeblood seeped into each batch.

Already, Bron's cheeks were ruddy, his eyes struggling to focus on my father. Laughter fell from his lips over nothing as my mother kindly suggested, "Dear prince, perhaps you shouldn't drink—"

That was when the two soldiers had arrived, Bron's and my father's highest in command, their expressions mirroring grave concern. "Your majesty," Elhn said with a swift bow. "We've just received word of bodies strung up in the trees of the Spring Forest, limbs torn apart, blood in the river..." He trailed off when my mother lifted a hand and glanced at me. "Apologies."

Grateful I hadn't eaten, I offered a tiny smile, my chest squeezing tight.

"My men?" the prince cried, the merriment fading from his face like an incoming storm clouding the sun. Standing, he wobbled on his feet, blinking harshly. "Good grief, what did you make me drink?"

My mother's lips pinched between her teeth. No one had made him drink anything. He'd poured the wine before any of us were even aware of what he was doing.

"Survivors?" my father asked, his thick fingers sailing around the rim of his goblet, unseeing eyes upon the table.

"No reports of any."

My father rose from his seat, the flora-shrouded snakes encircling the back of his gold and silver chair appearing watchful. "Let us talk outside."

Bron's general offered a hand when the prince tripped over nothing, then took it back when he was reprimanded.

It didn't matter that the Spring Forest lined a lot of the coastline, stretching from Gracewood and through to Errin. They were here. Yet again, they'd crossed over.

Enough of them to wipe out a portion of the prince's army.

After pacing my rooms for what felt like hours, I retrieved the prince's cloak and perched upon the window seat that overlooked the gardens below to follow through on my promise.

Invisible thread flowed from beneath my fingertips, and I willed it to match the same shade of golden brown as the cloak. The scent of the prince, sea salt and something sweet like burnt sugar, rolled off the weathered velvet.

His lips, full and soft and warm and unexpectedly rubbing over my skin, the specks of gold in his brown eyes... Those fluttering moths died, replaced by molten heat when a different set of eyes and lips entered my mind.

When I imagined it'd been Fang's cruel yet sensuous mouth to grace my skin, and his fingers so delicate at the arch of my ear.

Opening my eyes, unsure when I'd closed them, I folded the mended cloak in my lap and leaned my head against the glass window.

I wondered what Fang was doing, what his beastly king might have him do on a daily basis, and if he'd been amongst the murderers in the village town and Spring Forest.

Two attacks. Both brutal and swift and close together.

A thud on the door interrupted my fear-spiked thoughts, followed by another. I climbed down and sped across the room, knowing the scent on the other side did not belong to my parents nor any of our staff.

"Good evening," the prince said, fine lines deepening around his eyes and his hair finger-worn. "I do hope it's not too late, but I've come for my cloak."

"You're leaving?"

He nodded, his gaze never quite meeting mine. "Yes, it was foolish to come in times such as these." A wan smile wriggled his lips. "My mother always chides me for being too curious for my own good. An adventurous spirit."

I could empathize, so I smiled and handed his cloak to him. "I've repaired it."

The prince nodded once more, unfolding the cloak to look for where the tear had been while I leaned against the wood and studied him beneath the glow of the flames in the sconces on either side of the door. His low lashes shadowed his cheeks, mouth pressing into a thin line. "It probably isn't wise, as I'm sure my father has told you, to be leaving—"

The prince's eyes jumped from the mended tear to mine, wide and dark. "Gold."

"Excuse me?"

He tapped a nail upon the tear, and we both heard the tiny clink before he shook the cloak at me, blinking fast. "The stitching, *your* stitching, it's…" He gulped. "It's *gold.*"

No.

I could feel my face drain as I snatched the cloak and fumbled for what I'd done.

But there it was. Each perfect stitch was thick, woven gold.

Shit. I swallowed down the shock, the shame, the scared little youngling I'd once been that tried to resurface. "It would seem I chose the wrong color," I muttered, hoping he'd buy the excuse.

Scowl deepening, he fastened his eyes upon the cloak, evidently unsure.

"Excuse me while I see if I can have this undone." I could undo it myself, but I raced past him and down the stairs in search of my mother in the tower opposite mine.

Down the shadowed hall and up the stairs I flew, the heavy skirt of my tulle gown catching on the stones, causing me to stub my bare toes. Opening the door, I found their chambers empty and backed into the small entryway, my heart a lump of un-beating fear in my chest.

My father caught me as I descended and rounded the last of the stairs, eyes bright as they drank me in and sensed what I couldn't say. Gazing behind him, he then tugged me to a nearby cleaning chamber, tucked away from the meager light.

"Look at me, honey bee. Watch." I did, as I always had, while he made his eyes change from a deep green to gold and then to brown. Such antics had me in fits of giggles as a youngling, and as I'd grown, they had helped temper the storm inside me. The wild that awaited and sometimes insisted on release. His presence alone—the time he'd spend with me regardless of the reason—was usually enough to distract me.

It wouldn't work now. We both knew it, and after minutes of feeling my breathing quake, breaking over my lips, he released me and stepped back. "Go. Run."

So I dropped the cloak, and I did.

It wasn't safe to be leaving the castle right now. I knew that, and so did he. But I had to. The alternative, according to him and my mother, was far worse.

Racing out of the kitchen's exit once more, I then checked for soldiers on patrol and waited until their torches faded before taking off through the vegetable garden and into the fields beyond.

Gold.

The look of awestruck horror on the prince's face. The consequence of releasing such a secret into our world… I ran faster, harder, my blood pressing at every vein, each muscle tightening and bending.

It had first happened when I was young. I'd been mending my mother's favorite plum gown, the silken one she'd said had been my brother's favorite, and with images of her serene smile, the portraits of them together, it had just… *happened.*

I'd been excited, so sure she'd be pleased by what I'd somehow managed to do, but she and my father had looked at one another with fear-bright eyes and had then warned me to never speak of it.

To never do so again.

For years, I hadn't been permitted to mend a thing until one day, I'd done so against their wishes—proving to them that indeed it wouldn't happen again.

They hadn't seemed to believe me, but once satisfied that no sign of gold was amongst the thread, they'd nodded and said to confine any mending I did to my quarters.

It was in our blood, a part of our souls, to heal and build and repair and create and amplify growth. We could seldom keep it contained to nature. It was a song in our hearts, and when that song demanded freedom, it was painful to ignore its call. Just as it grew painful now to ignore the pounding rhythm inside me that begged to be set free.

I ignored it—I had to as I rushed through the forest, bounding over the familiar path and around each well-known boulder and snare.

I knew before I ducked under the small opening and crawled to my feet inside the cave that he wasn't here.

Still, I climbed through the tree to sit atop it, and there, I saw what had the townsfolk boarding up their shops and homes.

Blood.

Starlight twinkled over the water's dark surface, highlighting the darker strands marring it that wove along it like slithering snakes in search of a never-ending feast.

He wasn't here. He wouldn't be coming.

And instead of thinking about every horrific reason, I allowed the current inside me to pull me down.

And inside that darkness, I let go.

Mother was waiting in my rooms when I returned with the rising sun, her voice solemn. "Do you know what you have done?"

I shook out my hair and dragged my fingers through it, the glimmering blue that hung from the twisting wooden posts of my bed shielding my mother's expression.

"Of course, she knows," my father said from behind me, and I stumbled back into my bedchamber, taking in the weary lines of his face. "She's sealed our fates."

Though his words struck through me like a dull blade, there was no anger to his tone, only soft resignation. Eyeing his armor and the sword at his side, I asked, "Where are you going?"

"The prince and his men await us outside the city. We're to escort them back to Errin."

"You can't," I said, panic scratching at my voice. "It's not safe."

"Nowhere is safe," he grumbled, then forced a smile into place when my face fell. Collecting me close, he murmured against my hair, "Look at me, honey bee." Inhaling his scent, the blueberries I knew he kept tucked in a pouch upon his weapon holster, I met his tired green eyes. "Be brave."

My mother followed him out, leaving stifling worry in her wake. It clouded the room, my mind, and I was thankful when Linka entered to take me away from it. "Come, now. It's just a quick journey south."

I nodded, my arm in hers. From the balcony of my parents' rooms, Linka and I watched as my father, atop his midnight stallion, took flight with his soldiers and disappeared beyond the gathering dust.

# FOUR

**D**USK ROLLED OVER THE HILLSIDE, DRAGGING DAY INTO DEEP pinks and oranges to gift to the growing night.

This time, he was there, and upon seeing the sword resting against the rocky wall of the cave, I paused, picked it up, and then I waited.

"Sunshine," he said with feigned cheer as if I was anything but a heavy rain cloud. His boots hit the tree with a mighty thump that shook the dirt above my head, his steps lazy yet quick as he approached the mouth of the cave. "We need not train if you—"

As soon as he entered, I leaped at him, and without enough warning to remove his weapon, he ducked just in time to avoid losing precious strands of that creamy blond hair. "Opal."

I ignored him, ignored the sound of my name on his lips that made it sound more than the simple thing it was. "Fight."

After staring at me for unbending, fracturing moments, his blue gaze darkened. Finally, he unsheathed his sword. "Did someone piss you off?"

I didn't want to talk. Doing so would only lead to more anguish, more anger, as his people continuously slaughtered my own as well as humans, and he didn't care. He didn't care that their hatred, their malice, their greed, and their cruelty had pulled my family apart and would soon have us begging at the feet of mortals for refuge.

Refuge they now wouldn't give because of me, because in their eyes, all of us were monsters, abominations not to be trusted.

No, this crimson male didn't care at all.

I struck again, and our swords met in the air, moonlight flaying off the blades as they slid and then clashed between us. "Opal," Fang said once more, but I didn't take my eyes off his blade as I stepped back. "Fuck, what's gotten into you?"

I couldn't talk to him. I shouldn't have even been *associating* with him. No matter how innocent it seemed.

"Sunshine?" A question containing a softness that could be mistaken for concern.

I couldn't kill him. Even if I could, I wasn't ready to kill anyone, and we both knew it.

So I dropped the sword, and this time, I was the one to leave without looking back.

Guards were stationed on every corner outside the castle gates, many giving me disapproving glances as I moved through the bustling market quarter of the city toward the square.

I deserved their disapproval, most certainly, but not for any reason they knew.

They clearly thought it absurd that my mother would allow me to venture into the city streets, swallowed up by carriages and wagons ambling behind horses over the cobblestone and the vendor carts squatting before each alleyway.

But my mother, who'd been confined to her rooms since my father had left, didn't know.

"We have enough seedlings to last through the winter, my princess," Linka said beside me, her hands wrung tight around her empty shopping basket. "Herbs, too. Whatever else you might need, we can fetch for you."

I wasn't here for any of those things, and she soon discovered that as we crossed the square and headed straight for a dark alley. We walked to its end, the creek whispering through gnarled bushes on the other side unable to mask the scent of aged wine and roses.

I refrained from wrinkling my nose as we stood before the black-painted door pressed between a stone arch. The rock exterior was darker here, more of a creamy brown, some stones struck through with black rot and drooping, leafy vines. A stark comparison to the moonstone white and overflowing trellises throughout the rest of the city.

The door knocker was shaped into the head of a serpent, a sun rising in the copper plaque behind it. Our royal crest. Although she was an entity larger than any royal framework, she'd served Sinshell for hundreds of years. Though the curious would wonder whom it was that truly gained from her line of work.

I wrapped my hand through the metal, felt the rumored tingle right down to my fingertips, and then released it to thunk against the door.

"Princess," Linka hissed, belatedly realizing where we stood—whose door we stood before. "I forbid you to—"

"Wait here," I said and moved inside when the hinges creaked and the door opened on its own. Guilt punched at my stomach, but I'd needed an escort for the sentinels at the gates to so much as consider allowing me a brief absence from the castle, and though she'd protested, it had to be Linka.

I couldn't chance bringing anyone else.

The door closed soundlessly behind me, candlelight flickering and climbing from the half dozen giant candles perched upon the book-lined walls. I took three steps forward to stand on a shaggy patch of emerald carpet.

Wreathed in a fading patch of sunlight that cut through the red glass window to her left, the ruby-eyed female crossed her legs in the generous throne-styled chair behind her oversized desk.

"Bright one," the serpent sorceress crooned, the two glowing white snakes upon her shoulders stirring. "I've been waiting some time for you."

*She's sealed our fates.*

"Really?" Swallowing over the knot in my throat, I lifted the hood of my gray cloak from my head and tucked my hands within its folds to hide their trembling. "Then I am sorry to have kept you waiting."

The sorceress hummed as though she didn't believe me. A plate of cherries sat before her, the snakes curled beneath her voluminous waves of burgundy hair growing still. "You're too late."

I blinked, then frowned. "You said you've been waiting."

"Indeed, I was, but you kept me waiting too long."

"What do you mean?"

"I mean," she purred and stabbed a cherry with a toothpick. "Someone paid me a visit before you, and now I no longer hold the cards to your fate."

"How?" I asked, all the while something nudged at my muddied mind, piecing my confusion into something that shot an arrow of fear into my heart.

"You know *how*, little Princess. The creature who visited me?" Chewing the cherry, she grinned, the blood-ripe fruit staining her serpentine smile. "Well, your fates are intertwined."

Rocks pelted my stomach, roughening each slow breath.

Knowing I'd get nothing else from her, I inclined my head and made to leave when the locks clicked into place over the door. "Payment."

"But I did not have my fate told," I needlessly said, my fingers curling into my palms. Of course, she'd try to take something from me. No one stepped foot inside her den without leaving something of themselves behind.

"But you did. It may just take you longer to understand what the stars have planned for you."

My eyes widened, then shut, and I was thankful my back was turned so she couldn't see. "I'll send you any coin you desire."

"You know it is not coin I desire, my bright flame. Ten drops should suffice." I whirled to face her, my chest hollowing when she tapped the large black goblet upon her golden desk, then pushed the small knife toward me. "Ready when you are."

Tempted to close my eyes, I dug the point into the palm of my hand, ignoring the sting as I made a fist. The sorceress's gaze was not upon the blood falling drop by drop into the goblet but on my face.

Her head tilted when I caught her eyes, and her lips curved briefly, too brief to be considered a smile, her ruby eyes darkening a shade. "You look just like her."

Taken aback, I asked, "Who? My mother?"

The sorceress snatched the goblet, and I was glad, for I'd lost count of how many drops I'd given it. "Do give her my warmest regards." She rose and twisted away from her desk, the heads of her snakes lifting.

Not wanting to see what she had planned for my blood, I hurried out of her hovel.

"What in the stars has gotten into you?" Linka waited to whisper at me until we'd crossed back through the square, her once pink face now white. "You do realize who that was."

"Of course, I do." I lifted my hand, the cut already healing, for emphasis.

Stunned, Linka waited until we'd breached the waning crowds lining the street outside the shoe store. They were holding a sale— likely worried their creations would be spoiled should war creep closer to our doors and wanting to gather whatever coin they could. "Well, what did she say, then?"

"Nothing."

"Nothing?" she almost squeaked. "You do not visit the sorceress and leave with nothing."

Sighing, I blew some loose tendrils of hair from my face and righted the hood of my cloak. Even with it on, some still recognized me, but by the time they did, I was wading past them, too fast to chase down and greet or bow to. "She couldn't tell me my fate," I acquiesced. "She's already handed it to someone else."

Linka's arm tightened around mine as we climbed the small, steep hill to the castle gates, its moonstone rising high above the city and farms beyond. Another sun to blind us all. "Who would come looking for your fate?"

"I don't know, but probably no one," I said, having already wondered the same thing myself. A nod to the guards, and they let us in. "Whoever it was merely came looking for their own."

Leaving her inside the foyer to tend to the rest of her duties, I wandered to the library on the second floor, hoping the crackling of the fire and the treasure trove of books with their worn lettered spines would calm the rising wave within me.

I should've known it wouldn't. Placing the ancient history text upon the marble table, I gazed at the silver gilded portrait of my father and mother with Joon, my late brother. Their lips were slightly curved, but all three sets of eyes were smiling.

Another portrait, sans Joon and instead with a tiny me, sat upon the opposite wall.

As I looked at the paintings, at our similar gold eyes and hair, I tried to ignore the empty gazes—the lack of smiling eyes other than my own—and counted back the hours since my father had left.

The hollowing inside me yawned wider.

Soon. He'd return soon. The journey to Errin was a two-day ride unless he'd chosen to travel through the human lands and deliver the prince and what remained of his entourage straight to the king and queen's door.

A thud came from upstairs, followed by the rare sound of my mother shouting at someone. Whispers sounded from down the hall, murmured concerns and demands between the staff.

My eyes fell closed, the room suddenly too hot, too sweltering and small.

"Not now," I groaned between clenched teeth.

It didn't listen. I didn't listen.

I didn't run. Determined to beat the instinct this time, I walked, and when I reached the northernmost woods, I realized too late that I couldn't give in to it if I wanted to.

It was still daylight, for one, and this place, the damp soil under my hands as I arrived at the cave, was no longer a safe place to allow myself such an indulgence.

Resolved to wait it out, to think over the sorceress's carefully crafted words until they could no longer scare me, I stayed until nightfall. Inside, against the wall, the earth warm at my back, I watched my hands and arms shake, my feet fade and reappear, and willed my blood to cool.

The moon took a shape I couldn't see in the sky. He wasn't here, wasn't coming, and after hours of shivering while boiling inside, I knew I had to let go. That it was probably safe to.

About to, I opened my eyes at the sound of a soft crunch at the other end of the cave. "What is wrong with you." Not a question but an order for answers.

"Nothing," I said too quickly and jumped to my feet, hoping they'd hold me.

They did, mercifully, and staring at him as he approached, I felt every boiling blood vessel begin to cool as I drew in Fang's features. The moonlight behind his head wouldn't touch him, but it shone splashes of silver upon those angular cheekbones, their high rise toward those ice-sharp eyes stealing my breath.

"There's nothing I hate worse than people wasting my time." I would've scoffed if I'd had enough energy. "Tell me why you're shaking like a leaf in a storm."

Meeting those eyes, I immediately looked away, knowing I'd have to tell him something or leave. I had a feeling he wouldn't let me do that this time. "The prince visited."

Silence reigned, with the exception of the trickling water outside of our secret passageway.

"You could say it didn't go well," I murmured, hoping that would be enough to placate his need for an explanation.

A low hum left him before he said, "You are betrothed?"

I half laughed at that, sinking back against the wall as my limbs slowly returned to me. "I highly doubt it."

More silence. "You're disappointed then," he surmised, his head tilting in that predatory way as he studied me with bright eyes.

"Something like that." I ripped my lace gown with the small dagger I'd started wearing strapped to my thigh, his gaze a blistering brand upon my bare legs. "Did you bring your swords?"

In answer, he unsheathed both from his back. "You've taken to carrying a weapon."

"Dire times," I muttered, too thankful for the return of myself to remember I was yet again in a place I shouldn't be with a crimson asshole from across the ravine.

His voice lilted as he said, "So I've heard."

Annoyance arrived, thick and oily. I pushed the dagger back into its holster at my thigh, then snatched his short sword, the emerald in the hilt dark and shadowed. "Did you have something to do with that? The Spring Forest. The river town and villages."

"You know better than to ask questions you won't like the answers to," he murmured low, his other sword twirling in his hand. His eyes stayed fastened on me, ice-bright yet oh-so void.

"Very well," I said with an airiness I most certainly did not feel and did as he'd said, honing that fury into every limb, the clenching of my fingers around the worn hilt as I braced myself.

A wicked smirk deepened the blue of his eyes. "Shall we dance, sunshine?"

"I thought you'd never ask."

We moved at the same time, blades clashing and our smiles mirrored. My arm shook with the effort to keep his strikes at bay, my teeth gritting.

"You're sloppy this eve," he said, sounding bored when I feigned right, then lunged forward, his sword catching mine before his chest, the steel halving his grin when our stomachs touched.

Bouncing back, my breaths coming too fast, I panted, "I'm fine," and gripped the sword in both hands, ready for his downward arc.

I was on my back before I'd even realized he'd easily outmaneuvered me, the back of my head in his large hand, the blade poised at my throat. "Dead," he whispered from above me, every hard part of him aligned with the softest parts of me.

As though he had just realized this, he blinked, brows lowering over cobalt eyes. "You're huge." It was all I could think to say, the words leaving me before I'd thought about how he might receive them.

Those eyes widened, then narrowed with his rising lips. His teeth, stars, they were perfect, blinding in the dark, even his longer, sharper canines. "I suppose that is a compliment." His smile loosened. "Though what would you know about such matters?"

My fingers sifted through the dirt at my sides, readying to throw it into his eyes if need be and then shove him off me, when the sword fell beside me, and he rose. Only slightly, though. His hair sprinkled down over his forehead. His large arms caged me to the ground.

I'd never felt small. I'd never worried over such things.

Until now.

Until I felt an energy, primal and bloodthirsty, leaking from his enormous frame in a way that both shortened my breath and sent embarrassment spiraling toward my face.

When I failed to say anything at all, knowing he could likely feel the heat rising from my flaming cheeks, he then asked in a softer voice, "Did he kiss you?"

It took a moment for me to remember the prince, and even though I didn't deign to give Fang an answer—it was none of his business—he got one, his eyes probing mine, then every inch of my face. "Where?"

Swallowing, I rasped, "Get off."

Another infuriating smirk. "You don't want me to. You're just saying that to save face."

My teeth gritted, anger forcing me to admit, "He kissed my cheek."

His head lowered without warning, the tip of his nose trailing each cheek until he'd scented what he was looking for even though I'd bathed numerous times since, and he inhaled deep. Then with my hands darting to the back of his head, fingers curling into his shockingly soft hair to pull him away, he licked me.

"Did you just—?"

"Quiet," he said, a curt, gruff bark, and the arms beside my head lowering as he did so once more.

My toes curled. Something feathered its way from my chest to my stomach, tickling profusely. And then, as soft as rose petals warmed by the sun, his lips dragged in a caressing brush over the skin, over every inch of my cheek, a rumbling noise climbing his throat that made my fingers curl gently into his thick hair.

More. I needed more.

As though he could sense that, his mouth ghosted down toward my lips with torturous slowness.

Our eyes met and held for moments that stole the beat of my heart. His had grown dark. The pupil expanded, black spreading into a now deeper, oceanic blue. A shiver assaulted me, and then his lashes lowered, and so did his mouth.

That feathered sensation melted into liquid fire.

Tentative at first, his lips pressed gently into mine, finding where they'd fit—finding that they fit perfectly. Another low rumble left him with my shaken breath, my mouth parting slightly, enough for his lips to slide over mine, my fingers clenched in his hair. "I've never done this," he rasped, then scowled down at me as though his admission was somehow my fault—that him laying over me and kissing me was also somehow my fault.

That scowl, the annoyance that narrowed his eyes, told me that what he'd said was true. His kiss, though nothing short of breathtaking, the hesitation and slow evolvement, did too.

Everything in me stilled. That this young, ruthless god hadn't been kissed by a thousand females, or stars, even males, robbed me of speech.

His lips rolled between his teeth as he watched me. Then he shifted, and my hands decided to keep his head held within their desperate grip. "Me either," I finally whispered.

His nostrils flared with his eyes, delight birthing a smile I hadn't yet seen on him before. A smile that spoke of unbridled joy or perhaps even relief. "Thank the fucking stars," he said, his voice so rough, and then he stole my breath once again.

Any trace of uncertainty was gone. He kissed me as though he'd been tasked with the most important job in the universe, his lips holding mine in a firm promise for heart-thrashing moments before parting them for his velvet tongue to skim inside my mouth.

I moaned, uncaring of the strange sound as his hardness met my soft. One of his hands slid slowly down my side, tracing and marking every curve, to hook my leg behind his back.

A low growl coated my tongue, and I swallowed it greedily as well as his following curse. He ground his length into my body through our clothing as our tongues stroked, teeth nipping at one another's lips.

Copper filled my mouth, but I didn't care. I was lost inside this dark, magnetic space where nothing but this rainbow of sensation existed. The heat of him, his breath—always even and now breaking across my lips with every digging thrust of his hips.

My eyes opened to find his were too, and I felt myself falling upon rapid winds while lying upon the hard earthen floor as he sucked my lip into his mouth, teeth scraping. The slight tang of blood returned, and he shot up to his knees as though I'd taken the sword that laid beside me and struck him with it.

My heart raced, too fast for me to control my thoughts, let alone words, as Fang stared at me. Lips parted and tinged red, his chest heaved while he glared as if I'd grown another head.

Then without a word, he stumbled to his forgotten swords and dragged them with him to the opening of the cave. To the tree that would take him back across the gully.

"Wait," I managed to breathe out, pushing up to my elbows. "Fang."

His steps faltered, but he said nothing, did nothing save for disappearing into the night.

The silence in his absence screamed and eradicated the precious air remaining in my lungs.

On unsteady feet, I rose from the ground, shaking dirt from my hair and willing the wet away from my eyes.

I'd kissed him. He'd kissed me.

It wasn't just forbidden. Unless it could be proven that relations already existed before the second war, it was now treason to consort with the crimson.

That wasn't what terrified me, though. No, what terrified me the most was this residual feeling of emptiness, as though he'd taken something from me that I couldn't describe, couldn't make sense of, and I wasn't sure it was smart to attempt to.

Something I feared I could not get back.

At the entrance to the cave, I knelt and crawled out of the low-lying hole and stilled when I spied something in the grass to the right. Walking over, I kicked at it with my slipper.

Peppered nuts spilled from the pouch, and I didn't need to bring them closer to my nose to recognize the foreign scent lingering on the canvas. Such a snack wasn't permitted here.

Because it was eaten *there*.

The world shrank and tilted, the haze Fang had left me in clearing rapidly.

*Stars.* He'd...

Gazing back at the cave, I inhaled deep, then followed the trail, the strange scents, the signs I'd missed earlier while solely focused on trying to gather and control myself—and then all over again in a brand new way courtesy of Fang.

A howl came from deep in the woods, and then I was running, running and knowing I wouldn't make it, knowing they were miles and miles away, and that if I had any chance, I'd need to change.

And so with a flash, my heart twisting, then pausing inside my chest, I did.

My blood roared and vibrated, my vision darkening and my senses illuminating in a rush that used to make me vomit for hours when I'd change back. Clumsy from panic and the disuse of this form, I almost flew headfirst into a tree before my wings spread and tilted, and I swerved around and through its branches.

Higher, higher, and higher, I climbed, cresting the treetops of the woods, leaving them behind within precious minutes. The moon rose behind the castle in the distance to my left, but I continued south and followed the dense line of trees and foliage that skirted the ravine.

The soft orange light cast from the city beyond the castle gates lit the corner of my eye; the villages between the city walls and the woods beneath me dark and slumbering. That wasn't the case for others as I flew closer toward the mainland, Errin, the human's kingdom, tucked beneath the stars in the ever-stretching distance. Some villages, farms, tiny towns, and the old mine were nothing but husks, a darkness that might never see the light again.

Faster, I had to move faster.

I'd flown countless times as a youngling before I'd learned to control it, to conceal what my parents deemed a curse rather than a gift, but never this fast. The wind barreled into me, attempting to steer me north—back home—when I needed to keep going south, so cold as it ruffled every one of my downy feathers.

Unable to help it, I looked to the right, toward the ravine over the edge of the forest, the cliff's jagged edges and the trees on the other side visible even at night. Vordane spread beyond those trees. A lush, tree-populated entity of hidden gloom. Sprinkles of light glittered like faraway stars from its heart—the city across the river from the palace that watched over all at Vordane's northernmost corner.

Shadow Keep.

It had been years since I'd glimpsed it from the skies. I'd never visited. We'd never dare. To do so was as good as welcoming an untimely death.

The thought withered when the wind delivered screaming that tugged my gaze southeast. Banking, I surged, and it wasn't long before I saw it.

Flames, carnage, murder...

All the blood.

No sign of the prince and his soldiers. They had crossed the border, then, and were possibly already home. Which left only my father and his small troop, who'd been making the journey home.

Steel clashed against steel. Beasts dived on limbs. Blood sprayed like bursts of rain falling from the sky and puddled just the same.

My heart burned in my chest, ash flooding my mouth.

I was too late.

It was too late, yet I circled back to keep out of view and dropped beneath the trees, swooping through a vacant barn beyond them and out through to the broken fencing. The grass might as well have been concrete beneath my feet, I landed so hard, but I didn't shift.

A large shadow against a rotted-out stump, barbed wire curling in the wind behind me, I could do nothing but stand there and stare.

So many. *Stars*, there were so fucking many. Wolves of differing shape and color, some with wings, most double the size of any human man, snarled and lunged and ripped—

Too many of them to have crossed a makeshift bridge thrown across the ravine or river in the dead of night.

I stumbled back on my webbed feet.

Fang.

Me.

*My fault.*

A wolf, larger than any I'd ever seen before, crashed through the air and into the middle of the clearing, his maw stretching open with a roar so ferocious it shook my feathers and every blood-soaked blade of grass.

Cream furred wings, blackened with blood and gore, fanned and then tucked into either side of the horned beast's torso as it prowled through the throng.

The blood king.

The fighting didn't cease—but it wasn't fighting. My father's soldiers, Fae who'd been trained since their bodies had matured, fell like insects swatted beneath giant paws.

It was a massacre.

Move. I had to move, but to join the battle would guarantee my death, and the repercussions of that would spread far and wide.

I was the last living heir. An heir to provide my family with another.

But my father, bellowing with fury as he fended off three attackers, took a hit to his side. His white-gold hair was coated in blood, his face nearly unrecognizable... I couldn't just leave him.

I couldn't leave any of them.

If I shifted back, I'd hopefully still find that dagger strapped to my thigh, though I knew it'd do little good with beasts that quadrupled the size of my shifted form.

The largest beast—the king—advanced through the fallen, crushing them beneath his giant paws as though they were already soil that belonged to the land and nothing else.

My father, fending off attacker after attacker, weakening more by the moment, didn't see it coming.

I screamed, the sound little more than a honking call to the wild birds who'd long scattered—useless and pointless.

But he heard.

My father looked my way with wide eyes, no longer soaked with rage but with bright fear. Fear for me. His eyes darted to the trees, indicating, pleading for me to go.

I should've listened, but he couldn't expect I'd be able to move an inch as the wolf rose onto his hind legs and wrenched my father off the ground by his neck.

Then shifted as his paw struck, claws and fur punching deep within my father's chest.

The beast, now a male in a familiar black cloak, lowered to the dirt with my father's neck still in his fist, his other inside his chest, twisting, pulling, as my father released a silent scream and turned his eyes skyward.

Fang.

My stomach dropped, and my vision blackened as my father's lifeless form fell to the dirt, his glimmering heart in the crimson guard's— *in the blood king's*—hand.

Cheers and howls sliced through the clearing, through my airless chest, as the king, *Fang*, lifted my father's heart to his mouth and tore into it with his teeth.

Teeth that, just hours ago, had scraped over my lips.

My father's lifeblood cascaded over his and down his chin as he raised the dead organ toward the night sky, his kin's approval thunderous, vile, and deafening.

The few remaining soldiers couldn't be helped. I knew that.

So when my father's heart fell to the grass beside his dead body, I retreated, shrank back into the night in search of the forgiving light of day to end this twisted nightmare.

He'd lied.

All along, I hadn't been meeting with some rogue guard from the enemy's kingdom. I hadn't spilled precious words into Fang's ears. *Stars*, his name wasn't even Fang.

The monster of Vordane had multiple names.

The blood king. The king of wolves. King Dade.

And I was a fucking fool.

Before I could reach the barn or the husk of a farmhouse, I felt it, the warmth of eyes at my back. Twisting my neck, I found the king standing at the fence I'd just left—in the very place I'd watched him murder my father, his face stained with his blood, cloak billowing, and those blue eyes swirling with nothing I wanted to read into.

He didn't know. There was no way he could possibly know it was me.

All he saw was a large black swan.

And so I turned back and flew for the cover of the woods, hoping they'd shield me, that my wings would carry me the entire way home when my soul felt so heavy.

If he'd known it was me, I had no doubt that he would've easily given chase, yet I flew alone.

# FIVE

**D**AYS PASSED LIKE SEEDS SLOWLY FED TO THE DIRT.
My father's body was eventually retrieved and given to the soil behind the castle, a giant seed beneath the cherry blossom tree next to my brother. Flowers, white and luminous, had sprouted all around the tree's base, spreading toward our feet like tiny wishing stars.

My mother wept beside me, though no tears left her eyes.

I knew that type of heartache had to be worse than any other—the type that hurt with an intensity that stole your tears and refused to allow the grief to leave your body. For if it did, there'd be nothing left. Nothing.

To lose someone you love, a mate no less…

And it was my fault.

I hadn't told her. I wasn't sure I ever could. That I'd been tricked and so stupid. That I'd spent time with the enemy, never knowing, never thinking he was so much more than that.

He was our ruination.

*Look at me, honey bee.*

I wouldn't let myself shed tears. Not for the same reason as my mother, but because I wouldn't dare mourn him when I did not deserve to.

Our military had been whittled down to scraps, fear spiking through the castle halls as though winter had visited early.

No one remained to rally or strategize how to reinforce our borders and collect more people to train, be they farmers and traders or otherwise. There was only a silence so suffocating, I wondered if it would kill us before King Dade thought to finish us all off.

Elhn had been severely wounded, leaving my father's two generals scrambling to gather some composure in a city and kingdom inundated with peril. The captain and two other soldiers were all that remained of my father's destroyed unit.

"Princess." My mother's servant and closest friend, Edwan, bowed when I reached the stairs leading to her chambers.

I'd been avoiding her. An easy feat when she refused to leave her rooms, and now, I was trying to work up the courage to go check on her.

His sun-kissed face was pale and drawn, cheeks sunken, arched ears a harsh contrast against his bald head. In his trembling hands was a tray with broth and bread, and I gestured for it. "She still won't eat?"

"I'm afraid not, my princess," he murmured, lips whitened with worry. "It's been four days."

My eyes shuttered. "Has she drank anything?"

He inclined his head. "Some but not enough, and mostly wine."

We were a species who'd live for thousands of years, but that did not mean we couldn't fall prey to starvation like humans. It would take our bodies considerably longer to perish, but perish they would over time if not treated well.

"Thank you, Edwan. I'll do my best."

Gratitude wet his violet eyes, and he bowed once more before rounding the corner.

Up the stairs, the door creaked open with a thought, and I walked inside the dark, stale room. My mother's scent, lemon rose, was fading with her health, leaving the bitter taste of sodden leaves in its wake.

Rounding the half-made bed, where she lay perched against the pillows while gazing at the swaying drapes concealing the windows and balcony, I set the tray upon her nightstand. "Mother, make haste, the food wastes."

With a harsh swallow, she shifted a little. "I'm not hungry."

"I know," I said as I climbed over her legs to lay in my father's spot, his scent of lime and leather pungent on the pillow. My heart throbbed, guilt roughening my voice. "Me either, so perhaps we can starve together?"

And there she was, Nikaya, queen of Sinshell, her glare harsher than the sun. "You will do no such thing."

"You know I will if you do not eat." Clasping her cool hand, I squeezed it. "You must." Her long lashes fluttered, throat bobbing as I begged, "I cannot lose you too."

Gazing back at me with gold eyes so similar to my own, I feared she could tell, could read the guilt in my eyes and in my voice.

If she did, she didn't let on and gave my hand a weak squeeze in return. "Honey bee," she whispered, a broken nickname for the daughter who'd broken her heart. "One day, you will understand what it is to feel your soul leave your chest, to fight against your heart's instinct to follow." Licking her dry lips, she added, barely a sound, "One day, you will know what it is to find and lose your true mate." Reaching up, she smoothed her cool fingers down my cheek. "I would almost rather death for you, honey bee."

Unsure what to say, only that I wanted to keep her here, present and talking, I said, "I worry such a thing will likely occur before finding a mate is even a thought in my mind."

She smiled then, wistful and wretched. "You do not find a mate," she stated, color to her voice now. It was dark but color all the same. "The stars bring them to you."

I'd been told endless times before of how she and my father had come to find one another. At fifty years of age, it was past time she separated from her lover and grew up, her father had said, so a marriage was arranged with one of my grandfather's chosen suitors.

Two nights before her wedding, as townsfolk and villagers from all across Sinshell arrived, she met my father, a farmer's son who lived outside the woods by the border between Errin and Sinshell. A warrior not by choice but because he and his family had needed to protect their livelihoods of land and livestock. His mother had insisted he attend the wedding, for it was unheard of to miss such an event.

My mother, who'd of course been in love with another and not romantically fond of her betrothed although they were friends, had snuck out of the castle for a pint in the city. Hiding in a dim corner of the tavern, she'd watched faeries of all ilk drink, dance, gamble, and throw darts, lost to sorrow.

He'd sensed her before he'd walked in, he'd said. Unaccustomed to sitting idle, he'd decided to explore the city as night fell. Curious, he'd entered the tavern, drawn to her as a moth was to flame. Within hours, the wedding was canceled, and my father's family was already making plans to move their farm closer to the heart of Sinshell.

*You cannot fight a mating bond and win*, he'd told me. And so with a frustration born from wasted coin and our people's time, my grandfather had welcomed my father but ordered him to clean up the mess he'd caused.

He'd done so gladly and had replaced Elhn to wed my mother instead.

A fairy tale written and spoken of with great awe in the human kingdom.

But, as their many stories suggested, not all fairy tales ended happily.

"A mate you won't find, not in this realm." A cough followed her grim words, and I frowned. "The prince wrote us." She entwined a lock of my hair in her fingers. Staring at it, she said with little care, "He requests for you to stay with him for protection while they consider marrying you into their family."

"What?" I almost shouted.

Marriage. I hadn't thought I'd still be expected to… I'd thought

I'd ruined any chances of such an alliance when I'd spun gold into the prince's cloak, and he'd fled home.

Mother didn't startle, just smiled sadly and sighed. "Oh, the games we've been forced to play."

"Mother, I cannot—"

"You leave the day after tomorrow with the rising sun." As she scooped my hair behind my ear, her touch began to warm. "You will have their protection, and we need you safe. That is what matters right now."

I closed my eyes, wanting to protest, wanting to yell at her to get up and help me fix all of this. But she was, and she had, and the prince was our only way out.

She knew that.

"I don't know how to do this," I said, swallowing thickly. "But I will, though the blood king…"

"He will return, so no one knows you are leaving. Just you." Sharp eyes met mine, a command in them. "And me."

I was to take myself. I was to shift and fly.

Nodding, I took her hand. "I will do this for you, but you must eat." Her eyes rolled. "Mother," I said, softer now. "If I have nothing to live for, what's to stop me from flying across the sea instead?"

I awaited reprimand, a reminder of my *duty*. Neither arrived.

After long moments of staring at me with a vacancy to her gaze I'd never seen before, she brought my hand to her lips. "You should, honey bee. You should flee and never return."

We both knew I wouldn't, so she sat up while I fed her broth-dipped pieces of bread.

# Six

**T**HE POLINPHE MOUNTAINS ROSE ALONGSIDE ME, SILENT watchers of my lone journey east.

Their peaks stretched toward the clouds, blocking the perilous cliffs beyond them above the Night Sea.

The only way for ships to venture to our war-ruined half of Nodoya was via the Royal Cove, which was too often ambushed by waiting crimson bandits sent by their king.

*I've never done this.*

Hard to believe, and undoubtedly a lie, that the beast of the west, the king of wolves, had never dared to kiss another before. Rumor stated he was thirty-four years, had been brandishing a sword and upheaval for more than twenty-five, and could tear someone in half with his claws alone.

The tyrannical king had likely taken hundreds of lovers to his bed.

I squashed the intruding thought of it, the unexpected and unwelcome fury that accompanied it, and any imaginings of those too-soft lips on my own.

He would pay. One way or another, he had to—even if I died trying.

For I surely would.

Keeping to the trees, the foothills, and the quiet trail of farmland only broken by the Salt Creek and the nest of greenery surrounding it, I pushed thoughts of vengeance and guilt aside.

Mother had mercifully risen from her bed and left her chambers yesterday. I wasn't sure if it was for my comfort or because the kingdom needed her. I was merely thankful that she had. Now, crossing the border, the woods that stretched for miles and miles from the mountains at my left toward the ravine turned river to the right, I needed to fabricate an excuse to feed the human royals.

To explain my lonely arrival.

Perhaps, merely the fact that I was Fae would be enough to mollify them, though I knew most, especially the king and queen, knew better than to accept that.

I'd yet to discover if I contained such a gift, but there were those of us who could warp from place to place. Typically, they were either gold and crimson nobility—and powerful ones at that. As if the beasts needed more of an upper hand.

I was beginning to truly empathize with my grandfather, who had led the charge in ridding Nodoya of King Dade's parents. The threat they'd likely posed to our continent was now abundantly obvious for all to see.

A threat that had now unraveled with their son into a deadly promise.

Drying fields and sandy dunes that rippled toward the Royal Cove soon replaced the lush and rolling green as it faded behind me. Castle Errin sat in the southeast corner of Nodoya, stone and wood and mortar that shone in bronze and browns beneath the peaking sun. The city of Errin sprawled and climbed between it and the Royal Cove, a vast array of cream and color, buildings shaped from sandstone and brick squashed together with little thought for clear thoroughfare.

A kingdom easy to hide within.

I tucked that thought away, keeping it in the safe space of my mind beside the darker things I couldn't and didn't have time to release. Later. Perhaps years from now, there'd be time to give to those aching thoughts that matched the changed tempo of my heartbeat. A time when we could afford to reflect and vow to do better.

I couldn't see such a time for that existing. All I could see, even with the sand-crusted beauty below me, the waves rolling against the cliffsides and into the bay, was gore and blood and endings.

Village roads, little more than packed dust skirted by shrubbery and cacti, crawled to the glittering city, and I veered left away from them, toward the castle hidden beyond a giant stone wall.

A few guards looked up, most looked away, and I waited until there were no eyes on me at all before quietly drifting down to the fountains in a sprawling courtyard. A swan, black and peering around with slow arcs of its neck, was all anyone would see if they happened to spy me standing upon the stone ledge, water misting my feathers.

Looking up, I met the marble eyes of a statue, one of the gods the humans bowed to, his manhood exposed and a spear in hand.

"A black swan," said someone from behind. "Look, Georgette, do you see?"

Shit.

"Oh, my," said who I guessed was Georgette. "I do believe it's been years since I've seen a swan at all, let alone a black one."

"An evil omen, do you think?" asked her companion.

At that, I couldn't help but swing my head their way, causing both women, carrying baskets of bread and fruit, to squeak. They then hurried away from the fountain and into the adjoining city street.

An omen. I would've scoffed. Instead, I made sure I was alone before shifting and shaking out my stiff and tingling limbs. Well, given my parents' fear of my curse, only time would tell if they were all correct, and I hadn't the time to care.

Stepping out from behind the giant statue spilling water from his mouth into the algae-infested depths below, I crossed to the shade of some nearby maple trees while righting the emerald and olive skirts of my gown.

I'd kept it as simple as possible, knowing that was how the humans preferred it, the gown lacing up my back in tiny bows and covering my breasts and upper arms. The bodice seemed to squeeze my chest, or maybe that was my chest tightening, the closer I came to the wall of the castle.

My neck strained back after a horse-drawn wagon ambled past from around the side, soldiers seated in the back with empty baskets, to take in the height of that wall.

I'd been told about it, this wall and castle, many times, but too distracted by my own whims, the innocence I'd once harbored with too much grit, I hadn't listened. Guards were stationed at every corner in lookout towers that would grant them a view for miles in any direction, their bronze and silver armor gleaming in the sun.

"Halt," a female voice cried when I stepped out from the shelter of the trees and headed toward the courtyard. "What is your business here?"

*Here goes everything.* "Opal," I said, my name sounding strange. Foreign almost. "I am Princess Opal of Gracewood, here at the royal family's request."

A heavy silence ratcheted up my heartbeat, and then the silver metal gate across from me, not the larger one fit for horses and carriages but for single-file entry, opened.

Five guards, wearing armor and helmets, walked out and stopped before me, inspecting me from head to toe, then looked at one another. "That is her," one of them said, words muffled behind the metal encasing his face. "I've seen her before."

I surveyed the man, wondering if he even spoke true, before ultimately deciding it didn't matter as long as I was taken where I needed to be.

"Alert the family," the female said, then gestured for me to follow as two guards rushed ahead of us inside the gate.

We waited in another courtyard, more of those fountains gurgling, interrupting the tense silence, as the soldiers shifted and eyed me. Roses of every shade mingled in thick bushes lining the walkways leading to the curved castle doors and around the sides, thinning alongside hedge-lined pathways.

"Come," the guard said gruffly and flicked his hand toward the arched wooden doors that remained open as though I were a stray animal he did not want to sully himself with.

A shadow crossed the red-dressed floor. The prince, his smile and hands spread wide, stepped into the doorway, immediately taking the three circular steps down to greet me with a kiss upon each cheek that did not touch the skin. "Welcome, Princess." Standing back, he looked around, and his smile drooped a little. "Your entourage?"

"They already return," I said, surprised at the smooth lie.

After a nod and a glance at the guards behind me, he led me inside. Shocked, I hurried after him, more confused than comforted at how easily my lone arrival had been overlooked.

"I am sorry," he said as we crossed the entry chamber. Portraits of his ancestors hung on the walls on either side of the soft red carpet. "About your father. He was a good… man." He was no man at all, but a male of both great heart and power.

The doors shut with an echoing boom that made me flinch and forget about correcting him. The lit sconces guttered and then flared high over the stone walls. "Thank you."

"Would you care for any refreshments?" he asked, seeming so small now, his rich eyes dull in this place of after. After he'd left without a goodbye and made me think the worst. After my father had escorted he and his men home safely.

After they'd been killed while returning home.

All I could manage was a shake of my head and to entwine my trembling fingers.

Clearing his throat, Bron tucked his hands into the pockets of his dark brown pants. "My mother and father have been sent for. They might already be awaiting us in the great hall."

"They are aware then," I said, cautious as we walked down a long hall, deeper into this dark, foreign castle. "That we plan to wed?"

His slight cough and the falter in his next step drew my eyes away from the stairs that zigzagged, their wood clothed in that red carpet, up through the ceiling into the floors beyond. "We shall explain in due time."

His bland tone and the stiff set of his shoulders caused my mind to whirl. Though, surely, if they'd planned to do me harm, they'd have done so by now. No one had so much as touched me, and besides, they'd be foolish to.

Sinshell might have been a broken kingdom, but the human kingdom would need all the help they could muster if they stood a chance at surviving the blood king.

The great hall was void of anything but two thrones upon a wooden dais, wrapped within two steps. The polished wooden doors opened to reveal the king and queen already seated, their hushed bickering ceasing at the sight of us.

Forced smiles fell into place as they rose. Bron's mother, Sabrina, was aging at the eyes and mouth but beautiful for it all the same. His father, red-haired and rotund, dragged a finger over his graying moustache, then wiped his hand down his red and brown regalia. "Welcome, Princess Opal."

"We are so sorry to hear of your father's passing. It grieves us so to know that if our son had just stayed put during these trying times, then perhaps he would still live."

Bron looked at the ground, and I fumbled for a response, Sabrina's brown curls sliding over her shoulder as she shot a glance at her husband. "Thank you," I finally settled on as a cold weight pressed behind my eyes. "He is greatly missed."

The queen's words spoke of a reluctance to have her son anywhere near us more than guilt for not being able to keep a handle on him. Even so, that twinge in my chest worsened as all the many useless what-ifs returned.

"We've prepared your quarters for you," the king said with a clearing of his throat, shaking me loose from my tormenting thoughts. "We hope you will find them pleasing." Another look from his wife had him sputtering, "Oh, and of course, we will ensure no harm befalls you under our watch."

THE SAVAGE & THE SWAN | 61

"That is most gracious of you indeed, but I must ask of the plans to marry—"

"Child." Sabrina released a breath that sounded like more of a sigh. "May I be frank?"

I was no child. A fact she was well aware of. Still, given little choice, I nodded. "Yes, of course."

Stepping down from the dais, she walked toward me with her gown, a sky-blue mixture of ruffles and lace, trailing behind her. A silken gloved arm slid through mine. "I will show you to your rooms while we chat." We headed through the imposing doors before I could find words for the king or prince and straight to the stairs I'd passed on our way in.

Her arm stayed looped through mine the entire way, and though I waited, drinking in the dancing ornate sconces and the portraits on the wooden panels of the walls that were flanked by bronze and gold tapestries, Sabrina didn't say a word until we'd reached the very top of the stairwell.

Atop the four steep turns of stairs, a short hall led to only one heavy wooden door, the queen losing her hold on my arm as she struggled to get it open. I could've opened it for her just by willing it to, but I doubted she'd appreciate the display of our differences very much.

With a huff that sent spirals of curls from her face, Sabrina opened the door and swept a hand wide for me to enter first. Slowly, I did and recognized I was inside one of the square towers I'd seen on my journey into the city, this one likely the shorter one out of the four given the size of the stairwell and room.

The bronze, red, and gold décor had made its way into these rooms too. The bed, quilted in red with patterned gold whorls and tasseled throw pillows, sat in the center of the room. Two wooden chests of drawers on either side housed shining red metal lanterns, void of flame.

The sight of the crimson shade tempted my mind to dance toward gruesome places.

"There's a bathing room just through this door," Sabrina said, knocking on the closed wood and pulling me from my near-spiral. "The maids have provided you with enough essentials…" She eyed my ensemble, the lack of belongings. "I shall ask them to provide some more gowns for you and sleepwear."

I nodded, murmuring my thanks as my eyes flitted across the bare walls, the large golden trunk over by the lone arched window. "That's beautiful," I said, if not for something to say at all, as I stepped closer to take in the engravings upon it. The wood had been carved by an expert hand. Little creatures, squirrels and rabbits, played amongst trees in the gold-painted wood. A purchase, no doubt, from a Sinshell woodworker.

"Inside it, you'll find your first round of projects."

That pulled my hand away from the trunk. I spun to the queen, who stood poised, chin high with her hands clasped before her. "Projects?"

A small smile curved her lips, and then she sighed. "My dear, did you truly think we'd harbor a faerie princess for any reason other than to help? Surely, you are not so young as to be unaccustomed to such politics."

Against my urgent wish for them not to, my cheeks warmed. "What would you have me do?" Mending, I guessed, or perhaps crafting paintings or pottery.

The thought jarred and awakened as Sabrina's smile grew into something real and threatening. "Our son informed us of your ability to weave gold."

Breath sailed from me. "I-I don't," I started, then tried again. "I cannot just—"

"Spare me your excuses, Princess." Walking to the trunk, the queen opened it to reveal mounds of clothing inside, and I tripped back toward the bed. "Our armies have been decimated. The few left help to protect us, yes, but they won't be enough should trouble arrive on our doorstep. And arrive it will." She straightened, demure and unblinking. "We need more soldiers, and therefore more coin, our coffers draining faster by the month with every ship forced to turn away from our shores as they cannot risk the danger of trading with us."

"You... but I don't think you understand," I said even though her words made perfect sense. "It is not something I can just *do* on command. Honestly, it has only happened a handful of times. All of them accidental."

The queen nodded once, then looked at the ground, lips pursed. When her eyes rose, her voice lowered, deepened with warning. "Then I suggest you figure out how you did it, and do it again." I blinked, eyes stinging with an onslaught of tears that would never arrive. "A great many times, and should you prove yourself worthy"—she tilted a bony shoulder—"*then* we will discuss marriage."

She turned for the door, and I raced after her, pleading, "No, please. Wait."

It closed in my face, numerous locks turning on the other side before I could rattle the handle. "No trying to escape. You'll be captured before you even reach the castle walls."

I slumped against the door, terror a stake tearing slowly through my heart.

"Oh, and none of that faerie magic. Unless, of course"—she laughed softly, the sound more of a tinkling threat—"it involves providing us with gold."

Her steps downstairs were drowned by each stampeding breath burning past my lips. Swallowing thickly, I turned back to my new room. To my new home.

To my cell.

# SEVEN

THE LATE GLOW OF THE SUN LEAKED OVER THE WOODEN FLOORS, slowly chased away by the growing shadows.

I didn't light the lanterns nor the few golden sconces on the walls.

Upon the bed, I stared at that beautiful trunk, wondering how I'd gotten here—a prisoner and a murderer. As the moon formed the shape of a scythe, I surmised an ending of this nature was only fair, and perhaps this was exactly where I was supposed to waste my final days.

In a crimson and gold cage.

Beneath the low-lying arched window, the trunk mocked me—sang of promises I couldn't see myself keeping and finding a way out of. For even if I could summon the energy to do as I'd been tasked and weave gold thread into the garments inside, they would still not allow me to leave.

My mother would need to send for me, but that would require an army, of which we were now lacking with the remaining soldiers needed to protect our kingdom.

The room had grown dark by the time a servant knocked on the door, then opened it to deliver a tray that shook in her hands. Young and pale, the woman stuttered, "P-princess, it is awfully dark in here."

Before her next breath, sun-captured flames danced within the sconces on each wall, revealing her frightened blue eyes. I might not use magic to escape, but I'd use it as I would every other limb. It was a part of who I was, as necessary and vital as breathing. "Just leave it on the trunk," I muttered. "Thank you."

She did as requested, hurrying out of the room as though I would eat her for dinner instead.

I ate nothing, but I opened the window above the fish stew before flopping sideways over the bed to stare at the night sky.

The stars still twinkled, the moon still shone, yet it now felt as though they too mocked me from where they sat so high above us all—a foolish golden princess who'd fallen for a known enemy's tricks and had brought ruin upon all.

Morning brought with it a visitor. My eyes fluttered open when the door did, a near-silent creak of the hinges and a familiar scent alerting me to the prince's entry.

"Opal," he whispered as though I were asleep when he could see my eyes upon him. Closing the door, he leaned against it and brushed his hands over his cheeks. "I don't even know what to say other than I'm sorry."

"Did you know?" I asked, sitting up and pushing my hair back from my shoulders. "Did you know this was their plan for me all along?"

Toying with the hem of his shirt, he took a cautious step forward, gleaming boots meeting the soft red carpet. "Opal, you have an incredible gift. One that could help us turn this nightmare around..."

"My mother will be very displeased." I said the words with a low vehemence.

He received them for the warning they were, swallowing as he nodded. "I understand, truly." I scowled, twisting my legs away from him as he came to the bed and dared to take a seat beside me. "We will marry, okay? We will make Nodoya the great realm it once was, but to do that, we need your help first."

"Agreeing to marry you was help enough," I said before I could think better of it, my eyes widening at my own arrogance. "But you humans never are content with all you've been given."

A lilting smile shaped his lips, but it failed to fill the dark eyes that stared back at me. "True, but you must believe me when I say that if I thought any harm would befall you, I would not have gone ahead with this."

"Liar," I hissed, rising and taking the tray from the trunk. It clanged to the floor as I flung the wooden lid open, revealing rivers of color. "You'd have agreed anyway because you are no king. You are a prince, and you've little choice."

His jaw clenched, teeth gritted.

I sat upon the floor, tugging a velvet-lined cloak from the chest and spreading it over my lap. "Leave me, for it seems I have miracles to tend to."

"You did it before," Bron said with a forced, grating laugh. "Can you not just do so again?"

"If it were that easy, these garments would have been replaced with others by now, wouldn't they?" I knew I should have watched my tone and chosen my words more carefully, but I'd spent most of my life doing just that, and in the end, it had done nothing good.

Not for me nor those I loved.

"You can do this. I know you can. I've seen it." The prince stood. "And then we will have our revenge, Opal, this I swear to you."

Revenge.

The word had never sounded more attractive, had never caused my heart to refire in such a violent, deafening way. I wanted it more than I remembered wanting anything—knew that I would need it. I stared down at the rippling fabric. "We will die trying."

Bron's footsteps halted halfway to the door. "But try we must." He hesitated, then murmured, "I shall return tomorrow if that is okay with you?"

I said nothing, knowing that was his way of saying the time for lamenting my fate and dawdling had come to an end.

Once the door closed, the latches clicked on the other side, and I willed my heating blood to calm so I could try to focus.

There was nothing else I could do. I wasn't leaving this castle alive unless I'd given them what they wanted, and even then, the chances of that happening seemed slim. Still, it was all I had, and though I was tired, so stars-damned tired of being told what to do, I'd learned that doing what I wanted led to far graver fates.

Hours sped by, the sun dragging toward the bottom of the sky as I sat with that first cloak, now spread before me over the floor. Tears threatened, but I knew they wouldn't fall. Instead, they left an ache in my skull that I tried to infuse into my unachievable task.

By nightfall, all I'd managed to do was undo the previous stitching, ragged pieces of thread waiting to be rewoven with gold.

My fingers brushed and glided over every inch of fabric, and then I moved on to the next, a tunic made from fine cotton, and willed my heart to unspool before me into the awaiting garment.

Either it refused or something was missing, something was wrong, but I couldn't piece together what that could be, what that could mean, as I thought back to the handful of times gold had spun from beneath my fingers before.

Another tray of food was delivered, and my uneaten lunch taken away. I'd managed a few sips of water, feeling guilty when I'd remembered my mother and how she'd promised to make herself do what felt impossible when all she wanted was to fade away and allow her soul to find my father.

The door closed once more, the servant girl never once looking my way.

She'd be reporting to the queen, of that I was sure, and after tearing more clothing from the trunk and staring at it in dismay, the days spent eating poorly in my own kingdom and eating nothing here began to catch up with me. I grew dizzy, my eyelids unbearably heavy, and slumped over the clothing on the floor to stare at the filigreed ceiling.

A clack sounded upon the windowsill. I didn't move. Another bird hoping I'd throw them my uneaten food.

"Sunshine, what in the bleeding stars are you doing in this putrid place?"

# EIGHT

**S**ITTING AGAINST THE WINDOW FRAME WITH ONE BOOTED foot perched on the floor and the other upon the wooden sill, the intruder cocked his head. "I've been looking all over the countryside for you."

Not a bird. I wished it had been.

A wolf.

"Well?" Beneath the hood of his cloak, his eyes gleamed, roaming over me in a quick, assessing sweep. "Did they steal your tongue? I hope not." His mouth curved. "I am rather fond of it."

"You," I breathed, my heart finally restarting with a painful thud.

His smirk widened into a grin. "Me."

I scrambled back over the clothing, hands slipping on silk and chiffon. "No."

He watched from his perch, a brow poised high. "No?" His cloak absorbed the starlight as he tilted forward. "No, what?"

"You're... you're *him*, and you killed him."

A low laugh fell from sin-shaped lips, the roughened sound lighting his eyes. "Sunshine, though I do find your befuddlement amusing, you're making very little sense."

"My father." I climbed to my knees, my gown in tangles beneath and around me. "You killed him," I seethed through my teeth, each word fire, "and you ate his heart."

The blood king's lips pursed. "Oh, that."

A heavy silence fell like a noose to wrap around my neck, freezing my desire to scream for help, to alert the guards below the stairs that the enemy had breached their walls. That he might kill me.

"So it *was* you," he murmured, so soft, too soft, and I ground my teeth against the fluttering inside my empty stomach. "The black swan."

"What swan?"

"Don't even attempt it." Throwing his hand at me, he said, "We both know you were there."

About to call out, my intentions wilted when the king tutted. "I wouldn't do that. You'd hate for someone else to die because of you, now wouldn't you?" I swallowed, my eyes shuttering. "It wasn't your fault really. Sheltered, shrouded in a bubble of innocence as you were, why, I'll bet your only responsibility in this life has been..." He feigned thought. "To save yourself for breeding, perhaps?"

He hummed, receiving confirmation he hadn't needed when I said nothing. "As I was saying, even if you hadn't been guileless, how would you have known who I am?"

I wasn't sure if he was trying to alleviate the guilt that weighed my every breath or cause it to spread like a forest fire.

"Those from this side of the realm who have seen me rarely live to tell the tale."

"Why?" A useless, stupid question I shouldn't have set free.

"Why what?" Midnight rippled over his black attire, the breeze flowing around him to kiss my burning skin. "Why did I deceive you? That should be obvious." His words carried a dry humor I wanted to wring out of him until he begged for me to stop. "Why did I kiss you? Well, my pretty little broodmare, that should also be obvious by now being that—"

"*Enough.* Why did you kill him?"

"You're a little rude. Has anyone ever told you that?" He contemplated the thought, his tongue skimming his upper lip, and I directed my eyes to my shaking hands. "Perhaps you've been too spoiled in that lovely kingdom of yours. Manners, my black swan, are not archaic, nor are they barbaric. They are ingrained in our heritage and a part of who we are."

I nearly laughed at the absurdity, hissing, "You're the barbarian, a savage with no heart. Where were your fucking manners when you murdered my father, my people?"

A smile entered his voice, but I kept my attention fixed on my twisting, squeezing fingers. "We've all the time in the world for stories, but unfortunately, that time has not yet come."

I looked up when his other foot dropped to the floor with a controlled thump so as not to alert anyone to his presence. "Where are the others?"

"Who?" he asked, rising to his feet.

I didn't stand, didn't care that a monster was two steps away from looming over me even though I should have. "Your beast warriors. You're here to invade and conquer, are you not?"

"Not yet, sunshine." He erased those two steps, then crouched down before me. "Not yet."

His scent ran rampant, a flood of stained air I wanted to eradicate, and when his finger reached my chin, tilting it up, I snatched his wrist and glared into those wasted pretty eyes.

He smiled, breathtaking in a way he did not deserve, those dimples exposed. "There she is."

"Don't touch me."

"I do believe you're touching me."

Releasing him, I shifted back, and his eyes fell to the carpet. "Did you have a tantrum with your belongings?"

I didn't answer him. Instead, I rose to my feet and headed for the door. He was there, a gathering of shadow that formed a tall, broad-shouldered male in a second, blocking the door. "Enough dallying, tell me why you're here." He sighed when I stepped back and turned away. "Is it to marry the human toad?"

"You deserve nothing, and you will get *nothing* from me ever again."

"Opal," he said, right behind me, and I jumped a little when his breath washed over my neck. "Answer the fucking question."

I whirled, our chests nearly meeting as I seethed up into his face, "Or what? You'll murder me, too?"

His eyes narrowed. "You'd have been dead weeks ago if that were my intention."

That shocked and cemented something I didn't want to pay any attention to. "Just go." My voice broke on the last word, and I lowered back to the ground, dizzy once more and lacking the energy to parry with him, let alone alert someone to his presence.

"I didn't eat his heart," he said after a heavy moment, still behind me, his gaze burning into the top of my head as I tugged a gown over my legs. "I mean, usually I would, but I spat it out."

I snorted, my throat and chest too tight. "Because that makes the fact I will never see him again easier to bear."

He could say nothing to that, the silence stilted as though he was at a loss for what to do. Then he rounded me, and asked in an edged tone, "What are you trying to do?"

"I must weave gold into all these"—I lifted the dress—"and I'm tired, so please..." I whispered, exhaustion overlapping my fear and hatred of him. "Just leave already."

He bent low. "I will when you tell me why they're making you do such a thing."

I didn't, and I let him deduce from that what he would.

He didn't leave. He watched, eyes transfixed on my failing hands. I pulled away when he reached for one, and he said, "Trust me."

I almost laughed. "Never."

He nodded once but took my hand regardless, and I was too weak to fight him as he lowered to the floor across from me and said, "Try again." When I gaped, he grinned. "Go on, I dare you."

Frowning, I did and gasped as gold thread not only wove through the fabric but danced along the hem and neckline with such speed, the dress shone with it within a handful of stuttered breaths.

Blinking at it, then up at his contemplative expression, I asked, "How?"

"You did it. I merely... assisted." He released my hand and tugged the cloak free of my leg, placing it on my lap over the gown. "Again," he said, a cold demand.

I wasn't sure how it was happening or why I allowed him to touch me once more. I only knew it was happening, and I was grateful. Not to him, but just... relieved.

Within minutes, the entire trunk of clothing had gold spun through every thread of stitching, and with a feral grin, the king of wolves gazed at me beneath his long lashes. "We make a good team."

Reality slammed back in. I slid my hand out from under his silken, callused fingers and hurried to my feet. "We make a good nothing."

Collecting each item, I folded and placed them upon the closed lid of the trunk while the king stood there, watching silently.

"You should eat," he finally said, and then he was gone.

# NINE

**A**S PROMISED, THE PRINCE VISITED THE NEXT MORNING, HIS smile stretching into his cheeks. "You did it."

Indeed, the servant who'd delivered my breakfast had gone to inform them of the clothing piled upon the golden trunk. I'd remained where I was, lying over the crumpled bed in the same clothing I'd arrived in, as she'd left and returned with a friend to collect it all.

Now, still seated upon the bed, I was tearing at the mound of hard bread that'd come with breakfast, forcing little pieces down with sips of water. I'd almost thought it a dream, a trick of a misery-addled mind until the items were carefully carried away—the reason for the gold-embroidered clothing a ghost haunting my every thought.

"Opal?" the prince asked, unmoving from where he stood beside the open door.

"I wish to be alone," I finally said. Not meeting his eyes, I let my own slide away from the finery he wore.

"Mother says you are permitted to leave your chambers for a walk in the gardens..."

"I said I would like to be left alone." The bread started to crumble in the firm grip of my fingers.

The prince cleared his throat, then stepped out. "As you wish."

The door closed and locked, and it did not reopen until that evening as I was leaving the bathing chamber in a white satin robe I'd found hanging over a hook beside the shelves of bath salts.

"Good, you're clean. Herma was beginning to fret about the stench that might befall this room."

I didn't bother informing her that whatever stench I left in my unwashed state would not be detected by their inferior sense of smell, my fingers twining my hair into a loose braid that fell over my shoulder.

The queen finally met my eyes when I said nothing, her own widened with expectation.

Still, I remained silent, and she huffed, turning to the door and ushering someone in.

Two men carried three knapsacks each. All were promptly up-turned onto the red carpet before the now empty golden trunk. With swift bows, they then hustled past the queen with their sacks and left.

Sabrina gestured to the new mounds of clothing. "We will give you until the day after the morrow."

A shocked laugh slipped out. "You're giving me time limits now?" She folded her hands in front of her, straightened her posture, and I shook my head. "What happens if I fail to complete them on time?"

"Certain allowances might be taken away." With a coy smile, she spun for the door, her brown and gold gown dragging the unswept breadcrumbs with it. "Good night."

I stared at the closed door, then looked at the mountains of expectation on the floor, and decided to finish my chicken dumplings instead. They lacked the flavor, the love of the earth, from back home, but they weren't terrible, and after not eating well for a time, they probably tasted better than they truly did.

Afterward, I unlocked the door with a touch of my hand on the wood, smiling to myself as I left the tray outside, then closed it. A silly victory that did nothing but show a little defiance, and hopefully a hint to Herma, the servant, to keep out of my rooms.

✦

As I'd feared, the moment my fingers touched the thread of the finery I'd laid out before me upon the large single bed, nothing happened.

Nothing save for the stitching that was already there growing stronger. Unyielding.

While I was certain most humans would appreciate such a thing, I knew the king and queen would not and glowered at the clothing as though it had been created to dupe me.

"Need some assistance?"

My eyes shot to the window. How he'd arrived, so silent and undetectable, was beyond me. "How are you getting past the guards?"

"Warping," he said as though I were daft, and perhaps I was for not having considered that already. In my defense, I had defiant ungold stitching to contend with, and the blood king had mercifully flitted to the back of my mind.

Until now.

He climbed through as though he had every right to and crossed the room, hands tucked within the pockets of his long leather coat as he surveyed the space. "A pretty cell for a pretty faerie princess."

"It's not a cell," I lied. We were both well aware that it was.

Humoring me, it seemed, he didn't bite back, just dipped his fingers into the bowl of vegetable soup upon the nightstand. He put them into his mouth, and nausea assaulted me when his lips curled around them, and my blood rebelled, heating. Then he winced, hacking with his tongue out. "Stars above, that is fucking *foul*."

"So is your presence," I muttered, clearing my throat. "Kindly show yourself out."

"If this is about your father, I fear I cannot apologize," he said with a calm apathy that alarmed more than it angered. "Duty is duty, and I cannot falter from the path I've been set upon."

I tilted my head back to blink at him. "Your duty is to murder hundreds, no *thousands* of our kind?"

"If necessary, yes. Humans, too." He tapped a finger against the unlit lantern, and it sprung to life, flame bouncing. "I do not discriminate, sunshine."

I scoffed. A red haze caused a film over my eyes as I clenched my fingers around the scarf. "You're disgusting."

He took a seat on the bed, uncaring that I wished him ill, and folded his long legs beneath him, the wood groaning under our weight. "Give me your hand then, and let's get on with it."

I pulled my hands into my lap, and he watched the action with a maddening half-smile and tilt of his head, strands of blond hair creeping down to brush his forehead. "Why come here?"

His brows climbed, and he stared at me as if I should know why he'd shown up yet again. "Swan, any place you go, wherever you find yourself, I fear I am bound to follow." From the sharp edge of those words and the ice lightening his eyes, I couldn't convey whether he was pleased about what he'd stated.

My throat thickened, ire strangled by fear. "I would much prefer you didn't."

"You only say that because I killed your father and a great many other creatures." Waving his hand, he collected a robe and stole my own. "Be furious later. I've things to do after this."

Stunned once more, I didn't pull away. I glared down at the robe between us as though my loathing alone could peel back his skin but then noticed the contrast in the size of our hands, mine too tiny and nearly hidden by his.

Gold unspooled, flowing like a dotted river along the edging of the robe. My teeth knocked together, but I couldn't help it. Knowledge was power. "Dare I ask what things?"

"You may ask, but that doesn't guarantee an answer."

I sighed as he tossed the robe to the side and spread a large coat between us, our hands still joined. "Maiming, torturing, fearmongering…"

"Politics bore me," he said. "If you must know, I've a meeting with my uncle and two of my…" His nose twitched as he paused. "I suppose the easiest thing to call them is friends."

I wasn't sure if he was attempting humor or if he truly hadn't been aware that these so-called friends of his *were* his friends until now.

"Your uncle?" I said while he swapped the finished coat out for a gown. I'd heard next to nothing of the fearsome general who'd supposedly been the late ruler of Vordane's brother and best friend. Only that he was cruel, merciless, and hundreds of years old but still without a mate.

The king hummed. "Indeed, Serrin was once a very rotten fellow, and now I fear I am more rotten than even he." He looked up, teeth flashing. "It's a curse, this excruciating need I have to win."

I could barely dare to imagine just how wretched his uncle and whatever creatures he called friends were. "I assume one of those friends is the real Fang."

"Fanerin is his real name, which, of course"—he smirked down at the gown—"he loathes, so it's always been Fang." His fingers linked between mine over a new item of clothing. A gentle, cautious movement that I pretended to ignore. Beneath his lashes, he peered up at me. "Do you know my name?"

"The blood king."

That strong, straight nose crinkled.

"The king of wolves."

He nodded. "That one is much better." Scrubbing the stubble on his cheek with his fingers, the sound stiffening my every muscle, he said carefully, "But what is my birth-given name, Opal?"

"Dade Volkahn," I whispered, unsure why, and averted my eyes from his.

Silence permeated, and he cleared his throat as he selected another garment, fingers unwilling to release mine. The high collar of his coat brushed his arched ear as he bent forward slightly. "My mother was dead before she could name me, but my uncle knew the two names she'd been struggling to choose from."

I couldn't help it. "What was the other?"

"He never told me, still refuses to," he said with a huff. "The arrogant shit."

Asking him about his mother, how she'd died, seemed too

dangerous a road to travel with his skin upon mine, warmth unfolding from both our bodies into the fabric between us and heating the room.

Without words, we swapped out one item of clothing for another, Dade seemingly content with the mundane task. Surprising, considering I knew he was a creature with far more than paltry parlor tricks up his sleeve.

As the last few items of clothing joined the pile, I found myself too curious not to say, "I'd thought the blood Fae couldn't mend. That such things were not only beneath you but also not within your realm of power."

Vordane's king rose, stretching, and released a cold laugh as he waded to the window. "I'm not doing anything, swan. I'm merely opening the door for you to do it yourself."

He vanished before I could ask him what he'd meant, shadowed tendrils dissipating in his wake.

The prince arrived before lunch the following day, and I paused in my pacing of the room, fingers spreading over the violet and cream gown I'd donned when I'd woken from a restless sleep.

It was hideous, entirely too big, and constricting with frothy lace erupting in the giant skirts and over my chest, making my breasts appear bigger than their already generous size. But my soiled dress had been taken away, and other than being a reminder of home, of why I was here, it hadn't been much comfort either.

Dreams of blood and teeth and fur and feathers plagued me in the hours following as I tried and failed to piece the dream back together to make sense of something so scrambled.

"Good morning, Princess." Bron bowed, knowing he didn't have to but showing me respect all the same. "I know you might not be up for it, but I was hoping—"

"Yes," I said, already walking toward him and then past him out the door. My clenched and tense muscles jerked with each step. I needed the sunshine, the taste of rain that'd dampened the early hours of morning upon the breeze, and open space.

"Okay," the prince said slowly, laughing a little nervously as he followed me down the stairs.

At the bottom, two stone-still guards with those odd-looking helmets upon their heads glared at me. Bron said, "This way," and gestured to a hall a little ways down the one we were currently in.

It was narrower, less cluttered with ornaments and pictures than the other few I'd been in. There was no sign of anyone else, save for another guard stationed outside the wooden bracketed door Bron unlocked for us to step out onto a stone pathway.

A few feet away from the watching guard, I stopped and tilted my head back to the sky, inhaling deeply. The tension slowly leaked out of me as I exhaled and removed my eyes from the heavy white clouds above.

"You have been cooped up for some days now," the prince said as though he'd been searching for something to say, for some explanation for my odd actions.

And they would seem odd to him. To someone who hadn't any ties to their land except for what it could give them.

"It feels like it's been half a century."

The prince chuckled, and we continued along the hedge-lined path, wide steps taking us down the long length of the castle and into the gardens behind it. Green, dotted with bursts of color and fruit-laden trees, stretched for at least half a mile toward that impenetrable wall in the distance.

"You're..." the prince huffed, "incredible, Opal. Those garments..." We slowed by a marble bench seat with potted ferns on either side of it, and he turned to face me. "Mother has secured a sale for the lot."

"How much?" I wandered to the geraniums across the path, fingers gliding over the glistening petals, and watched their color sharpen.

With an audible intake of breath, the prince did too. "I'm not at liberty to discuss such matters. I'm sorry."

"Liar," I purred, throwing a coy smile at him over my shoulder.

His eyes left my fingers, the petals that unfolded over top of them, and met mine with a start. "I'm not sure what you mean."

"You're not sorry," I said simply and straightened, raising my arms and moaning with the stretch of muscles in my back.

Bron's gaze was heated, darting over my face to my chest when I turned back, and though I held no interest in the human trickster, I still smiled. My mother had been right about many things in her absent ramblings to me in our two decades together. Males, especially human males, were easily bested when played right. "Can you sense lies?"

I'd never been too interested in games of lust. As coddled as I had been, I'd been content to wait for an all-consuming love like my parents had found. A love that stretched the bounds of forever into eternity.

I hadn't the desire, but I'd also had little need to worry about such matters. The same couldn't be said now.

"Not in the way you think," I said and patted his arm before moving deeper into the garden, passing tomato vines and cucumbers. The workers with shovels and gloves moved on when they saw me approach.

Beneath an oak tree at the perimeter, I found another bench, this one wooden, and picked up a fallen apple from the ground. Bron joined me, slowly, as though curious of what I'd say or do next as I rolled the fruit over my gown, granules of dirt spoiling it.

"How long?" I asked, taking a bite out of the apple and finding it, as well as so many other things in this magic dry kingdom, lacking.

Bron slid closer to me on the seat, brows crinkled with confusion. "How long?"

"Until an army can be raised." Even as I'd said it, something inside me protested at the idea of the male who'd visited my rooms to help me thread gold dying upon a battlefield. Quickly, I squashed the feeling. He deserved nothing but the hardship and torment that awaited him. A death as gory and grotesque as what he'd given my father—if not worse.

"I'm not entirely certain."

I took another bite, chewing as I talked, and knocked the image of my mother berating me, of Dade's talk of manners, away. "You're not certain?" I swallowed, smiling at the prince's stunned face. "Or you merely do not wish to tell me?"

"Oh, I want to tell you," he said, his expression melting into one of heated interest. "But I'm positive I'll get myself in trouble if I do."

"Who's to know you said anything?" I arched a brow.

Chuckling, he reached out, brushing apple juice from my lower lip with his thumb. "If you can keep a secret..."

I fluttered my lashes. "Of course. You know we are adept at doing so."

He leaned closer, the crispness of his scent all wrong, his hooding eyes upon my mouth. "We hope within a month, but more than likely, it'll be a little longer."

"A month?" I nearly choked, lowering my voice to a whispering hiss. "Anything could happen in that time."

"We are calling for reinforcements from all over this side of the world, Princess. That and training them all once they arrive, well, it takes time. It's quicker than waiting, hoping, that one of the neighboring human realms across the sea might merely come to our aid."

No one would come. We were a land of myth and legend and death.

Gold was necessary—the only way.

Turning my eyes to the garden, I clenched my teeth, focused on the marigolds. He was right, and still, it hollowed something within me to think of all the horrors that could unspool from the shadows during that time.

"Opal." Warm, smooth fingers grasped my chin, shifting my face back toward his. "We will defeat him, this I vow," the prince whispered vehemently, then stole my lips.

# TEN

THEY WERE SOFT, BUT NOT AS SOFT AS I'D HOPED.

They were gentle, but with a firmness that spoke of barely leashed aggression.

They were nice, but five seconds was enough, so I pulled away.

"I'm sorry," Bron murmured, blinking down at his lap.

"I should head back." I stood, fingers fluttering against my lips. "I'm sure another delivery of clothing has arrived by now."

Bron joined me, and what had seemed like a short walk now felt as though it would drag into eternity, the silence between us a cold wind.

I wasn't satisfied that I'd proven the prince could be tempted to care for me, to help me, even if it wasn't out of the goodness of his heart. I was nothing but... hollow. A chasm, one that seemed to grow wider than the divide between our realm, had made a home within my chest.

I wanted to cry. I wanted to, yet I knew I wouldn't—couldn't.

At the top of the stairs, Bron opened the door to my cage and bowed. "Thank you for..." He stalled, sputtering roughly, "Well, for joining me."

All I could manage was a smile and made to walk inside to the new mountains of clothing I could see awaiting me on the floor.

A large hand gripped my upper arm, pulling me back slightly.

Bron whispered to my ear, stirring my hair as my spine stiffened, "You should know that I'm not really sorry." With a smirk curling his lips, he gazed at me momentarily, then released me and waded back downstairs.

Inside, I leaned against the closed door. The apple, still clutched in my fingers, had coated my hand in its sticky blood.

The king of wolves did not show that evening, and the following day, I remained in my rooms, determined to weave the golden thread myself.

Perhaps if I could, he wouldn't come back. At the very least, he'd have no reason to stay if he thought to pay me another visit.

And so although no gold laid before me after hours spent with different items of clothing, I was ready, frustrated but ready, when he arrived.

Though as shadow unfurled into a large male, it occurred to me that I was wrong. That as he slipped inside the window, boots landing silently on the floor, and pulled the collar of his coat as high as the sharp bones of his cheeks, I was never going to be prepared for all that he was.

A monster masquerading as a rare form of art.

The flames in the sconces on the wall guttered and swayed, the soft light and dark highlighting the harsh angles of his face, the sensual lips, and those eyes… I swallowed and looked at the open window, wondering why I'd never thought to close it.

"I'd open it," he said, with a crack of his neck, tracking my vision and line of thought. "Nothing keeps me from what I want."

Those words were like stones sinking inside my burning ears. As I fiddled with an apron in my lap, my skirts trussed around me on the bed, I laughed a little, the sound dry. "You want to toy with me?"

I couldn't not look at him as he took the same seat he had last time on the end of the bed, this time removing his boots before lifting his long, muscled legs. Pants that resembled breeches but appeared thicker wrapped around them, moving like water as he crossed his legs. My eyes bugged when I saw them mold over the largeness at his crotch, fire infusing my cheeks as he chuckled, and I looked away.

"I love to toy with you," he purred, hatred and heat filling my stomach. "It's amongst one of the many things I long to do more of with you."

"Before you kill me?"

His eyes thinned, thick brows dipping over them. Without removing them from my gaze, he reached out and snatched my hand, fingers linking instantly. "I'm beginning to wonder if that would please you." When I blinked, he added, "Admitting to something we both know I have no intention of doing."

I had to move away from the subject, from him, but alas, hundreds of garments awaited me, and though I hated it, I couldn't do this alone. "Let's just get to work."

His fingers squeezed gently. "Of course."

We were four pieces deep, my gaze fastened on the gold unspooling from beneath my hand, a gentle warmth floating through every vein, flowing through my fingers to their tips, when he asked, "Who else knows of your ability?"

"That I'm a swan?"

He lifted a golden brow, dragging a pair of fur-lined pants between us. "The shadows hear all, Princess." Noting my frown, he went on, voice so low I felt that heat return as I studied his lips to be sure of what he was saying. "The mortals have not only heard but spun tales of the only shapeshifter to grace the golden Fae, and so I'm sure some are also aware that the spinning of gold is linked to the rarity that is the black swan."

"Those tales likely mean nothing to them," I snapped, yet whispered the harsh words. "Only our kind, and to be honest, I'm not even sure why."

"Ah." The king of wolves smiled down at our hands. "They never told you."

"That it's a bad omen of some sort, yes," I muttered. "I've gathered that much."

The king scowled, eyes darting over my face from beneath curling lashes. "It's just the opposite." Sighing as though he were confused and annoyed, he tossed the pants aside and gathered a large gown. He lifted it into the air for it to fall over our legs, creating a gentle, brief, fluttering breeze. "The stars have indeed handed us some contradicting—*what the fuck?*"

Shocked by his outburst, the snarl that so suddenly roughened his voice, warped his expression, and raised his upper lip, I couldn't move as he lunged toward me, then knocked me back onto the pillows. Warm puffs of air, tickling and stomach snatching, trailed over my neck, lower jaw, and then finally, my mouth. "The toad kissed you."

The air he'd stirred with the gown had given the prince and me away. Enough time had passed, and I'd washed, that I hadn't even thought about the fact he might scent Bron on me, and to be honest, I hadn't really cared.

*Fool.* I was a damned fool to forget who was stealing inside of this cage.

He was not like most Fae who resided in these lands. He was a wolven beast with a heightened sense of smell that exceeded even those of us with the grandest senses.

A low growl rumbled near my ear, and I felt him shaking above me—shaking with unmistakable rage.

Now was not the time to provoke him. "Stop," I said as gently as I could, trying to keep my voice from wavering. "Please, it's fine."

But he didn't move, just released a violent curse and dragged his nose over my cheek. "You let him touch you."

Not a question, and so I didn't treat it as one, and merely waited with my eyes shut tight for him to get off me. A minute passed, maybe two, with him just breathing, low and deep and deadly, arms braced by my head, his nose pressed into my jaw.

He was holding himself back. From doing what, I didn't want to know. But for all my taunts about him murdering me…

No. Not like this.

I infused his name with every inch of fear crusading through me. "Dade."

It seemed to work. He rose, staring down at me with ocean-deep eyes, then cursed once more. Shaking hands swiped through his hair as he retreated back to the end of the bed and then scrubbed over his cheeks.

Another suffocating minute swept by. I couldn't look at him.

Unsure what else to do, I retrieved more clothing and his hot, stiff hand, keeping my eyes on the task. His fury didn't ebb. If anything, it became a thundercloud between us, and I grew tense, never daring to look at him as I waited to see if it would erupt.

"Why?" he finally gritted through his teeth as though he loathed to release the word.

"You're not the only one capable of games."

"Meaning?" he barked.

"You know exactly what I mean," I said, too soft, still unable to stare into those violent blue eyes.

My own glued to his clenching jaw, watched it spasm as he rolled his neck and grunted, "Fool."

"Excuse me?"

"You heard me just fine."

Simmering silence caged us, and we both remained focused on the clothing for taut minutes. Gold thread gleamed beneath our hands, shining brighter than any star. His hold so tense, his fingers twitched and squeezed mine.

I couldn't stand it, hated that I couldn't keep myself still, that I couldn't keep enduring the quiet, the frustration, the ire. He'd murdered my father, so many of my people, destroyed towns and homes, yet I couldn't keep my mouth shut nor make him leave. I loathed myself, loathed that he'd made that self-loathing worse. "It's none of your concern."

It was the wrong thing to say. For many reasons. The main one being that it propelled him into action. With a heart-quickening snarl, he launched to his knees. Clothing crushed beneath him, he gripped my cheeks in his hands. "None of my concern?"

His gaze held mine, searching and unblinking. "Dade," I tried again, reaching up to wrap my hands over his. His head lowered, nostrils flaring, and then...

He kissed me.

Hard, possessive, erasing—his lips coaxed and claimed, and I tore at his hold on my face and shoved at his chest, slapping his hands away. "*How dare you?*"

His ragged breaths floated over my mouth. "Play what games you think you must, sunshine." His face was void of anything welcoming, blank and ferociously cold. "But do not let him do that again."

Then he was gone, leaving little more than half the clothing glittering with gold.

# ELEVEN

**A**NGER AND SHAME BECAME A PIT OF SNAKES WITHIN MY chest and stomach, writhing and strangling. After sleeping for all of half the night, I had to escape my rooms.

The queen's servant girl had arrived, displeasure crinkling her features when she'd taken the incomplete clothing on the bed and floor. "I'm not feeling well," I'd said, toneless, and she'd nodded before leaving to inform Sabrina.

I was certain I'd be paid a visit from her majesty before sunset tomorrow if I hadn't finished, yet I felt no panic at the thought. No sense of urgency. All that remained was the blood king's scent, his vicious kiss, and that never-ending self-loathing.

Rounding the outermost pathway to the rear of the gardens, I slowed my steps when giggling floated from the northern end. I turned, just slightly enough to make out moving color—pinks and greens and blues—and updos of chestnut and black curls.

The princesses.

I'd yet to meet them, sequestered in my gilded cage as I had been, but I'd heard rumors of their beauty, their cutthroat antics at court, and of their ages.

The twins, Myla and Claudia, were eighteen years of age, and the older sister, Rosabelle, a mere ten months younger than her twenty-three-year-old brother, Bron. Some said Rosabelle was a bastard due to her slightly darker coloring and hair, while others say she was adopted, found on the stoop of the castle.

I didn't know what to think, and I hadn't any thoughts one way or another due to not caring about human politics and their rumors.

But as they continued to laugh in the vine-shrouded courtyard atop the gardens, I could feel their stares upon me while I continued my walk. Perhaps they didn't know I could hear them, or perhaps they knew my hearing was better than their own and did not care.

"Bron intends to care for her," one of them said.

Another cackled, nearly hollering, "Eldrid wouldn't hear of it."

A quiet, firmer voice said, "The faerie princess stands more of a chance at marriage to the idiot than one of his braindead lovers, I'll tell you that much."

"Rosabelle," one of the girls gasped, "she's a bloody faerie. Don't be absurd."

Rosabelle said nothing else as the other twin whispered, "She might be pretty, but her ears are odd, and so is the way they carry themselves, as if they're water in the midst of freezing."

"So still," murmured her sister. "It's creepy."

I pricked my finger on a thorn just to glimpse the color of my blood. Dark crimson bubbled, and with my back turned to the princesses, I lifted it to my mouth and sucked. A mistake, immediate and scalding memories flooding my mind—life-changing and too bitter to ever be considered sweet.

"…he's even said he won't marry her," one of the twins was saying now. "Something about not being malleable enough."

Rosabelle snorted. "Figures."

Their conversation dwindled to some misfortunate courtiers as they retreated inside the castle, parasols left on the brick and white teacups upon a large metal table, its cream paint flaking.

Eyeing them as I walked past, I considered all they'd said and waited for the anger to arrive. Waited for the upheaval of my stomach at the knowledge I'd been played for a fool yet again.

It never came.

I couldn't decide if it was because I'd experienced worse or if it was due to the fact I already knew I would never marry the human prince.

All I knew was that I needed to get out more, perhaps befriend a princess or two, if I planned to escape this place alive.

As though my dragging mood had summoned him, the prince soon sauntered through the gardens, his smile as bright as the fading afternoon sun. "Opal, I've been looking all over for you."

"Oh?" I tilted my head, smiling and withholding a laugh. "There's really only one other place I could be."

His answering smile could only be described as insufferably buoyant, as he went on to say, "You haven't been informed? You're free to roam the halls as you please, any garden you like." Instead of feeling shocked or even excited, suspicion flooded. Grasping my hands, the prince grinned wider. "Mother has agreed a marriage between our two kingdoms would be beneficial," he rushed out. "A fitting way forward."

Beneficial.

*Fitting.*

I pursed my lips to keep them shut, slowly taking my hands from his so as not to make him concerned. "Well, this is... unexpected." *And utter rubbish*, I thought.

Why would the queen lie to her son in such a way? To have him inform me, and therefore keep my hope alive enough to keep working for them?

Staring into his gold-flecked eyes while he muttered about the conversation they'd had over breakfast, his hands moving animatedly, I watched him scratch the side of his nose three times.

The timing of his appearance in the gardens, not long after his sisters had gone, leaving only us, the insects, and perhaps a loitering groundskeeper, said this had nothing to do with his mother or the king.

He was lying.

"Hello, murderer."

Vordane's king didn't talk or falter as he crossed the room from where he'd warped inside by the door and retook his seat upon the bed. Silent, liquid movements now stilted, he gathered clothing and my hand, and we got to work.

"You seem… tense," I goaded once we'd reached the second to last pile.

"Fucking furious is what I am," he rumbled, jaw shifting and his hand clenching over mine. "You reek of him."

"He didn't kiss me," I said after a minute had stolen precious air from my lungs. "He did find me in the gardens, though."

His head lifted, features twisted with displeasure yet no less striking. "How lovely."

Looking down at the bed, I hummed, and we soon moved onto the last pile.

Because I was an idiot, and because I hated him, I went on, casual and unbothered by the overwhelming heat that rolled off him and flooded the room. "He said he plans to marry me, has spoken with his mother, and she has taken it under consideration."

His feral expression slackened, fading into something too dark to be named.

"What?" I asked with an air of feigned impatience.

"Truly, sunshine…" He seemed to stare right through me. "Can you not smell rot when it crouches before that pretty nose of yours?"

I let him feel every ounce of rage inside himself, hoping it burned his black soul, and then, with a calm that threatened to shatter the ice in his eyes, I said, "I'm well aware of what hides and festers in this kingdom, and that I have no place here."

The room cooled within an instant as his fury morphed into confusion, his stumped expression nearly comical. "Then why?" His thick brows flattened over his eyes. "Why do any of this?"

"For now, I have no other choice."

It still seemed to escape him that he was the reason. "You do, and you know it," he snapped, leaning over the garments to grip my chin.

His eyes sank into mine, refusing to release them, as he murmured, "We can leave right now."

"You can, and I hope that you do, but I cannot." Pulling his wrist, I bared my teeth when he wouldn't relinquish his hold on my chin and ignored the tight flutter in my chest when he smirked. "You wouldn't return me home, and even if you did, you'd kill us all soon after."

The wolf king's smile dropped, and he rose from the bed. "Someone comes." Looking from the closed door to me, he held out his hand. "Let's go."

"No."

"Now is not the time for you to be petulant about your father—"

The handle twisted, someone fumbling with the locks and cursing.

"Opal," Dade said, voice shockingly soft, as were his eyes. Pleading, I realized, and then the door burst open, and he was gone, the prince stumbling inside.

"What in the witch do they need so many blasted locks for?" he grumbled, slamming the door behind him with a breathless laugh. "Shit, that was loud." Straightening, he removed his coat, slurring, "Did I wake you?"

The scent of ale wafting from his unsteady form into the room was enough to make my head spin as I inhaled it. Drunk as he was, he evidently didn't see the clothes on the bed and floor, most threaded with gold. "No, Prince."

He waggled a finger at me. "Someday, I will be king." He stopped at the side of the bed, his leg mere inches from my bare foot. "And I will need a queen to rule beside me."

So focused on the reek, on the garbled words leaving his smiling lips, I didn't see it coming.

In a breath, he'd fallen over me, smacking my head into the wall behind the bed. "But one must always sample before they commit." His hands were suddenly everywhere, sliding down my sides to my thighs, pulling at my skirts hard enough that I heard numerous tears.

"Bron," I said, my voice squashed in my throat as I struggled to push at his shoulders. "I cannot allow this, please." I pushed harder. "Bron, you need to go."

"It won't take long," he said, as though that were all the encouragement I'd need to submit.

I'd never submit, but his body, draped so heavily over mine, and my fear held me trapped as his wandering hands made their way to my breast and between my legs. My knees clamped over his hand, and I groaned, teeth snapping as I tore at the other hand tugging down the bodice of my gown. "Stop," I hissed. "*Stop it right now.*"

He just laughed, mumbling low words. "I'll make you feel so good. God, your skin is so soft." Then his hand broke the confines of my knees, reaching my undergarments and brushing over them, and I screamed.

I screamed, and all the frustration, all the fear, all my pent-up power made its way into my hands, thrusting him off me with enough force to send him over the edge of the bed and flying to the floor with a violent thump.

In a rush, I sat up, my heart racing.

Cursing, Bron groaned, clutching at the bedding to help himself stand. "You little faerie bitch," he spat, rubbing at the side of his head.

My teeth gnashed when his eyes met mine, and then I grinned, wide and daring, as he struggled to his feet. Before he could so much as touch the mattress, I allowed my power to spill and gather into a bubble of thorn clouded air around me, shocking him enough that he paused as I sent them all to him.

The air slammed him in the chest, stunning him while thorns pierced his exposed skin. Eyes wide, he gaped and then slumped to the floor.

I swallowed and scrambled off and away from the bed, unsure how such a petty gathering of air, typically used for cooling and gardening, had worked on the prince in this way. But it had, and my eyes squeezed shut. "It worked," I heard myself say, over and over while frantically pulling down my tattered skirts, and then I tripped backward into a hard pillar. "It worked."

Not a pillar but a male.

Strong hands gripped my upper arms. "Fury heightens things in such beautiful ways, my swan."

"He…" I blinked and blinked at where the prince's foot stuck out from behind the other side of the bed. "He tried to…"

"And he'll never dare try again."

"Fuck," I said, bile coating the word, my throat. My palms dug into my eyes, my chest on fire. "That fucking human *fuck.*"

Dade released a low laugh that quickly died. "I'm done playing this game now." Dropping my hands, I whirled to find him staring at the prince, at the asshole who'd tried to steal even more from me. "Let's go."

Stepping back, I looked at the window, then at his waiting hand. "When did you get here?"

"When you pushed him off you like the sack of horseshit he is." His arms came around me, unyielding as the night sky bled and shifted behind him, and he warned, "Hold on."

"No," I screamed, but it was too late, the sound stolen by the ice we'd warped into, color blurring, objects remolding, time clutching then readjusting… and then it stopped with a ferocity that stole every ounce of oxygen from my lungs.

My head swam, and I coughed, my stomach threatening to evict the lamb shanks I'd had for dinner onto the gleaming white stone floor. "What have you done?" I all but screeched, my hands fisting my hair. The room we were in, its never-ending stone and wood ceiling, closed in on me.

"I rescued you. You're welcome."

"Rescued me?" I did shout then, a crazed bout of laughter following as I advanced on him and ordered, "Take me back right this second."

"Why? So you can marry the prince toad and find a way to defeat me?" He laughed, low and insidious. "It won't work, and not only because I cannot be defeated, but because he will never be permitted to marry you."

"I was going to work for my freedom," I said, not knowing why I even bothered.

His brows lifted. "By seducing the prince into helping you leave?" Taking a lock of my hair, he twirled it around his finger, thumb brushing the golden strand. "If tonight was any indication, you'd have failed." His eyes flashed. "Creatures like him don't wait. They take."

He released my hair, and stupefied, I spun in a circle, taking in the grandeur around me. The intense contrast between the beauty that befell my eyes to the overgrown, gnarled, and worn exterior I'd seen from the sky some years ago while taking one of my rare and daring flights.

Before I could absorb the lifeless stone walls, the domed ceiling, and the giant black doors of what appeared to be a grand foyer, my hand was snatched, and I was dragged deeper into what I knew had to be Shadow Keep.

"Dade," I warned, tugging to no avail to free myself from his hold. "Stars help me, if you don't—"

He whirled on me, and I tripped backward, grateful for his grip as my other arm spun to keep me upright. "You'll what?" he seethed, eyes shards of black-specked ice. "There's no escape, not from here, not from me, and should you try..." He let those unsaid words fill the small space between us, then continued toward a giant marble staircase.

It flared at the bottom, thinned in the center landing, then flared again at the top to join with matching marble railings that appeared to be supported by row after row of carved trees. It dawned on me then with enough force to thicken my tongue and swell my throat.

I was indeed standing in the middle of Shadow Keep.

We climbed, me with my heart pounding painfully inside my chest and he with brutal determination in each graceful step, until we reached the central landing. The floor there was made entirely of that gleaming stone with no carpets or clustering furnishings in sight.

The only décor was the arched window above the landing, large and filled with crimson glass, the others along either side oval and their glass a gray so light, it was nearly clear.

We veered left down the hall, passing door after closed door, their brass handles shaped in the face of a snarling wolf, and then we reached another flight of stairs, but this one was stone and far less grand.

I noticed another set that matched on the opposite side of the palace, keep, whatever this place was, but little else as I was led high up into a shadowed hall that housed two rooms. The one straight ahead was blocked by arched doors big enough for a beast to clamber through. The one we walked toward had a single, smaller door, and it was open.

Without pause, I was gently released and thrust into the dark by a hand at the small of my back. I froze mere feet inside, my eyes catching on a white poster bed with gray furred bedding and tasseled silk pillows, a long deep red chaise at its end. Bookshelves in a matching white wood spanned two walls, nightstands with twisting birch legs poised either side of the bed, and then I glimpsed three other doors.

I didn't see where they led to—bathing and dressing chambers, maybe—I turned back to the king as he said, gruff and clipped, "You seem rather fond of gilded cages..." He curled a finger at the door, coaxing the heavy wood toward him and effectively trapping his cruel words inside. "So here's another, my lovely swan."

# TWELVE

## Dade

THE PATH TO GLORY WAS PAVED WITH BLOOD AND GORE.
And bone-melting lust, it would seem. Though in nearly a lifetime of training with my uncle, he never went into detail about much else. Sex was a release, he'd said, and desire a curse. We fuck to be rid of it, but only if doing so did not detract from our goals.

Love would be our end.

An unexpected surprise—the intense attraction a nuisance I'd thought might need to be eradicated until the stars intervened, and well, here we were.

A swan princess, a prized jewel that had not been seen in centuries, was now cornered within my keep. She could run, she could shift, escape and fly herself home, but we both knew it would be futile.

We both knew I'd enjoy the chase and perhaps leave a trail of bloodied violence in my wake.

My swan was easily drowned in useless feelings such as guilt, so she'd stay right where she was, feathers splayed beneath my paw.

"My king," drawled Fang from the drawing room. "Why do I scent a bird in our midst?"

The scent of her should've been a dead giveaway during our handful of visits to that cave, but my hunger was such that I cared little about her sweet, airy fragrance and more about her lithe body. Every perfect curve, her laughter, and the way her eyes would change from bronze to molten gold with her turbulent emotions.

I should have never confided in Fang, but being that he was the closest thing I had to what most called a friend, I sometimes did. "Because you're sticking your snout where it does not belong."

I made to continue down the hall when he chuckled and said, "Scythe is positively overjoyed, you know." Sighing, I turned to lean against one of the dark oak doors while Fang finished chewing his leg of chicken. "Already sharpening his claws. Swan is a delicacy."

The circular marble-topped table shook with my rising rage, rattling the cutlery he didn't bother using. "Then it is within your best interest to make sure those claws stay sheathed."

His low laughter trailed me as I swept down the hall to the stairs that spiraled down into the kitchens.

Staff bowed and went about their business. I made haste to Merelda, the head cook, who was reprimanding a young pixie, and cleared my throat.

Though everyone else in the kitchen stilled, their fear and unease circling the too-warm rooms, Merelda did no such thing. The cook had been running these kitchens since before I was born, and therefore I'd surmised it was impossible to evoke utter obedience in someone who'd spanked you with a wooden spoon for stealing fresh sugar daisies.

The pixie's pale green eyes flicked to me, then to Merelda, and sensing she was no longer hearing a word, Merelda dismissed her with a wave of her favored threadbare dish towel before finally deeming me worthy of her attention. "King."

I watched the pixie dart around me, my lips wriggling, then tilted my head down at the rotund cook. "You terrify her."

"No more than you do," she muttered, heading to an awaiting tray on the wooden island behind me and dumping a spoonful of batter onto it. "What can I do for you, Daden?"

As always, my teeth clenched, but she was the only one permitted to call me by my true name. "We have a guest."

"Just one?" She didn't remove her attention from her task, slopping heaping globs of what smelled like oats, raisins, and brown sugar onto the tray. "You're losing your touch if you return with only one prisoner."

"Sarcasm," I said, dragging my finger over one of the perfect globs, groaning a little as the sweet ingredients caught fire over my tongue. "Delicious."

She swatted me away with the towel and a scowl. "Get to the point." The tray was moved out of my reach. Wise. "What's this guest got to do with me? You don't feed prisoners."

"We'll need to feed this one three times a day and give her whatever she so desires."

"Three times a day?" Her golden brows shot up with her head, brown eyes blinking as she surveyed my face. "You've..."

"That will be all," I said before the entire room became aware of information I'd rather they not be privy to. It wasn't that I was ashamed. This feeling, nagging and incessant, forbade such a thing. I just didn't care to give them all something else to gossip about as they prepared our meals.

Merelda's gaze tracked me until I disappeared up the stairs. The palace, often referred to as Shadow Keep, was abuzz with activity, murmurs in halls and behind closed doors as the staff all tended to their duties.

I sensed him before I saw him and withheld a curse in the hall atop the stairs as he exited a small sitting room where he'd been waiting and fell in step beside me. "We need to talk."

"Oh?" I ached to tell him to fuck right off, but instead, I asked, "What of?"

He gestured to the now empty drawing room, Fang long gone, the remnants of his dinner still upon the table. Nothing but bones. "You know exactly what of," Serrin said as soon as he'd pulled the doors shut behind us. Such a thing would not keep passersby from overhearing, not when many of those were faerie shifters, so I masked them with a thought, trapping our words inside. "The black swan was thought to be nothing but a fable, but now we know it is not."

"She is not," I corrected and leaned a shoulder against the wall. "Her name is Opal."

Serrin's blue eyes narrowed. "It matters not. You've brought our foretold doom straight to our door, *inside* our stronghold. Worse than that…" His thick brows scrunched with his face. "You seem fucking happy about it."

I ran my tongue over a canine, smiling to myself. "Do not worry yourself. She wouldn't hurt a fly." I straightened and sank a hand through my hair. "I will need legion one ready to journey at sundown."

"You have their princess, and we've killed their king," Serrin needlessly said, his expression rolling into slack shock. "Is the queen next? They will fall, and what will your swan do then?"

"What the swan does or does not do is of no concern of yours," I gritted. "We head to the cove. While I was visiting Castle Errin, I heard talk of ships arriving at dawn the day after tomorrow."

"Dade."

I'd turned for the doors when his next words stopped me.

"I fear what the stars have in mind for you, for all of us, if we proceed now that we know of her existence."

*When feather meets fire, vengeance will expire.*

Anger burned brighter than any prophecy mapped out by the stars as I rounded on him, and growled low, "Are you suggesting we stop? When we are *this fucking close* to total annihilation?"

"Total annihilation was never what I had in mind, my king, only revenge on those who stole our hearts from us. You've nearly enacted all we'd set out to do, so perhaps it is time to put another plan in place." He squared his shoulders and braced his feet apart. A battle stance fitting for his demand. "Now, we must make them submit."

I stared at him for untold seconds, and then, as though it was rising from the deepest depths inside me, a graveled laugh trickled out, growing louder as I grabbed the rough fabric of his red tunic within my fist and bared my teeth. "You dare tell me what I do and do not need to do?"

All my fucking life, this cretin had bathed me in stories of murder and heartbreak and retribution. At the age of five years, I was handed a blade and told to wipe my tears and cut down that which had caused them.

He'd *never* given me reprieve, yet here he stood, asking it from me.

To his credit, he did not tremble, and he did not waver as he pushed through his teeth, "I merely wish for you to succeed and not fall, Dade."

Glaring at him, nearly nose to nose, I seethed, "You made me, honed me into all that I am, so don't you dare stand here and act as though you do not know any better—act as though you do not know me." His tunic slid through my clawed fingers, tearing as I unclenched them and shoved him away. "If we falter, even for a breath, we lose the advantage. We lose this war. *That* is what you told me. *That* is what I know to be true. So keep your prophesied worries to your fucking self."

The doors opened and slammed on his face as I stormed through.

I waited, claws long since retracted inside the beds of my nails, until the raw fury Serrin had stoked to life, the ember that never extinguished inside me, was reduced to a controllable smolder.

Outside the door to her rooms, I stood, listening. Her heart wasn't racing as fast as it had been when we'd arrived, but oh how it still danced, pumping blood into those gorgeous extremities, fueling each stride as she paced on the other side of the door.

I never saw her coming. Along with so many other fables, the swan princess was just a story told around campfires and before bed. Some were true stories of past events spun with fiction, others entirely imagined to frighten younglings or entertain brethren or would-be nightly companions.

All this time, she'd been a myth. A myth now given flesh and blood and burning golden eyes.

Mine. She was all fucking mine. And Errin's perfect prince now had a glowing mark upon his back. His death would arrive far sooner than we'd predicted. Far sooner than what was wise.

He'd have ample time to ponder his regret for touching my creature while locked within the bowels of my keep, his blood collecting slowly beneath his hanging feet.

As though she could scent the flare of my ire—the air warmed with my hunger for vengeance—the pacing on the other side of the door ceased. Smoothing a hand over my already perfectly tousled hair, I opened it with a grin.

And was struck in the head by a candelabrum.

I swayed but only momentarily, catching my swan atop the stairs with my arms looped around her.

She squirmed and raged, legs flying behind her to kick me in the shins. I didn't care. I barely felt it. I carried her back to her rooms and set her on her feet, taking in her swirling golden eyes and the heaving of her ample chest.

Noticing where my attention had landed, she snarled. I smirked. "You are displeased with me."

I kicked the candelabrum out of the way and closed the door as something trickled down my hairline.

"You killed my father," she said for what seemed like the hundredth time. "You deceived me, tricked me, and kidnapped me." Her smile was anything but comforting yet still shockingly beautiful as she growled, "Displeased is far too mild a word, *King*."

Lifting my hand, I collected some blood from where she'd struck near my brow and rubbed it between the pads of my fingers. "Try another one, then."

"What?" She glared, marching backward to the bed when I advanced.

"Another word. Loathing, contempt, ire, hatred, disgust…"

Stopping, she narrowed her eyes and then dropped them to the furred carpet before the bed, long lashes cresting her cheeks. "Just… go away."

"So you can try to escape again?" I asked, intrigued and humored. "Tell me, sunshine. Why wait until I arrived when you could have easily found another way out?"

Her silence was telling, loud in the way it spoke of all we both already knew.

"Because I'd find you," I said, gently, softly, clasping her chin in my bloodied fingers and lifting her eyes to mine. "Wherever you go, no matter how far, nor where you hide, this"—I rubbed the blood on my thumb over her bottom lip and watched her pupils explode with her rush of breath—"will never fail in uniting us should one of us seek the other, and my swan…" Her eyelashes fluttered, my thumb brushing, tempting those perfect lips to close around it.

I grinned, my cock harder than it had ever been before in my life, pushing at the confines of my pants in such a way that I knew when she swayed into me, unable to stop herself, she could feel it.

My lips skimmed her temple, a low groan accompanying my words as hers wrapped around my thumb to be introduced to her silken tongue. "My darling swan, never will there come a day, a night, a fucking minute of time when I won't need you near."

I vanished before I did something reckless. Before I bent her over that bed and lifted her skirts to explore the flesh I knew my words, my touch, *stars*—my fucking presence alone, had dampened.

I vanished to my rooms, and in the silence, the roar of my blood in my ears helped drown the one that ravaged my throat as I gripped my length and rid the need she constantly stoked to life.

# THIRTEEN

## *Opal*

T HAT VIOLENT ROAR, THE ONE THAT ARRIVED MINUTES AFTER
he'd left my rooms, echoed through the walls and sank deep
into my bones, urging my fingers places they'd rarely ventured
before.

I wouldn't do it, refused to because of him.

Ignoring the desire, the ache that lived and breathed like a second
entity inside me whenever he was near, was akin to dragging a knife
over slippery flesh, hoping the blade didn't slip or slice.

I couldn't let it. Not after what he'd done, the magnitude of it all,
and not when I now knew who he was.

My enemy, born and raised to be nothing but as the many rumors suggested.

To take him inside my body would not only cause shame but it
could also cost me my life to let my guard down in such a way, regardless of whatever the stars had decided.

It was not the decision of fates so far removed from us to decide
how our lives would unfold, not when handing our faith to them meant
certain peril—more bloodshed and death.

Yet I could not leave. I could not step one foot outside that door with the intention of escape. He'd know. He'd follow. To flee home, though my heart bruised with longing to do just that, would be selfish.

I would bring darkness to our city gates, to our people, and they'd already seen and endured so much.

In an effort to stave off thoughts of cherry blossom trees, torn hearts, and wide, pleading eyes, I'd discovered the rooms were stocked and luxurious enough to suggest that maybe the king had indeed not intended to kill me. That maybe, he'd been waiting to steal me. That or they'd once belonged to his mother or one of his lovers.

I discarded thoughts of the latter with bristling annoyance.

For hours, meals delivered and left outside my door, I sat upon the irresistibly comfortable bed and paced each length of the room, thinking, regretting, worrying, trying to conjure a strategy that might end this madness.

But when madness was all we knew, all any of these savages knew, what hope was there to garner something else?

The answer came with the rising of the sun, its golden glow leaking between the thorn-knotted branches obscuring the two windows on either side of my bed and the view of the river in the not too far distance. Instead of acting upon it, I dragged my breakfast inside and savored each bite before deciding on sleep.

This was not the type of plan that could be planned, but rather, came down to sacrificing oneself in order to survive—and maybe, just maybe, it would provoke change. Whether it would work, I didn't know, and though it would sicken me to try, the days and nights ahead seeming endless, one thing was painfully clear. Without the gathering of more forces from across the sea, we had nothing else.

I had nothing else.

All I had was *him*.

The king of wolves. A savage monster that, for reasons I was only just beginning to wholly absorb, purred and preened at the mere scent of me.

The door opened without any resistance as it had some hours ago when I'd retrieved my food.

It would seem the kitchenhands had been quick to take note of what I did and did not eat—providing me more fruit with breakfast and lunch and smaller portions of meals.

I half wondered if the king had requested that no one enter my rooms or if the staff merely did not wish to. Though I was willing to wager that when I returned, my bed, that I'd already made myself, would be remade and the tray consisting of a carafe of water and my mostly eaten dinner would be gone.

The hall was silent, eerily so, as I gathered my hair, still damp from the quick bath I'd taken upon waking long after the sun, and walked toward the closed doors at the end of the hall.

Without needing to check, I knew whose rooms lay beyond the intimidating large wood. Engravings of thorns and vines twined throughout the enormous arched barriers, his scent, smoke and cedar, pungent inside his lair.

But he wasn't in there. His rooms lay empty, yet I didn't bother trying to turn the brass handles. They'd be locked, and even if they weren't, I didn't want to see what horrors lurked inside.

His scent alone was a trap, a tempting call to lure me into certain darkness. Already, I stood upon the precipice, readying myself to leap into the shadowed depths below, painfully aware that I might never return.

And though I was certain I could do it—certain that I had no other choice—I didn't get the chance. I wound down the staircase, and the giant one after that, and came to a stop in the grand foyer, turning this way and that.

No one, not one single soul, had passed me by. No one stood at any of the alcoves and doorways. No staff, no guards, no king.

Instead of walking out through the main doors, where I knew sentries, as silent as they might be, were standing, I veered left across the foyer and rounded the back of the stairs to find a parlor at one corner—walls of bookshelves circling a chaise and a gleaming black piano—and then moved on to the pair of looming doors behind the staircase.

Roses, red and yellow, stained the oblong sections of cut-out glass, sunlight dripping through them and down the varnished wood beneath. They opened soundlessly when I willed them to, exposing a terrace beyond and two silent sentries who didn't so much as turn to look my way. Stepping stones, circled by tufts of grass and tiny white flowers, paved the way from the stone terrace to the emerald-green lawn.

More roses, alive in reds and blacks, unfurled in rows of circular beds before a giant hedge. As I waded closer, my skirts gathered away from the dew lingering upon the grass, I discovered it was not a hedge but the entry point of a maze.

"A game," said a deep voice from behind.

I whirled, my pulse skidding and my heartbeat pounding, to find a huge male with dark brown hair tucked behind his ears. His smile slowly spread to his near-black eyes as he chewed on a bone small enough to pick between teeth, his fingers tucked within the edging of his trousers.

I didn't trust the feigned casual stance—that he wouldn't be on me within a failed breath if he thought it necessary.

"If you dare," he continued, raising a dark brow.

"I'm not fond of games," I returned, glad my voice remained steady.

He noticed my glance at the guards some yards away on the terrace, his smile climbing higher into his cheeks, dimples popping. "Yet here you stand."

Every muscle coiled, ready to spring into feather and flight. As if he could sense that, the male just laughed. "Fear not. I've been warned not to harm you, swan."

"That's… lovely," I muttered.

"Indeed." Those dark eyes slid over me, a slow perusal that raised every hair on my body. "Others have been given the same order, though I would not press your presence upon certain… people."

I frowned, sure there was a clear message behind those words, one I couldn't read, but I nodded. "Where is he?"

"The king?" he asked, knowing full well that was who I meant. "The royal cove."

My stomach sank, and my half-formed plans withered. The gold, all that gold he'd helped me to weave, and he'd just… kill the merchants before they could so much as barter for it.

Boiling. My skin boiled with each tense breath, and I turned away from the tall, staring creature to collect myself momentarily before asking, "You did not wish to go with him…?"

"My name is Fang. I was given orders to keep an eye on things here. You are free to roam the grounds, but might I caution you to wait until the king returns."

*Fang.* The king and his wishes could go rot. All that gold thread…

I took a step toward the maze, needing away from yet another beast wearing the skin of a Fae male—needing away from this place and its king and his every abominable action.

"Princess." A warning I refused to heed.

I rounded the opening in the hedge and allowed myself, even if just for a little while, to get lost.

# FOURTEEN

## *Dade*

I KICKED THE FALLEN LAD'S SHOULDER, TOEING HIM TO HIS BACK from the rock on which he'd died.

What remained of the captain's face after landing on the rock was too bloody to make out. It mattered not. I crouched down and patted his pockets, sniffing, finding what I needed inside his coat.

"Captain Lesands," I murmured so Scythe would hear, "was given minimal, basic orders."

"I don't understand." He said what the rest of us, if we had half a brain, were thinking. "Where's the gold, then?"

We were not after the gold woven from myself and my swan. No, we were here merely for the sport of it. Keeping the gold-embroidered clothing from leaving our shores was but a bonus.

A bonus that further kept the human king and queen from gathering foreign armies to our land.

We hadn't been given misinformation. I'd heard it myself, and the wolves who'd eked out a living in the human villages and farms, glamoured to appear less than what they were—had backed that information up with their own findings.

Three ships were to enter the Royal Cove after sunrise. Only one had done as predicted, all its inhabitants now dying on the sand at our feet, dead, or swimming out to sea to take their chances with the ruthless beasts of the ocean instead.

I stomped toward the water where Scythe was holding a flailing man's head beneath the surface, his eyes gleaming as the man came up for air, sputtering and coughing.

He growled into the gent's face, "Where are the others?"

"Others?"

He shoved his head back underwater, then tore it out by his hair. "The other ships, you useless fuck."

"I do not know of—"

His words were cut off as Scythe shoved him underwater once more. Though we didn't need him to tell us what I'd already figured out.

A gull shrieked overhead, flapping away as eagles and crows began to swarm, lured by the scent of blood and dying flesh. Gazing up at them, then down at the parchment in my hand, I read over the meager contents again.

"So we have coordinates and one task." Scythe released the man when he went limp, the sea swallowing his head and then his torso, and brushed his hands over his leathered vest. I squinted at the frothy bay, thinking out loud. "Collect the goods and set sail immediately. No goods, but we have two missing ships."

"A decoy." Scythe frowned at the harsh glow of the midday sun.

We'd arrived before sunrise, but we hadn't attacked when the ship anchored in the cove. No, we'd waited for the king and queen's regiment to arrive. When no one had, we'd watched the human sailors, listened to their lilted accents as they'd talked amongst themselves on board, then realized from their careful conversation that something was amiss, and they'd had no plans to leave their ship.

So we'd decided to remove them from it ourselves.

"Pile every single body and limb back on board," I roared, scrunching the parchment in my hand, then setting it aflame. "Leave the ship in the harbor but set it on fire."

"A message." Scythe flicked blood from his cropped head of black hair. "I like it."

"We've indeed been duped," I said, annoyed beyond reason to have my suspicions confirmed. "They must have scaled the cliffs beyond the castle. That or they lowered or just tossed the clothing to the other two ships."

Scythe followed my line of vision to the beach, the gray blurs of the seaside village that'd been vacated long ago, to the city beyond. "Should we head that way? We can cut them off as they leave."

"It won't work." I was the only one amongst our legion who could fly. Vordane had three legions. Scythe commanded legion one, legion two belonged to Fang, and my uncle commanded legion three—the only legion with flyers.

I governed and outranked all, but not even I was riddled with enough wrath and greed to send my warriors over guarded land in hopes of reaching the sea and ships at the cliffs beyond. Such a task would require more than one legion unless accompanied by foot soldiers, maybe even some of the grunts still undergoing training.

Taking the cubs out for missions they were not yet equipped for would not only see many of them killed—such wasted potential—but it would enrage many.

I was never in the fucking mood to deal with disgruntled mothers.

"We return home," I said at long last, tearing my eyes from the city of Errin and all the cretin that awaited me inside. Their deception rankled, and I was certain they'd hoped for just that as much as they'd hoped their stolen product made its way safely from our waters.

I wondered how they felt about their missing captive. Now my captive. My swan.

The thought made me feel a little better about being tricked, and many warriors gaped at me, perplexed as I waded through them all wearing a smirk.

Oh, those human royals would be mighty pissed. Why, I was willing to bet they hadn't even alerted my swan's dear mother. For it would reveal them to be the bumbling fools they were, as well as anger the grieving widow to the point of war.

I'd send an anonymous tip myself, knowing the gold queen would send every soldier, every able-bodied creature, to Errin—eliminating many from both kingdoms. Perfect. Far less work for me.

Alas, I'd come to learn my swan would most certainly not appreciate that.

Oh, how she fucking enraged me.

Stars, I loathed her and all she stood for. I loathed her nearly as much as I wanted her. I'd been cursed. I was sure of it. The bird was both my remedy and my affliction.

Fortunately for all, I'd never been afraid of hard work. The human royals could wait. The itch to lay eyes upon my feathered princess could not.

In a flare of bone-crunching flame, I shifted, the minor wounds I'd garnered on our hunt healing. While the warriors hefted and dumped body after body onto the ship, I leaped at the hillside, claws sinking inside soft sand and blades of grass, wings unfurling as I withheld a rumbling roar and shot into the sky.

# FIFTEEN

## Opal

**S**ILENCE CREPT AFTER ME LIKE A SHADOW AT MY BACK. Birdsong from the trees above waned and died, rustling leaves stilling. Gazing up, it was as though a glass ceiling had rolled overhead, trapping the world outside and me within.

Fine hairs began to stand upon my bare arms, the warm breeze no longer. The air had grown thick, frozen, yet I could still feel each breath enter and leave my body. One foot moved before the other, carrying me toward the first corner of the maze.

In that corner sat a garden gnome, and as I wound deeper inside the maze, another and another, all dressed in differing painted clothing of red, yellow, green, and blue. Some wore top hats, others bonnets, and upon each of their faces were tiny secretive smiles. They guided the way, and I found myself eager to discover what the next one might look like with each new corner.

The sun didn't leave me, but its warmth was no longer, and the shade with each passing turn caused my skin to prick and pebble with gooseflesh. Roses, in deeper blacks and reds, hung from many a thorny branch in the hedge, all in perfect bloom.

On my sixth turn, I gave in to the urge to reach out and touch one. Silken petals firmed and yielded beneath my fingertips, and then the ground shook, and I clutched my hand to my chest as roots slithered out from beneath the hedge.

I scrambled back, but it didn't matter. Like snakes in a feeding frenzy, the roots raced after me, and I fell flat on my back, bones rattling. A scream was trapped inside my throat, unable to be released as I rose to my bruised backside and frantically tried to pluck at the roots that'd circled around my ankles.

Dade would say this was a perfect example of how carrying a weapon could save my life. Yet I had none, knowing I'd probably not be permitted a tool in which to slay him.

Groaning, I tugged and pulled to no avail. Panic scored through me, my heart kicking at my sternum when the vines didn't budge. They climbed higher, nearing my knees, thorns ripping and trapping my skirts.

*Shift*, I told myself. I had no choice but to shift.

I closed my eyes, swallowed thickly as my legs began to grow numb, and then rational thinking reentered, and I leaned forward to wrap both hands around the vines. Thorns cut into my palms, my blood only aiding my intentions as I compelled the plant to calm, to stop moving.

My breath, a long-forgotten thing, burned as I watched the serpentine vines slowly still, then gently unravel themselves from my body.

I didn't wait, wasn't willing to believe I could afford to. I climbed to my feet, urging feeling to return, and spun around to head back. To head back to the enemy I was growing uncomfortably familiar with. I'd much rather finish what he'd started than waste my people's chance out here by getting maimed by plants or some other creature.

I reached the end of the hedge-lined path when they moved. Closing in, they slid together in a patch of greenery and roses so thick, I wasn't sure my meager powers could convince them to do otherwise.

Cursing, I turned, the vines now slithering back under the hedges, and raced across the soft trimmed grass to the other end. If the maze wanted me to earn my way out, then that was what I'd do.

Rounding the bend, a line of garden gnomes blocked my path, and I blinked, swearing I had seen a few of those gnomes already when there was a blinding flare of light.

My arm shot up to shield my eyes, and when I lowered it, I found small faces with determined expressions and weapons bigger than they were in their hands.

Little Folk.

"What do we have here?" asked the white-bearded elf.

"A trespasser," hissed a tiny thing beside him—a youngling wearing a pair of overalls smaller than my palm.

It didn't matter that they were little. I shifted without thought, without thinking of the risk, wings flapping and taking me high above the giant walls of the hedge. The gnomes, Little Folk, became nothing but colorful dots below me as I climbed higher, my wings spreading wide with the gathering breeze.

I caught it, soaring over the hedge. At my back, Shadow Keep blocked my ascent from view, but not from those in the vegetable gardens to the west of the hedge, nor the workers in the orchards and wheat fields that stretched for a mile or more toward the east behind a large building with a horse-dotted training yard before it.

Greenhouses sat in three clustered rows beside the fields, and as I breached the never-ending hedge—trees. Dense woods spread from the west to wrap around the northernmost corner, crawling toward the east.

Toward the ravine, the place I'd once found solitude, and had since handed me chaos.

Lost to my musings, the melancholy for all the darkness that lay behind and ahead of me, I banked and dropped beneath the thick foliage of trees and entered the woods. I had to return. I knew that even with the king gone, he could still be alerted to my absence, and if this singular plan of mine was to work, then the last thing I needed was to make him too distrustful of—

A net swallowed me, pulling me toward the ground.

Feathers ripped and splayed, and I shifted back right as I hit the earth, my teeth singing, ankle groaning as I slipped on the netting and rolled to my side. Pushing up and peering through the mesh, I found myself surrounded by Little Folk.

They gawked, weapons slack at their sides or forgotten on the ground.

A white-haired female came forward, her dark blue eyes seeming too large for her small head. "A black swan."

Another female hurried by her, snatching the knife from her lax hand and snapped, "Well, don't just stand there, free her." Clucking her tongue, she approached me, slicing at the net, and then hollered, "Rosanne! Put the kettle on." She looked back at me, her huge eyes smiling bright. "We have ourselves a special guest."

Shock held me immobile as the rough netting slid down my arms, and I gazed around the small clearing I'd wound up in. Gingerly, I pushed to my feet, absorbing the tiny creatures that rushed out of their homes inside of fat toadstools, thick tree trunks, and the flower beds surrounding both.

Burrows emerged, rock thrown aside and more of them scrambling and spilling onto the grass. "You truly are the Little Folk."

We hadn't any in Sinshell for some decades, many fearing they'd been extinct or moved on after the first war.

"We prefer the term Elf." The white-bearded male drifted closer, his cheeks ruddy and shifting as he smiled. "But you may call us as you see fit."

"Elves," I breathed, blinking hard, still taking them all in.

"How do you like your tea?" asked the female, head tilted.

Tea? I stepped out from the netting, walking back a couple of steps toward what I hoped was the entry to the forest. "Just moments ago, you were ready to kill me."

"Kill you?" The female balked. "Oh, my dear, no. We merely teach trespassers a lesson, and then we let them go." I froze at that, thinking perhaps it was time to take flight again when she continued, "They might be missing some hair and shoes, but that's to be expected."

"Shoes?" I couldn't help but ask as two teeny tiny younglings hurried through the circular throng of Elves and into the clearing with a tea tray.

The bearded male stepped aside, and sketching his hand behind him, he peeled back some of the foliage. "The young ones enjoy them."

Indeed, behind him amongst the tall grass and wildflowers, a few of them clambered over what appeared to be a castle fashioned out of slippers and boots and leather dress shoes. The latter were few, and they would be, being that they were worn mostly by human males in Errin.

Ignoring the impulse to walk closer and inspect the laughing children, the windows cut out of soles, and the battlement made from the rubbery base of a rainboot, I asked, "And hair?"

"Oh," the female said, dragging my eyes back to her as she prepared the tray of tea, "that is merely to cast misfortune on the darker souls, the rotten ones who wished harm to befall us."

I found myself following her request to sit when she gestured to the empty grass behind me and smoothed out my tattered skirts over my knees as I did. "How does one do that?"

A tinny voice, likely undetectable to human ears, came from below my knee. "We boil and weave their hairs, then make lovely soft blankets with them." I shifted my leg, peering down at the young female who wore a gap-toothed smile and her brown hair in pigtail braids.

"Fink," hissed who I guessed was her mother. "Give the princess her space."

But I found myself returning the youngling's smile and offering my hand.

Her mother gasped when her daughter, delighted, climbed on, latching onto my fingers as I lifted her to my leg. There, she sat, watching me receive the tea I was sure to finish in two sips from the white-haired female. "And what's your name?"

"My mama's name is Beshal," informed Fink, who then pointed at the white-bearded male and said, "and that is my papa, Harro, and that is my uncle and aunt, Gretz and Pilon."

I nodded their way, still smiling as Fink introduced me to more of those gathered nearby. Most returned it, some of the young scuttled behind their parents' legs, peeking out from behind them every so often with shy smiles.

The tea, although barely there, was divine—a mixture of bergamot and sunshine that warmed my chest and relaxed my shoulders. I was offered more and found I could not refuse when Beshal scowled.

"No one tells that female no," Harro, who I'd guessed was her spouse, laughed jovially.

"Why are you here?" asked Fink. "You belong in storybooks, in tales told before sleep."

I raised a brow at that. "I'm not that old."

Fink laughed, but Beshal said, "The black swan has not been seen for many a year and has long thought to have been bled from your bloodline forevermore."

I nodded. "I know." Unsure of what else to say, I shrugged, laughing weakly. "Well, here I am. Another one."

"And in the king's clutches, no less," griped Harro, his bushy brows covering his beady chocolate eyes. "So yes, what brings you here?"

"He stole me," I said simply, for it was true and the last thing I'd ever do was protect the likes of Dade Volkahn.

No one spoke for a minute, the only sound the trilling of birds and the sea in the distance, crashing below the cliffs.

"But you are outside the keep. You could fly home at any moment."

"Don't be foolish." Beshal glowered at her spouse. "The king of wolves would find her, hunt her until her final days." She looked back at me, her eyes twinkling with knowing. "No, she is exactly where she ought to be."

I smiled and sipped my tea.

# SIXTEEN

## *Dade*

**A** FUCKING TEA PARTY.

I'd been flying across the southern farmlands of Vordane when something began to crawl beneath my skin. Landing in a paddock, I startled the shit out of some cattle, then shifted back and opted for faster travel when the feeling didn't abate.

Warping inside the Keep, I knew instantly that something was amiss, so I interrogated Fang until I feared I'd rip his head clean off, and there she was…

Sitting amongst the fucking toadstools and flowers, drinking tea with the elves.

Fang had nearly pissed in his trousers when I'd appeared before him on the terrace after finding Opal's rooms empty, her scent leading outside. "Where is she?" I'd growled.

Collecting himself with a curse, he'd straightened from where he'd been taking a nice little nap against the pillar. "She wanted to explore the maze."

"And you just let her?" I glowered. "*Alone?*"

"They won't harm her, I'm sure."

I'd snarled, rippling into shadow inside the maze, only to discover her scent led up into the sky, trailing toward the woods beyond the maze, and then vanished suddenly. I'd landed and traced it again upon the breeze, following it into the trees.

To find her smiling, drinking tea as though she hadn't skirted danger and made my stomach churn and twist in such a disgustingly foreign way. Elves surrounded her, sitting in the grass, standing before her with enraptured faces, and one even perched on her leg.

"My king." One of them finally noticed I was in their midst, standing by a tree, and my swan... oh yes, that was panic in her eyes as she lowered her thumbprint-sized teacup and glanced my way.

I tilted my head, eyeing her. *What have you been up to?*

She looked away, helping the tiny creature off her leg and setting her onto the grass. "Thank you for the tea," she said to Beshal, whose eyes bounced back and forth between us as she carefully placed the teacup upon the tray. "It was the most delicious I've ever had."

Beaming, Beshal forgot all about my presence and curtsied. "Please do come back."

"I'd love to."

I withheld a grumble and waded over, snatching my swan by the arm. The elves took note but wisely didn't say a word as they scrambled back toward their homes, and I took my swan back to her rooms.

Inside them, a shadowed breeze still fading from our arrival, Opal whirled on me. "That was so rude."

"Rude?" I kicked the door closed, perplexed to the point of near-laughter.

"You just... just"—with a groan, the swan flung her arms out— "*took me*, and you didn't even offer them a greeting."

"What do the elves care for greetings?"

Her eyes widened, gold jewels catching on mine. "You mean to tell me you do not even know them?"

"What's to know?" I eyed the bookshelves, tiring of this conversation. "They are Little Folk and of no importance or use to me."

Anger lit her eyes, and I found myself struck stupid by the glow of them, the way the high rise of her cheekbones reddened. Her mouth, the perfect pink bow, spread, but then her lips closed. I couldn't look away as I watched that ire rapidly melt, replaced with a deceptive calm. "Why?" she said at last.

I could hardly stand to blink and did so quickly so as not to miss a moment of staring. "Why what?"

"Why do you want me here? What *use* am I to you, especially given what the stars have foretold."

She went there, straight there, and I should've known she'd muster up the courage to eventually. Why, watching as she was forced to grow into herself, to adjust to her ever-changing surroundings, adapting to things that happened to her while she hoped to control and reverse it all... stunning and fascinating.

I placed one foot in front of the other, my leathered armor still reeking of blood and terror, and took note of the way her heart pounded harder, her skin flushed deeper, and her entire body locked.

But those eyes, they didn't waver from mine.

A sheltered princess, most certainly, yet one who'd made it her mission to absorb everything in the world around her, searching for things others couldn't afford to waste time looking for. She ignited intrigue and study like nothing else ever had, and I knew, even without the stars meddlesome intervening, it would be so regardless.

Opal didn't move even though the rational part of her, the part that thought me nothing more than a savage beast, longed to. Her scent infiltrated, flooding deep, and I groaned lightly as my head swam with it, and my blood heated and bubbled with desire.

Fingers coated in dried blood slid under her delicate chin, and her eyes closed when my head lowered. "Because my troublesome swan, I prefer to keep my most worthy adversaries right where I can see them," I whispered, her eyes reopening as my nose bumped gently into the side of hers. "Right under my snout."

I tore myself away at her sharp intake of breath, the air between us growing taut enough to snap with leashed need, and forced myself to the door.

"Wait," she rasped.

My eyes closed briefly, and then I peered over my shoulder.

She wrung her hands before her, her mettle shrinking with her shoulders, and then she turned for the window. "Never mind."

Her torment should have satisfied me, but instead, it worsened that pit of foreign feeling inside my stomach, causing it to crawl into my chest.

"You could just take her," Scythe suggested, tearing a chunk from a glossy red apple and grinning around the fruit. "We are nothing but savages after all."

The thought alone, of her struggling and wailing beneath me, as I'd seen happen to some females before during attacks, disgusted me now as it had then.

"No," I barked. "Savages we may be, but we are not thieves." Scythe raised a brow in question, knowing I was indeed a hypocrite. I didn't care. He knew. He'd been there when I'd made it extremely clear that I would not tolerate such abuse. "Only vermin take what is not offered willingly."

He nodded once, returning to his apple. "Wine then. She is sure to forget how much she loathes you with some wine in her soft belly."

I gnashed my teeth at him, and he laughed, flinging his middle finger in the air as he bowed and left the war room.

It was now empty, save for Fang and myself. He and Scythe had stayed back after the meeting with my uncle about the human royals' clever deception in the cove. It would seem the golden thread had indeed left our shores, but we hadn't the desire, nor the worry, to seek it out.

Let the humans barter with it.

No one would come to their aid, no matter how much gold they accrued and sold. Those across the sea had to know it would be suicide to involve themselves in a war that did not concern them.

They'd take their gold, make their faulty promises, spill lies easily as humans so often did, and meanwhile, we would continue. We were close now. Only the queen remained, and those in her court who could not be trusted once we took their land for our own.

"Scythe wouldn't know what to do with a female unless they landed in his lap," Fang said, snatching my attention from the coordinates on the map of Nodoya.

The red stakes indicated the landmarks already destroyed. They covered lovely fat little chunks, like blood trickling through a snow bed. The black indicated the three remaining strongholds to be taken.

Castle Gracewood, the city of Sinshell, and Castle Errin.

The latter was a little optimistic and possibly unnecessary. Though the idea of sharing a realm with humans did not bother me as much as it did some of my brethren, it still irked. Mainly due to their dubious attitudes and cunning assertion of power.

They did not strike. Their ilk slunk in the shadows and skipped over skirmish.

And they said we, the Fae, were creatures with no morality.

"Luckily for Scythe," I murmured absently, my eyes dragging from Castle Errin and sweeping over the woods and river into the land beyond. "That is often what happens." How the Gracewoods had shared their land with mortals for all these centuries was something historians failed to explain in thorough detail.

They said that ten ships entered the harbor many a year ago, intent on exploring a realm other sailors had passed on their journeys. A realm shielded in fog and mist with sand more gold than that of any coin.

Rather than battle with them, the weaklings of our kind—the gold Fae—had invited them to stay and sold off a portion of their land in good faith. In hopes of garnering trade opportunities with more of the human filth across the sea.

The opportunities indeed came, and with them, the humans bargained their way into more land from the Gracewood line, their kingdom now taking up nearly half of Sinshell—and renamed the southeastern corner of our continent after their first king—Errin.

Yes, it would prove interesting to take back that which never truly belonged to the mortals. However, I could not foresee how doing so would benefit us too greatly. For they indeed had helped the continent of Nodoya and its two originating kingdoms to grow in wealth and opportunity.

"King?" Fang lobbed a peppered nut at the map. "Stars, have you been smoking the hazel?"

He knew better than to ask such a thing, so I needn't have bothered answering and instead scrubbed my fingers over my chin. "What of the crossover?"

"We could use it again, but wouldn't your swan have informed her mother or somebody of its existence by now?"

Doubtful. "Send your legion there at first light to see if it remains."

Sharpening his favored dagger, Fang nodded. "And how does she fare after her journey in the maze?"

"She was having tea with the elves when I found her."

"What?" Fang barked with a laugh.

"You heard me just fine," I grumbled and knocked the placeholders from the map. They rolled across the table into the Night Sea.

"Well, well," Fang drawled and tossed the rock he'd been using to the table. "I do believe this swan most certainly likes to keep you on your toes."

"She cannot stand the sight of me," I admitted, every word gritted. "Yet the stars themselves have ordained it. I do not understand."

Flames danced higher in the sconces on the wall, no daylight visible in the windowless room that had been spelled to keep anyone in the dungeons down the hall, or anywhere else, from overhearing.

"Have you thought about doing something nice for her?"

I scowled. "I saved her from being mauled by the human swine, did I not? Then put her up in lavish accommodations with three meals a day."

Fang bit his lips, then released them with a grin. "Maybe you should gift her with something she likes then?"

"What's not to like about her rooms?" Blinking once, I wondered why she wouldn't have appreciated my rescue and all I'd given her since, then demanded, "And why would I do that?"

The asshole laughed, then sobered upon realizing I'd meant every word. "Oh, my fucking stars." Straightening in the chair, he clapped his hands between his spread knees and bent forward. "Okay, first you need to find out what she likes, what makes her happy, then give something to her with an apology for taking her away from her new elven friends."

"Why the fuck would I apologize?" I asked, incredulous. "She is mine, not theirs."

"The golden ones are… different." He nodded. "From what I've seen and heard anyway. So I wouldn't think the swan is too fond of being treated as though she were property."

"But that's exactly what she is," I said, confusion causing my fingers to buckle as my claws threatened to erupt. Safely delivered and secured—she would forever belong to me.

Fang stared at me for moments that only incensed, then shook his head and stood.

Gritting my teeth, I spat out, "Regardless of the fine print, she likes frivolous bullshit like flowers." I flung a clawed hand at an empty cup and saucer on the table, then leaned over it. "And fancy tea and pretty ideals such as peace."

Fang lifted his shoulders, eyeing my black claws, then let them slump as he meandered to the door. "So give her flowers and fancy tea." With a look over his shoulder that I couldn't decipher, he said, "We both know you cannot grant her that last one."

He'd been gone a while before I finally retracted my claws, leaving gouges in the map and the wood beneath it.

# SEVENTEEN

## *Opal*

REMAINED IN MY ROOMS THE NEXT DAY, UNSURE HOW TO proceed or if I even had what it took to see this insane idea through.

There was no other way.

Yet as I'd sat upon the bed, arrows and circles of light spilling in from between the vines and branches concealing most of the windows, I'd contemplated what I'd been about to ask the king the previous day.

When I'd told him to wait.

I had been hopeful he'd walk right back to me, and then I could kiss him, but I should've known before the word left my mouth and his razor-sharp eyes had met mine over his broad shoulder that it wouldn't be that simple.

He wouldn't have believed it. Not now. Not yet.

A book was splayed over my lap, nursery rhymes from the mortal lands, and a handful of grapes entering my mouth, when a brief bang on the door echoed, and he sauntered in.

Swallowing, I closed the book and set it atop the small pile next to the bowl of fruit on the nightstand. "Do you always just enter rooms without permission?" I inwardly winced. Idiot. I was such a stars-damned idiot. All my life, I'd harnessed the skill of biting my tongue, but around him, the one creature I had to, I failed to protect myself in that way.

Dade pursed his lips in mock thought, leaning against the door. "Well, yes." A grin, magnificent and eye-reaching, made my stomach jerk. "I am the king, after all."

I read the words his waning smile delivered... *And it would be wise to remember that.*

"I did knock." He sighed then said a moment later, "Take a walk with me." A gentle offer I could not refuse.

I still tried, for that was what he'd surely expect. "I'd rather not."

His breathy laughter was talons and heat, a soft threat that grazed the skin. "Your lies are sweet, truly. But I've got time. I'll wait as you feed me some more."

Wanting my eyes off him, I peered down at my lavender gown. Simple, versatile, and laced around every edge in white, it fell from the tops of my breasts to my ankles easily as though it were a nightgown.

It was one of my new favorites, but too plain if I hoped to seduce a king. "Fine," I said, and his brows rose as I did from the bed. "But let me change first."

Expecting him to leave and allow me some privacy to do just that, I crossed the room to the closed door on the same wall as the bathing chamber.

Inside it, rows of gowns for varying occasions hung in peaches, creams, lilacs, blues, emeralds, whites, and lemons. A studded sitting chair was perched in the corner, an ornate silver table beside it, so one could sit and eat or drink as whomever used this room decided on which article of clothing to wear.

The cloaks were velvet, silk, and thick wool. The nightwear was tasteful, even if some of the lace concoctions left nearly nothing to the imagination. I wasn't sure I'd ever dig deep enough to find the courage for some of those.

My fingers fell upon a white dress with a heavy underskirt. Its bodice hung low enough to tempt but not enough to sully.

"Do you like them?" The king's voice came from behind, and my hand flew to my chest.

He stood in the doorway, leaning against the wooden trim with his hands in the pockets of his trousers. "I picked the colors." His gaze left the garments and draped over me like a cool breeze in the midst of a hard summer. "The colors I thought would best suit your skin tone, your hair..." He blinked once, his eyes finding mine. "And your eyes."

Words evaporated from my mind.

Every single one.

I stood there, fingers falling slack to my side as the king's eyes left mine to slowly roam over my face. They sat on my lips for a paused moment, long enough for me to remember the airless weight of his own upon them, and then swept down my body. "Leave that one on."

Words returned in a rush, spinning me where I stood, as I said with a harsh exhale, "But surely something nicer—"

"It's perfect. You're perfect." Dade backed out of the dressing room and into the bedchamber. "Let's go."

Unable and unwilling to argue, because I was fond of the dress myself and also because it felt as though something had snuck inside my brain and mixed everything into an unrecognizable mess, I followed him silently out into the hall.

We rounded the staircase and followed the quiet all the way to the bottom. In the foyer, the king stopped and turned to me so suddenly, I nearly crashed into his chest. He steadied me with strong hands upon my shoulders. I told myself not to recoil and to stand still while I gazed up into those cerulean eyes. "Would you like some tea before we go?"

His hands slowly slid down my arms, leaving chills in their wake. "Tea?" I asked, perplexed enough to scrunch my brows. "I thought we were taking a walk."

The king's jaw flexed, and he nodded as if to himself. "Right. Yes, of course." Taking my hand, he led me through the grand foyer, through those formidable arched doors, and out onto a beige stone landing that curved with the three steps beneath it.

I slowed, the king forced to do the same, and turned to stare back up at what had been my prison this past week. Shadow Keep was indeed a palace, its gigantic exterior rising higher than my eyes could reach from our angle. Black stone intermingled with off-white slabs of concrete, creating a monstrosity most might consider abandoned if they didn't know any better.

Leafy vines, thorn-ridden and out of control, covered more than just the windows of my chambers. They curled over every available space, making the stone almost invisible beneath, light and dark peeking through in small patches. The doors before us, and the statues of wolven beasts with wings high up on the ledges of the rooftops, were all that seemed unscathed. Though moss crawled over the centuries-old sentinels' heads and bodies, the stone cracked in some places, the monstrous spread of greenery and thorns had merely curled and woven around them.

"A trunk of gold coin for your thoughts?"

"It's... beautiful," I heard myself admit, transfixed. "And nothing like you would expect."

"It is a deterrent, yes, but I mostly just prefer people not to think I live in a shiny palace with all the glitz and frills."

I turned to the king, laughing a little. "But it is just that inside."

Dade winked—my stomach kicked—and then collected my hand again. "Many don't know that." Taking the steps down to the fountain, another winged beast at its center, water spraying from its open maw, the king added, "And we do not have all the pomp..." He flicked his free hand. "The paintings, trinkets, vases. I removed most of it."

I watched the moss deepen in color as we neared the edge of the square fountain's low wall, watched it slither and writhe as though begging someone to touch the sun-warmed ledge. I didn't, knowing a trick when I saw one. Such moss was grown with enchantments to snatch at the limbs and clothing of unwanted guests. "Why?"

"Less work for the staff. All that dusting must be rather tiresome."
I made a face, and he noticed, for he said, "You think I'm joking?"

"Most certainly."

A shocked, quick bark of laughter. "Fine. It reminded me of my parents, of those I never knew, and I couldn't stand it."

The desire to ask more about them thickened my tongue. We avoided the road leading away from the Keep toward the river through the trees and veered down a stone path. Hedges, dotted with blood-red and snow-white roses, sat perfectly trimmed on either side of us.

The sudden stillness, the question sailing from my parting lips, made me all too aware of the gentle grip of his enormous hand around my own. "How old were you when they died?"

"Barely more than a week."

The cold detachment in those words struck me as did a harsh, unexpected slap of empathy. To have never known my parents... For all their many faults, I still couldn't fathom it and did not even wish to try. "Have you been told much about them?"

"Enough," he said, tone curt. "Mainly how they died in the first war." I'd already known that but not the particulars, of which he surprised me by stating, "Your grandfather and his general lured and captured them, trussed them up on flower-choked poles to be made an example of, to threaten into compliance, and then he tortured them before slaying my mother and thus beginning the war."

I stopped as we reached the Keep's edge. A giant dark metal gate loomed at my right, shrouded with whorls of leaves and blocking the entrance to the side of the palace. "They did no such thing."

"They did, and for nothing more than fear of those greater than them." His hand released mine, but not before he brought it to his lips. Soft and with his eyes locked on mine, they pressed into my knuckles, then fell away with his touch. "Believe what you will." He walked on through the opening gate, the stone path no longer and grass beneath our feet. "Your lot always do."

I followed him behind a rosebush and then a large grouping of shrubs beyond that until we emerged into a slow-rolling clearing that caught my breath and expelled it all at once. Emerald grass danced in the autumn air, wildflowers and bluebells rustling, petals scattering on the current of the wind.

And beneath it, a river, its surface like that of blue glass, winding and curling, cutting through the heart of Vordane—separating its ruler from the rest of the land.

"There are bridges hidden amongst the forest-heavy parts of the river, and they're always guarded." Dade's hair swept back, every inch of his marble-hewn beauty available to the eye when he turned a few steps below where I stood. "The city across the river lends itself to both home, ship, and business owners. There's a florist, botanist, herbalist, apothecary…" He went on, but I found myself lost in the movement of his lips, the perfect plushness of them, and the white teeth that would reveal themselves as he spoke of this place, this place of nightmares and death, with such ardent affection.

The movement of his mouth ceased, and I feared my cheeks would pinken as those lips curled into a knowing smirk, so I looked at the city across the river, the tiny glimpses of a lie I'd been made to believe my entire life.

If there were nightmares in this land, then they were hidden well, for all I saw was magic, vitality, and, judging from what he'd believed to be true, a ruler stars-bent on justice.

Revenge against those who had taken something irreplaceable from him.

I wasn't sure where he'd heard fables of torture about his parents, but I did know that it couldn't be true. I'd make him see that. Before all this was over, the truth would live on.

I cleared my throat, asking, "Can we cross it?"

"Another day," the king murmured. "Or eve. The dancing lights over the river are something else entirely."

Those words raked over me in the form of a shiver as I stared at the clustered wood and stone homes and shopfronts, the streets that wound it all tightly together into the shape of an imperfect diamond. I couldn't make out much beyond the heart of Vordane, nothing save for many wood-shrouded areas, possibly some creeks and village towns.

"Why did you bring me out here?" I asked, no ire in the question, just blatant curiosity.

"You, ah…" The king dragged his attention to his boots, the breeze catching his loose tunic and plastering it to his firm chest. I swallowed, removing my eyes from his muscular torso when he looked up. "Well, you seem to like the gardens."

"We, the golden ones, born with flowers in our hair," I muttered, though I couldn't help but smile. "I should be offended by your assumption."

His brow crinkled in a way I found far too endearing for a male who'd ripped my father's heart from his chest before tearing into it with his teeth. "It's not merely an assumption, but watching what you seem drawn to."

My breath dried and vanished.

*Him.* I was drawn to him, and remembering just who he was and what he'd done seemed futile given our circumstances—but I could never forget.

As if reading my darkening thoughts, Dade sighed and retrieved something from the shoulder holster I'd assumed was void of weapons. Not so; he'd merely glamoured them so no one could see. "Here," he said, closing some of the space between us to offer me a sapphire hilted blade. "Should you decide to run into the maze unassisted again. No iron, so don't bother coming for my heart."

Those last words were low, frosted. I didn't tell him that I doubted the elves would meddle with me, nor that I hadn't thought about sinking a blade beneath his flesh. Carefully, I reached out, the sun glinting off the gathering of sapphires in the hilt before my hand wrapped around the leather.

Seeming as though he wasn't sure what to do with himself, the king's eerie stillness was no more. He shifted, boots pressing heavy into the grass, and brushed a hand over his cheek and into his hair.

He'd given me a weapon, believing I wouldn't thrust the blade into his back when he turned and waded over the grassy mound to the pathway back to the palace through the bushes.

"I can take care of myself, you know."

"Hence why I gifted you with the dagger," he said. "You're welcome."

A groundskeeper passed us on the path and bowed but did not look our way as I hurried after his king. "Dade."

He stopped upon the steps, lashes spreading from a jeweled eye that peered at me over his shoulder. "Why did you bother teaching me? When you'd never planned to let me live."

"You still think I intended to kill you?" He scoffed. "We both know that is impossible." He headed inside, and confused, I trailed him up the stairs, thinking he was heading back to my rooms, stunned when he walked straight ahead to the doors of his own.

"But you could have done it then," I said, my skirts clenched in my fist. "You had endless opportunity."

"I should've killed you, yes, and perhaps I once did intend to." He opened the doors to his rooms, waiting for me to walk in ahead of him before he continued. I shouldn't have, but I did, and was immediately taken aback by the enormity of the chamber, struck still beside a low-lying chest of drawers with few trinkets on them.

"The first time I saw you sitting on that hollowed-out tree, I knew I had to—after using you to get to that father of yours, of course." He went on before I could send the wolf skull masquerading as a vase on his drawers sailing at his smug head. "But even having just met you, the mere idea of doing so, of harming you in any way, made me feel odd. A little ill." His eyes narrowed on me. "Are you a witch playing at being the swan heir?"

I gave him a blank stare. "Not funny."

"Fine. Would it curdle your blood to know that I like to play with my food before I eat it?"

My tongue threatened to poke a hole in my cheek, and I set the skull down with a *thunk*.

A roaring laugh scrunched every one of his lethal features, warming and remolding them into something else—something that curdled my blood for the wrong reasons—something I'd rather not see yet knew I would do so again whenever my eyes closed.

They swayed over him, then over his room, the bed twice the size of any other king's with its bending dark wooden posts and the two oblong windows on either side shrouded in red glass and copious vines. On one side of the bed perched a dark oak desk before a window, inkpots and parchment lined and piled neatly, and a small dining table with two seats. On the other side, upon the wall above another chest of drawers used as a nightstand, stretched a map.

Thick reddened blotches of ink had been splattered upon Sinshell—upon the landmarks he'd poisoned and murdered.

Tearing my eyes from the map to the king, who stood wearing that infuriating mask of indifference, the weight of the dagger in my hand increased.

And I raced from his rooms to my own.

Indecision and disgust and hatred and something else I didn't want to acknowledge had my limbs tangling in the bedding until the moon had risen high beyond the windows.

Darkness gathered in patches over the floor and in the corners of the room, broken only by lighter shadows that bobbed and drifted.

*Look at me, honey bee...*

The dagger, tucked under the nightstand, was already warm in my hand when I bent down to retrieve it as though it had been ready and awaiting use.

I didn't know what I was doing. All I knew was what I was feeling—this broiling, unbearable ache that shattered in scalding waves behind my dry eyes. It fired every limb into action, my breathing into sharp shards of air, and encased my heart in a protective barrier of ice as I exited my rooms.

The hall was empty. No guards stood outside our doors for protection. I was willing to wager the king thought himself protection enough. The cocky, insufferable monster.

*Would it curdle your blood to know that I like to play with my food before I eat it?*

His soft tone, brutal words, had haunted me for hours. For years, my people had lived in fear and worry that soon it would be them. That soon he would come for us all—leaving no trace of us behind save for the healers I'd heard he'd stolen from us to help his own people.

Even then, they'd be bred into the blood Fae's history until our heritage was so diluted with theirs, those stolen gold Fae healers would soon be wiped from most everyone's memory.

No more.

I couldn't bear it, this torturous game of lust-addled hatred and fear. Fear of him, fear of myself and of what he stoked to life within me, fear for my people and what would become of them should I fall prey to a murderous king and lose myself. Either in death or...

I couldn't even fathom the thought of it, but this entity inside me, this fate-ordained disaster that seemed like some type of gruesome jest of the stars, made me feel it anyway.

I wanted it gone—over before it unfurled into something that would cost our people everything.

One of the doors opened with a thought, and shocked, I just stood there for a moment as it swung far enough to reveal the darkness within.

When I was certain the swaying shadows over the floor were just that, I crept inside, and the door closed with a near soundless click behind me. My eyes slowly adjusted with each careful step taken toward the ginormous bed.

In it, upon his back and shirtless, the king slept. His bare chest, sculpted by the stars and scarred by his own deeds, rose and fell. His arms, boulders of muscle, were folded behind his head, exposing tufts of golden hair in his armpits. His lashes crested his cheeks in curls of shadow, perfect lips parting with each soft breath.

Our kind wasn't prone to such things as snoring, though I had thought the wolven blood Fae, even while not in their beast form, might do so. His scent—stars, his fucking scent was everywhere, and dizzy from it, I halted by the side of the bed, overrun with the urge to think this through, perhaps find another—*no*.

Teeth gritting, I threw myself onto the bed and pressed my blade to his thick, exquisite neck within half a failed heartbeat.

He smiled, a slow reveal of his teeth while his eyes remained closed. "Do it," he purred throatily, and then his eyes opened, blazing and hooded. "*Mate.*"

Blood trickled as my hand trembled and the blade slid against his skin—that word said aloud cleaving all that I was in two.

His smile didn't wane, but his arms unfolded and came around my body, hands gliding up my back. One clawed finger scraped over the gossamer, tearing the sheer white nightgown. That claw took its time traveling the expanse of my spine until my nightgown drooped over my arms, my breasts nearly exposed.

The king's eyes never left mine.

The blade slipped from my fingers, clattering to the floor as the king swatted it away and grabbed the back of my head.

My mouth crashed into his. Desperate and starving, I collapsed over him and my lips parted his, teeth catching his tongue.

He groaned, flipping me to my back, and loomed over me with glowing eyes. His head lowered, a rough laugh dancing over my mouth a second before he nipped my upper lip. "You truly wish me dead, sunshine?"

His wings, although not visible in this form, unfurled as shadows upon the walls, rendering everything except for him in total darkness. I didn't, couldn't answer. Horror tried to form a place in my vacant mind when my thighs parted, allowing his body to settle against mine.

He chuckled, the sound deliciously heated over my seeking lips. His forearms rested on either side of my head, fingers smoothing my hair from my face. "If you did, you'd have aimed for the head and not my throat, mate."

I growled. "Stop saying that."

A golden brow quirked. "Ashamed, are we?"

He knew I was, and I wanted him to know, as I hissed, "More than you'll ever be able to comprehend, savage."

If I'd offended him, he hid it well. Dade hummed, then recaptured my lips for a quick taste, murmuring between teasing brushes, "I want to properly shame you…" I felt him tremble when my hands slid over his back, muscle and sinew shifting. "I want to feel you, to torture you with my mouth, fingers," he groaned, "my cock." He swallowed, his voice changing, graveled. "I want you slick, so slick that your pulse will forever quicken at the mere thought of me."

I moaned, pressing my hands into his toned waist—pressing him against me. His hips began to rock while his hand trailed down my side, taking my ruined nightgown with it. With his eyes on mine, he tore his mouth away, lips skimming my chin, journeying slowly to my thudding pulse. He pressed his tongue against it, and we each exhaled a sharp breath. Dragging his mouth over my chest, he then lifted high enough to gaze down at my breasts.

"Fuck," he groaned, and then he was squeezing, licking, caressing, and driving me so wild, I was writhing underneath him, on fire and burning higher with every breath.

On his knees between my spread legs, my tattered nightgown split apart once more with a slow swipe of his claw. It tickled over my stomach, stopped right before my mound, and then retracted as Dade ripped the fabric with his hands before gazing at what lay beneath. He cursed again. "Do you always sleep with no undergarments?"

"I-I…" My voice was too thick, too useless.

"Do not answer that," he rasped.

Unsure what to do with my hands, with my naked body on display beneath this giant male, his eyes twin pools of burning ocean upon mine, panic raced in.

And then he touched me. His eyes remained on mine, and he touched me with such careful precision, his lips parting with a low groan at what he found. "I fear I might explode in my pants."

"Take them off," I urged, suddenly desperate for the sight of him.

He didn't, and I frowned. Then featherlight fingers, fingers that had ripped heads from bodies and decimated entire towns and villages, touched me as though I'd break if he did not do so with extreme care. Up and down, they brushed over me, turning for his knuckles to do the same. They caught my folds, opened them slightly, and I moaned long and loud, delirious in a way I'd never experienced before.

Noticing—noticing everything—Dade repeated the action, swapping his knuckles for the pad of one thick finger, but not before he dragged his tongue along them.

Hypnotized with no breath left inside my lungs, I watched his eyelids flutter. Those heavy lashes lowered with his hand as he stroked and circled, and I twisted my lip between my teeth as every limb tingled and my blood heated beyond anything that could be considered safe.

"Kiss me," I choked out, and he was over me in an instant, still working me toward a slow entrance into oblivion.

Our lips met and parted, his tongue matching the circular swipes of his finger. "At first," he said, his voice so deep that some of his words cracked, "when I realized what'd happened that night in the cave, that I had bonded to you, I couldn't believe it." His breath rushed inside my mouth. "I didn't want to..."

His finger crawled to my entrance, toying, and we both moaned.

"But when I saw you again, I knew, even as a swan, that this was real, real in a way that felt right, no matter how much I thought to refuse it. And now..." He circled again, dragged his teeth over my chin, along my jaw, and licked my erratic pulse. "Now that I've got you in my bed, in my arms, on the brink of breaking beneath me..." He groaned, teeth clutching gently at my skin. "I can see that the stars made you just for me."

I couldn't talk, could hardly stand to believe a word he said, let alone try to swim away from the feelings his touch, *that he*, was drowning me in. My eyes widened when he rubbed me, and his nostrils flared as his hooded gaze darted all over my face, reading and learning.

I heard his pants loosen and felt his skin burn against mine, though he hadn't moved to rid them. "You said..." I swallowed hard, catching the back of his head when he made to rise. "You haven't done this."

"I didn't lie." He hissed when his length replaced his fingers. He didn't enter my body. He ground into me, harder than stone and perfectly positioned, and I was flailing over the side of a cliff, just waiting to be pushed.

Crazed with sensation, I tilted his head to lick the blood from his neck. The cut sealed shut beneath my tongue, and he shuddered, sliding harder against me. Stars cluttered behind my closed eyes, our labored breaths a violent song in my ears.

"Opal," he groaned, and my name had never quite sounded like that, like a vow made with four simple letters.

A wave swept in, and I was thrown off the cliff, completely submerged beneath all that he was as he rocked into me, my head caged in his hands while I struggled to open my eyes and draw breath. His own eyes were a furious blue, his thumb at the corner of my lips as he choked on a curse and stilled. Something warm spilled over my lower body—and didn't stop until I'd quit shaking and my lips grew slack against his.

A satisfied growl climbed up his throat, filled my ear as he dropped his head into my neck, where it stayed for fracturing moments. Then he rumbled, rolling to his side and keeping my body aligned with his, my head placed under his chin above his thundering chest, "Don't you dare leave."

And I didn't.

Not until morning arrived when he was called away at dawn.

# EIGHTEEN

## *Opal*

**S**HADOW KEEP MIGHT HAVE APPEARED ABANDONED FROM the outside, but inside, it was alive and overflowing with the hum of activity.

And I was tired of staring at the same walls, riffling through the same pages of books that couldn't hold my interest, and of my own twisting, dangerous thoughts.

Upside down and inside out, they twined and separated and un-raveled only to knot into bite-sized chunks of growing anxiety that would always end with me pacing the room.

Yesterday, I'd stayed in my rooms, feeling the king's indecision and need as though it were my own. For as much as I hated to admit it, it was my own. He hadn't knocked, hadn't entered as though the place belonged to him—for it certainly did—and I hadn't had the guts to seek him out.

Today, even amongst the steady vibration of life on the other side of my cell door, I could feel his absence. That and my own self-loathing were my constant companions, and I wanted to be rid of them.

*The stars made you just for me.*

Growling, I collected my tea tray and decided I'd return it to the kitchens myself. He wasn't here, and I shouldn't have cared if he was.

I was on a mission to save my people, this entire realm, so encountering him was part of that plan. Using him, taking advantage of what the stupid stars had ordained, was all I had.

But I knew it was no longer that simple.

*Mate.*

There was no questioning it, no fighting it, though that was exactly what I'd been trying to do since that night in the cave. I'd keep fighting it. I vowed to. Rejecting a mate, a bond forged between two souls, was not exactly common, but it happened time and again.

Though in rejecting one's mate, they typically did not see them again or at least did their best not to. For an untold period, I was stuck with mine. So I had to discover if there was a way to reject the inevitable as others had done while also being in such close proximity— while all I could think about was shredding his flesh from his bones at the same time I fantasized about shredding his clothing from his stupidly magnificent body...

The door opened silently, the hall empty outside, as per usual, and I shook my thoughts away.

One day at a time.

It'd been two since I woke alone in his bed, his scent as smothering as the furred blanket he'd draped over me, and I'd gained no clarity. Only more torment to accompany a new breed of want that now laid nestled beneath my skin.

It seemed to purr at the thought of him, at the memory of his smooth skin sliding over mine—

"Princess." I stopped at the bottom of the stairs and blinked at the young pixie. She curtsied, spindly fingers lifting her apron from her long, delicate legs. "May I take that for you?"

I should have said yes. Instead, I offered what I hoped was a sweet smile, my cheeks still warm, and asked, "Actually, I was hoping I could see the kitchens?"

The pixie blinked, her green eyes large and her pink lips slack.

"If you don't mind," I tacked on. "It's just... well, I'm terribly bored. I would love to offer a helping hand, but I understand if that would offend you." Such things were true. To take over someone else's task was akin to making them feel or seem inferior, and though many had tried to adapt to a more kinder way of thinking over the thousands of years of our existence, it still stuck with many. "I'd be happy to merely deliver it and then see myself to the library."

Eyeing me curiously, the purple-haired pixie nodded once. "Okay." Sweeping her hand behind her, she said, "Allow me to escort you, then."

Relieved, I followed eagerly, nearly losing a spoon from the tray. "What is your name?" I asked as we rounded the stairs and moved swiftly down the long hall.

"Gwenn," she said, then smirked. "I know yours, Princess Opal."

I smiled. "Then now we are even." At the top of a spiraling set of wooden stairs, knots of oak in the railing worn smooth under my hand, I couldn't help but prod some more. "How long have you served your king?"

"The king employs us all," Gwenn said, and I almost tripped down a step in surprise. "We are paid handsomely." She turned at the bottom, smiling wide with pride-filled eyes. "After six years of saving, I've purchased my parents' home for them." She stepped back as I stepped into the warm glow of one of two large rooms. "Soon, I hope to start saving for my own."

"Gwenn! What have I told you about bragging?"

Gwenn made a face at me before turning to the older female. "I'm not bragging, Mer. I was just telling the princess that we are not expected to serve. We do so willingly here in Vordane."

I didn't miss the jab in her words, no matter how succinct nor sweetly said—nor did I miss the way the female called Mer tensed at the long wooden counter in the center of the next room, her back to me.

She turned, her golden ringlets pulled into a tight, low bun at the base of her thick neck, and scowled. With a cluck of her tongue, Gwenn ambled back over to me and took the tea tray from my hands. "What brings you down here, Princess?"

I gestured to where Gwenn had skipped off to, a row of three sinks with soapy water frothing from two. "I wanted to return the tray."

"But we send someone to do that for you."

"She wanted to explore, Merelda," Gwenn said, returning with a threadbare towel that Merelda snatched from the pixie's damp hands without removing her eyes from me. "Clearly," Gwenn said with a twinkle in her eyes, "a tea party with the elves wasn't enough excitement for her."

Merelda's brows creased at that, deepening the lines upon her face. She had to be twice my mother's age, her impatience proving that beyond her looks. "A tea party with the elves? What in the star-forsaken crud do you mean?"

"You didn't hear?" Gwenn said. "They have been telling anyone who'll listen. Beshal is mighty thrilled with herself. The black swan"— she wandered over to a mound of dough and plucked up a rolling pin—"dining with the elves, here to save us all."

Merelda's displeasure returned at that, and she hissed over her shoulder at the pixie. "The only thing you'll need saving from is that rolling pin meeting your forehead if you talk such nonsense again."

Nonsense? Saving them all was indeed a stretch. I wasn't sure I had it in me to even bed the king, let alone lure him into a pretend game of love that might soften his heart.

"But the prophecy—"

Merelda clicked her fingers, and the pixie's voice disappeared. Gwenn frowned, her lips still moving, then stamped her foot and scrunched her face before storming out into a leafy garden beyond an open arched door.

With a loaded sigh, Merelda watched her go, then looked back at me. I knew that look, had seen it upon many a face during my short life, so I braced myself—chin up, shoulders squared, fingers linked before me, and a small, patient smile in place.

"Child," the cook, head cook I was guessing, started. "A warning to you, if I may?" It might have been a question, but it was worded as a warning.

Still, I nodded, my eyes trained on her stern brown gaze.

"I don't know why you're here. I don't know what you've got tucked up your silken sleeve, but I will say this—he might be infatuated, but he is still a king, and to usurp a king, especially one as powerful and revered as he..." She puckered her lips, tossing her towel over her shoulder. "The consequences would ripple for generations to come. This must end with yours. With him. No one else needs to bear what he has been forced to."

"I don't know what you mean," I said, and honestly at that, for even though I'd contemplated it, I knew I could not kill him, knew I'd need to turn the blade on myself after if it came to that. "He brought me here, and as much as I wish to leave, I can't. I can't because there's..." I stopped and swallowed, releasing a slow exhale.

"There's little to return to. It's all perishing." She said what I could not, not unkindly but in an even tone that spoke of no mercy and brutal facts. "Your land, your wealth, and those you love."

Again, I nodded. "I do want to fix this," I admitted, a little uneasy for doing so. "I do, but I don't know how, and I am no murderer." My words held more grit than I'd intended.

"Like Dade is," Merelda said, brows high.

I drew in a sharp breath, knowing this was going nowhere and that perhaps the little I could do would go nowhere too. "Do not worry." I smiled faintly. "For I can save no one." My chest constricted at hearing those words out loud. "And your king is well aware of that."

Merelda studied me for a moment, then tilted her head. With another sigh, she crossed to a basket of fresh fruit and plucked out a mandarin. "You might not be able to save anyone, but I hear you like fruit."

Stunned, I watched as her warm hand took mine and placed the mandarin in my palm. She closed my fingers over it. "A monster will forever be a monster, you beautiful fool, so quit losing sleep." With a pat on my hand, she released me, murmuring quietly as she drifted back to the counter. "But do remember that even the most violent of beasts can be brought to heel."

The cook's words stayed with me as I wove through the halls to the library tucked away in the long, narrow parlor beyond the grand staircase. A fire was crackling in the hearth, stalling my steps outside the open doors, but I sensed no one inside.

Tame him. It was evident that the cook, who I supposed knew this beastly king the stars had tied me to well, believed something was in him that many people—perhaps merely my own—could not see.

Trying to comprehend that when all I could see was blood spray and all I could hear were screams and the scent of smoke and the dead was impossible, yet... something told me I wouldn't be standing here if that were not true. I would not be roaming shelves that towered from the floor to the ceiling, branch-made ladders leaning against rows to reach the higher shelves, if I thought all was lost.

I'd have gone home to spend what little time we had with what remained of my family and friends.

Edging a thin gray novel from the shelf closest to the fire, I grinned at the faded title. *A Love and A Lie.* Rounding the piano, I set it upon the small stack I'd made on the oak table that had been marked by many a hot teacup, and then I stilled.

Fine hairs rose at the base of my neck. Gooseflesh pebbled my arms, and my every sense pricked, on high alert. The parlor had two entry points—the first sealed by two giant armchairs, the second the way I'd entered. I could move them, or I could face whomever it was out in the hall.

Or I could sit down and wait for them to appear.

I chose to collect the books and leave the way I'd arrived. As foolish as it might have been, I had faced worse, surely...

The hall was mercifully empty.

Yet when I rounded the stairs, I heard soft footfalls from behind and spun around.

No one was there, but the black tapestry, a white wolf with wings of flame howling at the glowing full satin moon, swayed.

And the scent of earth. Sweat and earth.

Tucking that knowledge away, I took the stairs at my usual swift stride, perhaps walking a tad faster, and nearly tripped on the steps leading up to my rooms when I felt someone behind me.

I turned at the top, my heart beating in my throat, and found no one there as I carefully slunk backward toward an alcove housing a statue. I bumped into it, cursing when it teetered and spinning fast to right it.

A hand fell upon my hip, warmth heating my back, and I swallowed a scream. The books raised in both hands, I whirled, ready to strike them over the head.

Then Dade's voice blew soft against my cheek. "Have I ruffled your feathers, my pretty swan?" He laughed when my breath shook its way past my lips, catching the books before they toppled to the floor. "What in the stars were you planning to do with these? Book-bludgeon me to death?"

Snatching them back, I thwacked him in the chest with one. An attempt to make him back up a step or ten. An attempt that failed.

"Don't you have innocent people to slaughter?" My cheeks burned, and I refused to meet his eyes, choosing instead to stare at his throat. The fine hairs that dusted it, crawling up and over that fiercely hewn chin.

"I've already crossed that off my to-do list," he stated with such irritating indifference that I wished I had hit him with the poor books. "I wanted to see you." I blinked when he carefully caught my hand. He placed it over my still pounding heart, his fingers, his entire hand, overlapping mine. "Your heart races."

So large that hand, as it sat there a moment, and I lost the little control I'd had, finally meeting his blue eyes.

They were a bright turquoise, watching his hand leave mine to travel up my chest to wrap around my throat. "Such a delicate, perfect neck." His voice was an edged caress. "Why, some would call it swan-like." He grinned then, wicked and every inch the wolf he was, and then it faded from his eyes as they fell upon my lips. "I wanted to see you yesterday. The urge to lay eyes upon you a burn that never ceased. But I knew." That huge hand tightened for a second, then slackened, his thumb brushing my thrumming pulse. "I could sense that you were not ready. Your shame, your self-loathing... it keeps you from me."

"Dade—"

"I wish to lick you," he groaned, effectively muting my meek protest. "Here." His hold on my neck loosened, his touch crawling slowly to my chest. "These," he rasped, fingers tickling the bare mounds of my breasts before dragging down to my stomach. "Here." His hand roamed over my hip, sliding over the bone and moving down to my ass. He squeezed it, groaned deep, and set fire to my veins. "Here. And lastly..." His eyes connected with mine, a darkening storm on the cusp of downpour within as he cupped me hard, and I shuddered. "Here. I want so badly to taste you again, to take my time with you, to savor every morsel of greedy need this pretty cunt will spill over my tongue."

Trapped within the imagery of all he'd described, I could do nothing but begin to burn and stare into those intense eyes. He gazed back, waiting, watching, wanting. His desire clouded the air I struggled to inhale, the musky wood growing thicker with every second, and I forced myself to blink.

I found my voice, barely, and found it was embarrassingly breathy, whispering, "You cannot just say..." I swallowed. "All of that."

I tried to peer around his shoulder, praying we were alone as I'd thought but not knowing for sure. His lips curved. "Why? It's true, and I know you'll enjoy it just as much as me."

Reaching between us, I removed his hand from me. I had to before I did something else foolish—like rock into it to feed the hunger he'd stoked to life.

The king watched me, brows hovering low over his eyes. Before he could goad me into anything else, I blurted, "Where have you been?"

He sighed as if I'd woken him from a good dream. "Nowhere important."

Right. Staring at him, hoping some of the heat beneath my skin would recede, I waited for him to move. It didn't, and he didn't, so I huffed and ducked past him.

"What were you so afraid of?" he asked when I neared my rooms. "Just now when I returned? I won't delude myself into believing it's still me."

"I don't fear you." I walked faster and opened the door. "But I do despise you," I said primly, then slammed it behind me.

I heard his laughter and his words through the wood I leaned back against, trying to catch my breath. "Indeed, you're all I fantasize about too, mate."

The beginning of a smile wriggled my lips. I scolded myself and dumped the books upon the nightstand.

I woke with a heaving gasp.

A fine layer of sweat covered me from head to toe, my nightgown sticking to my body while my heart thrashed and wailed.

Inside the lukewarm bath, I sat with my knees tucked to my chest, watching the sun slowly chase away night and waiting for the remnants of my nightmare to fade. Beasts of blood and shadow and dagger-like teeth rolled into velvet green hillsides with children running, smiling, then screaming as those shadows crested the valleys and covered everything in crimson and night.

It was no nightmare, and that was what made it all the more terrifying.

In the gardens, I wandered through the dew-dotted grass, discovering plants I'd never encountered in our lands, yet with an inhale, I found I knew them all the same. Before the vegetable garden that ate a good portion of the western side of the castle grounds were two long rows of medicinal plants, herbs, and spices.

It was no secret our healers were being used by their armies, but seeing it and some of the plants from our land made it all the more sobering.

The Keep was quiet when I returned, marigolds and thinsilver tucked within the long, flowing sleeves of my sky-blue dress. The bodice was loose, the velvet covering the chest area shifting and sliding in a way that might have felt slightly improper back home as if it were a nightgown or paint smock.

But I was far away from home, and I found I quite liked the freeing cotton fluttering around my ankles. It was as though whoever created it had thought to bring nightwear to daywear and had found the perfect balance.

I knew such things were usually created by the gold Fae, but I was no longer naïve enough to believe the crimson did not have talented dressmakers of their own. I made a mental note to ask Gwenn the next time I saw her.

A russet-haired faerie, one of whom I'd not seen before, waded past me as I rounded the stairs to the foyer inside. I nodded, offering a brief smile, but she did not look up to meet my eyes. In her hands, her trembling hands, I noticed, was a pail.

And bloodstains on her apron. Fresh, I discovered when I inhaled.

Stars. What horrors was he unleashing now? And upon his staff? They seemed to respect him. Feared him most certainly. But I couldn't deny the awe and loyalty of his people.

My hand squeezed the marble railing. I told myself to leave it alone. I wasn't here to ensure his staff was well taken care of. I shouldn't have been here at all.

A clang sounded from somewhere deeper within the Keep, and heartbeats after it, another whiff of blood. My feet carried me off the bottom step and down the hall that contained room after room, most of them grand and unoccupied, and eventually, took me to the kitchens.

Losing the scent, I backtracked, knowing all too well that Dade wouldn't have lost it. He'd have already found the source with senses far more powerful than most of us. The irksome knowledge only fueled my quest to discover what had happened, so I turned back and found a closed door halfway down the hall. It wasn't locked.

Knowing I was alone, for now, I opened and closed it behind me, shrouding myself in total darkness.

Bright light flared from my fingertips, and I found myself inside another hallway. A hallway just as beautiful as the one I'd vacated seconds before. So why, I wondered, was it so dark? And spelled, I realized, warded to keep the groans I could hear coming from the other end from seeping out into the Keep. I followed the noise, the rancid scents of death, blood, and other bodily fluids, down into the slow-sloping darkness.

The air grew colder with each step down the cleverly hidden ramp masquerading as a hall. A sharp turn at the end, followed immediately by another, and I shielded my eyes, the warmth in my fingers snuffed. Flames danced in sconces upon the walls of what appeared to be a dungeon. Cells, iron-barred cells, all of them empty save for the ghosts of souls long perished, lined one of the long stone walls of the narrow space.

On the other side, chains and other torture devices hung from the stone and the ceiling in at least ten different places, and in the center, chained to the ceiling and the floor, his arms and legs flayed wide, was a swollen eyed, bloodied prince.

"Heddo?" he mumbled around the metal gag strapped to his mouth. "Who 'ere? Who?" His head whipped side to side as though he could see where I was. But he couldn't see, or else he'd have known I was now standing right in front of him, my fingers pressed to my mouth and my stomach sinking to my toes.

Prince Bron was hardly recognizable. If it weren't for his scent, smothered as it was beneath the sweat, blood, and other less than appealing fluids, then perhaps I wouldn't have even known it was him.

*Where have you been?*

*Nowhere important.*

My teeth snapped together.

The chains clanged, and Bron moaned, a sound akin to a blubbering wail following, snot and blood exiting his nostrils. I backed up, unable to remove my eyes from the ribbons of blood covering him, the cuts, deep gashes, and bruises and the recently cleaned space on the floor beneath him.

I had to help him. He'd tried to have me without my permission. Against my will. He might have been heavily intoxicated, but I wouldn't make excuses for him.

He was just as much a monster as the creature who'd rescued me from him.

Yet surely I couldn't just leave him to die.

But I couldn't make my feet move or find a way to help him either.

Tears threatened, but my eyes remained dry. Slowly, I waded back out of the haunted, narrow cave made for pain and murder until those shadows again collected and darkened with each turn.

At the closed door, I waited. I waited until I heard footsteps pass, Gwenn's voice and laughter intermingling with another's and eventually fading on the other side.

Then I returned to my rooms, where I sat on my pretty bed and stared at my useless hands.

# NINETEEN

*Dade*

S NOT-NOSED PRINCELINGS ARE NOT SO EASY TO STEAL BUT easily lured.

I caught ours the morning before returning to find my swan in the hall outside our rooms—the mere sight of the arrogant fuck's face enough to make my blood boil when I thought of how she'd allowed his unworthy lips to grace hers.

I'd given the warriors instructions, then I'd warped back to the Keep to lay eyes upon Opal. Which had nearly earned me a book to the face.

I still smirked at the thought of her using a book as a weapon. She could fight, most definitely, yet she so often forgot her own strength in the face of fear.

The prince had been sent a letter from a friend of mine who excelled at imitating handwriting. A letter from my dear Opal stated she was on the run and requested to meet with her alone near the Well of Wishes. The ancient well sat a few miles from the border between Sinshell and Errin, deep enough into Sinshell's land that the human soldiers did not see us coming.

And neither did the prince. Although he was idiot enough to believe the letter's contents, he wasn't so stupid as to arrive on his own.

His eight comrades were now sea dragon bait thanks to legion three, and after watching in horror as they'd flown over the cliffs to dump his men into the Night Sea, the prince had little choice.

He'd glared at me, indignant even as fear rolled off him in a putrid wave. "W-what do you want?"

I'd grinned. "I thought you'd never fucking ask." Then I'd knocked him out with a fist to the face before instructing my uncle to see to the prince's delivery to my dungeon.

What I wanted was his guts oozing between my bloodied fingers, my talons still embedded in his stomach. What I wanted was to devour my swan in front of him, to show him what it was to have her be a willing participant, to show him that he'd never, not in this life or any after, know what that was truly like.

What I wanted was his fucking head on a pike atop my keep, but I could not be hasty. No, I'd take my time in getting there. I would savor every moment and make him regret the day he first laid eyes upon my mate with extreme care and attention to every fine detail.

Swinging one boot in front of the other, I dragged my fingers over my instruments, blood splattering onto the stone floor. Oh, the things they'd seen and done. I chose the scissors for my next task, noting they were gleaming—evidently not used as much as the hacksaw, hammer, and varying other devices.

The prince moaned and whined. I whistled, thoughts of Opal beneath me in my bed never too far from the forefront of my mind. If I were being honest, too often it was the only thing I could think of.

*Kiss me*, she'd said, so rough—as though it'd tainted parts of her to make such a plea.

I opened the scissors and sliced them across the asshole's abdomen.

The way she'd shuddered at my touch, shaking as she began to come undone in such a slow-building, blissfully torturous way.

I closed the scissors around the tip of his nipple and snipped.

Agony. She'd been ensnared in the most exquisite type of agony, mostly naked beneath me, breasts heaving and her skin flushed and misted, her eyes struggling to focus, to stay open at all when it had arrived.

Blood gushed over the handles and my hand, and with his screams nothing but white noise, I then stabbed him between the ribs.

When it all had finally gathered enough to break, and she'd over-flowed with pleasure, shaking relentlessly with it, as I'd spilled myself all over her.

Another stab, this one to the gut, the scissor blades separating while still inside his stomach.

"Dade." Her voice came to me. So soft, so fucking sweet. A summer fruit given soul.

And fuck did she taste just as sweet. So divine, I wanted to devour—

"Dade." A half-shouted growl this time, followed by a touch at my elbow.

I recoiled, whirling and yanking the scissors from the prince's gut while doing so, blood flicking through the air to splatter at Opal's feet.

The prince screamed, garbled and continuous, but I could barely hear it.

I heard nothing as Opal's gaze flitted behind me to the mangled prince who'd tried to steal her maidenhead. Who'd tried to steal what was mine. Who sought to use her for his own gain, marry her, defile her, humiliate her...

I turned and said, "I'll be right back, dear prince." Then I slogged him in the face hard enough to send him into black nothing.

"Sunshine," I said between my teeth, both enraged and ecstatic she was within touching distance of me. Touch her I did, taking her gently by the arm and leading her out of the dungeon.

Her head kept twisting over her shoulder, her reluctance to walk away from what she'd seen evident in her weighted steps. "Where did you find him?"

I sent flame into the sconces of the dark hall, and they danced toward the vine-patterned ceiling. "That matters not. What are you doing down here?" I stopped when we reached the spelled hallway, firelight flickering in her eyes.

"I..." She chewed her lip, then released a rushed breath. "Well, I was looking for you." Her cheeks reddened as she said gently, "I couldn't find you, so I followed your scent."

I scowled, unsure if I'd have believed her if it weren't for the embarrassment, that annoying shame she was so fond of harboring, entering her voice, skin, and those golden eyes.

"You said you'd show me the city," she went on, her hands scrunching in the skirts of her creamy gown of lace and satin. "At night, and I've been waiting but..." Her nose crinkled, and fuck if I didn't want to lean down and nip it, then kiss it, then do the same to those sin-infused lips. "Are you going to kill him?"

Already, noting the way her eyes kept darting around me, over me, I knew she wouldn't let this go. She wanted to know more. I could tell her.

Or I could live up to the abomination she thought me and take advantage of her curiosity for an evening outing and steal some more time with that luscious mouth of hers.

I tossed the scissors I hadn't been aware I was still holding over my shoulder. They hit the ground with a clang. "Fine. Let's go."

If she thought I didn't notice what she was doing, she was both beautiful and delusional.

And I was a fucking fool for allowing it.

# TWENTY

## *Opal*

**"W**HAT IS IT EXACTLY YOU WISH TO SEE?"
The king seemed reluctant, annoyed, and I knew it
was because I'd taken him from his task of torturing the
prince. He'd washed his hands in the kitchens, instructing me to wait
at the top of the stairs, but when he'd returned, a carriage already
waiting below the Keep's steps, I saw either he'd done so in a rush or
his skin was stained.

It would forever be stained with his acts of brutality.

Inside a carriage as dark blue as the night sky, I twisted to face
Dade. He was staring out the circular window, but I knew he wasn't
seeing the hedges we ambled past, the fountain, nor the willow-lined
road we'd begun to roll down.

It might have been new to me, but he'd seen it all before. I missed
taking such things for granted in my own home. The walls, the trea-
sures kept within, all just things until they'd been stripped away from
you.

"The clothing boutiques," I finally admitted. "I find myself rather
fond of your fashions, the comfort of the gowns and nightwear, the
materials. I wish to meet the people who craft them." In part because

I wanted to see if they were slave workers, golden Fae stolen from my kingdom.

"So you can remake clothing of a similar fashion?" Before I could say yes, he added with a slight sneer, "For when you return home?" He looked at me then, and in those blue eyes was not the same creature who'd cornered me in the halls outside our rooms the day before, the creature who touched me with a violently gentle reverence that melted and seared.

In those eyes loomed the predator he'd always be.

The monster who'd damned and killed hundreds of souls, who was responsible for the deaths of thousands of others, including my father.

I'd taken him from his next kill—had thought to distract him because even though I couldn't stand Bron, I couldn't have him die in that nightmare of a dungeon. Not when the repercussions would be vast, and he could be of use in sending an important message.

And so I'd lured the wolf from his captured prey by offering myself as his next meal, yet I was evidently foolish and flailing.

And failing.

I swallowed over the swelling in my throat, wishing he would blink already. Wishing things were different. That he wasn't who he was, that he wasn't all the horrors he'd committed, and that I could climb into his lap and erase the winter from his eyes.

"I think we both know that I'll never return home." That seemed to do it. The king blinked, his eyes narrowing with the lowering of his thick brows. "So I would like to spend my time doing things that I enjoy." The lie flowed smoothly, softly, from between my lips. So much so, that I wondered if it were because there was more truth to the words than I'd known until I'd set them free.

If this were any other male, any other time, any other life, I'd love nothing more than to see to the things I loved the most. Mending, perfuming, exploring, and gardening.

But those things were a waste of time and selfish. I'd discovered so the hard way. My people were dying and would continue to.

Dade released a breath through his nose, his nostrils flaring slightly. "You would like to spend your days with your passions? Mending and gardening?" A little lift to his lips, then he said, "But I hear you already spend a lot of your time in the gardens."

I tilted my head, then looked out the window. "Define a lot, my king."

"I think my cock just ripped the seam of my pants." I coughed, dragging my eyes from the lights that had begun to twinkle through the window and back to the smirking king. "Say that again."

I scowled. "No."

"Yes," he purred.

"Do you grow…" I scrunched my nose, irritated that I didn't have the right words and deciding on, "erect whenever someone calls you their king?"

"Erect?" he said, delight lighting his eyes, raising his brows. He laughed, then reached out a finger to trace down the bridge of my nose. "Only when my mate does."

I snapped my teeth at his finger, grinning. "My mate you may be, but you are not my king."

"Ah, she admits it. Then why did you say it?" he asked, all velvet curiosity.

"It was a barb," I stated coldly. "Sarcasm. Do you know what that is?"

"Do you know how erect I am?"

I smacked him in the chest on reflex, playfully and without thought.

He caught my hand before I could retract it and brought it to his mouth for his lips to glide over the skin of my knuckles, eyes never leaving mine while he listened to my heart whoosh and thud. "Look," he murmured to my skin, eyes darting behind me.

He scooted over the leather seat to my side as I looked out the window. Breath tumbled from me and through the open glass into the night beyond. Up ahead loomed a bridge large enough for two carriages to cross at once, the river reflecting the vegetation and large rocks that nestled along it, as well as the night sky.

"Here they come," the king said, his voice at my neck, stirring tendrils of hair and warming my skin. We left the bridge with a gentle thump, then meandered through a cropping of giant oaks and the gaps between. Starlight sprinkled over the leaping squirrels and packed dirt roads and pathways.

Not just starlight, I soon discovered as we exited the foliage and entered a clear grass valley, but lights. Dazzling and blurring, they lit up the heart of Vordane in neat lines that stretched farther than I could see seated inside the carriage. Though I suspected that unless I was in the air, I still would not be able to capture all that awaited us.

Streets, cobblestone and narrow, were filled with two-story cottages made of brick and wood and stone. Shops intermingled amongst them as well as smaller homes. A cluster of manufacturing halls, thatched and worn but well-loved, was the first to appear through the window, their chimneys expelling puffs of smoke that dissipated inside the night sky.

A distillery. A metal shop. A carriage repair shop. A cookware supply shop... the signs were all the same and hanging above the wide metal doors, a few locked and sealed tight for the night.

At home, we had some similar sheds crafted for such things and more, for there was surely more upon the other side of the carriage that I hadn't seen, but nothing as tidy, as large and as obviously needed, as any of what gathered before and after my eyes.

The city was a coiled, jeweled serpent, homes and shops glued to one another in a loving, untidy yet organized fashion, light swaying from windows and doorways, from fires and sconces and torches. I'd entered another maze, this one crafted in straight, square lines that stretched farther than I could walk in a day.

Peering closer, the king's heat at my side, I waited. I waited, and I watched the groups of citizens we passed by. Some were huddled on doorsteps, gossiping and laughing. Others were serving patrons outside of squashed and spacious restaurants.

Many were looking straight at us and bending at the knees.

I sat back, forgetting not for the first time just who I'd journeyed here with and wondering why in the stars I hadn't seen it. The hatred, the fighting, the thievery, and the unrest.

With a ruler such as the one seated right next to me, the stories were endless. Tales told of the vicious Vordane and its smiteful king who governed his people with a talon-sharp fist.

I was grateful when the king tapped the ceiling, and the driver pulled the horses to a stop. Dade climbed out before me, and before I could deny him, he grabbed me by the waist and set me upon the uneven cobblestone.

I gripped his arms, then righted myself and pulled away, turning in a slow circle to see where we were. At the end of a street that stretched into forever, most of the lights out save for two sconces outside a large wooden door with many a metal lock.

The door was open, laughter and raucous noise emptying out onto the street from inside. I nearly smiled, relieved to have found some truth to the tales we'd all been told, and steeled my shoulders for what may greet us on the other side.

But the king walked past the door, and I frowned before hurrying to keep up, wondering where he was going.

He stopped outside a darkened store, knocked once, and murmured words to someone I couldn't see when the white door with its blue trim opened a crack. "Of course, my king. Come on inside. I'll just be a moment."

The king looked back to where I still stood in front of a dark bungalow that sat between the tavern I'd thought we'd be entering and what I soon realized was the king's preferred dressmaker.

Her shop was lilac painted walls, lavender-scented candles upon every surface, and fabrics that tempted me to drool as I flitted about like a fly at a picnic.

When the female returned, a brunette with sharp honeyed eyes and short curls that bounced around her neck, she curtsied.

"Apologies, my son needed the last two pages of his book read to him or he'd have screamed the place down."

Dade chuckled. "A tyrant in the making is what you have, dear Olivianna."

The female grinned, gathering her layers of sheer blue skirts and nearing me. Familiar. That they were familiar enough with one another that she would keep her king waiting while she tucked her son into bed made something sour in my stomach.

"Princess Opal, it is a pleasure."

I waved her off, my annoyance dripping away as Olivianna showed me around her store and told me of how she'd fallen into dressmaking after she'd been forced to repair her mother's best dress. "I'd not only soiled it with wine but tore it on the window ledge while climbing back inside my parents' house."

Afterward, over tea, she divulged that her son was conceived that night, and although she was not in contact with the male who'd chosen to be with another and to serve in one of the king's legions, she thought it was a sign.

"It wasn't even that I'd mended it that well." She leaned closer, laughter in her eyes. "It was that I'd enjoyed it and had wondered what it would look like if I'd made some more alterations." She poured herself a smidge more tea from a crystal teapot. "So I began to dismantle some of my clothes, and not long after, sought a business loan from my parents."

"What did they think?" I couldn't help but ask. "Of your son, and the male who just left you to raise him alone."

She stared down at her tea, then lifted those eyes that I now guessed were often smiling. "They didn't know until I was a few moons from giving birth, and by then"—she shrugged—"I was making just enough to keep my new store afloat."

"So you live upstairs?"

Olivianna nodded. "There are two rooms, a kitchenette, and a washroom. Besides, I do my best work at night when Ryon is sleeping."

She winked as she blew on her tea. "After a wine or two. So I like to be close to everything I need."

We left soon after, Dade loading up the carriage that was now parked across the street in front of a run-down looking butcher with a mountain of fabric.

Guilt gnawed at me, a nibble that wouldn't cease. It wasn't as if he hadn't paid Oliviana—as well as allowed her to kiss both his cheeks—for the sack of coin he'd left upon the table next to the book he'd been reading said she was paid handsomely.

No, as much as I loathed to admit it, I didn't need the material. I wanted it, of course, my heart singing at the sight of all the various cottons and silks and rayon, but I shouldn't have taken it so far as to actually take it.

I'd not only distracted the king from his murderous ventures, I'd used him to gain something I had no freedom to enjoy.

I had to get over it. I had to grow used to doing such things.

For it would take far more than some pieces of fabric to keep him from hurting more people.

"I don't know what to say," I murmured, gazing at the colors attempting to swim out of the storage compartment beneath the driver's seat.

"I'd say you should thank me, but I'd rather you kiss me instead."

My cheeks instantly burned, the driver busy but still well within earshot.

Dade brushed his thumb over my warm cheek, then jerked his head to the side of the street we were standing on and took my hand. "Have a drink with me."

"Oh, I couldn't," I said, no longer in the mood to see the violence of this city.

"Nonsense. I saw the way you eyed it earlier."

The tavern seemed too dank, too dim, to house a royal such as Dade, yet oh-so-perfectly fitting for the beast that lurked beneath his skin.

Behind him, my fingers caught in the curl of his, I watched him prowl toward a barrel-made countertop, all eyes upon us. Their attention was ignored, as was any greeting thrust his way, as Dade leaned over the counter to say something to a silver-haired male with piercings along one arched ear and eyes a blue so deep they were nearly purple.

I stayed behind him, watched the way the muted glow of a fire lamp turned his blond hair to a murky, shadowed sandy hue, and studied the broad expanse of his back beneath his black tunic.

The one he wore tonight was tight, though I didn't think it was due to it being ill-fitting, but rather, due to the fact that he fit it too well. Muscle shifted, bunched and straightened as he pointed at something on the dark shelves behind the bartender. One leather booted foot was kicked over the other, his weight leaning into the aged wood that balanced atop the barrels and appeared to have been cut from a ship.

Throwing a glance around the mostly empty tavern, I pulled my fingers from his, noting the fear in some lone and older patrons who were finishing their drinks with feigned casualness. There was more curiosity than fear from a group of females, and even hunger in those who were giggling, trying to build up the courage to approach their king.

The easy way the king had communicated with Olivianna flushed hot irritation through me. I hadn't realized I'd been making a face until the females smiled ruefully and retreated, and Dade turned around, a decanter and two glasses in hand. "Shall we?"

I gave him a flat look, and he shook his head with a grin before jerking it to a set of stairs over by the edge of the countertop. We climbed them, finding a few small tables perched before a floor-to-ceiling triangular window overlooking the dark street below. Grime and stars knew what else covered it, but even so, I could still make out the rows of lights, the city of Vordane beyond.

Dade kicked a chair out for me, and I took a seat as he rounded the table and slumped into another with grace a male of his height and muscular build shouldn't have. The chair didn't even groan.

He poured us each a glass of what smelled like vanilla frosted wine. "You scared them off."

Confused, my eyes shot to his, but he was smiling down at his glass. "The females." He popped the crystal stopper back on the decanter and lifted his glass to his lips, his gaze to mine. "You acknowledged the bond, made sure they could scent it as well as see it."

Ice trickled down my spine. "I did no such thing."

Dade half rolled his eyes, his throat bobbing as he swallowed and sat back, one knee tossed over the other. "I'd be inclined to believe you if it weren't for the fact that I have a fucking nose, sunshine." With a pointed look, he stated coldly, "I scented it, too."

How I hadn't, unless I hadn't been able to when I was the one emitting a silent threat, I didn't know.

Dade set down his glass, already just a long sip from being emptied. "I suppose the visit to Olivianna's riled you up, primed you." He smirked, a dimple appearing. "It matters not. I rather liked it."

I guffawed, lifting my glass to gulp two much-needed mouthfuls, and nearly moaned. "Shit," I breathed, lowering it and staring at what remained. "This is delicious."

"I thought you might like it."

"And you can bed whomever you like," I blurted, unsure why but knowing I didn't want him thinking I cared more than I was willing to let on. "Most kings do."

Dade's upper lip curled, fingers clenching around the stem of his glass. "You dare insult me?"

"How have I insulted you?"

"Honest answer?" he said to which I nodded. "By suggesting that I would bed someone else, especially when we both know what we know…" He let his words trail off, and I was tempted to put voice to what he hadn't said, so that perhaps others could know the king wasn't the bed-hopping animal most believed him to be.

Of course, I couldn't. A better, more cunning female would have ensured the news had spread through half the kingdom by now.

A better princess would have stuck an iron-infused knife through his heart and ended this insanity already.

"Why?" I finally asked what I'd longed to, still not entirely sure I believed him. The way he'd touched me, kissed me, tortured me all said it couldn't be true. Yet the rational part of my brain said otherwise. That it was instinctual, a desire so wild, our inexperience in matters of lust and sex had no room to breathe. To exist at all.

Knowing exactly what I was referring to, Dade tortured me some more with a knowing gleam in his eyes, seeming to mull over my question. Noting my growing impatience, he rubbed his lips between his teeth, then exhaled a loaded breath. "It's a distraction, swan." He swallowed, his lashes dipping with his simmering eyes to my mouth. "I know that now more than ever."

Something began to fizz inside my chest, my blood, at hearing that clipped admission. That I was a distraction, yet here he was, this almighty king, just allowing it...

I coughed, asking low with my words lumping together, "So you mean to tell me that you refused any offers?"

"Offers?" he said, humor soaking the word. "Most are too terrified to so much as try, and those who dared were only interested in my"—his nose scrunched a little—"many titles, I suppose."

"Oh," I exhaled, slouching in the chair. "Okay then."

He stared, unblinking and still quietly bristling.

I bit my lip to keep from smiling. "If you're waiting for an apology, you will be waiting for all eternity."

He snorted, draining his wine and thumping the glass onto the table. He leaned forward, voice soft and eyes hard. "What I'm still waiting for is that kiss."

I raised a brow. "Why don't you skip around the corner to Olivianna's and ask for one?"

"I do not skip." Dade's brow furrowed, and he sat back, studying me for a moment. His eyes swept up and down my frame, and I looked away as he said, "Our friendship truly bothers you."

I stared out the window, watching a flock of birds fly below the moon. My bones itched with the desire to do the same. "If that's what you wish to call it."

Dade was quiet a moment, then he hummed. "She is extremely

pleasant on the eyes, and she curses like no warrior I've ever battled with."

My hands fisted. I brought them under the table. "That's lovely."

He said thoughtfully, "She is lovely, yes. Though I do wish she hadn't cut her hair. It was much better before. You see, she could bend down before me and undo my pants without one of those ringlets bouncing up—"

"Shut up," I hissed, standing so quickly the chair screeched across the floor.

Dade gazed up at me, one arm slung over the back of the chair, a finger lazily rubbing at the bristle beneath his bottom lip. "Something the matter, swan?"

"You," I whispered heatedly. "You're the fucking matter. I cannot stand you. Take me home."

He grinned. "Home?"

I growled, and he laughed, raising his hands. "But of course, your majesty. Lead the way."

My teeth glued together as I did my best not to stomp down the stairs, rage a fire burning each breath as I ignored the few patrons brave enough to remain and hurried outside to the carriage.

"Insufferable beast," I muttered, letting myself inside before he could manhandle me.

"Beast?" he asked, climbing in after me and making sure his giant body nearly squashed mine as he stuffed himself on the other side. "I thought you golden ones were the creative type."

"You could've gotten in on the other side," I huffed, snatching back the skirts of my dress he'd sat upon. I gave up when I thought it would tear and stuck my nose to the window, pleading for the night air to cool me down before I did something foolish, like smack the king of wolves across his smugly handsome face.

"Where's the fun in that?"

I swallowed a myriad of colorful curses. My annoyance with the barbaric king, with myself, kept me from enjoying the scenery. The jealousy and the embarrassment kept me from being able to see much of anything at all.

The savage laughed, sudden and sharp enough to still the air in my lungs. "Fuck, stop it." I glared at him, then squeaked as I was hefted into his lap, the carriage jostled. "I was only messing around. I meant none of it."

My glare was erased by a blink. "None?"

The humor faded from his face. Those taut cheekbones lowered with his softening smile, his touch cruel in the way it so gently curled a thick tendril of hair behind my ear.

His gaze followed, his finger then falling down my arm with deliberate slowness as his eyes met mine. "None at all. Olivianna is my uncle's youngest cousin, and he knew of her ability to craft fine clothing, so he hired her not long after her babe was born to make me whatever I desired."

She was young then, as suspected, but not so young that she would take advantage of a king to better her life when she knew the bargain she'd struck was already more than she'd have ever dared hope for.

The same could never be said for myself, and for that, I almost envied her. Not only for her freedom to create for a living, to live a life of her own and on her own, but because I felt like half the female she was, knowing I was every inch the opportunist I had almost believed her to be.

I hated it, wanted to hate everyone so that I could quit hating myself whenever he touched me, looked at me, so much as came near me, though surely, I couldn't hate it forever.

I had to have faith that maybe one day, I would be okay with taking advantage of this mateship, of this beast king and his desire for me. The salvation of so many was worth the ruination of one soul.

"What are you thinking?" Dade murmured, his hand framing my face to keep my eyes upon his. They were searching, patient and impatient at the same time. I had a feeling that feat was not common for this male.

"Why would you do that?" I whispered. "Say all of that? Especially when you'd just insisted you had never done anything of the sort."

Dade hummed, his thumb rubbing over my cheek, eyes trailing as it landed upon my lips. "You should know by now that I love to watch things squirm," he purred, and my lips parted instinctually, the hardness I'd tried to ignore but now could not twitching beneath me. "I love to watch you squirm the most, especially when it's over me."

My tongue flicked his thumb, the coiled band of heat inside me tightening.

Hearing his rumbling groan, it snapped. I gripped his face, those smooth and rough cheeks, and I kissed him.

Gone was the guilt-heavy exploration that had kept me from taking what I wanted before. There was only want, pure and scorching, and tongues and teeth. I tilted his head. He tilted mine. My body leaned and pushed—needing that hardness in his pants to rub against me just a little more, a little higher... I moaned when Dade pulled back.

With his fingers floating down my cheek to my chin, he tilted it up, whispering, "Open your eyes."

I didn't want to, knowing what he'd see inside them—all the permission he did not need to give me everything I burned for.

"Open them," he said again, firmer, a dark order I could not ignore.

I surrendered, lashes hovering low, my lids heavy but not as heavy as the weighted need inside me that awaited attention.

Dade's lips parted, a small bead of blood bubbling near the center of his bottom lip. "You're the most exquisite creature I've ever seen." His words were hushed as though they weren't words he'd planned to say, and his brow furrowed.

My fingers crawled, thumbs brushing his thick, soft brows until his lips wriggled. A hand at my waist tightened over my hip, then lifted the thin material of my gown to inch up my thigh. "Want to know why I could never throw you in the dungeon like your prince? No matter what vitriol you spew at me."

"No," I breathed, but he knew that was a lie.

He smirked, and I fought the intense urge to lick those dimples. His fingers neared the apex of my thighs, and I leaned back a little, making room for them to brush over my undergarments.

"Because," he said to my chin, teeth nipping. His other hand pulled my head to his, his nose skimming mine. "Because your eyes, your heartbeat, and your body tell me the truth." My eyes fluttered closed, his lips whispering over my cheek, fingers reaching where I needed him and rubbing. "You want me. You might loathe it, but you cannot reject me because it burns you alive to even consider it."

My breath quickened, thighs clenching.

"Feel good?" He asked what he already knew, then expelled a rough breath over my mouth before kissing it ever so gently and murmuring, "You're so damp for me, sunshine, so warm and needy." Then a sharpness pressed into me, and I stilled as he hushed me, a claw dragging down the material to slice it open. "I have to feel you."

The carriage bounced over a boulder, but the king didn't lose his hold. His mouth rejoined mine, hot, seeking, and I feared I could die with his lips on mine and not even notice. Not even care.

He was smoke and heat, and I was panting, mewling, as he stroked me to dizzying heights, his free hand roaming my back, fingers sinking into my hair and his palm gripping my face. I rocked over him, against him, unable to breathe yet uncaring if it meant I'd lose his lips on mine.

"Melt for me, swan," he rumbled against my tongue, then sucked my upper lip. "Let go."

His finger pressed, flicked, and sparks ignited, my eyes opening wide, hair everywhere as I rasped, "Stars, I'm…"

The king growled, and I was tossed over the seat, my legs spread, skirts tearing and bunched at my waist, and then his mouth returned as his length ground against me.

Heated eyes gazed down at me, his hand twisting in my hair, and I clasped his cheek, whispering to his mouth, "Harder, wrap my leg around you."

The command caused him to still. Then with a flare of his nostrils, he did as I said and cursed violently, his giant body folded over me, desperately seeking his own pleasure as I flew toward mine.

Some failed breaths later, his eyes flashed as a silent roar parted his mouth. My spine arched, tilting my head toward the sky watching through the oval window.

He twitched over me, my skirts soiled and ruined. I didn't care. I wanted more.

I didn't feel the wood of the carriage against the back of my skull. All I could feel was the king's teeth scraping down the curve of my neck, his tongue lapping, lips sucking.

For all his inexperience and my own, never had I thought I'd become this. This wanton, insatiable creature who would throw more than caution to the wind.

I'd sacrifice almost anything for more of this male. To keep his hands roaming my sides, his mouth at my pulse, lowering to the peaks of my breasts, his approval a throaty hum as my fingers explored the thick strands of his hair, sinking to his scalp.

Yes, I'd sacrifice my soul for the king of wolves. That was why in moments of clarity, I would rebel against the desire to give all of myself to him.

I would use this inferno intent on destroying me to my advantage—however few those may be.

We hit another bump. The king snarled, rising when the carriage quit shaking, then returning to me. But I rubbed my head, laughing even as I winced, and after a moment, he did the same.

Dade helped me sit up, catching my face and bringing my forehead to his lips while his fingers roamed my hair.

"I'm fine," I laughed out.

He huffed and kissed my forehead again, then sighed and tucked me over his lap while he tried to make me presentable. "We'll need a bigger carriage."

Something cracked inside my chest, but I ignored it. Easy to do when I remembered what those fussing hands had done—the lives he'd destroyed.

Back inside the Keep, he left another lingering kiss on my forehead, and I laughed when he scowled at the shake of my head. "Good night, savage." Like me, my beast was not sated, not in the least.

But he was thoroughly distracted.

He grumbled out a, "Good night, swan." His petulant expression evoked a small laugh from me as I closed the door on his face and waited.

# TWENTY-ONE

*Opal*

T HE PRINCE WAS SILENT WHEN I ARRIVED, AND IF NOT FOR THE fact that under the firelight, I could see his chest rise and fall, I'd fear him dead.

I peered around the walls, light flaring from my fingers and skirting over damp rock. A door sat on the far side of the narrow dungeon, various torture devices lining the wall behind Bron, and on the one closest to me upon a rusted hook was a set of keys.

Hearing their jangle, Bron stirred, his eyes still too swollen to see who was here. He grunted, then released a wheezed exhale loaded with defeat. I paused mere feet from him, studying the damage to his torso, wondering how much longer he'd live if those wounds weren't tended to, and then I saw the scars.

They'd been healing him. They'd been healing him to keep him alive. To keep giving him more agonizing pain.

A flicker of affection warmed my chest at the knowledge Dade had done this, in part at least, for me. To avenge me.

I couldn't let that stop me from doing what I had to do. If the prince was here, if he died, then who knew what would become of the human royals' plans. We couldn't risk them and my mother joining forces in that way, regardless of whatever armies they might gather from across the seas.

The thought of those forces marching upon this land, decimating it in the way the blood king had done to so many patches of our own, caused my gut to curl and my heart to drop. Vordane, its peace, and its shocking normality was not its ruler, yet its occupants all had blood on their hands.

The blood of innocent people.

It had to end. All of it.

I unlocked the shackles from the prince, and he fell to the ground with a groan that made me freeze and glance around. My heartbeat thundered in my ears, almost loud enough to drown out Bron's mumbling.

When I was as sure as I could be that no one was coming, I lowered to the ground and slid various keys into the chains holding the gag in his mouth until one finally clicked, and the hideous headpiece fell to the bloodstained stone.

"Come on," I whispered, tugging at his arm while he rotated his jaw with a wince. "It's now or never."

"Opal?" he croaked, one eye opening just enough to confirm it was me. "Stars, you're alive."

I tried not to be offended nor waste more time and hauled him to his feet. "*Move.*"

He finally listened, standing on trembling legs. After a few wobbles that almost sent us both crashing into the ground, he found enough balance to stumble toward the doorway that led into the darkness. "Hold the wall," I instructed, then told him to wait when we reached the end of the cold hall that would take us back into the Keep.

It was a gamble, but I had to believe it would pay off—that we'd both make it out of this alive. We waited, Bron's breathing a steady whistle, his weight heavy as it leaned into my side. I blocked it out and focused on catching any sounds on the other side of the door.

Nothing save for the occasional creak and groan of the ancient fortress.

"Okay." I willed open the door. "Quiet as you can, okay? And quick."

Bron nodded, and I half dragged him out into the glowing hall. In the dead of night, the sconces were dimly lit, but that they were lit at all wasn't something we could afford.

I snuffed each one out as we neared them until we crossed the grand foyer before the stairs. We stumbled through a brisk walk to the other side, past the library and those eerie statues that had seen generation after generation of Volkahns and stars only knew what manner of things drift through these halls.

The doors leading outside weren't locked. No sentries stood upon the terrace.

"Not normal," Bron mumbled. "Not normal, is it?" he said again when I didn't answer.

It wasn't, and though I shouldn't have needed to confirm that, I still nodded. "We don't have the time to worry." We kept moving. Through the gardens, a pail of carrots overturned in our haste, passed the stables beyond, and into the shrubs that grew thicker as we slowed behind the training pens.

Bron bent at the knees, breathing heavy, wheezing enough that I knew he was stopping himself from coughing. "Where are you taking me?"

I was tempted to roll my eyes. "Anywhere is better than where you were, so why ask? We need to reach the woods." I blinked at the darkness, the fields of wheat swaying in the night breeze, and said, "That way," while pointing at the wagons parked aside the field. "We run to each wagon, and we don't slow until we've breached the trees."

Bron smothered a cough. "I can't see shit."

I took his hand, cringing but tugging. "You'll be fine."

We ran from wagon to wagon, dodging pitchforks and half-dug holes filled with manure, and though I tried not to, all I could think of was how easy this had been so far. Too easy. So easy that I knew something was wrong.

Not even the kenneled hounds beyond the pens and stables had stirred.

Something was terribly wrong, but we couldn't turn back. I couldn't turn back. We had no choice but to see this through. We continued northeast through the woods, Bron unable to sustain the hurried pace and slowing to a dragging walk a few miles out from the ravine.

From what I hoped was the crossover.

"Keep walking," I said, knowing I had to head back before night bled into morning. "Along the ravine, look down, and you'll find a hollowed-out tree. It's a bridge."

Bron's blood-covered face, sweat streaking through the brown smudges, creased. "You're not coming with me?"

I continued as though I hadn't heard those tempting words. I didn't wish to go anywhere with him but to see my mother again, just one last time... I swallowed. "Climb inside the tree and walk through to the cave beyond, then follow the forest east for a few miles until you see the lights of Sinshell."

"Opal," Bron said. "Your mother has been frantic. She's threatened our family. Why do you think I even met with the blood king?"

I wasn't sure what to say, the thought of my mother enough to make words fall into ash over my tongue. "You need to hurry," I mustered, backing up from the clearing for the cover of the trees. "Tell her I am well. That you saw me, that I helped you leave, and that the lot of you should do *nothing* for the king treats me well, and I've got a plan."

That would remain to be seen after what I'd now done.

I might as well have taken another dagger to his throat and actually stabbed him.

An idea struck me when Bron hesitated, and I bent down, searching for a stick. Standing, I infused it with all the heartache and love that warred within me, warmth spreading from my fingers over the brown wood—turning it gold.

Bron gaped, one swollen eye now open halfway, and took it from me with a shaking hand.

"Deliver it to her. She can feel it, see it, know all of what you say is true, and then she will see to it that you are cared for before you journey home." Each word was ice crusting my lips, for he didn't deserve it, and if my mother knew, she would see to it that he never returned home…

*Later*, I reminded myself. I couldn't allow the oily sludge that filled my veins to change my plans. He would get all that was owed to him. But first, he had to be of use. He had to see my mother. He had to return home to Errin.

Bron's throat moved, and he nodded. "Are you sure?" He threw a glance at the trees behind me, the Keep that loomed far beneath them, miles through the dark but its soft glow still visible through the dancing leaves. "Now is not the time to be a martyr. He's a fucking monster, Opal. He will kill you."

I smiled then and retreated into the dark. "I'd rather he kill me than try to take what does not belong to him."

Bron cursed. "I was not myself. I swear to you, I wouldn't have actually—"

I gritted my teeth. "Save it, and if you could be so kind as to return the favor of saving your life by keeping away from the drink and uninterested females, and doing as I've said, then that would be thanks enough."

Bron stared after me for untold minutes, and I waited behind the thick, rough trunk of a giant oak until finally, the grass swayed, and his scent and footsteps faded on the breeze. In his absence, I felt no relief, no sense of accomplishment at duping a murderous king.

I felt nothing but the gathering wind curling my hair back from my face, sweeping inside the folds of my nightgown. I was still wearing the same undergarments. The same pair that contained a rip right over my center, his seed long since dried on the material.

His breathy voice, the hushed cadence of his groans, the simple yet determinedly curious, bone-melting way he touched me—the time between his dominance over my thoughts was growing slimmer and slimmer with each passing day.

I knew he'd be made aware of the prince's escape as soon as it was discovered. I knew I was the first person he'd interrogate, blame, and he'd have every right to. Perhaps I'd even take Bron's place in that dungeon.

Yet I continued walking back, dodging rogue tree roots, sharp ferns, and moss-covered rocks until the scent of wheat and roses arrived. When I rounded a gnarled tree, its branches twisting enough that I ducked before stepping over a log, I then scented something else.

Whirling to the right, I found the king.

Leaning against a giant rock that reached his shoulders, he peeled the skin from an apple with a small knife, his eyes not on his task but on me. "I trust our dear prince will have a safe journey home?"

The same clothes from this evening still graced his form, rumpled from our tryst in the back of his carriage. My throat dried, fingers clenching and unfurling at my sides. His tone might have been pleasant enough, but it was his empty gaze that gave away the lurking danger behind his question.

The keys upon the wall. They'd been left there for he or his warriors should they need them, but they'd also have known of far better hiding spots.

He'd left them in plain sight. The unlocked doors. The lack of sentries.

"I-I..." I stammered, fear creating a lump in my throat as my heart ceased to beat.

"You think I didn't know what you were up to?" he asked, tearing a bite out of the apple, the knife glinting. "Did you think I wouldn't wonder what you would do when you discovered the vermin in my dungeon?"

I had nothing to say to that. Nothing that would help. No excuses. I didn't want any. I'd done what I'd done, and I'd take whatever punishment he dished out.

Still, he waited with unnerving patience, eyes glowing brighter by the second.

I tried to find the words and tripped over every useless one.

"Don't you ever wonder what it was like before? There's been enough violence."

I refrained from gulping at the feral twist of his features, the immediate darkening of his eyes. "Yet your freeing him will only bring more."

"But you..." I shook my head, incredulous and confused. "You... you just let me free him."

"I-I-I most certainly did," he mocked with a cruel curl of his upper lip. "I wanted to see what you would do—and now I know." In smoke and shadow, he vanished, and dismay filled my entire being like a cloud blocking out the sun.

I couldn't breathe. My vision darkened. My legs began to quake.

Would he kill me? Hurt me? I'd known something was wrong, so terribly wrong, but I hadn't thought it would be anything like this.

That he would test me. Knowing I'd fail, he decided to test me anyway, and he was an asshole, for he knew I'd have chosen most things over him. Mate or not.

I slumped against the tree, my hands tunneling into my sweaty, tangled hair. Tears crested, and I closed my eyes over the burn.

I'd betrayed him as he'd guessed I would.

I'd betrayed him knowing I'd be caught—perhaps wanting to be. Perhaps hoping that if he hated me the same way I had to hate him, then this would be easier.

I'd betray him again and again if it meant helping those he'd hurt.

There was no way out. Not for either of us. This torment, this deadly game of lust and war, would have no winners. Still, I vowed to endure whatever else I had to. Even if it left me torn for all eternity.

Even if my soul continued to unstitch itself from my heart.

I returned to my rooms uninterrupted, numb, and exhausted enough that I prayed whatever punishment awaiting me could wait until morning.

The sentries were back at their posts. Eyes trailed me. I didn't look anywhere but straight ahead, using what remained of my energy to keep my head held high—wondering if Bron had even made it over the crossing if the king had known what I was up to.

I had to believe he had. That he'd see my mother, my people, and give them some measure of hope in the form of a useless golden twig.

The morning arrived with breakfast waiting for me outside my door. Bleary-eyed from only managing to capture a few hours of sleep before more nightmares and my torn conscience got the better of me, I carried it inside my rooms without daring a glance at the giant closed doors down the hall.

The bread grew stale by the windowsill, my tea cold and half-drunk in the delicate teacup as midday ruptured through the crawling ivy over the windows.

And still, I waited.

I waited for something that never came, and after drawing myself a bath, I fell asleep upon the fresh furs that'd been placed on the end of my bed while I'd been gone. I woke right before dinner was delivered, but instead of taking it inside and closing the door, I dropped it onto the small table and walked back out into the steak-and-mushroom-scented hall.

The doors to the king's rooms were open, and I chanced a quick look behind me, knowing there was nothing there save for statues and ghosts, then peered inside.

The bed was made, the décor untouched by dust and fresh books sitting upon his nightstand. I wanted to see what they were, to take a closer look at that map with its horrible red splotches, but I couldn't move.

Maybe that was due to it being another trap. Or maybe it wasn't at all, and my paranoia had reached perilous heights in the king's unnatural silence. Where was he? His scent smothered his rooms, made my blood hum to go in search of him, the most recent bite of it leading toward the stairs.

My feet carried me to and down them before I could think better of it, and as I twisted around the last one to follow that scent, a scream raced up my throat.

"Going somewhere?" An imposing male stood by a statue half his size, a statue of his baser self—a wolf.

I stopped. "Who are you?"

In his hand was a dagger, its edge glinting under the candles floating in the crystal chandelier above our heads. "Scythe."

Flicking my eyes from that dagger to his scarred gaze, I nodded. "I suppose I was looking for the king."

"You suppose?" he asked with a tilt of his head. That scar, I had to wonder if it was the reason for his uncouth name with the way it curved through the sealed skin of his missing eye. "It was cursed," he said then, surprising me. He raised the tip of the blade to his face. "To never open, never regenerate and heal."

The other was a green so velvet, like moss after rain. "I'm sorry." I didn't dare ask what happened, knowing without asking that he would never share that information, as something told me it wasn't a battle injury.

"Why?" He sheathed the blade in a holster at his hip, his gray tunic falling over to conceal it. "You didn't do it."

"I know, but I just mean…" Flustered, I curled my fingers at my sides. I clenched them, forcing out, "It must have been agony."

His upper lip curled over glowing white teeth. "Many things get the title of agonizing, swan. But this"—he pointed at his missing eye with his thumb—"this deserves no such honor."

I did my best to swallow down the boiling shock before it could move over my face. It must have anyway, for his grin grew truly menacing. "You should return to your birdcage now."

"I'm not a prisoner."

He sketched a hand toward the giant dark doors. "Then, by all means, allow me to escort you out."

The rain hammering against the Keep, tapping ceaselessly at every window, made my face scrunch. Curiosity won out when I eyed his pants, the mud-splattered boots and the weapons that were surely hidden beneath. He'd just returned from somewhere. "What were you doing with the dagger?"

"Admiring it."

I ignored those biting cold words. "You thought I was up to something?"

He lifted a shoulder. "I wouldn't have hurt you if that's what you're getting at." His grin turned feral then, entering his eye in a way that made it glow a brighter green. "Our dear king would never forgive me."

"So you would if it weren't for that?" I wasn't afraid, nor was I angered. If anything, I appreciated the honesty. Lies were an old comfort that I now found myself tired of encountering.

Which I think he deciphered when his eye narrowed and his mouth closed, his stiff stance loosening somewhat. "If you were not his mate, your feathers would be a pretty little vase filler by now."

I laughed even as I inwardly winced. He only eyed me with more suspicion, but his expression slackened when I released a heavy breath. "You think me the enemy when I have killed no one."

"You don't need to have blood on your hands to be a murderer," he stated coolly. "Besides, you released the scummy human prince, proving your untrustworthiness. Mate to the king or not."

"I did because another kill doesn't repair anything." I leaned against the stair railing. "How can you support it? All this death?"

Scythe huffed. "The same way you and yours supported it when they moved against us in the first war." Taking one step closer, he whispered heatedly, "You started this. Maybe not you, but your family."

I found nothing to say to that. There was nothing to say when words were becoming so few and futile against numerous allegations.

He smiled, not kindly, and turned on his heel to head down the hall. "Fear makes monsters out of beasts, Princess. Remember that next time you find yourself so ready to condemn."

I watched the darkness of the hall take him, then returned to my rooms and stared at my cooling dinner. And I waited some more.

Two days passed with the same mind-bending routine. I supposed it was safe to assume he wasn't coming for me. That no one was coming for me.

But it was never safe to assume anything with the king of wolves.

For the first time in days, I left my rooms and ventured downstairs, the relentless rain outside splattering the Keep's windows. The vines that encased the exterior created a violent rattle and tapping as thunder boomed overhead.

I didn't dare go farther than the library, though my curiosity, this insufferable tugging beneath my skin, had me longing to delve deeper into the Keep.

He was here. He'd been here for three days. I'd felt it. Listened to his late return each evening to his rooms while wondering if he'd acknowledge me in mine. He never did, and on the fourth night of silence, the bad weather heightening the edged vibe that'd filled the Keep since its arrival, that incessant longing won out.

I didn't know what I would say, only that when I reached the landing below the stairs leading to our rooms, I had to follow the sound of his laughter. Up the set of stairs that led to the other side of the highest floor in the Keep, a place I hadn't yet explored, I trailed his scent, the noise escaping into the halls, and discovered an enormous room.

A ballroom.

Glittering silver chandeliers hung from the rose-painted ceiling, and beneath them were columns wrapped in more vines. Twinkling fireflies bounced inside of tiny glass orbs that looped around them and floated throughout the room.

Flames danced in black sconces and flared with the energy in the giant space, and given the raucous, wild barking laughter and activities, they were roaring toward the ceiling.

I halted in the doorway, unsure what was going on when it dawned on me that nothing special was taking place. This was no ball, but it was a party of some sort.

Naked females danced together around a large velvet-looking circular chaise in the corner, and my eyes widened when a male approached one and spread her legs, hauling them up around his neck until the female quit laughing. Her back arched, her head and shoulders the only parts of her remaining on the large chaise as the male feasted between her thighs and another crawled over her, his member nearing her mouth.

"A black swan darkens our doorway," Fang drawled, seated upon a giant throw cushion with a brunette, a pipe between his lips.

"Fuck," a red-haired male with a deep scar cutting through his cheek muttered from a table overflowing with drink, cards, and piles of coin. "Tres, fetch the king."

A golden-haired male who I assumed must have been Tres thumped his ale to the table, coins bouncing. "You fetch the king."

"Just do it," snapped a raven-haired female beside him.

"The asshole can do it himself," Tres said, picking up his ale. "And as if he doesn't know there's a bird in here."

"What did you call me?"

"Shit." Fang slowly rose from the floor, his stunning female companion pouting. "*Brim,*" he warned.

"You fucking heard me, *asshole.*"

The tankard went flying, narrowly missing my head as I stepped aside, and it clanged into the hall behind me.

It happened so fast, and just as it did with the king, I barely saw it. A series of slight crunches, night coalescing in shadowed tendrils, and skin turned fur. The males were full wolf by the time they collided in the air over the table and took a chair with them to the floor.

The chair splintered into pieces. Growling, snarling, and cheering erupted, but it didn't last longer than a collection of short seconds.

From the other side of the cavernous room, in a corner I couldn't see that faced the naked females upon the circular chaise, came a snarl lethal enough to rupture eardrums and haunt dreams.

Dade took his time. In a loose steel-gray long-sleeved shirt that gaped at his chest, giving a glimpse of the fine hairs dusting his sun-warmed skin, his long legs—thick thighs hugged tight by black pants—ate the quick to clear space of the ballroom.

The silence became so complete that each thud of his knee-high boots grew into an echo.

With one dark glance my way, he sighed and looked at the mis-behaving warriors who were now in their Fae forms, standing ramrod straight, waiting on reprimand.

"Change back," Dade ordered, and then the males were wolves once more, formidable in size and height, but nowhere near the monstrous size of their winged ruler. "Walk home and stay home until told otherwise."

The red wolf left first, the black and gray following, both their tails tucked between their legs.

"You too," the king said, and I'd been so busy watching the wolves slink past me, the red one stopping to sniff at my leg, that I hadn't realized he was talking to me.

I blinked, and he sneered, walking toward me when I didn't move. "Do you really want to enrage me any further, swan?"

"I just..." Too many eyes, even some of those fucking again in varying spaces of the room, were on me. I squared my shoulders and tried again anyway, looking directly into the king's cold eyes. "I need to talk to you. Please."

A brow rose. "Please?" He swung one foot in front of the other, slowly stalking forward. "My, my. Well"—he gestured to the hall—"by all means, lead the way."

Snickering followed as I stepped out, and he trailed, the doors closing behind him.

I couldn't keep my gaze from the glossed, engraved dark wood. "Something bothering you, sunshine?"

He knew very well what was bothering me, and still, I said, "What were you doing in there?"

The king leaned back against the wall, tucking a hand inside his pant pocket as he eyed me for a heated half minute, then sighed. "What did it look like I was doing?"

"Well, I couldn't see you, but there were naked females, and they were…" My cheeks grew warm, and I looked down at my bare feet, feeling so incredibly small. Useless and stupid yet again.

"Fucking. They were fucking. Say it with me."

I refused, and the king laughed without humor, the airy sound raising hairs all over my body. Taking his hand from his pocket and rubbing his jaw, he stated in a bland tone, "We are warriors, but we are also family and friends, and we enjoy the finer things this long eternal life has to offer just like any other creature does."

My stomach sank so hard and swift that I feared the little food I'd had for dinner might hurl itself up my throat. "That means you—"

"You used what I feel for you against me, but I am the fool for letting you."

"So you retaliate in this way?" I asked, each new breath sharp and slicing. "What would you have me do?" I surprised myself by asking. "If you were me, what would you have done?"

"Swan," he said, and I'd never heard him say it without inflection, as though it were just a word. "You seek empathy from a male who has none. You are a bird, and I am a beast. Now run along before I ponder the possibility of crafting a flag of victory from those lovely black feathers."

He left me with his harsh yet undeniably true words and closed himself back inside his den of debauchery.

I wasn't sure how long I stood there with my eyes and chest burning, but when I heard something thump against the closed doors, followed by growling and laughter, I forced myself to head back down the hall.

My foot had barely met the cold marble of the landing when that scent—sweat and earth—returned. But too late for me to realize it was yet another foe.

"He might not pluck those feathers…" Heated breath washed over my shoulder. "But I will."

Something smacked into the side of my head, and then there was nothing.

I ended up in the dungeon after all, though it wasn't Dade who'd brought me here.

"Serrin," the male said with an unnerving amount of calm when he returned and realized I was awake. "Uncle to the alpha king and his advisor." Wading toward me, he observed the metal that'd been looped around my neck and grimaced. "My, this is unpleasant, but you see, I've been left with little choice."

The chain was tight, but not so tight that I struggled to breathe and talk. My hands were bound behind my back with what burned like rope. "Where is he?"

"They left this morning to terrorize a little town named Tulane. You might know of it?"

He indeed knew that I was more than familiar with the town by the border of Sinshell. The Well of Wishes resided there, as well as a creek that contained healing stones and algae. It wasn't just those things that spiked a nail of fear through my heart, though.

It was the people. Tulane was a farming town. What remained of my father's extended family still lived there. I wondered if the king knew that, and judging by the gleam in the blue-eyed male before me, I was guessing he did not.

"You know my family lives there. That more innocent people live there."

"Perhaps not anymore," Serrin said, grimacing again. "I would say all is fair in love and war, but we both know this war and"—he waved a hand at me flippantly—"whatever it is you and Dade have been struggling with is anything but fair."

The male who, besides being gifted with similar-colored eyes, looked nothing like his nephew knew very well that we were mated.

Serrin circled me, the scrape of his fingers over his short, dark beard mingling with his booted steps.

He was patient, waiting for my curiosity to drown my stubborn desire to remain quiet. "What is it you want?"

Footsteps ceased, his shoulder-length brown hair falling over one eye as he came to a stop before me. "To end this once and for all." He procured a dagger from a sheath at his waist and stepped closer. "He'll forgive me, and I hope you do, too, as I'm merely doing what he should've already done. Now change."

Confused, I asked, "What? Why?"

"Just do it." When I didn't, he sighed and circled behind me, then thrust the tip of the blade into my arm. I screamed. No one would hear me, I knew, but I couldn't help it as my blood fizzed and warred against the iron that tried to poison my veins.

I shifted, wings flapping, the chain around my neck tightening, the other end now in Serrin's hands instead of hooked to the ceiling.

"Stay still, Princess," he ordered, but I continued to struggle, my neck throwing itself around, instinct screaming to flee, to be rid of the metal around it.

I might have been a bird, but I was half the size of him, and I couldn't help the urge to swing my beak at his pawing hands. He evaded me. One by one, he plucked the feathers from my body, the sharp pinch enraging me to the point of getting tangled up in the chain on my back.

"That's it," Serrin crooned, looming over me now, a hammer and large nail in hand. His boot landed upon my leg, the hammer striking the nail hovering above my wing—once, twice…

I passed out and came to with both wings staked to the stone floor, feathers, too many of them, being gathered in a large sack over by an empty cell.

"You're awake," Serrin said, clomping over. "Good. Now, I must send some feathered treasure to the dear golden queen, but of course, a threat cannot be delivered without a healthy dose of blood. My apologies, Princess. I know it's easier for you to heal in this form, but I need you to shift back if you wish to fly again."

Knowing better than to ignore his warning, I did as requested, agony rushing in and blackening my vision from the two holes in my lower arms.

"A few days and they should heal nicely. I missed the bone," he said as if he'd done me a favor.

I couldn't talk. I feared that if I opened my mouth, I'd wail like a babe and scream until my lungs gave out.

But it wasn't over yet.

He hauled me up to sit against the wall, then tore at my gown until I was wearing nothing but my canary yellow undergarments. No, he wasn't satisfied until he'd plunged the knife inside one of the wounds and twisted, holding the limb over the sack of feathers.

Blood gathered and spread over the luminous black, collecting in a thick layer that would soak clean through the feathers and cream canvas. Shreds of my gown were tossed inside. "Your mother must surrender, swear her fealty to our king, and then we can be done with all this," Serrin muttered as though I'd agree, and then he was gone.

The butcher left. He left, and I was left half-naked with blood pooling beneath me on the ground.

# TWENTY-TWO

## Dade

*Fourteen years old*

"**O**N YOUR FEET, BOY."

I spat a glob of blood at the dirt, my head ringing and my sword beside me. I could stretch out and reach it, but I couldn't. Every part of me was chipped—my very bones brittle and aching.

"Dade," Serrin barked.

I pushed to my feet, too slow for his liking, and landed flat on my ass as his steel-toed boot collided with my gut. My breakfast left my stomach, burned its way up my throat, but I'd been here before.

Every damned day. Morning, noon, and night, I was tortured beyond reason, but the reason was always the same.

My uncle came for my jugular. "Do you think they'd be proud?" He released a snide laugh. "You're a disgrace. Now get on your fucking feet," he roared with a vehemence I couldn't ignore.

I understood his pain. I felt it every waking morning when he forced me to before my eyes had fully opened. My father had been his best friend, his idol, a mate found in a brother.

And he'd never let me forget.

I snatched up my sword, and we danced. I struck, left, left, right, then *feigned a turn, catching him off guard. It only served to enrage him further, his attacks no longer practiced caution but life or death.*

*The shock of it could've killed me, but he'd been this furious many times before. Just once, the first time, as I'd lain in a pool of my own blood, unsure if I'd see the sun rise again, was enough for me to take his deadly rage seriously.*

*We fought until I was shoved back against the wooden fencing, other warriors of similar ages going through their morning stances and routines in the pens across from ours.*

*I could feel their eyes on us, hear the general bark at them to clear out as I pushed back against the steel that came for my side. My teeth bared, blood boiling as Serrin's eyes clashed with mine, the hatred and grief and frustration in his too much to break away from.*

*Trapped. I was trapped, and he'd never set me free.*

*I wanted to avenge my parents' deaths. I wanted to rule this kingdom with a brutal, furred fist. I wanted to make sure everyone knew the price of crossing a Volkahn.*

*But I also wanted to follow the others as they left the training yards and returned to their homes or barracks. I wanted to fly with them, fight with them, and I knew I would, but... when?*

*When would I be good enough to live a life outside of my uncle and his bloodlust? When would I be able to laugh with the others as they trained and fought together? When would I be treated as a growing king and less like a beast that would never be tamed? When would I be able to follow a female around who'd piqued my interest rather than eye the female warriors from afar?*

*When would I be able to fucking breathe without being berated and reminded and beaten and controlled?*

*A roar tore from somewhere deep inside, shocking us both as my skin hummed but did not catch fire with the change. "If this means so much to you, why don't you just become king?"*

*Serrin's eyes flared, and he pulled away. Just when I thought he was done with me for the morning, he spun back, the side of his blade catching* me in the shoulder hard enough to slice through my leather tunic and graze my skin. *"You ungrateful—"*

I let go, unraveling into a darkness so complete, a burn that split apart my breathing and bones and remolded everything into more. Sharper, fiercer, deadlier—it happened so quickly, faster than ever before, that my uncle had no time to react.

I snarled, teeth poised over his throat, my growled breath pluming the frigid air. Pinned beneath my paws, claws sinking into his shoulders, Serrin looked something other than crestfallen and furious.

For the first time in my entire life, he stared at me with fear.

It swam in his eyes, flooded and seeped through his pores, and I inhaled it deep, drunk from a growing power stronger than anything I'd encountered from my maturing body before.

A thunderous growl left me, uncontrolled and steaming the air, dampening his cheek. His hands rose, his eyes collecting pain to accompany the fear as my claws sank deeper.

*"Dade,"* he ordered, though it lacked the usual sharp conviction. *"Dade, return. Change back."*

Bone crunched beneath the weight of my paws, his blood running between them into the dirt by his head.

He tried again, voice softer, more gentle than I'd heard before. *"Dade, please. You must change back."*

I snarled, teeth closer to his cheek, tempted to take a bite—just one. Though I was sure his flesh would taste like sour milk, he had to learn. He had to pay.

*"Your mother wanted you,"* he said, shocking me. *"You were a surprise, of course, though she knew your father was lying. That he'd planned your conception. She didn't care."* He laughed, the sound wet. *"She didn't care because from the moment she realized you existed, she loved you. She loved you with a love so pure, she cried every time you did when you arrived."*

I eased back on my haunches, but only a little.

*"Not even a week,"* he continued. *"She didn't even get a week to learn how to stop feeling your pain, your hunger, your confusion as if it were her own, and your father... when he left for the annual meeting of the bridges,*

*he'd had a mere three days. Just three fucking days." He enunciated each word with a clenched jaw as though it took everything for him to keep the grief welling in his eyes from escaping.*

*I retracted my claws. He hissed, the wounds steaming the cold before they slowly began to close.*

*"He was gone a day too long. That one day was enough to have your mother pacing, torn between her two greatest loves. I said I would go. I begged for her to stay, to wait until morning when the rest of the guard would be ready to leave with her. She said she would."*

*He swallowed, and it sounded as though it hurt. "She promised," he rasped, tears slowly leaking from his eyes now. "And I know he'll never forgive me because I went to bed. I did not stop her that night when she left you with the nursemaid and ran. She ran to her mate, to her death, and she did so with hope that whatever was wrong could be fixed, that he would be okay, though she knew and could feel otherwise."*

*I whined low, peeling my paws from his shoulders, bone grinding under my weight, and stood over him instead. But I wouldn't let him leave. Not yet. Not until I'd heard the rest. Not until I'd felt that organ inside me blacken and perish just that little bit more.*

*Serrin sniffed, groaning before he went on. "When we reached old bridge later the next day, they were gone. It would be another two days of riding and flying through Sinshell until we found them hanging from flower-trussed poles, blood leaking from everywhere, and Kenton Gracewood demanding we agree to his terms, or they would die."*

*His grief melded with my own, climbing higher into a fury that scorched through every vein until I felt it embed deep within my soul.*

*"Those terms?" Serrin said, a dry laugh following. "To send you to a human kingdom, either Errin or across the sea, to be raised as one of them so that you would not know all of what you could be, and therefore not bring the doom they feared you would. The foretold bullshit from a deranged sorceress who claimed you would be the end to the Gracewood line."*

*A low rumble slipped between my teeth, and I gnashed them, my uncle smiling sadly. "Exactly," he said. "They created their own doom when Althon's father slid that sword across your mother's throat and then into* her heart. And though your father had been tortured for days to agree to their terms, his agony was so violent that it shook the earth. It set him free, and thus the first war began."

I hadn't realized we'd gathered a small audience, but not even the generals and trainers cared to tell the other wolves to fall back in line. No, they did not care to talk at all, to interrupt any part of what my uncle was saying, though I was sure they'd heard it before. Some of them had even been there. The misery and unjustness, the crime that had gone unpunished, kept them rooted to the spot or quietly drawing closer.

"It ended just two days after, as you already know, with a spear through your father's eye courtesy of Althon Gracewood." I moved back enough for Serrin to sit up. "We were outnumbered severely, but when Joon, the Gracewood prince, fell too, they pulled back. They called an end to the battle of their own making, as though they were the judge, jury, and executioners, and we were nothing but beasts expected to blindly obey."

That name chanted through me, cursed me, and I welcomed it, bowed to the desire to crush it from existence—Althon Gracewood.

Serrin wiped a muddied hand over his cheek, leaving dirt in its wake but uncaring. "She ran with hope, and in the end, that was what killed your mother. The hope that creatures would not be good and kind, but fair and just. Hope kills," he hissed, climbing to his feet. "So kill it first and fight. Let this entire continent know they made the gravest mistake of their miserable lives when they stole from us."

I shrank back into myself, more bruised and battered on the inside than out, but something had changed.

Something had irrevocably changed as I turned in a circle and took in the grim faces surrounding our enclosure. Some just stared, horrified, others had tears in their eyes, and some of them nodded in confirmation that every word Serrin said was true.

I'd known it was true. I'd known, but I hadn't known how scalding the details of that truth would be—the brutal chill of them frosting through my bloodstream to freeze what remained of my heart.

I picked up my sword, barely feeling its hefty weight over the new one that had now become a part of me.

*Serrin grinned, his eyes wet, and nodded. "There you finally are, my king."*

There was no unearthly way I could ever touch someone else, but my swan didn't need to know that.

Just as she didn't know I was standing in the middle of a once beautiful town named Tulane.

Of course, I enjoyed watching her jealousy drown her need to hate me. I enjoyed it, and I wanted more of it, but I couldn't stomach the idea of seeing her. Not yet. The mere sight of her inquisitive golden eyes the previous night, so hopelessly lost as she'd stared beyond me into the ballroom filled with gamblers, fighters, fuckers, and royalty, tempted me to torment her some more.

It wasn't as though she didn't deserve it.

Flame danced upon my palm, its burn nothing compared to the ice my swan had left me with. She'd toyed with me. Tricked me. Tried to seduce me into becoming a malleable puppet easily remolded and duped.

My swan would soon learn just how well such games would work out for her.

Yet as I went to reduce the town to cinders, something stopped me, and I launched the flame at a smattering of trees instead, my teeth gritting as I hollered, "Clear out."

"No burning today?" Scythe asked, hurrying to my side with an armful of books and liquor.

I trudged through the blood-riddled puddles caused by the rain and the fall of their beloved well. "If we burn everything, then we have nothing to take for ourselves when the time arrives."

Knowing I was right—I was always fucking right—Scythe turned back to order the wolves and our new friends to stop their pilfering and file out. Beneath my gore covered armor, something began to itch at my skin like a parasite.

A few precious moments passed before I remembered I'd felt this itch before.

I tore the metal off, charging for the horses, then growled and shifted when it didn't abate, choosing to fly ahead instead.

The wind howled in greeting, flooding my ears, each whoosh of my wings unable to propel me fast enough as the ravine opened into the sea below and the itch beneath my skin warmed to a steady burn.

Snarling, I dropped with bruising speed to the cliffside.

Opal. I knew it before I warped to the Keep and found her minutes that felt like an eternity later. Righting my shirt as I raced into the dungeon, that burn now searing, I tripped to a stop as I rounded the doorway and caught sight of her.

Naked and caked in blood upon the dungeon floor.

A crunch echoed, but I knew it was no one. That it was nothing but the stone organ inside my chest, rupturing with each rusted beat.

The door at the other end of the dungeon creaked and groaned. Serrin entered with a pail of soapy water in hand and a healer trailing him. He stopped, the healer almost walking into him and then slowly stepping to his side. "Dade," he said, blinking.

My vision turned crimson.

He'd touched her. He'd… he'd hurt her. He'd fucking put holes in her perfect body.

He'd plucked her feathers, some floating about the room, a sack of them resting beside her against the wall.

He'd terrorized my swan.

"Dade, n-now just l-listen." Serrin set the pail down and edged closer. "It's not as bad as it—*argh*."

Gripping him around the neck, I launched him at the wall. He smacked into it with a boom loud enough to crack it. A sickening snap was heard beneath the crumbling of mortar and stone before he fell limp to the trembling floor.

The commotion stirred Opal—her choked gasp tearing me in two.

My fists curled, claws cutting into skin, my body torn between wolf and male and the desire to finish him off. To make sure he could never see her or so much as touch her, or anything else, ever again.

Then she said, "Tulane," and I wanted to turn those claws upon my chest and throw myself at her bloodstained feet to beg for mercy. To ask what this life of *before* was, what she knew of it, and how we could make it together if she'd only forgive me.

She wouldn't. She'd never forgive me. Hence why I was a bastard who just continued to make sure of that fact.

So instead, I hurried to her, hushed her, and pushed her hair from her face before gently removing the chain from her bruised neck. Blood still rushed from a deep wound in her arm, and I covered it with my hand, willing it to stop, to seal. It did, but it would only hold for so long before needing proper medical attention.

My stomach turned, rage and worry gnawing at each other and charging into each ragged breath I drew. Stars, the blood. Blood was fucking everywhere. Her other arm ravaged, too but neater, as though a stake had been driven straight through her flesh.

Looking at the sack of blood-soaked feathers, I swallowed thickly. "Swan," I rasped.

Her eyes fluttered closed, and I carefully collected her into my arms, nodding at the healer who was watching on with a watery brown gaze. "Follow me."

# TWENTY-THREE

## *Opal*

I WOKE IN A FOG, THE SILKEN WATERS OF SLEEP PEELING AWAY like a soft sheet being pulled down my body.

An ache, dull and tempered by healing hands, lingered in both arms. When I peered at them, daylight streaming in through the windows beyond the bed and pushing my eyelids closed, I saw nothing but lightly stained bandages.

A low whine followed me into another dreamless sleep.

When I woke, the stars were out, the moon glazing over the beast prowling in circles at the end of my bed.

The white-furred giant made it five paces before needing to slink into a narrow turn and then paced again. I watched him, mesmerized by the liquid grace of each powerful step. Those paws, the muscle in his legs, he could stomp a hole right through the floor if he wanted to.

But it was the wings that stole my breath. The fur upon them was so light they appeared leathery at first glance. The hair grew dense toward the edges then spread into creamy feathers. They rustled, those giant wings, tucked close to his side but occasionally shifting when he released a huffed breath.

Needing some water, I pushed up onto my elbows and nearly choked when I set the glass down to find the beast stalking toward the side of the bed. Those eyes were the same cerulean blue, drinking me in, unblinking as he folded himself into a sitting position next to where I laid.

His snout was canine, larger than my head, but the horns that curled out into harsh bends behind his furred ears were like nothing I'd ever seen on a creature before. They shone, a deep glittering bronze, both sharper than blades at each severely pointed end.

It was said that the firstborn son or daughter of the king would bear horns. A feature that set them apart from the rest of their kin. A crown for the alpha of all beasts.

The king of wolves tilted that giant head, and finally, he blinked.

I blinked back, then realized he was waiting. I wasn't sure what he wanted, but I soon wondered if this was his way of asking if I was settled enough with his appearance for him to come closer when he released another huff, dark nostrils flaring as he lifted a paw and let it thump to the floor.

I swallowed, unsure yet also certain I wanted him closer.

And that was always the problem with this male. I feared I'd forever find myself stuck someplace between want and hesitation.

Then I remembered. Tulane.

I lowered to the bed and faced the opposite wall, ignoring his low whine.

Another day passed, my limbs too stiff and achy for me to endure more than a trip to the bathing chamber.

Still in his beast form, Dade continued with his pacing of the room, sometimes choosing to lay upon the furs on the floor, his giant snow tufted tail swishing while he slumbered.

His eyes flashed open, and I frowned, laying the book I'd been trying to read on the bedding next to me. A knock sounded seconds later, Dade's snout in the air as he scented who it was, then growled low, as if annoyed, when Scythe entered.

He closed the door behind him, a smirk upon his full lips as he eyed his king. "Not tired of playing guard hound yet, my king?"

Dade growled harsh enough for his lips to peel back over gleaming white fangs.

Scythe, still smiling, tucked his hands inside his pant pockets. "Relax, I'm just here to inform you that your dear uncle has finally woken. He suffered a broken neck." Scythe's attention crawled slowly to me. "But he'll live."

Dade rose, quicker than I'd have thought something of that size could move, and began to pace again, this time slower, as though he were pondering something.

"Serrin," I said, forcing my eyes from Dade to Scythe and away from the memory of a blood-hazed dungeon. "Did he end up delivering the, uh…"

"The package?" Scythe finished for me. I nodded, and he watched me for a moment, then released a rough breath and leaned back against the door. His black tunic, lined with crimson stitching, flattened against his hard chest as though the heavy fabric were crafted to move with him like air. "No, it's been destroyed."

Something in those words told me that he wasn't exactly thrilled with the waste, but that he would not dispute it.

I nodded once more, curling some of my hair behind my ear as the memory of each pinching loss, feathers plucked as though they were brambles amongst skirts, rippled over me in a cold wave.

"He hasn't shifted back," I said, partly curious as to why and also wanting to fill the tense silence. To divert his attention someplace else. "Is there a reason?"

Scythe read the question I didn't ask, *is something wrong?* And that curl of his lips returned.

"His senses are better in his baser form," he said. "All of ours are, but his, well, they are unrivaled." His smirk broadened into a dazzling smile. "Get used to him, swan. He won't return until he's ready."

For the remainder of the day, I mulled over that, and when dinner arrived this time, I noticed an extra meal upon the tray.

Instead of eating at my bed as I usually did, I set it at the small table in the corner on the far side of the room. The space between the nightstand and the bookshelves was cramped, and I didn't delude myself into thinking the king would fit on the chair opposite me even in his Fae form.

But there was enough space between the bed and the shelves, the white furs he'd napped upon between the watching beast and me, for him to come closer if he so wished and eat something.

Unsure if he'd shift back or not, I set his plate on the ground. The king didn't so much as look at it, bright eyes never leaving me. His tail flicked behind him, those eyes moving to my plate and then back to mine, a spark of impatience within.

He wanted me to eat.

That made two of us. My arms trembled a little as I removed my cutlery from the tray and cut into the juicy slice of lamb. Dade's tail stopped its swishing as I chewed, and after a few more mouthfuls of green beans and meat, I set my cutlery down and stared at him.

I hadn't seen him eat once in the days we'd been sequestered in my rooms. Of course, he might have done so while I'd been asleep, but I highly doubted he'd have quit his brooding to make time for it.

His eyes narrowed, and I said, "You need to eat too." They narrowed more, and I smirked. "I won't be eating another bite unless you do."

He snarled, the harsh grumble raising the hair upon my now steady limbs.

I didn't relent, but I did pluck up his plate of food from the floor and cut the bone from the meat. Then I sliced the lamb into four large pieces and motioned for the king to come to me.

We both stilled.

An order. I'd given the monster of Nodoya an order, and while in his beast form at that.

My breath sat tight in my throat. Dade's head cocked as though he were amused as he considered me.

My shoulders sagged when he didn't move, and I tried a different approach. "Please." The whispered word broke a little, surprising us both. But then he moved.

Slowly, his eyes never leaving mine, mine never leaving his, the king's giant body swayed with each powerful, lazy step he took across the carpet. I kept still, so still I wasn't sure I was breathing, as his snout rose higher than my forehead, tilting downward for his gaze to meet mine over the long muzzle.

His scent was more potent in this form—smuggling inside my every extremity and locking up each muscle as I wondered if one large bite would tear my head clean from my shoulders.

His mouth opened, long tongue peeking out, and then he sat, though his head still loomed over mine. Unable to stop myself, I reached out with a tentative hand, watching those eyes to see if he'd snap, and when he merely waited, I gently stroked his mane. Instantly, my fingers disappeared inside the impossibly soft white fur, and I pulled them back with a start.

Dade licked his lips, and I looked away, stabbing into a piece of lamb with my fork. "You should probably lie down, unless you want me to stand." As always, he was too close, too huge, and far too much for such a confined space.

He did, and I stopped myself from balking at the sign of submission.

A wolf king at the feet of a swan.

It took great effort to keep my hand steady as I delivered the fork to his mouth, which now sat nearly level with my chest, and his ears pulled back, as did his head.

I scowled. "You don't like lamb? I don't believe you."

He huffed and swung his eyes to my free hand. It dawned then. Of course, he didn't want me to use a fork. He wanted me to hand-feed him.

My stomach sank as I glanced at that mouth, the ginormous dagger flooded darkness within that would shred my entire hand in under a second. Dade stared at me, waiting, knowing I was at war with myself yet again and offering me something he wasn't used to giving anyone else.

Patience.

He wouldn't hurt me, I reminded myself. The bond we shared made that nearly impossible. At least, he wouldn't hurt me physically.

My heart, my feelings, did not fall under that protect at all costs mentality—for he hadn't a heart of his own. But when his nose gently nudged my hand, I wondered if somewhere behind those watching blue eyes, he was now learning that mine must be protected too.

So I picked up a piece of lamb, and with it in the palm of my hand, offered it to the king.

A flash of something moved behind those eyes before he lowered his head and gently licked the meat from my hand with his soft tongue. But when I made to pick another piece up, he grunted, and I sighed before snatching my fork to take two bites of my own meal, which had now grown cool but no less delicious, the beans soaked in a glazed caramelized onion sauce.

We continued in this fashion until all that remained were the vegetables. I set the plate upon the floor. "You can lick those up yourself," I said, smiling when he released an irritated breath.

He ate, and satisfied, I helped myself to a glass of water, then tipped some into a small bread dish upon the tray after placing the tiny bread rolls onto my empty plate.

Though the size of his nose made it difficult, the king still lapped all the water from the bowl, but turned his head when I offered him more.

The following morning, the king refused breakfast but agreed to eat lunch. Of course. Meat and vegetables in this form were probably all he'd tolerate. The porridge would only make him ill.

That evening, the king dozing before the fireplace, I ran myself a bath after dinner, thankful for the time alone yet also fearful that he might leave in my brief absence.

I should've known he'd protest at the wooden barrier and bust it open at the first sound of pain that left my mouth. Still, I slid inside the warm depths, vanilla-scented bubbles frothing near my chin, and gritted my teeth.

I'd barely noticed the healing wounds upon my back, the numerous tiny yet deep cuts that had nearly healed, until the water reminded me of how many feathers I'd be missing when I next shifted. I was almost too afraid to find out, praying that enough time would pass before I did and that many would have grown back beforehand.

"I'm fine," I grumbled. Peeling the bandages from my arms, I set them over the ledge and selected a sponge from the windowsill to carefully drag over the healing wounds. "You can leave now."

We both knew he'd do no such thing. He slumped to the ground right outside the bathing room, his head almost filling the doorway.

I sighed but finished washing before allowing myself a moment to just sit inside the warm, creamy water and breathe. A wet nose at my arm roused me from sleep, and I forced myself not to startle at the sight of Dade's narrowed gaze inches from mine.

"Okay," I said, righting myself in the tub and then remembering I was naked. It didn't matter that he was a horned beastly wolf, nor that he'd seen me naked before, I still ordered, "I'll get out if you give me the privacy to do so."

He stared at me in a way that could only be described as mocking, then took his time turning in the small space and heading back into the bedroom.

He didn't close the door, but when I looked over my shoulder before climbing out, I couldn't see him. Wrapped in a cloth, I padded from the bathing room to the large robe in the next and selected a peach satin nightgown that fell to my knees.

Dade was slumbering upon the floor, one eye flicking open as I dragged a comb through my damp hair while walking back to the bed. I set it upon the nightstand, then gingerly pushed my legs underneath the bedding and listened to the wind howl outside, unable to sleep.

The thorns upon the vines clattered into the windows, the fire in the hearth guttering.

"Dade," I eventually whispered, not sure if he was asleep, if he

204 | ELLA FIELDS

ever truly slept while in my rooms. "Your uncle is being held some-where, I assume. You can come back now."

He said nothing, and after some moments of staring at the ceil-ing, light and dark throwing each other into the shadows of the moon, I knew it didn't matter if the threat was contained.

Scythe was right. The king wouldn't return until he was ready—until he'd spent enough time alone with his anger and shame and whatever else ailed that dark, strange mind.

I had to wonder if maybe he wouldn't come back until I'd for-given him. And maybe I could forgive him this, but there were too many other things I could not.

In any case, Scythe's visit had been more than a mere message about his uncle that anyone could have delivered. It had been a check-ing in of sorts. Dade was a king, a tyrant but still a king, and this king-dom was now without one and an advisor until he chose to come back.

I had a feeling his uncle and advisor, the same male who could now not be trusted in the king's eyes, was the one who'd govern in the king's absence. Which left his most trusted warriors, the same war-riors who liked to bed females in a ballroom under many a watchful eye while others gambled and drank themselves stupid.

I might not have known them well, but I knew that Scythe and Fang were ill-equipped to hold this place together for weeks. They'd likely never had to do such a thing before.

Dade had to know that, had to be well aware of that, given all else he was so keenly aware of in this form, yet...

"Dade," I whispered again, harsher this time.

He sat up, eyes bright in the dark, horns dipped in moonlight.

I was crazy, most certainly. A fool for the way I cared when this would be an opportune time to take advantage of this murderous king. To swoop in and take back some of what he'd stolen from me and so many others. I could alert what remained of our forces—could send word to the human kingdom—if I could somehow leave this room or get a message out of Vordane.

But none of those things were possible, even if I could do them.

He would chase me. Wherever I went, whatever I did, he would know, and he would follow.

Nevertheless, I would continue with this asinine quest. But I was selfish, so I'd take advantage of this king while also feeding my starving heart—this invisible need that would inevitably be my end.

Keeping my eyes on his, I rose and patted the end of the bed. Dade didn't move, didn't so much as shift his gaze toward the bed.

Stubborn asshole.

Withholding a groan of frustration, I tore my eyes from his and scrunched the bedding in my fist. Fine. If he wanted to sulk in his beast form upon the floor for the rest of his miserable days, then—

I looked from the bed to him and nearly laughed.

He would break it. Perhaps even if he were careful, the wood would still bow and bend and snap beneath his considerable weight.

Right. I stood and marched to the door. Dade reached it in one leap that shook every piece of furniture in the room. He growled in warning, blocking my exit.

I propped my hands upon my hips and raised my brows.

He sat on his ass and lifted his nose into the air, every inch the spoiled royal brat, even as a wolf.

Sighing, I said, "I thought we might be more comfortable in your rooms."

He stared, then blinked, then twisted and marched to the door on the opposite side of the room—to the door that I'd never dared open, never dared to even near, before now.

I opened it, knowing what I'd find and not entirely sure that merely closing it would mean it would never be used again, then paused in his dressing room.

A dressing room that was almost the size of the bedroom we'd just left. Reds, grays, blacks, and a small smattering of whites and creams were all I could make out in the dark.

Dade huffed and rounded me, soft fur grazing my leg and hand, waiting for me to lock the door behind me.

Satisfied when it clicked, he strutted into the bedchamber, then

paused, blocking my entry as he sniffed the air. I waited in the doorway, the moon bouncing off the pristine dark bedding on the gigantic bed, as Dade sniffed every corner, every item of furniture, then
climbed onto his bed.

It groaned but otherwise seemed plenty big enough for him and
even myself. Yet I halted, thinking perhaps I should just tell him I was
okay and make my way back into my own quarters.

Dade waited, head upright, shadows dancing around his pricked
ears and those deadly horns, and I sagged with defeat and relief, crossing a woven carpet and climbing onto the monstrosity to sit beside
him.

After staring at him for endless moments, I gave in to the urge
to crawl closer and laid my head upon a pillow soaked in his scent. I
was tempted to roll my face into it, tempted to rip it to shreds with my
hands and teeth while swallowing as much of him into me as I could.

Then he laid his head down below the pillow next to mine, eyes
searching, fur rising and falling with each breath.

Beautiful was too small a word to describe him. He was magnificent, terrifyingly intimidating, and so utterly enchanting it captured
each trembling breath. Despite every natural instinct I'd been born
with screaming not to, I surrendered to the newest one. The one I was
still struggling to come to terms with—the instinctual need to be as
near as possible. I surrendered, and I curled closer to trace his muzzle, the silken white fur between his eyes.

They closed at my touch, his tongue wetting his lips when I continued over his head to the horns. Stone. Twisted, sharp twins of stone,
they were warm and smooth under the pad of my finger.

Wings, tucked into his side, rustled when I dragged my finger
down to his soft ears, and I couldn't keep from smiling. "You want
me to touch them too?"

He opened one eye in answer. My smile remained as I settled
back against the pillow, thinking it was best we both sleep instead.

A nudge from a cool nose at my arm had me conceding, and those wings flicked out, stretched wide to skim the floor, downy feathers brushing my cheek. "Show off."

A fire roared to life, lighting the silver stones in the hearth, but I couldn't drag my tired eyes from the magic beside me long enough to admire the stonework. They drooped, Dade's breathing evening out, his heartbeat a slow drum near my ear that lulled me to sleep as I nestled closer.

I woke some hours later, sweat misting my forehead, and realized why. A wing had blanketed my entire body. My face was buried in fur, a snout evicting even breaths that stirred the hair at the back of my head.

Smiling, I rolled over to gain some air, noticed it was morning, and happily drifted back to sleep.

# TWENTY-FOUR

## *Opal*

**E**ARLY EVENING BROUGHT A HALF-NAKED MALE WITH IT.
Chin on his palm, his other hand toying with my hair, Dade watched me with a smile in those lupine blue eyes as I stretched my legs and forced my own to stay open. "I never partook in the festivities," he said by way of greeting.

It took me three confused blinks to gather what he was referring to, and relief swaddled me so tight that I sat up. He hadn't been with any of those females that night in the ballroom.

He passed me a glass of water, and I guzzled the lot. "You may do as you wish."

I tried to crawl off the bed, to set the glass by the books on the nightstand and to leave. He was back. He was back, and now I didn't know what to do with him.

With myself.

The glass fell to the carpet on the floor, rolling under the bed when an arm looped around my waist and threw me beneath a large, toned body. Dade stared down at me, a fresh cedar scent rolling off him. He must have bathed while I was still asleep. "What I wish for is you."

Stunned, I gaped at him for searing moments. "You watched them," I said and immediately wanted to smack myself.

Dade's brows gathered. "I have at times, yes. You'd be hard-pressed to find someone who wouldn't." He grinned then, strands of blond hair falling over his forehead, curling around those sharp cheekbones. Both dimples deepened, my fingers itching to touch. "You even watched. I saw you."

He had me there, and I bit my lips against the heat wanting to rise into my face. "I was shocked."

"You were curious." His smile drooped into something deadlier, then he lowered until his naked chest was almost pressing into the satin covering mine, and murmured, "But if it bothers you, I won't look ever again."

I knew a vow when I heard one, especially given in that deep, rasped tone. "Truly?" I still asked.

My lips parted, breath sailing between when his eyes dipped to them, then down to my chest. They returned to mine fevered, his nostrils flaring. "My lovely swan," he purred. "My bittersweet neme-sis, I'm beginning to fear there isn't anything I wouldn't do for you."

I gasped at hearing those words and the way his lower body fell into mine, my legs spreading before I could think better of it. I couldn't think.

He erased everything rational, and the aggressive shine that deep-ened his eyes, causing the muscles to flex in the powerful arms on ei-ther side of my head, said he knew it. "Princess," he said, voice hoarse. My hands grabbed his cheeks. My body arched into his. His eyes shut-tered as he choked out, "Fuck," before slamming his mouth over mine.

Fire filled every extremity, my heart an explosion of failed beats as his mouth pillaged and plundered, and it was all I could do not to melt into the feathered mattress beneath us.

A clawed finger skimmed my side, gooseflesh rising in its wake, and then the other. The straps were next, then both hands returned to fist the bedding beside my head as my nightgown fell in strips with each thrusting slide of his lower body over mine. "I liked that nightgown," I panted when his mouth gave me reprieve, and grazed my neck and chest.

"I'll buy you twenty more to tear apart," he muttered to my breasts, breath hot and ragged, and I mewled as his warm mouth closed over a beaded nipple. He sucked, then licked, then moved to the other to give it the same attention. His eyes flashed up at me, watching, learning, knowing. Gently, his teeth scraped over the delicate skin, his question more of a search for confirmation. "Like that?"

"Love that, but come back." Desperate, I clasped his hair between my fingers, pawing at his back when he gave that luscious mouth to mine, and then pushed at the waistband of his pants.

They left his body with one movement, and I froze at the feel of him, the heat of his smooth skin near boiling. "Need you," he whispered, husked and nipping at my lips. "Like I've never truly needed anything until now."

I nipped his lips back, then licked at the tiny pearl of blood I'd spilled. "Do it," I pleaded, too soft for it to be the taunting dare I'd intended.

Dade stiffened over me. His head lifted far enough for his eyes to search mine. I gazed back, my heart thundering against his, my tongue tangled in all the words I wanted and refused to say.

*Take me, possess me, reduce me to nothing but yours.*

He read the unsaid message loud and clear, a shuddering exhale shaking his broad shoulders and leaving his nose. My fingers dug into his muscular back, my thighs tightened around his waist, and my heart thrashed like the wounded animal it was when he didn't devour me.

No. Instead, the monster kissed me sweetly, earnestly, as though I were porcelain that would shatter if handled without care.

My eyes smarted with tears, and I closed them, sinking inside my own peril as I kissed him back. A soft caress for every shaken breath, rubbing and melding and incinerating. I lost myself so thoroughly that when he reached between us, a finger pressing and then entering, I released a loud moan.

"Exquisite," my beast breathed against my mouth, removing that finger just far enough to slide it back in and torture me all over again. He stopped when he reached the barrier, the one I'd thought he would decimate with the same skilled cruelty he was known for, then retreated and moved down my body.

I mewled in protest, but my reaching hands were no match for his eager mouth. He licked my breasts, my stomach, tongue dipping inside my navel, giant hands squeezing my hips, then he paused at my mound.

A heated exhale burst over my slick skin, my legs twisting in the bedding on either side of him as he drank his fill with his eyes. A graveled curse was all the warning I had, his mouth falling over me. He might have been unpracticed in the art of bedding a female, but I knew I wouldn't know even if I'd had experience in this arena myself.

In long velvet strokes, his tongue ravished me—tasted me from thigh to thigh. They shook so violently, I half feared they'd rattle the bed, my fingers in his hair tugging and pulling. *More.*

More, more, more...

He answered my call, finding that place he'd been purposely avoiding to give himself time to explore, and a single coaxing drag of his tongue over it was all it took. I shuddered and moaned, my thighs trapping his head between them, and my body curling toward the ceiling as an ocean of pure rapture held me under for blissful moments.

I was released gently, the barely-there kisses Dade pressed to my center violent in comparison, and I pulled him away, desperate for his mouth to return to mine.

He loomed over me, lips glistening and his lashes bobbing low. "Never in my entire existence have I tasted anything quite like you."

My breathing was still uneven, my heartbeat sharp and bruising, but I wanted more. Wanted it bad enough that I managed to whisper hoarsely, "What do I taste like?"

"The stars and the sun and mine." He licked his lips. "All fucking mine." I clasped his chin, pulling him closer, wanting to see for myself—just *wanting*, needing more. Dade's hooded eyes widened with a flash, his lips curling. "You surprise me."

"Shut up and kiss me, savage."

I swallowed his laugh, then his groan as my tongue swept into his mouth, tasting my own essence. The way it combined with his caused my head to spin.

But he pulled away, breathless and suddenly seeming so unsure of himself that I wondered if he was the same male I'd been stuck with these past weeks. "I will hurt you."

At that, I smiled, my nose brushing his as my thumbs danced over his stubbled cheeks to coast beneath those long lashes. He released a panted breath, arms trembling, and I whispered, "You've already wounded me beyond repair, so why stop now?"

Wrong thing to say.

The king peeled away, lust battling with something I couldn't name in his eyes.

Shocked, I sat up, scrambling for him and hating myself for it but too afraid he'd back out of an agreement I'd thought we'd already made. "Wait." He stood, his perfect backside stealing my attention, the muscular thighs collecting shadows and starlight as my panic rose higher.

His order was low, barely more than a grumble. "You may return to your rooms."

"Excuse me?" *Unbelievable.* Annoyance trampled panic. A wild noise nearly exploded, but I swallowed it. "I will not be returning anywhere," I said, shifting back over the bed and crossing my arms and legs.

Dade halted by the chest of drawers, his entire frame stilling. "That wasn't a request. It was an order."

"Come and punish me then, for I refuse to obey."

Peering at me over his shoulder, the animal that prowled beneath his skin shone back at me through his eyes. "Careful, swan." A warning wrapped in two deceptively soft words.

"Or what?" I taunted, proud that I'd kept my voice steady when he slowly turned, and my insides quaked. "You've made a mess between my legs. Prior to that, you made me a promise you haven't kept."

"Did I now?" he mocked, then took two large, calculatingly slow steps to the edge of the bed.

My eyes dragged over his terrifying yet undoubtedly impressive manhood, my stomach dissolving into butterfly-flooded lava. They roamed over the sharp definition of his hips and abdomen, then lifted to the wings that flared in shadow behind his back and arced over the walls to block out the moonlight.

As if my gaze were a feathered touch, he groaned.

Finally, I met his eyes. I met them, and I dragged my teeth over my bottom lip before purring, "It sure seemed that way to me."

His head tilted, and then it was his turn. His gaze was utterly inhuman, growing wilder as it crawled between my legs, swayed over my breasts, and then shifted to my face when I threw myself back over his bed and tangled my hands within my already tangled hair. "Honest answer?"

The bed dipped with his weight. Fingers curled around my ankle before slowly moving up, up, up, and stopping at my thigh. "Always," he said, strained.

The admission burned, my throat and my tongue and my lips. "I don't think I could leave even if you really wanted me to."

He froze. Then he was back, above me and staring down at me, so fast that I squeaked as he said roughly, "You torment me."

"So," I said to that addictive mouth. "Torment me back." My legs wound around his back, feet pressing him closer.

Another groan. "You will regret it." Yet he was still aligning himself, prepared to strike and kill as soon as he'd been given the go-ahead. "We both know you will."

I wouldn't lie to him, not like this, but I found myself wanting to when he looked at me like that. As though I were a blade he adored yet would continuously puncture himself in the chest with.

That was impossible. The blood king had no heart, no feelings outside of his own, but maybe, judging by the fear flickering on the surface of those depthless, stormy eyes, he had a soul.

A soul I would destroy.

Gently, I clasped my hand over his cheek, brought his forehead to mine, and kissed his nose as tears stung my closing eyes. "Maybe I will, or maybe…" I kissed his mouth, his sharp exhale burning over my lips. "Maybe it will be the one and only thing I could never regret."

His arm slid under my shoulders, his hand trapping my face to his as he fused our mouths, and his body crashed into mine with intense precision, erasing my maidenhead and my faulty plans.

Dade swallowed my scream, fingers at my hairline smoothing sweaty strands, his cock lodged inside me and so hard, so huge, that I feared I'd burst—rupture at every seam.

Countless labored breaths rushed free, and I didn't. I didn't break, and he kissed my lips, my cheeks, my eyelids. When they slowly opened, my muscles unlocking and melting, even while the slicing ruination still burned, my savage was watching, waiting. "I'm sorry."

Stunned, I gaped at him, certain it was the first time I'd ever heard him utter those two words and concerned. Concerned because he couldn't. He didn't know what they meant. He didn't know what true remorse was. Yet looking at his pained expression, those unearthly features creased with worry, perhaps he did.

Perhaps he was learning.

I melted even more, my stiff limbs unspooling, fingers reaching for his sweat-misted brow. "Sorry for claiming my virginity, or sorry that you've hurt me?"

He huffed out a brief laugh, the deep sound jolting my heart, lighting his eyes, and reminding me of the fire between my thighs. Humming, he stole my fingers and brought them over my chest for his mouth to skim. "I'll never apologize for the first." Mirth left his eyes then. "But yes, I am sorry I hurt you. That I've"—he swallowed thickly—"that I've caused you such pain."

The room swirled behind him, my heart both sinking and soaring, but he kissed me before I could order him away from me.

Before I could wail at him and demand he explain that apology to me in full.

I was glad he did, though—glad for the meeting of our lips and the gentle shifting of his unsure yet desperate body moving inside mine—for I knew what he was apologizing for.

And I didn't want it. I wouldn't have it.

But I would have him.

Our skin slipped and heated, and within moments, maybe a minute, Dade was no longer kissing me. He was grunting and shaking, and I knew he was restraining himself.

Fascinated, I pulled his face away from mine to study him, the corded lines of his throat, the bunching sinew in his shoulders and arms, the half-drunk, glazed look in his eyes—a tempest waiting to be unleashed.

"Let go," I whispered, smiling a little.

"But I…" He groaned, his hips moving faster now, instinct drowning clumsy inexperience and flooding my body with an unexpected heat as he plunged into me, over and over, and I moaned. "Fuck," he ground out, his head falling back, muscles spasming, shadows shaking the fire into ash, and his teeth bared.

In awe, my stomach coiled into a knot of need that had my thighs clenching around him, I watched. I watched his breath hiss between his teeth, his chest rise and fall in violent heaves, as he withdrew from my body and spilled himself over my stomach.

Then he fell over me, catching his weight before I was squashed and nuzzling his nose between my neck and shoulder with a thundering rumble of harsh breath. My hair curled with the heat of it, my slick skin sticking to his. "Stars almighty," he rasped and pushed himself back inside my body. The pinching sting was easy to ignore when he kissed under my chin. "I have to," he grunted. "You feel so good." He pawed at my side, squeezing my hip. "So fucking good, I never want to leave."

"I'd say I've created a monster, but a monster you already are."

He huffed, fingers clenching at my hip, his not so flaccid length firming more inside me. Tiny needles of pain sparked, but I laid still, content to ignore it for I didn't want him to leave either.

Then he sniffed, and move he did, carefully rising to his fore-arms. "You're bleeding." But that wasn't disgust or worry in his gaze. It was lust.

With a rough growl that evoked a shiver, he withdrew from my body and lowered between my legs, fingers tipping my thighs wide apart when I attempted to close them. I tried to rise onto my elbows, wanting to clean myself up and rid the desire that'd fogged my brain.

"No," he warned, and I fell back at the power behind the word. "It's your turn."

"I've had my turn, and I wasn't aware that was how this works."

"It works however we want it to, *mate*." He drove that last word home with knife-sharp brutality. "You've gifted me your innocence, and now I want to further enjoy it."

I tried to stop my eyes from widening. "As you said, there's blood." I waved a hand at my lower body. "Down there."

His grin was nauseating in the way it so quickly flattened my resolve and drove this never-ending hunger higher. Wild. This male turned me into something too curious, too insatiably wild.

I hated myself for finding that I loved it, but I knew it would never be enough to stop.

I smirked when he dragged his thumb through me, parting me, then brought it to his nose and inhaled. "Savage indeed."

He grinned, licked his thumb, and then he licked me.

He didn't stop until I was writhing. Until my head thrashed in the pillows, and my thighs held him prisoner once again.

"Swan," he said, groggy as morning breached the windows in the form of lighter shadows.

I'd fallen asleep upon his chest as soon as my thighs had un-clamped from his head. With a wicked, arrogant smile, he'd dragged himself up the bed and gathered my limp body into his arms.

I didn't like how well I fit inside them, next to him, atop him—it was all too perfect, too unbearable in the way I already hated the idea of his absence. "Mmm?"

"Marry me."

Ice rained over me in a wave strong enough to evoke a shocked laugh. I searched my addled brain for something, *anything* useful, and mumbled, "That wasn't a question and no." I peered up at him, wondering if I was dreaming, if he'd lost his stars-damned mind.

He just smiled, eyes remaining closed, and whispered, "Will you please marry me, swan?"

My stomach fluttered. "Much better," I said through a laugh, and then I killed the flutters. "But the answer is still no."

He grumbled, shifting and turning his face into my chest and releasing a dramatic sigh. His mouth opened, pressing gently into my breast. His kiss grew hotter, wetter, as he continued to torture me from the brink of sleep. I'd had a few hours, maybe. I had no idea. But I felt both deliriously exhausted and more alive than ever before.

I made the mistake of moaning, of pushing into him when the hand at my backside drifted down behind me and felt between my legs. "Just knowing you lay here with my seed all over you is enough to make me starved anew."

I caught fire in an instant, and he grinned, rolling me beneath him and pressing his mouth into mine. "This time," he murmured between drugging kisses, "this time will be the last time I empty myself over your body instead of inside it, so when I have a tonic sent to your rooms tomorrow," he cursed when I gripped him, gently squeezed the soft-coated steel within my small curious hand, "you better drink it. Unless..." He grinned again when I froze. "You want a babe growing in your womb."

Horror threatened to steal me and rip me from this deadly yet safe space I'd found.

He noticed, brows furrowing. "Where'd you go just now?"

"Nowhere, just... no talk of babes," I said, and realization dawned, his features falling lax.

*Pretty little broodmare.*

He nodded, about to open his mouth, but I released him and shoved at his chest.

He chuckled, rolling to his back and tucking his hands behind his head as I mounted his upper thighs and rewrapped my hand around him. "What makes you think there will be a next time?"

He wisely said nothing, but I relented. Deciding I'd tease him, I gazed down at his manhood. "Fine," I said. "I suppose it is somewhat impressive." I loosened my hold to swipe my thumb over the engorged head. "So thick, long, and angry-looking..."

He paused mid-groan. "My cock looks angry?"

"Needy?" I offered, to which he shrugged a little.

"You're not wrong." His teeth took his lip, then those lips spread into a disarming smile. "In fact, you could even say it's desperate."

"Oh?" I played along. "Desperate for what?"

The king hummed, throaty and stomach flipping. "To visit his new home."

I laughed, slapping at his chest, and he pulled me down to his side to steal my lips. "Show me," I said, still holding him. "Show me how you like to be touched."

With his hand at the back of my head, his arm molding my body to his, his fingers sank into my hair, massaging gently. "Sunshine." Beneath hooded eyes, smiling, glazed eyes that I knew I'd see whenever I closed my own, he studied me, then murmured, "I'll take anything you give me and still combust within seconds. You can do no wrong."

Grinning, I thought to test that somewhat sweet declaration that threatened to join the other ruptures in my heart and squeezed him. Hard.

He cursed. Thick lashes bobbed low, then reopened over blue pools of fire.

Shit.

As though he'd read my thoughts, he smirked, then kissed me until my every breath burned as badly as my body.

# TWENTY-FIVE

## *Dade*

**M**Y COCK SLID BACK INSIDE HER WITH NO ASSISTANCE.
She was ready, dripping ready for me. This time, there was no muted scream traveling down my throat, but a garbled cry, choked and silenced by her own shock as I planted myself deep and let her feel me.

Let her feel everything.

I'd experienced the pleasure of bringing myself to orgasm countless times by my own hand, the finest of wines, cuts of meats, and the sweet taste of victory. Yet nothing, absolutely fucking nothing, felt quite like this.

I was certain nothing in the entire universe would feel like her—a haunting song unraveling in violent creation beneath me, enveloping me, squeezing me, ruining me for all else always.

To be inside her, to move with her, to kiss her, was to have her sink beneath the marrow of my bones, enabling her to haunt me forevermore.

My teeth scraped over that soft, sweet-scented skin, nipping, dragging—I was damned near feral with the urge to make sure I lived inside her the way she would me.

Soft mewls soon grew rasped, her satin thighs slipping over my own and my hips. Deeper, I delved, my hands fisted in her hair and my lips climbing the elegant column of her throat. I kissed her pulse, then I gave in to the impulse that was thrumming through me too hard to ignore any longer, and my teeth pierced her flesh.

Opal stilled, her climbing hands at my back trembling over my wet skin. I couldn't stop, kept my teeth there, the coppery essence of her slowly invading my mouth and sinking into my taste buds. My hips pinned themselves to hers, then rotated.

A gasp, and then her hands flew into my hair. I felt my eyes widen, thinking she'd pull me away, but no, she pushed, cradling my head with those tiny hands.

She wanted more.

My blood roared, a growl of approval leaving me, and I sucked and kissed where I'd marked her and kept circling my hips, pressing into her as she moaned and squirmed beneath me.

Her heat tightened around me, and I tore away from her neck, whispering so she knew, so she couldn't yell at me about it later, "I've marked you."

Her golden eyes were glossed, lids heavy, and she panted between the slow curl of her perfect bow-shaped lips, "I know." Her leg moved, nudging at my side, and I read the intention in her eyes, placing a kiss on her ankle as I rose higher and tucked her leg over my shoulder.

I sank a little deeper, my eyes threatening to roll skyward. "Shit," I breathed. "Fucking shit." Shaking my head, I forced myself to check her, my attention getting snagged at her chest. Her tits heaved, sweat collecting between them, rosy pink nipples begging for my tongue. I gave it to them, her breathing sharpened, and murmured, "Does it hurt?"

"Yes," she admitted, voice quaking when I stilled. "But it also feels good. So good."

I released her breast, frowning down at her. "Want me to move? I fear I won't last long if I do, and I'm quite happy to stay inside you like this until we're forced from these rooms."

Her eyes twinkled, fingers trailing over my shoulders, dancing into the sweaty divots. Popping one in her mouth, she smiled around it, and I might have released myself a little inside her at the sight. "Are you saying you'd allow someone to take me from you?"

Outraged, I snarled. "Never."

Dragging her thumb over my bottom lip, her eyes following the movement, she said in a tone I couldn't decipher, "That's what I thought."

"You thought right." I nipped at her thumb, then stole it with my teeth and tongue, loving the way her golden eyes flared and her body curled into mine. "From the moment I saw you, before the bond noosed itself around our souls, I realized if I'd wanted anything before you"—I swallowed over a growing tightness in my throat, in my chest, and kissed her finger—"then I hadn't truly wanted it at all."

"So you came back," she whispered, blinking slowly.

"I came back." I brushed her hair from her cheek, then said, "I told myself it was for the right reasons, but Opal..." Breath rushed from me, my tongue tangled with things I shouldn't be saying but couldn't hold inside. "I'm worried." My voice lowered to a graveled whisper. "I'm worried I don't know what that is anymore."

Her lips spread, tongue darting out to wet them, then she dragged her thigh back around my waist and gripped my face. "This." My eyes sank into hers, the warmest most hypnotizing gold, her words like a promise staked to my soul. "This is what's right."

My mouth ravaged hers, and we rolled, hands threaded into hair, hearts thrashing in tandem—lost to ourselves once more.

Sleep soon took her, took us both, but when I felt her ass move against my cock, it left with a speed I'd never encountered before.

I kissed her arm, her shoulder, nuzzled her neck and moved her hair atop her head to grant me better access.

My stolen princess woke moaning, the sweetest song I'd ever heard, and clasped the hand I had at her waist, moving it around her body—moving it lower and parting her thighs.

Fuck, she was magic. Everything about her made just for me.

Her warmth unfolded around my finger, already wet, the scent of our previous lovemaking only driving my need higher when those luscious thighs spread wide. I shifted closer, lifting her leg back and over mine, and eased back inside paradise.

A croaked, choked sound left her, but I took my time, sinking all the way in and rubbing her shoulder with my lips. I made to remove my hand to grip her breast, but Opal pressed it back between her legs, at that nub of nerves that, when coaxed the right way, made her blast apart.

My gut tightened, my cock twitching inside her as she stole my pointer finger and twirled it around herself. I let her lead the charge and slowly withdrew from her body, both of us groaning when I slid back in.

We said nothing, and nothing needed saying. I fucked my swan until she detonated with a silent cry, my fingers now at her neck, around it and gripping gently, forcing her eyes and lips to mine as I pounded every ounce of pleasure from her body with slow, hard thrusts.

She didn't curse me out when I spilled myself inside her this time, but she did turn, her head stuffed under my chin and her arms slithering tight around me, fingers dancing over my back. Our legs tangled, and I held her close, as close as I could without suffocating her, and lost myself within this strange dreamy realm.

With my fingers in her soft hair, twirling, rubbing gently at her scalp as she drifted off to sleep, I wondered if that was what the mating bond did. I knew it would tether souls, enrich an attraction that already existed, and allow you to feel when that part of your existence was in trouble, but I'd never heard about this.

This unexplainable feeling inside my chest that burned and cooled and terrified and thrilled.

A few hours later, the sun was up, as was the rest of the Keep, but though I knew she had to be sore, my swan still hungered as much as I did and reached down to touch me, rousing me from sleep. She wanted more.

I couldn't refuse her. Even if I wasn't afraid of this being the last time she so freely gave herself to me, I still didn't want to. I wouldn't leave her. I refused to even if I could. Not until I'd felt her come undone around me one last time, that lithe body rupturing and shaking and fingers clawing as though I were her only tether to what I'd already found.

True magic.

Opal laughed and pushed at my shoulders, trying to remove my lips from her neck and failing.

She'd bathed, but nothing would ever remove my scent from her. I would make sure of it.

"Stop," she said, her laughter falling into a tiny moan, her touch at my shoulders too weak for me to believe she truly wanted me to stop. "You'll make me all disheveled before we even arrive."

"That's fine," I murmured, and tilted her head back to capture her sweet mouth.

She opened for me, whispering, "If you don't quit mauling me, we might wind up in a rather compromising position that could alert the drivers."

"Darling swan…" I licked her upper lip, grinning when her eyelashes fluttered. "Nothing would please me more than everyone knowing I've had you." I pressed my mouth to that soft lip. "Multiple times." Then her lower lip, then stole them both when she grabbed my head and tilted hers, her greedy tongue in search of mine.

Memories of the previous night, those early morning hours, hadn't left, and neither had she. By some miracle, I'd drawn her a bath in my rooms, and she'd stayed, only leaving to dress after we'd washed one another in the giant bathing pool.

I'd followed, of course, fearful she'd slug me in the chest with venomous words laced in regret but also just needing her near. It was instinctual, not of this world, a compulsion within the bone and blood, to make sure this creature of mine never roamed too far from me.

In her dressing room, I'd sipped tea that'd been delivered while she'd perused the many gowns hanging before her. Somehow, I'd convinced her to spend the day, what remained of it anyway, with me by tempting her with another trip to the city of which I knew she was already fond of.

Her fingers had brushed over the yellow, stalling briefly. "Why not choose that one?"

Opal's shoulders had stiffened. "My mother says yellow washes me out."

I'd nearly choked on my tea. "How can a color cleanse you?"

She'd laughed, turning to look at me as though I'd told a joke, and she was waiting for me to deliver the punch line. When I'd waited, sipping more tea, she shook her head. "It means it does not suit my complexion."

"Anything would look good on you," I'd stated, setting the tea down and tugging her between my spread knees. "But nothing more than me."

I'd managed to steal her into my lap as well as a kiss between her bouts of giggling before she'd wriggled off me, leaving me hard, aching, and with that damned feeling of soaring while not moving at all.

She'd settled on a midnight green gown that had no bodice, floating from her shoulders to her ankles with jeweled beading in the neckline and flowing sleeves. I approved. I'd have approved of a sack, nothing at all, really, but this gown made easy work of accessing those creamy legs.

And hopefully what waited and wanted for me between them.

The carriage lurched, and she snarled, the cutest fucking sound I'd ever heard—kissing me once hard on the lips and then pushing me away with adorable force. "Where are we going anyway?" she muttered, combing her fingers through her gentle curls.

Leaning back against the window, I watched her right herself, wondering if she knew the effect she had on others, on me, and raised my brows when she scowled.

"Dade."

"Yes?"

Her face creased with displeasure. Again, adorable. "Did you hear me?"

"Couldn't hear a thing thanks to that beautiful face of yours."

She tried to appear miffed, but her lips wriggled. "Savage."

"We're visiting the art gallery," I said, smirking and then straightening when we bounced over a boulder. An indicator that we were almost there.

"You have an art gallery?"

I fixed my sleeves and pushed my hair back. "You do not?"

"I, well," she started, and I peered over to find her staring out the window to the warehouses beyond. "We make and sell art." She looked at me then. "And now I suppose your lot are selling it for a higher price?"

I didn't deign to answer. A poor thing to do, as it would surely ruffle her feathers, but I had to select my words carefully. "Some of your people, Opal..." I scratched at my cheek, my stomach coiling as the carriage rocked to a stop. "They don't burn or get slain in battle."

I made myself meet those fiery eyes when she hissed, "What do you mean?"

"I mean," I nodded to the driver when he opened the door, climbing out first to ensure that I was the only one helping my swan down, "some surrender. They aren't slaves, though they do live and work here now."

Opal refused my help, and I half-thought she'd shrink back inside the carriage in one of her rages. We walked down the street in silence, and I forced myself to wait, to give her time to absorb what I'd said. Though I did steer her around muddied puddles from the storm, and down a narrow alleyway that cut through to the riverfront gallery on the other side.

"But you loathe us," she said finally. "You loathe us and you kill us."

"I kill those who resist and who are owed death for what they have taken from me."

"You seek to conquer us all, to force us into lives we do not want.

You burn our homes and our livestock and our people, and you care *nothing* for what you have done." Her words grew harsher, lower, and twice I kept her from tripping. "Now you mean to tell me that is not true? That my people willingly leave us to create a life here with you and your fellow savages?"

I let her rant for a few minutes longer, then pulled her beneath the shade of a willow tree alongside the one-story cottage. "Finished?"

"No," she said, her cheeks heated with ire. "I watched you." Her eyes glossed with tears. "I watched you murder my father and his soldiers. I watched you tear into his heart with your teeth and end his existence." She closed her eyes, and when they reopened, the tears were gone, but I knew what I'd done would forever remain. "I watched you," she rasped.

"Opal," I clipped when she turned on her heel and headed to the door of the gallery.

Inside, I nodded to the owner who was at the front desk. He tipped his head to a hall on his right, telling me she'd gone that way, then bowed.

I nodded, thankful I'd had him ensure the gallery was closed to the public until our visit was done with. I had a feeling it was going to end rather prematurely.

I found her at the end of the hall, admiring a painting of a burned out village. Weeds sprouted around a water well, grew in patches by collapsed doors, and charred earth birthed new wildflowers along the long-unused road.

*Indulge her in the things she likes my fucking left testicle.*

Fang was an asshole.

"If you say this is beautiful, I might actually stab you this time."

*Shit.* Still mad then. I shifted on my feet, sighing. "I know you will never forgive me."

Opal turned to glare fire at me. "Of course I'll never forgive you."

I looked behind us down the hall, the owner pretending to busy himself with menial tasks at his parchment-strewn desk, then stole Opal's hand.

THE SAVAGE &THE SWAN | 227

She cursed, tugging it free by an alcove around the corner. "You dare touch me? This building is riddled with the pain of my people."

"While that may be so, it's also healing for them—"

"Healing?" she spat. "Oh, right. You stole those creatures for your arsenal too."

"I didn't steal anything," I said calmly, and was proud of myself for keeping my beast at bay. "They had the choice. Fight or leave."

"Fight?" Opal's eyes glimmered, wide pools of hatred that speared me in the chest. "They'd have lost. You know it and they know it and that's why they are here and that's why their talent hangs upon walls they'd rather see burn."

She was wrong about that. For although there was resistance when newcomers first arrived in Vordane—of course there would be—we snuffed it by indulging and spoiling them until they'd all but forgotten about where they'd come from.

Though just like the female standing before me, some of these artworks said they'd never forget.

We also had close eyes on them, though they were not aware of it, and little problems had arisen. I wasn't foolish enough to explain all of the above, and instead, offered, "They live good lives here. Fair lives, and perhaps one day, they may even return home."

"Return?" she asked, staring at me as though I were the biggest fool alive. "Return to what exactly?" Her head shook, as did her hands as she dragged her fingers through her hair. "You honestly don't get it, do you?"

I frowned, unsure what to do or what I should say. Opal's eyes shuttered. "*Stars*, Dade. What did they do to you to make you believe that any of this is okay?"

I tilted my head, trying and failing to understand. "I don't know what you mean. I am a king. I was raised as such."

"That is the damned problem." Opal licked her lips, and I longed to just pull her close and sniff her hair, run my fingers through it, slow her heartbeat under my touch. "You have been raised to be the problem, and so thoroughly that you do not even see what you are."

"I know exactly what I am," I said, keeping my tone smooth. "A king of wolves, a righter of wrongs, and now…" I took a daring step closer. "I am also your mate."

My swan gave me that look again, her lashes beating hard over searching, stubborn eyes.

Panic gripped my voice, making it hoarse. "Tell me what I can do." I clasped her cheeks, imploring, "Please. Tell me what I can do, and I'll do it."

"There is nothing you can do. He's gone."

"I know," I said, nodding once. "I know, but I want to try. You have to at least let me try." And I would. Stars, if I could rid the hurt brimming her eyes, that stunted her heartbeat, by bringing her small-minded, dickhead of a father back from the dead, then I'd fucking do it.

Her eyes studied, her hands rising to remove mine from her face, but then she sniffed, and I felt her grow tense. "You would truly do anything?"

Fuck, didn't she already know that? "Any fucking thing," I said, vehemence deepening the vow.

"End this war," she said instantly and without hesitation. "Put an end to the bloodshed, to the revenge, to the unnecessary heartbreak. End it now."

I staggered back, my hands falling loose, my every reason, every plan, scattering like cards on the breeze as those golden eyes met mine with disgust. I wouldn't. She'd known that yet she'd still asked. "I can't do that."

"You can."

I caught her wrist when she brushed past me to leave. "Opal, I can't. It's not over yet."

"It's over when you find the fucking heart to say it's over," she hissed. Uncaring that the owner could hear, her eyes raked over me, and she laughed coldly. "But that's just it, isn't it, my king?" She backed up, leaving me with, "You don't have one."

She hurried down the statue lined hall, not one look given to the artwork upon the walls, her golden blond hair floating behind her.

Watching her leave, her scent clouding my mind and causing my hands to fist at my sides, an idea struck me so hard that I nearly shifted. I stalked after her down the hall and around the corner to another. "Marry me."

Opal didn't stop, didn't so much as falter. She continued on as though I'd said nothing at all.

"Marry me and it will end."

She stopped then, slippers catching on the oriental carpet as she whirled around, her hair flying over her cheek and settling over her shoulder. "Do you mean that?"

I took my time though I wanted to run to her, to throw myself at her feet and gaze up at her with nothing but honesty. I took my time and slipped my hand through my hair, forcing out a rough breath. "Of course, it will take time to arrange, and I cannot be ridiculed for plans that are already underway in the meantime, but..." I halted before her and met that golden gaze. "Yes, sunshine. I swear it will end once you are my wife."

"Then we marry tomorrow. We do not need a giant celebration."

I chuckled, unable to help it, and when she scowled, I did what I'd been longing to and brought her to me, even as she pushed weakly at my arms. She gave in, staring up at me with hope-filled eyes as I curled her hair behind her ear and whispered, "I will need to write your mother, of course, but once we have her permission..."

Since the moment I'd taken her from that human tower of filth, I'd hoped and tried to make plans for just this, to make her nothing but mine in every way, all the while knowing it might be impossible. I could force her hand, as I was now. Only now, I knew there was a large part of her that both hated and wanted me in equal measure, so it felt less like taking and more like coaxing.

I'd coax her for all eternity. She would be mine in this life and any that came after.

Opal melted into my touch, my hand cupping her cheek, and said on a resigned breath, "Then yes. If you make haste, I will marry you."

"You could at least try to sound excited," I said as irritation spiked without warning. "You would be queen, and together, we would unite the two kingdoms in a history-making—"

"Contract," she said, pulling away and strutting over to a nearby portrait of a young girl with a braided crown and a one-eyed kitten on her lap. "What we'll have is a contract, nothing more, but yes," she said, moving on to the next image of a hillside village by the Night Sea, "we will do what you seem so fond of doing."

"And that is?"

Her fingers lifted, the sway of them and her body hypnotizing as they hovered over a frothy wave. "Righting wrongs."

I smirked, even as my heart both soared and sank, then moved in behind her to wrap my arms around that glorious waist. "Whatever you say, my swan." I felt her hum in approval, and I kissed her bare shoulder. "Whatever you say."

# TWENTY-SIX

*Dade*

"**T**HE BIRD IS JUST USING YOU," FANG DECLARED FROM THE corner of the war room as he dropped into a chair. "It's a trap."

Scythe rumbled his agreement and thrust his hand toward the door, the other at his hip as he circled the large table. "Wouldn't surprise me if this was her plan all along."

I said through my teeth, "To marry me?"

"To bring you to your fucking knees, moron, via her cunt."

"Fucking watch it," I growled at Scythe.

"No," he snapped, and my hackles rose when he stopped and stabbed a finger at the map now spread over the wall. "First your uncle, now this?" His upper lip curled. "She's hypnotized you." His fingers flicked and fluttered at me. "Put some voodoo witch spell on you."

"They're mates," Fang needlessly reminded him. "Of course he wants to please her."

"You shut the fuck up. Since when does being someone's mate mean handing over the keys to your fucking kingdom?"

Fang pressed his lips together.

I rubbed my brow. "Since I killed her father, and she will never forget it."

"We know," Scythe said, grinning as though the memory pleased him. For the young pup who'd been found in a puddle of blood by Fang's family, it undoubtedly did. "We were there, helping you."

"Enough," Fang said, sensing my patience was at its end. "So this war ends." He nodded. "Fine. Okay." He shrugged. "Good. It grows dull anyway."

"We've other potential problems to worry about now the humans appear to have made ties across the sea," I reminded them. "War never ends, even when the battle stops." I downed the ale in the tankard before me. "History says that best."

Though our history suggested otherwise, tension had always brewed between the two ruling families of Nodoya. Hatred, greed, envy, and lust for power was a song in all of our veins, and given the right means—of which I'd been handed in the untimely death of my parents—no one was above destroying things to get what they wanted.

The difference between me and history was that I did not deceive and trust in shadows to veil my actions in the form of assassinating, bedding, robbing, and other less tasteful tasks of sabotage to have my revenge.

I trained, I waited, and then I openly declared war.

"What of the queen?" Scythe asked, staring at Castle Gracewood upon the map. "She will be an issue, no matter if you marry her daughter. We killed her mate."

"We could kill her daughter too, yet we have not," Fang added.

I gnashed my teeth at just hearing *kill* in the same sentence as Opal.

"Give her Serrin's head," Scythe suggested as he took a seat. "That should do it."

My uncle rotted in the dungeon beyond the war room door. He'd been permitted one meal a day of bread and stew and was forced to clean up his own filth at the end of each day. I'd made sure he was given nothing to relieve himself in.

It wasn't enough. His death would not be enough. But die he would. "Not yet," I stated with heavy reluctance. "He needs more time with his demons first." Not to mention my fist in his face until his eyeballs leaked through his nostrils.

"It is indeed a trap," Fang said again, staring at the map on the wall.

"You think I do not know that?" I'd written Nikaya as soon as we'd arrived home from the gallery three days ago, and her response had been swift, her penmanship steady even though every word had indented the parchment with her longing to see me suffer and her daughter's safe return.

I hadn't been sure what to expect. I did not know the female. But I did know that she'd been presented with little choice wherever it concerned me for nearly four years.

She would give me her daughter. How remained to be seen until the letter had arrived this morning. Permission to wed, permission I did not necessarily need, had been granted. Her only request being that the wedding be a private ceremony.

A private ceremony at Castle Gracewood.

"We take two legions," Scythe said. "Leave one to protect Vordane, hide two amongst the Gracewood forests, and legion three at the base of the Polinphe Mountains." He nodded as though satisfied this could work. "They can fly across the Spring Forest at the first sign of trouble."

Legion three, usually under my uncle's command, was now split between Scythe and Fang if I were busy, but otherwise, it was under my command.

"Who would signal this trouble?" I asked, staring at the varnished wood of the table leg, not seeing anything but all the many ways in which this could go disastrously wrong.

"Release that mighty roar." Scythe laced his hands behind his head. "As per dramatically usual."

I gave him a bland look that Fang caught. He swung his legs up onto the table, dried mud crusting the bottom of his boots. "We can also collect some trusted golden Fae, have them ready to send up a flare."

"It's a private ceremony," I reminded them through gritted teeth, an opportune time to leash and slay a beast.

I knew, though, that I was too far gone to turn down this opportunity. I would make my mate my queen—no matter the cost. We would make it work.

We discussed it until we hit yet more snags, and then I shelved it. "We'll reconvene tomorrow. I've a swan to find."

Scythe scoffed but said, "Sure, allow her to continuously lead you to your doom." Yet the tail end of his sentence lost its bite, and he slumped back in the chair against the wall. "Does she know of her mother's response?"

"Not yet," I said, and waded to the door.

Fang's laughter stiffened my spine. "May we come and gauge her expression, then? You know, just to let you know if we think she is truly wishing for your demise."

"Follow me and die."

Their howling laughter had me itching to turn back and thump their heads together, but I pressed on.

Fang was right. It was time to see how my swan reacted to the idea of her unwanted mate landing in a trap.

# TWENTY-SEVEN

## *Opal*

**B**ESHAL'S EYES WIDENED, THE TEAPOT SHAKING IN HER HAND. "Marriage?"

In the days since the king had presented me with the opportunity I'd been waiting for, I'd done my best to occupy myself while trying to wrap my mind around all that I'd agreed to for the sake of my kingdom.

But I was being dishonest if I thought that was all I'd been trying to make peace with. For this thrill, this gathering elation in the pit of my stomach and chest, said it was so much more than a mere contractual agreement.

It meant potentially giving in to what I felt. I just wasn't sure how to do that without forgiving him for all he'd done. And forgiving Dade Volkahn of his many atrocities...

I took the offered tea and sipped. "Yes. Is that citrus?"

Beshal nodded, Fink hiding amongst the gathered skirts of my gown with her friend Thompson, who'd been shy when I'd first arrived but shaking with excitement when I'd lowered my hand to lift him onto one of my crossed legs. "Mandarin and lavender, dear. My favorite for this time of year."

Indeed, the leaves were collecting in piles now, winter's kiss upon the air.

Beshal sat upon a small rock, her tiny booted feet swinging beneath her apricot frilled gown that looked more like an oversized apron. "My," she said, clucking her tongue and drinking some tea. "I cannot imagine it. Our king. Married. It seems like just yesterday we'd hear that uncle of his hollering at him after he'd done something egregious to displease him."

I wanted to hear more about Dade and his uncle, but rustling sounded.

Harro exited their home in the base of an elm tree, pushing past ferns that served as a fence with a tray of what appeared to be nuts in hand. "Princess, you're just in time for some peppered nuts."

I thanked him and took one while Beshal filled him in, and bit down too hard as a memory came forward from the dark. The memory of lying in that cave, fighting the need to shift and finding that pouch of peppered nuts that one of Dade's warriors must have dropped on their journey across the crossover and through the woods to slaughter my people.

I was to marry the monster who'd killed my father.

I swallowed, not tasting anything but the sour essence of regret.

Did he regret it? Would he go back and change the past if he could?

I wanted to believe he would. I wanted to believe so many things that I feared would be a mistake to ever believe in again.

Harro released a rumbling laugh. "Marriage? The crimson king?" He bobbed over the rock he'd taken a seat on with his fading laughter. "Well, I do not think so."

"Do you think the princess would lie about such a thing?" Fink said, her head popping out from under the sea green of my skirts. "Besides, Papa, he loves her."

I nearly laughed at that. Love.

Dade Volkahn wouldn't know the first thing about love, let alone being in love.

As I lowered my empty teacup, I was hit with the startling realization that I didn't either. That maybe, if this was all this life had to give, then I would never know what it was to fall in love. Lust, most certainly, but never true love.

Fink gazed up at me, her smile dreamy. "What's it like to kiss a king? Especially one as handsome as he."

*Liquid fire*, I immediately thought. The type that extinguished all thought and sensibility. The type that melted with a mere hint of touch.

"I'll beg your pardon, youngling," Beshal sputtered. "Mind your tongue."

Harro grunted. "And that imagination, please."

I smiled, hoping the dipping sensation inside me was not present upon my cheeks, and carefully tapped the pad of my finger under Fink's chin. "Who says I've kissed him?"

Her secretive smile gave me away, but she only whispered, "Your expression, my lady." Then Thompson grabbed her ankle, and she squealed, ducking back inside the rayon skirts to catch him back.

"You're apprehensive." Beshal eyed me curiously with her head tilted. "It's smart, I suppose," she said, nodding. "This ah, arrangement will surely put an end to this feud, but is it what you want?"

It was and it wasn't, and I didn't know how to answer that.

Harro's brows furrowed, then he jumped to his feet, nuts flying from his hand. "He comes." Rushing forward, he made to snatch the younglings from my skirts, but the king was already here, and I smiled even as my heart sank. That he'd come looking for me when, aside from leaving a black rose outside my rooms for the past two evenings, he'd been content to leave me with my thoughts, did not bode well.

"It's fine. You are safe." I reached out a hand to Dade when he appeared, smoky shadow curling around his typical attire of black, his long leather coat twisting in the breeze behind him and revealing a black vest underneath. "Our king loves a good cup of tea."

Dade's eyes narrowed, his impatience to take me and tell me whatever it was that had made him come in search of me apparent in the thinning of his lips and his stiff shoulders. "I do indeed, but we've things to discuss." He surveyed me. "Where is your cloak? It's cool out."

"I forgot it, and those things can wait five minutes," I said, retracting my hand and helping myself to another cup of tea. Though I was curious to know what *things* he was referring to.

Harro and Beshal were as still as the stones surrounding us, the two younglings inside my skirts the same.

"Opal…"

"It is delicious," I said to my tiny cup, and sipped before looking back at Beshal. "And we were in the middle of a conversation. It would be rude to leave before we are done."

One second passed. Then two. On the third, he finally caved and asked, "Dare I ask what this conversation was about?"

I snorted a little, smiling up at him. "You, of course."

His blue eyes blazed at my taunt, lips curling slightly. "Wonderful." Sighing, the king lowered to the grass and crossed his giant legs. He waved his hand. "Fine. Proceed."

I hadn't thought he'd give in, and his commanding presence suddenly seemed too much, both too stifling and freezing, to fit here on the ground with us.

But fit he was trying to do.

Thankfully, Beshal launched into action, pouring her king a tea with only a slight tremble in her hand. She marched around the small stump holding the tray and nuts, pushing through the grass that reached her shoulders, and lowered before Dade. "Here you are, sire."

We waited in tense silence as Dade sniffed at the tea, his nose crinkling in a way that caused my lips to itch with the beginning of a broad smile. I pinched them, watching as he lifted the little teacup to his mouth, tasted, and swallowed.

Harro seemed to be holding his breath, eyes wide on the king, feet stuck in place in the grass and his beard shifting in the breeze, while Beshal watched on with smiling, eager eyes.

The two younglings still hadn't moved, but I wasn't fooled. I knew they were waiting, too.

"Delicious," he finally said, seeming a little surprised as he took another sip, ridding what remained before handing the teacup back.

"Another, my king?" Beshal asked, already backing up toward the teapot.

"No," he said simply.

"Thank you," I added, irked by his rudeness.

Dade's attention swung to me, his smile lethal yet warm. "Thank you."

I returned his smile, then forced my eyes back to the elves. "I was informing them of our plans to wed."

Dade's silence created another thick wave of tension. I ignored it, so did the younglings, Fink choosing then to expose herself.

Her head popped up, arms leaning over a mound of fabric as she looked at the king. "May we come to this wedding?" she asked, and her mother made a noise I couldn't decipher. Fink's cheeks pinkened. "My king."

"You must excuse her," Harro found his voice then. Stammering a little, he stepped forward as though he'd retrieve his daughter and send her home. "Fink is but a handful of years old."

"It's quite all right," I answered for the king, who looked at me. His head tilted, those unblinking eyes seemingly asking what it was exactly I'd told them. *Enough*, I answered with a smile, then said aloud, "We are not yet sure where the wedding will be held, but I would love nothing more than to see you all there."

"That is actually what we need to talk about," Dade said, tone clipped. "Now, if you do not mind."

I pursed my lips, too curious to know what my mother had said. I was aware he'd written to her, and it appeared he'd received word. "Fine."

"Sire," Fink said, and I leaned forward to place my teacup on the stump. "Is it true you breathe fire?"

Dade released a shocked grunt of a laugh, his features returning to stone as he muttered, "Breathe fire?"

"Yes," she said, standing upon my leg now and revealing her friend's head. "You know, like a dragon."

"There are no dragons on this continent," the king said smoothly, and I wanted to smack him for the flat expression that darkened Fink's face. Dade looked at me, then sighed and said to the young female elf, "No, I don't breathe fire. Though I suppose it would be a handy trick to have."

Fink grinned. "Oh, indeed it would be."

"One of the things I can do," the king said, a glint in his eye as he leaned toward us a little. "Is this." Fire erupted from the grass behind him, moving slowly in a burning circle to his bent knees.

Fink's eyes threatened to pop out of her head, while her mother shrieked and her father raced to grab her, other elves now appearing from the woods to see what all the commotion was.

"Wow," Fink breathed, reluctantly climbing onto my hand with Thompson as her father gestured for her to climb down immediately.

Save for the breeze rustling pieces of Dade's thick hair onto one side of his forehead, he didn't move as the fire disappeared as quick as it'd arrived.

Such ease with deathly power shouldn't have been permitted—especially in those who would seek to use it for their own gain. A twinge of empathy flared for how my grandparents had felt, for the fear of Dade's parents, who'd both harnessed ungodly powers of flame and shadow, unimaginable strength, shifting, and warping.

But it was more than permitted. It was star-given, and to argue with the fates in such a way was futile.

And while I could empathize, it was growing more apparent that the murder of Dade's parents was just that. Unjustified murder.

The elves scrambled back a few steps, bowing to their king as he rose and offered me his hand. Fink waved from the forest floor, Thompson already bounding toward the play equipment fashioned from stolen footwear.

I smiled, waving back before placing my hand in the king's. "Thank you for the tea and the marvelous company."

We were nearing the gardens when Dade's hand squeezed mine and tugged me closer, his voice warm at my ear as he purred, "For the tea and the marvelous company?" I bristled as he chuckled. "My, you truly are a well-mannered, dutiful little princess, aren't you?"

I tore my hand free, pulling my shoulders back. "I'd rather be well-mannered than rude and arrogant."

"I'm rude?" he asked, and I nearly laughed at the way he'd done so, as if perplexed, and also the fact he'd wisely not denied his arrogance. "How so?"

"You interrupted us and then stared down your nose at them until I all but forced you to join us, and then you could not even thank Beshal for the tea."

"It was good tea," he admitted, and I spun before him, waiting for him to understand what I'd just spelled out. "I was not rude."

"You were."

"I am their king. To gentle myself in such a way would make me appear weak."

"Weak?" I laughed. "It would make you appear as though you *care.*"

"Perhaps I don't," he said then, brows raised in defiance, eyes of dawn gazing at me down the strong bridge of his nose. "Did you think of that?"

I felt my skin warm under that gaze, and said quietly without enough thought to stop myself, "Some weeks ago, I would have believed that. Now, I'm not so sure."

His feigned apathy didn't waver. We stared for a stretched moment, a moment that rippled and heated and charged and lured as my thoughts ran astray. Thoughts of him above me, behind me, beneath me, all over me, hours spent inside me...

Dade sniffed, his eyes darkening as though he could scent what those thoughts, *what he*, did to me.

Of course, he damned well could. Inwardly cursing up a storm, I cleared my throat. "So, this important news?"

He didn't so much as glance around the empty terrace before

saying, "Your mother responded. We are to marry at Castle Gracewood in a private ceremony in two evenings time."

Two evenings.

I might be home as early as tomorrow. Relief hit me so hard, it took me a moment to even imagine what that would look like. To walk through my own city, the archways and crowded corners of my own castle, and the gardens…

My eyes itched, stung, but I swallowed over the boulder of emotion in my throat. Home. I would be going home. A place I hadn't dared think about too much in recent weeks for fear of never seeing it again.

For fear of finding that I preferred the company and kingdom of a king that had tainted this entire continent with his vengeful schemes and actions.

But it had begun with us. My family. A fact I'd largely chosen to ignore. Not only because I hadn't been there, and I did not know enough, but because it did not excuse all Dade had done in the slightest.

Private. Gracewood.

"Something wrong, sunshine?" The king's snide words snapped me out of my trance.

I blinked hard before running a hand through my hair, forgetting I'd woven it into a loose braid before heading into the gardens earlier and ruining it.

I didn't care. Flustered, I gazed up at him, finding nothing but cold assessment in those eyes as I wondered out loud, "Perhaps this is not wise after all." I did not think my mother a killer. She'd marched with my father's armies many a time but often refrained from hurting others if she could avoid it. She was a healer, a defender.

But he'd killed her husband. My father.

Her mate.

Not to mention, he'd stolen me—her only living heir.

Dade's eyes warmed a fraction, his shoulders falling as he slid his hands inside the pockets of his tight black trousers. "How so?"

I reared back, withholding an incredulous laugh when it dawned on me. He knew. Of course, he already knew.

He merely wanted to see if I'd hide what we both feared.

"Don't do that," I snapped, then turned and hurried inside. He could take his precious wedding and shove it up his—

Hands looped around my waist at the stairs, and I squeaked. Dade turned me, loomed over me, brows dancing low and his lips curved. "What is it you think I'm doing?"

"Testing me."

He pressed closer, and my back met the marble railing. "Can you blame me? You've not been to see me since I agreed to your terms."

"You've not been here," I retorted, hating that I sounded miffed by that fact.

"I have, but I've been training a faction of my warriors that were under Serrin's command, as well as riffling through the reports delivered by some of our scouts and preparing things for when we leave tomorrow."

"Reports of what?"

"I'm keeping tabs on those human royals, of course." He hummed, a finger dragging up my arm, heating flesh in its wake, and stopping under my chin once he'd tilted it closer to his lips. "Especially that prince you seem so fond of."

Outrage roughened my voice. "I am *not* fond of him."

"You saved his life, betrayed me to do so."

I could say nothing to that. I had done both those things, and despite my actions, he was trusting me. He was putting a great deal of trust in me by telling me those two seemingly insignificant facts about his whereabouts.

"I've been waiting," he said then, his lower body pushing into mine, hard, hot, and I immediately tingled all over. "Hoping you'll return to my bed, that you'll simply just return to me."

"I want to," I admitted, far too breathy than I'd have liked.

Husky and low, he murmured to my cheek, "So why deny yourself? Why deny me?"

"I thought you'd come for me," I released another truth, closing my eyes against such foolishness. "You never did."

"I did. I left you presents."

The roses. Smiling, I reopened my eyes, turned my head until our lips almost touched. "Unlike you, I cannot sniff you out from beneath the door when I am in bed and likely asleep."

He pondered that as if he hadn't considered it before now, then groaned as if frustrated. "Come now then. We can talk more in my rooms."

Hypnotized, I allowed him to lead me up the stairs but halted when we reached the landing to our rooms—when I saw those large doors that would open to reveal a memory-stained space of another time.

"It's like another world," I heard myself say, fingers pulling from the king. He turned to me, confusion dancing within his eyes. "Being in that room with you, all those hours..." I shook my head, smiling even as something inside me screamed to walk closer and kiss that disappointment from his annoyingly handsome face. "We've too much at stake. We leave tomorrow. We cannot be distracted in—"

"I want you."

Such simple words. Such simple words with drastic complications.

"We will enter that room of yours, lose ourselves in one another, and risk everything by arriving at Gracewood sleep deprived, distracted, and infatuated."

"Infatuated," he repeated, as though tasting the word quietly.

I walked closer and took both his hands in mine, allowing myself that much when I wanted and needed so much more. I burned with it and squeezed as I implored, "Dade, this is not a game to be won any longer. This wedding... it could turn into another war. My mother is wounded. Gravely with the loss of my father, and I won't lose her, too."

He blinked slowly. "I won't harm her."

"Your armies will join us, will they not? It will end in another massacre if my mother does something foolish from a place of grief."

"No," he said, and relief flooded me. "It's just you and me making the journey, taking the risk, a risk I am willing to take a thousand times over because I fucking want you."

A throbbing started inside my chest. He wanted, and to him, it was that simple, that important. I had to wonder if he truly had never wanted something in this way before. If maybe his willingness to take such a risk was a result of never knowing true consequence. If maybe, he knew nothing of complications beyond the physical—beyond what he could only see.

And I didn't know how to make him understand when I wasn't sure that was possible, when he'd stated himself that he was a male without empathy, and when it would mean acknowledging things better left alone.

So I nodded, falling into him when his hands left mine and drifted to my face, lips brushing my forehead. "She cannot die, savage. You hear me?"

"I do. We will marry and return home."

Home. Again, that word, used for two entirely yet not so different places. She would be safe, but the king, this king of mine that I didn't want but now could not bear the idea of seeing harmed… "What if she tries something?" I said, peeling away and rubbing my chest. "What if she tries something, and…" and I couldn't voice the dark thoughts. "Why don't we just wait?"

He cocked his head. "Wait?"

I nodded fast. "We could wait. Wait until we can reach a better agreement. Perhaps more solid ground on which we can wed."

"No, thank you." Dade captured a curl that had strayed from my braid and looped it around his finger. "We will go anyway."

I laughed, my eyes watering. "Lovely manners. Why don't we marry here?"

"Your mother would not agree," he said, eyes upon my golden hair. "And for her to believe I care about you, it must be this way. She must see that despite any ideas she might have, I will do this regardless."

He was quite possibly one of the most powerful creatures on this continent, if not the most, but outnumbered, that would not matter.

The king sounded amused. "Swan, are you concerned for my safety?"

Dropping my hand from my burning chest, I grinned, shaking my head as I walked to the door of my rooms. "Good night, Dade."

"Daden."

I whirled, blinking back at him in confusion.

"My real name, though I would prefer it never used, is Daden." When I continued to stare, he smirked. "We leave at sundown."

Daden.

He'd gifted me with a secret—a name I'd never heard though I didn't doubt was real. Flutters had swarmed and warmed my chest ever since hearing those quietly uttered words, the vulnerability that lurked even quieter beneath them.

A vulnerability he'd hidden so well that I wouldn't be surprised if no one else knew it existed beneath that veneer of calm deadliness. And tomorrow...

I paced my rooms, uncertainty flowing through me and creating dark thoughts.

What if he was hurt or worse, he was killed? What if others were hurt and or killed?

She wouldn't harm me, my heart, not without good reason, but to see the blood king fall was reason enough. Except she did not know. My mother had no idea what he now meant to me.

I had no idea what he now meant to me.

When dinner arrived, I collected my plate and kicked the door closed. Pausing beside the bed, I eyed the table on the other side where I'd fed my beast.

*Mine.* Whether I was okay with it or not, that was what he was. A king. A savage. A murderer.

Mine.

When I'd first met him, it had felt as though a string had looped around my waist, tempting with daringly gentle tugs to be closer, nearer.

Over the span of weeks, that string had grown into rope, and now, I was in chains—bruised and sore for fighting a brutal pull that would never fucking cease.

I didn't bother knocking and opened the door that connected our rooms via his large dressing chamber. I knew he was there. I hadn't heard him leave, and I cared nothing for his privacy when I'd already seen every powerful inch of him.

Dade opened the door at the other end, hair deliciously mussed and his head tilted, releasing soft light into the dark chamber. Curious ghostly blue eyes drank me in and paused on the fish pie in my hands. His nose wrinkled at the scent, then he stepped back.

Two sconces on either side of that monstrous bed were lit, and I kept my eyes averted from the perfectly pressed linen I'd once tangled so thoroughly. "Not fond of fish?"

Dade gestured to the square table beyond the far side of his bed that sat flush between two large windows. Two chairs perched neatly beneath, his dinner untouched atop. "No, but I'll endure the stench if it means you'll dine with me." He untucked a chair, and I nodded my thanks, the nightgown I'd changed into sliding over the gray velvet padded seat.

"You've already bathed," he said, seating himself on the other side and pouring a glass of wine. "Vanilla." He handed me the glass.

There was only one, and my heart warmed as I took it, my fingers brushing his. "We can share, and yes. I was..." I blew out a slight breath, admitting as I removed the lid from my dish and set it aside, steam wafting into the air. "Nervous, I suppose."

Dade, quiet for a moment, sliced into a steak as big as my head, blood oozing out and slowly pooling over the white plate around the steamed vegetables. "Are you not excited to see your mother?"

"Yes and no."

He nodded, understanding my fears, for I knew he harbored similar worries, his teeth plucking the large hunk of meat from his fork.

I cleared my throat and cut into my pie. "What do you know of yours?"

"My mother?" he asked, brows furrowed and food still in his mouth.

I smiled at my plate, shoveling the fluffy pie into my own mouth and nodding.

He swallowed and sliced into more of his meal. "Not much besides the basics. She was fond of politics, swimming, and cooking."

"A queen well-suited to the throne of Vordane."

He ignored the slight mocking in my tone. "She also loved the piano, though rumor has it that she wasn't very good. My father had hoped for a demure wife, I'd heard, and instead, he wound up mated to a female who challenged him at every turn." His nonchalant tone did not stop those words from making me meet his smiling eyes. "He liked chess, battle, of course, and sailing."

"Sailing?"

He chewed and swallowed more meat before answering. "He owned a fleet of ships, and he and my uncle would often set sail twice a year under the guise of trade." I ate some more as he went on, my chest growing tight for all he hadn't gotten the chance to know for himself. "A male of few words, supposedly, but a keen observer. Prone to terrible tempers every other full moon should someone test him, but otherwise content." He sipped some wine, his eyes downcast. "Many say he was unnervingly quiet but friendly."

My appetite waned; the delicious, buttery crust that dissolved over my tongue struggled to slide down my clogged throat. Neither of us looking, we both reached for the wine at the same time, the king removing his hand when I pulled back. My cheeks warmed, but I took it and greedily drank a few mouthfuls.

"How did your parents meet?" I shouldn't have asked. I was a glutton for punishment, but it mattered. Even if he hadn't known them himself, they were a part of him, and they mattered.

"My uncle, actually," Dade said without inflection. "He'd dragged my father to the great lake beyond the city when he'd heard of a group of females competing in a swim competition." A roguish smile brightened his features. "My father apparently protested as he'd had plans with two females later that evening and didn't want to run late."

I nearly dropped the wine as I set it down. "Two?"

Dade nodded, his knife sliding with ease through the bloodied meat, then gathered some vegetables to scoop over the top. "Supposedly, he was a little too friendly with females, though not in an overt way, but privately." I waited as he ate, his full lips darker, wet from his food, when he continued, "Serrin promised they wouldn't be late, but in the end, he did not return home until three days later."

I laughed at that. "Your mother gave him a hard time."

"No, she knew what she wanted when she'd climbed from the lake and saw him standing there." He sat back, fingers dancing around the wineglass, his eyes dancing on me. "They hired a room in the city until they were satisfied their bond was uh… welcomed."

My skin grew tight, too hot in an instant. I looked away, returning to my food. Yet I couldn't keep from wondering if that was what I'd done—if that was what we'd done a few nights ago—welcomed the bond.

His sweltering stare, the burning air between us, was answer enough.

We ate in tense silence, Dade's attention a furnace I couldn't force myself away from, yet I didn't look at him.

A grating and toe-curling chuckle erupted, but he rose from the table before I could glare at him. He retrieved a book from the bottom of the small pile upon his nightstand and stared down at the age-worn brown cover.

"I didn't take you for a reader."

"It is hard to find the time with so much murderous intent, I will admit." I balked, the wine souring in my stomach, then his head lifted, and he laughed again—loud and utterly genuine. "Your expression just now."

The sound—stars, the deep, melodically guttural timbre that vacated him threatened to decimate me where I sat. "You're not funny," I said, though my tone betrayed me, and I pinched my lips to keep my smile leashed.

He huffed, stalking with that lazy yet lethal grace back to the table, and retook his seat. "Here." Sliding the book over the wood, he instructed before returning to his meal, "Open to the first page."

Carefully, I plucked up the book, watching him eat for a moment. He seemed to be waiting while appearing as though he cared nothing of it as I set the book in my lap and appeased my curiosity.

A female, brunette and smiling in a way that would undoubtedly make nearly anyone want to please her, gazed back at me with deep blue eyes. Below a high, marbleized cheek, a lone dimple popped, brown curls falling around a heart-shaped face as though created to help soften the eye-drawing yet cruel sensuality.

Next to the beautiful female's image was another. This one of a male of similar brutal beauty. His bone structure was not softened by anything, least of all the eyes that smiled yet remained a deep, dark blue. His near-white hair fell to his shoulders in thick, messy waves, his lips not as full as those gracing the male seated across from me.

I looked back at the female, noting Dade drew that feature, as well as the intimidating structured edges of others, from her face.

From his mother.

Beneath the two singular, painted portraits that were finger smudged by littler hands over many years and glued to the first page of a book of outdated nursery riddles were their names.

Vern and Maya Volkahn.

Swallowing, I closed the cover over the souls that haunted the male sitting across from me and gently placed the book upon the table. "You have her cheekbones and forehead." I gestured to my own, then my cheeks. "A slight set of dimples, her lashes, and her lips."

Dade paused, slowly straightening and lowering his cutlery.

I continued. "Your father gave you his hair but a shade darker, and that deep, ocean blue that sometimes takes hold of your eyes."

Pressing my hands over the skirt of my nightgown to keep the tremble that arrived hidden, I managed a small laugh. "Oh, and his strong nose."

"Strong nose?" he asked, his head tilting.

I nodded. "That perfect bridge with just the right amount of thickness and length."

He stared for a moment, then his features creased as he sat back and released another glorious yet brief bout of laughter. My cheeks burned when he settled and stated with deliberate slowness, "Thickness and length."

"King of jokes now, are we?" I coughed to smother my bubbling laugh. "Don't be so lewd."

"You said it, not me." He grinned and smoothed some rogue strands of hair back from his forehead. "So you like my... nose."

The way his eyes shone with remnants of mirth had my thighs clenching together. "I do," I said, not willing to add what he already knew—that I liked many other things too—and so I quickly said, "They're both incredibly beautiful. Stunning. Your parents."

His smile drooped, and I felt my heart thrash at what he'd just done, with all he'd shared with me, and therefore I had to gently say, "I am honored to see them, that you would show them to me." I had a feeling he never shared those portraits with anyone.

He watched me for a crushing half minute, then nodded once. "All pictures of them were removed as soon as I came of age enough to give orders to my uncle and not the other way around."

"You did not wish to see them?"

"Not as reminders, as weapons, no." His gaze fell to an empty space on the table. "But just as my parents. Eat," he said, and stood abruptly to return the book to its home by the bed.

He took his time, placing it exactly as it had been with a careful type of reverence. A reverence I might have been envious of if not for the fact that he'd also gifted me with the same attention.

Longing fluttered into something else, something wilder and untamable, and when he waded back, I forced my attention to the food I'd been carelessly shoveling into my mouth.

Almost done with dinner, I sent my gaze over the room while I drank some more wine, admiring the wood of the strange bed and the ghastly skulls atop the fireplace mantel and drawers.

"Are those your parents?"

He knew what I was referring to and refilled the wineglass when I set it down. "They are my warrior kin, my friends, you could say. Bond, Reline, and Nerin. I matured with them, and they died in battle. The last two this past year, and Bond in the first year." His mouth twisted, the decanter hitting the table with a thud. "He was never one for such things."

"Yet he fought anyway."

"Despite my best attempts to force him home"—he scooped some remaining vegetables onto his fork—"yes, so they serve as reminders."

I waited as he ate, then asked, "Reminders of what you've lost?"

"Of what I stand to lose more of." Such dark iced words.

I nodded, understanding even if I hated that I was able to. He would do whatever it took to ensure he never lost anything else again—even if that meant taking over the entire continent.

"Your uncle," I said, curious. "He's alive?"

"He is, though I cannot say for how much longer."

I clasped my hands together in my lap to keep from reaching for the wine—for him. "You should free him."

Dade's eyes left his plate, ensnaring mine as he pushed it aside. "Free him?"

"He's your uncle," I said, trying to find the words even as the new growth of feathers at my back still itched in this form. "He was trying to protect you. To end this war of yours by making my mother submit."

"He serves himself and himself only," he said roughly, his jaw rotating and then clenching. "He always has. He hurt you, maimed you—"

"I am healed."

"He betrayed me when he wounded you, and I care not for his reasons, only that he did."

My mouth dried under the blanket of those cold, graveled words.

I tried a different approach, knowing that sentencing his uncle to die was not what he wanted. Not really. He wanted to send a message to ensure no one else laid a hand on me, and he'd hurt himself in order to do so. "He raised you."

Dade's jaw shifted. He reached for the wine.

"He raised you," I said again, softer now. "He took care of you, did he not?"

He drained the contents of the glass and placed it down hard enough to crack it. Uncaring, he rubbed his fingers over the bristles around his mouth, the movements fluid yet not of the form that sat across the table from me. "He did."

"That's it?" I said, aghast. "He is your blood, and I will not be offended if you choose to allow him another chance."

"He placed a dagger in my hand on my fifth birthday and did not let me drop it until I'd killed one of three rabbits he'd released into my rooms."

I froze. Dade reclined in the chair, the wood creaking as he laid his leg across his knee and gazed beyond me into the past. "I couldn't catch one with the blasted blade, of course, and frustrated, I accidentally shifted and killed it that way."

"You cannot control the shift until you enter maturity."

"Right," he clipped. "That didn't matter, and it didn't matter that I puked all over myself when I shifted back, in tears upon this very floor." His eyes roamed to the end of the bed. "He made me do it twice a week until I eventually lobbed the heads off all three rabbits with a blade."

My chest throbbed with the image of such a young male losing himself to bloodlust. "Shit..."

"And then it was badgers. A year later, the training yards, where he beat me until my bones groaned and I silently raged beneath every blow and the reminders he'd spew at me about my parents being dead."

"He..." I blinked and released a choked breath. "He used their deaths as fuel."

"Of course," Dade said, as though it were normal, as though that were okay. "Understandably, as it worked, yet as the years bled by, his grief waned."

"But your purpose never did."

"He'd done too thorough a job. My generals, the older warriors, everyone spoke of my father as though he would return at any moment. The tales Merelda would tell me of her and my mother cooking together in the kitchens..."

"They were friends," I guessed, then frowned when I remembered the head cook and our conversation. "But Dade, she wouldn't have told you those stories to hurt you, to incite a need for revenge."

"I know that, but it doesn't matter." His voice lowered, deepened, his eyes like ice as they met mine. "It didn't matter when from every angle, at every available opportunity, I was reminded of them. Vern and Maya Volkahn are breathing ghosts in this palace. They still roam the halls in the hearts of many, and they'll never forget."

"Love makes things impossible to forget," I whispered, not meaning to.

Dade hummed, then dragged his finger over his bottom lip. "I couldn't love them. Not like they do. I never had that chance, and so they made sure I would never forget something I'll never know."

Silence crawled in, not unwelcome but cold all the same, as we both absorbed all he'd said.

As I'd grown to fear and suspect, my mate had been raised as a pawn. A weapon made from the many broken hearts of a fractured kingdom.

A tool used for retribution.

It was all he'd known. He'd known nothing else in order to know better or otherwise. This land, his people, and their memories were all he had.

Until now.

I stood, unaware of my intentions but knowing I had to give in to the tug on those chains. They pulled, and I followed until I was standing before him and his leg slid to the floor, eyes sharp as they stared up at me. "Do not pity me, swan," he warned with a roughened edge.

"Never." I tried to smile, felt it wobble as I wondered of all that could have been if things were different. If we'd met under the circumstances our parents had met their mates and their parents before them.

As two royal brats who'd spend their days mating and making plans for the day they'd take over the throne, thinking it exciting rather than a responsibility that could both save and destroy lives if not taken seriously enough or taken far too seriously.

I fell into his lap with the realization that if this had been the case, if we'd met without blood on our souls and scars on our hearts, then we wouldn't be permitted to marry. You could not stop a mating bond, but never in the entire history of Nodoya had a Gracewood and Volkahn tried to wed.

It would never have been allowed.

In mere hours, we would change history.

I wrapped my arms around his neck, holding him tight, so tight I could feel our hearts thunder together. Dade's arms slowly came around me, his nose nuzzling into my neck, mine tickled by his hair. "What are we doing?" His voice was muffled by my skin.

"Hugging."

"Okay," he said, sounding a little baffled but not relinquishing his hold in the slightest. After a minute, his body hard as steel beneath my thigh, he whispered, "You make me forget."

I squeezed my eyes closed.

Those words were all I could think of as I forced myself away from the pouting king and returned to my rooms for a restless night's sleep.

# TWENTY-EIGHT

## *Dade*

S LEEP ELUDED ME, AND THOUGH I LONGED TO, I DIDN'T DARE step into Opal's rooms to watch her dream. Not only would it likely frighten her to find me there, but I would be tempted to crawl into that bed next to her and pull her close.

Too close and we'd do as she'd said—lose ourselves in one another, time dripping away like the waters in that ravine until it coasted into a racing river eaten whole by the ocean.

I did not mind the idea of that at all, but I could understand her hesitancy. She was scared, terrified of what was to come. Most of all, the conflicting feelings that being with me aroused.

Dawn leaked through the windows of my rooms, her scent a stain I never wanted cleaned, when sleep finally took me. Lunch was awaiting me in the war room when I arrived, still shaking water from my hair after bathing in haste.

I snatched a leg of chicken, tearing into it as I unspooled the plans Fang and Scythe had come up with in my absence.

"Get enough beauty sleep, sire?" the latter asked, entering the room and taking a leg of chicken from the tray before propping himself in the chair on the other side of the table. "That swan of yours must have quite the appetite."

The leg of chicken smacked into his face before he saw it coming. He snarled, then grinned when I peeled my lip back. "You'd be wise to never mention her in a sentence like that again, you one-eyed fuck."

A whistle. "Oh, a one-eye insult." He feigned a pout. "No goods were delivered to your rooms overnight, then." He tossed the bones onto the tray, one missing and rolling grease onto the map of Gracewood taken from the wall and spread over the table. "Poor beastly king. Has she rejected you?"

"You know she hasn't," I grumbled, though it sometimes felt as though she still could, and I loathed how much that terrified me.

Scythe was silent for a moment, then kicked his feet under the chair and leaned forward. "She won't. I saw the way those weird eyes watched you while you showed off those ghastly horns and wings in her rooms while she healed."

I didn't allow him to see what those words did to me, and instead, kept my attention fixed to the map, the markers placed where the warrior camps would wait in the mountain range, The Spring Forest and Gracewood Forest. "We'll see."

He wrapped his knuckles over the table, nodding. "Make it back alive, and yeah," he knocked some markers aside, replacing them with a dagger that cut straight through the map and the wood beneath. "We will."

"Those spies we haven't heard from this past week?" Fang arrived with parchment in hand, his expression grim. "They're dead."

I gestured for the parchment, but the lettering was thick, wrong—as though whoever had written the message did not want their identity traced. I lifted it to my nose and scented sun and some type of berry. A female's scent.

"Ballsy move on their part." Scythe whistled. "Makes one wonder where they found such courage."

We knew all too well of the human royals attempts to gather more forces. "We send more spies, two flyers only," I said. "Just to check in."

"Then what?" Fang asked.

Rubbing a finger over my chin, I eyed the map, the kingdom of

Errin by the sea. "That depends on what they find, but I vowed to end the attacks, remember?" I closed my eyes and cursed. "Those were Opal's conditions for marriage. No more violence."

Both males said nothing, then Scythe exhaled out, "Fuck."

I sighed. "Indeed." I'd already deceived her, and to do so again was akin to poisoning myself and then waiting for the damage to be unveiled, but I still said, "When they return—"

"*If* they return," Fang muttered.

I glared but nodded. "Have word sent to me. They have two days."

Fang guffawed. "What if they can't find shit in two days?"

"If there is something to find, find it they will before returning well within that time," I said, cold and matter-of-factly. "Otherwise, we assume them dead and make other… arrangements. There is no time to waste."

Apprehension swarmed, tension brewing inside the drafty room. For the first time since I was a child, I hoped not to head into battle.

Shadows coalesced and separated as I warped into the middle of the foyer right after dinner, of which I'd eaten in the war room after leaving Scythe with a list of instructions a mile long.

He would oversee the running of the Keep—a task he wasn't entirely thrilled to be given. Fang and the warriors were already gone, journeying across the river to their given hideouts, deputy generals assigned and ready.

Opal rounded the corner from the library. "Where have you been? I've been searching for you for hours."

"Busy," I said, readjusting the sleeves of my shirt.

"Busy with what?"

My eyes shot to hers, which were simmering with suspicion as they dipped over my face. I swallowed the urge to snap. My blood was pressing at my skin, my inner beast prowling, unsettled and anxious over the many looming yet hidden threats headed my way.

That wasn't her fault. It was my own, and though I didn't deserve her and had all but forced her into this tenuous alliance, the last thing I ever wanted was for her to fear me.

"First of all," I said. "I had trouble sleeping being that yet again, you made me do so alone and aching, so I woke late with my fist around my extremely angry cock." Her eyes flared, lashes fluttering slowly, and I smirked when she pinched her smile between those pearly teeth. "Secondly, there are a great many details that go into running a kingdom, as I'm sure you are aware." I stepped closer, her scent calming some of the tension. "Though I hope we return as soon as possible, I do not know how long we will be."

Not mollified in the least, my swan lifted her chin, exposing that long, delicate neck. "You reek of deceit."

I had to touch her, couldn't not, and so I closed the gap between us and gently clasped her cheeks. My eyes swam into hers, even as something weighted tried to hold the lie between my teeth. "Sunshine, I've finally got you." At her raised brows, I grinned. "We both know I do, and so I would be a fool to jeopardize this." I kissed her forehead, then her cheek, her whispering sigh sinking inside me and turning my stomach. "Us."

I was burning in the deepest pits of the underworld while standing on perfectly solid ground when her hands closed over mine, and those gold eyes stared up at me, hopeful, trusting, relieved.

Erasing any emotion from my features, I ignored the guilt gnawing at my chest and waited for her nod.

I slid her fingers through mine, lowering them between us. "Ready?" The room began to fog, shadows returning and gathering force.

"No," she said, followed by a nervous laugh. "But let's go."

Within moments, we arrived under the cover of growing darkness, my feet planted on an unfamiliar stone floor.

And nearly stumbled into a bed as Opal raced away from me through the shadows.

I didn't dare send flame to any of the sconces or candles, my eyes adjusting with each passing second until I could make out where Opal stood by a large wooden door. I smirked as she turned one of two locks. "That won't keep anyone out."

So quiet it was barely a sound, she turned the last lock. "It might give us time should we need it."

I let her believe what she felt she needed to and set my sights on the large room. Her scent flooded the space, even after many weeks without her presence. The bed, half-veiled in blue netting and dressed in cream and lavender, was constructed from white stained oak and perched in the center of the far wall.

Along that wall, passed a nightstand riddled with dust-sprinkled books and a glimmering tiara, was a door to the bathing room and another that likely led to her dressing room.

I turned to the long row of shelving behind me and a dressing table cluttered in spools of material and piles of half-mended clothes. Upon the shelves, I discovered more books, notebooks, perfume bottles, and feathered quills by a cluster of inkpots.

I plucked up a perfume bottle and uncorked it. Opal was quick to snatch it from my hand. "Careful, that's my favorite."

"Vanilla rose and..." I sniffed the remnants lingering in the chilled air. "Like a brown sugar. Caramel?"

Opal hid her smile behind the crystal bottle, then recorked it and gently set it back on the shelf next to the many others. "You cheat with a nose like that. Though it would be handy next time I..." She trailed off with a slight puckering of her brows.

"Next time you what?"

"I was going to say next time I make some." She threw her hand in the air, forcing a quick smile before strutting away. "But who knows if that will happen or when. It's stupid."

I followed her, not liking her tone, the hint of sadness within. "It's not stupid. You make it yourself?" I turned back to the shelves. "All of those?"

"Yes," she said, sounding farther away.

I found her inside the doorway of her dressing room, frozen solid before a frilled gown.

A wedding gown.

Her disappointment bled into the room, made me long to tear the dress from its hanger and rip it to pieces.

"So it's not what you would have chosen," I said for her and moved in to place my hands upon her hips. "But you will do that gown a favor, make it all the more beautiful by allowing it to grace this body."

I heard her swallow, and she leaned back into me slightly with a tremulous sigh.

"Come." I turned her into the room and toward the bed. "We should sleep before someone hears and discovers us." When she hesitated, I offered, "Or we could go find your mother and let her know of our arrival. It would be the courteous thing to do, would it not?"

Opal spun around then, grinning. "Do not remember your manners now, savage." Her smile fell, and she sat upon the bed, quietly removing her slippers. "It will just lead to trouble."

"So we hide until we marry," I said, finding that humorously unattainable.

"Basically, yes."

Stubborn, clever swan.

I kept my boots on and walked to the window seat to view what laid beyond. Mountains rippled through the dark veil of night, my brethren slumbering but on guard, not a tiny glow of campfire in sight.

The reek of too many different flowers and plants perfumed the breeze, dragging my eyes to the gardens beneath the window that stretched toward the fields and forest in the distance.

How many nights, I wondered, taking a seat upon the cushioned bench, had my swan sat right here, mending garments, reading, bottling perfume, and daydreaming while I'd been out there. While I'd been across the ravine, miles away from her castle, plotting and plundering and plucking their people off. In death or surrender, it did not matter. I'd taken and taken, and I'd felt nothing for it save for a sense of righteousness because justice was never served.

It was delivered in the dead of night by a horde of beasts and their vengeful king.

"I've been a king since before I learned how to say the word," I said quietly to the window I gently pulled closed. "Yet I've never actually felt like one."

I wasn't sure she'd say anything when a minute of silence passed, but then Opal whispered, "You had no time to wrap your head around the idea of it." The bedding rustled, and I looked that way, her golden hair spilling over the pillows. "A king is what you've always been."

But was it all I'd be, and what I'd continue to be? Only the stars knew.

"I'm not fond of the idea of becoming a queen," she shocked me by saying. "I don't *hate* the thought of it, but I don't know..."

"You're not sold on it," I said, smiling a little. "A ruthless queen you will make, though, my gentle swan."

She stifled her laughter, then sighed and asked, "You think so?"

"I know so," I said instantly. Forcing my eyes from her shifting form beneath those blankets, I looked back out the window. "Those not in power would set fire to our souls to hear us talk of such things."

"They don't understand."

"No," I agreed, watching the moon spray light over swaying sunflowers. "I don't suppose anyone understands much of anything they've yet to experience for themselves."

Opal shifted again. "Come lay with me."

"Next to you or inside you?" I hoped for the latter all the while hoping she'd say no because I wouldn't be able to, and it could give our presence here away.

Opal just giggled, smothering it with her hand as I rose from the window and gently kicked off my boots at the side of her bed.

Her smile drooped, teeth taking her bottom lip when I removed my vest and loosened my tunic. She lifted the bedding, and though I knew I'd overheat, I didn't tell her not to bother.

I'd be closer to her under it.

Her hand snuck beneath her cheek, lashes shadowing them both while she surveyed me getting settled, my head upon the pillow next to hers. "You seem nervous."

I pushed up on an elbow to better see her. "Would it make me less kingly to admit that I am?"

Her free hand tapped my nose, her eyes smiling. "It would make you honest."

I took the opportunity to ask, "Honest answer?"

"Always," she whispered.

"Were you afraid? Living here while I was out there..." I swallowed, unable to say the rest.

"Taking your vengeance," she finished for me, and I could only keep my eyes locked on hers. "Yes," she said. "Though it was more a fear from feeling helpless, my gift not really a gift at all yet still something I had to hide, and no one really knew why."

I wondered over that for a moment, but I didn't need to wonder long. "Because you will be my end."

Horror engulfed those eyes, gold turning a liquid orange. "You know I cannot harm you."

I bit my lip and smoothed a rogue curl from her forehead. "I do adore seeing you try." She smacked my hand away, and we both laughed silently. I sobered, wanting to know more. An odd sense of urgency to know everything erupted, ridding me of patience. "So you were trapped in here, protected at all costs, bottling your perfumes and writing journal entries about evil young kings."

Her flat expression said I had her pegged, and then she said, "I did not write journal entries. I sometimes draw and write stories. Fictional," she said, and though it was dark, I saw her cheeks color, "but yes, they were fun in keeping me entertained."

"What type of stories?" I wriggled a little closer, the bed groaning, and felt the heat rising from her face. "Oh, my. Filthy swan."

"Not like that," she said, laughing again. "But there was some uh, kissing and the like, I suppose." At my amused expression, she harrumphed. "I was young, okay?"

"And extremely sheltered," I added, to which she nodded. "Bored, too."

Her head tilted a fraction. "Don't you humor me, savage. I still won't let you read them."

I would read them. Better than that, I would convince her to let me read them. "Whatever you say."

Our hands brushed, and I threaded our fingers, watching her as she watched me. "What do you think tomorrow will bring?"

"Me in a hideous fluffy gown for one." The humor faded, apprehension creasing her eyes and thinning her lips. "I wish I knew. But I suppose I will have breakfast with my mother, and you will hide until things proceed according to plan."

"I do like plans, especially when they work," I said in an attempt to ease some of her anxiety. It failed, and I squeezed her hand. "What do you want to happen?"

It was as though she hadn't truly thought about that, her brows furrowing and her eyes darting over my face as she finally did. "Honest answer?"

"Always."

"I don't know." My chest caved, then she said, "All I know is that I want you, I want everyone, unharmed, so I guess that means I want us to marry and then leave."

My throat tightened. "And you will come with me."

"I agreed to, did I not?"

"You agreed to marry me," I said, and immediately wanted to punch myself for it. "That was it."

Opal just gazed at me as though she could see right through me for melting seconds, and I felt my hand grow clammy in hers. "We both know that will never be it." Relief washed in, and she whispered, "You are really not yourself."

I licked my lips, thinking we'd best end this conversation and go to sleep. Well, she would sleep, and I would pretend while listening to every sound in this foreign castle I'd once planned to reduce to rubble.

My stupid mouth had other ideas when Opal shifted closer. "Talk, say what is wrong."

I closed my eyes, counted to ten, then murmured, barely a sound,

"You do not forgive me, and I cannot make you, but I want this." I opened my eyes, clasped her cheek. "I want you every day, every night, always." Her eyes swam, wet and so bright. I rubbed my thumb beneath one. "I'm selfish, I know, and undeserving, but could we maybe…" *Fuck.*

"Could we what?" she asked, so low, so sweet.

I rushed out, "When we return, could we try?"

Opal's lashes fluttered, lips parting as understanding dawned. "You mean a real marriage."

I nodded, my entire body numb with fear of rejection. *Lie to me,* I almost said. *Just fucking lie to me.*

My swan stared and stared, the heat of her, the heat inside me, unfurling and gathering. I couldn't breathe, didn't dare open my mouth to try for fear of sending her from this bed, from reach of me forevermore.

Wound so perilously tight, I didn't see her intent, just felt my heart roar in my ears when she pushed me flat onto the bed and curled herself over me.

Her answer came in the form of hands in my hair, tugging it back. In the searing bliss of her tongue at my throat, then teeth sinking into my neck. Stars flashed throughout the room, the type that only we could see. A heat so encompassing that sweat broke out over the both of us as my blood broke through my skin and spread itself with greed over her awaiting tongue.

She'd sealed our fates, the stars plan for us, our bond—her tongue lapping at the punctures, gentle and drugging swipes.

There was no hesitancy in our movements. Clothing peeled and tore, collecting around our limbs and thrown across the bed to the floor as I rolled and stared down at her.

At my mate.

Fire shone in her eyes, a fire I knew she saw mirrored in my own, and then I captured her bloodstained mouth, her thighs rising, hands seeking. They roamed my back as my tongue tasted what she'd done. The vow she'd made that outweighed and mocked things such as engagements and weddings.

She'd pledged herself to me, mind, body, and soul, and there was no turning back.

Wild with the knowledge, with the taste of my essence on her lips, the synchronized pounding of our hearts, and the power thrumming through my veins in a way I'd never felt before, I sank inside her. She was ready, her need for me so strong I could scent it upon the stifling air.

Opal gasped, and I covered her mouth with my hand, my eyes falling into hers as I groaned softly and cursed. She nipped me, and I grunted, planted deep inside her and feeling her body shake with a devilish little laugh.

I grinned, then removed my hand, replacing it with my mouth and kissing her hard. In slow thrusts, I loved her, brought her to a shaking climax swiftly. I held her as I did and bit her shoulder to contain my roar while I did the same.

But my swan wasn't done.

A flash of her eyes, and then I was pushed onto my back. I allowed it, still catching my breath, and then cursed when she squeezed my length and glossed her lips over my cheeks. "Smile," she whispered, kissing one with a flick of her tongue, and I withheld a laugh that gave her what she wanted. Her hand squeezed again, a tiny growl leaving her as she licked... my dimple.

She then moved to the other, her tongue precise as it swiped and dipped and her hair tickling my overheated skin. "I've wanted to do that for so long."

"You wanted to lick my..."

"Dimples, yes," she supplied, then kissed a pathway down my chest.

I cursed, torn between wanting to devour her divine mouth and never wanting her to stop everything she was doing. "Stars, you fucking ruin me."

She hummed. "That would only be fair."

Her teeth scraped over my pec, fingertips tracing and scoring into every dip and ridge of my torso. I shivered from head to toe. *More*, I urged silently. *Stroke me, torture me…* a groan rumbled from me when those delicate fingers rubbed.

"I want to poison you," she said to my abdominal muscles, and they clenched, the admission heated and soaking into my skin. "The way you've done me."

My heart slammed, my words thick and throaty. "Poison me, sunshine, and don't you dare think twice."

Her eyes flicked up to mine, riddled with lust. A desire so potent, it matched what I could scent building like an inferno between her thighs. They flared, a luminous liquid bronze, and then she moved lower.

"Swan," I warned when she reached my cock, but she had to already know I was covered in her release and mine.

Apparently, she didn't care. Her lips wrapped around the head of my cock and sucked hard enough to make it and my eyes bulge.

Satisfaction curled her glistening lips as she watched me twitch, hard as steel in her tiny hand, but she didn't stop. She sucked and bobbed her head, taking as much of me as she could into that sweet, hot mouth.

Just when I thought I might die if I held back any longer, her other hand slipped down the base of my cock to rub my testicles.

"Fuck," I spewed, and lifted her from my genitals and over my stomach, my breathing embarrassingly ragged.

She pouted. "What?" Then she blinked and bit her lip, unsure. "Shit, did I hurt you?"

"If by hurt you mean sucking until I nearly exploded down your throat, then yes," I said roughly, "you're fucking killing me."

"Oh." She tried but couldn't hide her smile.

I didn't let her gloat for long, lifting her back until she felt me waiting beneath her. Her eyes hooded. Lashes cresting her cheeks and her bottom lip in her mouth, she straddled me and then eased me inside perfection.

The sight of her, that long golden hair curling over her breasts, her mound slick with our coupling, and me disappearing inside her sweat-misted body...

I sat up and gripped those glorious hips. Opal moaned with the new depth of me inside her and curled her legs around me.

My mouth at her chin, crawling along it, my hand in her hair, tilting her head back for my teeth and tongue to graze her neck, I rasped, "Move those hips." She did, and we both hitched a breath. "Good little swan. How does it feel?" I dragged my lips over her throat, then nipped at her chin. "Having me so deep inside you."

"Like I could burn and be thankful for it."

I snarled low, not expecting such a frank, swift response—let alone one that would steal my next heartbeat.

"How," she started, then swallowed and lowered her forehead to mine, arms locking around my neck. "How does it feel for you?"

I smiled against her cheek, rubbed my lips over it, and tightened my hold at her hip while moving my other arm around her lower back and squeezing her close. Her breasts, damp and lush, squashed against my chest, her heartbeat dancing with mine. "Forever." Her eyes flicked open, wide and searching. "It feels like forever, a right I never want to get wrong."

Her mouth fused itself to mine so hard, we fell back onto the bed.

Over me, my swan writhed, her hips circling, grinding, and her hands in her hair when she rose and ground down hard. We both cursed, a growl I couldn't contain if I'd tried releasing when she began to shake, to fracture, her body riding mine on instinct, chasing a high she would get nowhere else.

From nowhere but me. "My mate," I whispered, in both shock and awe.

"Yes," she moaned, and I lost it.

Taking her to her back, I pushed her leg over my shoulder as she came apart. A silent cry widened her eyes, and inside them, a feral gleam reflected back at me from my own. I shuddered, my entire body aflame as I jerked and grunted like the animal I was and emptied myself inside her once more.

Our lips met, glued themselves still, as we both panted into one another's mouths. "I don't hear anyone," Opal whispered, fingers trailing down my back as I kissed her once, twice, twenty times, growing more obsessed with the taste of her each day.

"Then we're not done." I kissed her one last time, and she smothered her laughter in the pillow when I flipped her onto all fours.

# TWENTY-NINE

*Opal*

**A** ROOSTER CROWED HOURS TOO EARLY, AND I SHIFTED CLOSER against a hard chest.

On the fringes of sleep, I felt his finger trail up and down the indent of my spine while he whispered barely-there words to my hair.

Through the tiny cracks in his voice, I heard, "I'm sorry."

I fought the urge to tumble into dreams, listening, trying to make out more of what he was saying. "I'm sorry"—his lips pressed to my forehead—"for taking him from you, for breaking your heart before I thought myself worthy of it, before I knew better." A heavy exhale stirred my hair, heated my skin. "Before I knew what it was to love."

Though closed, my eyes burned along with the battered organ in my chest. His touch lulled, his repeated murmurings singed, and I didn't know anything anymore, but when he whispered, "Sleep, swan," I let myself drift away from it all while still trapped within his arms.

Morning arrived with a bang, the door rattling.

And a male sprawled on his side, head propped on his hand and staring down at me, his legs tangled with mine.

*Mine*, echoed throughout my blood.

I'd done something insane in accepting that, this bond, yet staring at him, those adoring ice-blue eyes, it felt like one of the best things I'd ever done.

*A right I never want to get wrong.*

I reached for him, for the patch of sunlight sliding over his tousled white-blond hair to touch his sculpted cheek, that dimple.

The bang came again as Dade drawled, "Your mother wishes to see you."

Shit. Where were my clothes? I rolled to the edge of the bed, Dade's soft chuckle behind me, and snatched my torn dress from the ground. "Thank you for your help," I said, sarcasm heavy.

Dade's finger appeared over my shoulder, my undergarments hanging from it. I snatched those too, quickly stepping into them and tugging them up my legs.

He hissed, "Stars, that ass."

I glared at him, but it softened when I saw the heat in his eyes, that bare chest I longed to rake my fingers down, to feel every ridge like a washboard beneath my—

"Opal," my mother shouted through the wood. "I know you're in there. Open the door."

The king bit his lips and rolled over to drag his pants on while I stuffed my arms through the dress and raced for the comb on my dressing table. It was a little dusty, but I had to wash my hair anyway and pulled it through the knotted and sweat marred strands while hurrying to the door.

I paused, looking back at the bed.

Dade smirked, sprawled over it on his side again, bare-chested, but at least his pants were on. "Shirt," I whispered.

He made a face that said he didn't quite catch what I said, and I made one back that said he was a damned liar. He laughed again while I undid the locks and opened the door.

In my haste to get somewhat presentable, I hadn't fathomed what it would feel like to lay eyes upon her again. My mother's hair, a shade darker than mine, was pulled back into a tight bun at her nape, not a honeyed strand out of place, and those same colored eyes...

Fury melted from them, and I was pulled into her arms. I hugged her back, inhaling her lemon and rose scent and clutching her tighter than I ever had before.

Rearing back, she sniffed, her hands still upon my arms, but her eyes fixed beyond me.

Upon the half-naked king on my bed.

Queen Nikaya was no fool. She could scent it as well as see it all over us, yet she said nothing. She just stared, too long and too hard for me to think any good would come from it.

No good would ever come from her and Dade looking at one another.

He'd killed her mate.

And I'd just made my father's killer mine.

Dizziness swamped me. As if sensing it, my mother swallowed and promptly patted her hands over my cheeks, shoulders, arms. "You're okay?" Those hands shook, rising to my face again and holding it. "You're okay."

"I am," I confirmed. "Mother, Prince Bron..."

"I know all about the cretin and all about the larger one who stole you from them." Her voice deepened to a low growl. "From me."

"I fear I simply had to wreck your plans, Nikaya."

I winced. *Shit.*

"You," she seethed, pushing past me. "You will rot in the deepest, darkest depths of—"

"Mother," I snapped, taking her arm before she drew any closer to my bed. "Enough. We have an agreement." I didn't look at Dade, found I couldn't when my mother's eyes fell upon me, tear-soaked with rage. I took her other hand, imploring, "I have made an agreement, and we must not break it." I said those last words slowly, carefully, begging her to rid her mind of revenge and schemes. "Please."

Her eyes swam over my face, her fingers shaking as her lips parted, and she again looked back at the king. Her eyes closed as she turned away. "Breakfast in twenty minutes. Just you."

Then she was gone.

I stared after her, then swung the door closed with a thought and pushed my hands into my hips.

My hung head snapped up, lips curling into a sneer when Dade muttered lazily, "So that went pretty well."

"You should go now," I said, traipsing to the bathing room as everything he made me forget threatened to reduce my heart to ashes. "Do your disappearing act."

"Opal," he called, a warning within not to walk away, one that hinted at him knowing I wasn't so sure about any of this anymore.

Not when my mother's pain lingered in the room with the cause of it.

"Please," I demanded, then I closed the bathing room door.

A knock sounded, and I sank deeper into the bubbles, my knees tight to my chest. "I told you to—"

"Princess?" Linka.

I nearly jumped from the tub, but she cracked open the door before I could, one bright blue eye peering inside and widening when she saw me.

She opened, then closed the door and cupped her hands over her mouth. "You're here. You're really, really here."

She rushed to hug me, forgetting I was naked, then retreated, her cheeks turning a dark pink as we both laughed. "I'm here."

She lowered to the stone floor, her apron spilling around her, and gaped.

"How are you?" I asked, deciding I'd better wash myself and get to this breakfast before my mother came in search of me again.

"Me?" Linka almost shrieked. "How are *you*? Oh, my stars. What did he do to you? Are you okay?"

"I'm fine," I said, understanding her concern, for I would feel the exact same way. I squeezed the cloth out and hung it over the side of the tub, offering her a small smile. "I'm truly fine."

"But," she started, sputtering out, "Queen Nikaya says you plan to marry the crimson king. How in the stars are you fine?"

"Because," I said, searching for the right words. I wouldn't go around flashing the fact I'd found a mate in our sworn enemy. That would not be helpful, nor would it be wise. "It is the right thing to do. The only thing to do," I added when it looked as though she'd protest. "So fetch me a drying cloth, please. We have a kingdom to rescue via marriage."

Linka's eyes bulged, but she laughed when I did, then fetched me one from the shelves by the door, unfolding it as I climbed out. She studied me as I wrapped myself and walked into the bedroom.

No king. I was both thankful and a little disappointed.

"You seem... different," Linka observed, heading to my bed before I could stop her. "And why did I catch a whiff of sex..." Her eyes grew impossibly huge then, and I stopped outside the dressing room, hoping she would say no more.

That hope was futile. Linka dropped the sheets and ran over to me, her pointed chin trembling. Spindly hands reached for me, then retreated. "He didn't, did he? Oh, stars, let me fetch the healer—"

"Stop," I said, the order unmistakable and causing her to freeze at the door. I released a slow breath, then said, "It wasn't like that." Lifting my chin, I met her eyes, then squared my shoulders at the horror sweeping across her face. "It's not like that. Not at all."

But there was no relief. There were no whispers for more details. There was nothing but that fear and an evident disgust staring back at me.

Before she could leave, I asked her one last thing. "Please, do not tell a single soul."

Her back was to me, her hand around the door handle, and she didn't answer. The door slammed behind her, and I slumped to the unmade bed.

Upon the nightstand, light catching the jewels and snagging my attention, was a familiar sapphire hilted dagger.

Despite the hovering cloud of uncertainty, I smiled at what it meant—at the return of the gift I'd once attempted to use against him.

After a near-silent breakfast—terse with things none of us would say—I checked my rooms, found no sign of Dade, then went in search of my mother who was in the mending room on the second floor.

We needed to talk, and I wouldn't let it be about livestock, trade, nor the dwindling numbers of both.

With the marriage alliance, we would fix all that and more. And soon.

A commotion outside lured me toward the nearest window in the stairwell. A wagon ambled by the castle gates outside, loaded with crates of produce, two younglings in the back waving gold and red ribbons.

Footsteps ceased above me. "Oh, thank the fucking stars."

Edwan, holding a mound of ruined material, hurried down the steps to where I stood, his violet eyes watering instantly as he bowed. "I heard you were back, and I'm relieved you're okay, but please," he said, swallowing hard, "please tell me you'll stay."

I frowned down at the material, bright color shredded, others crinkled and singed. All of it likely repercussions of my mother's moods. "She's been that bad?"

He hesitated, then nodded. "I love her," he rushed out. "The stars know I do, but I haven't been able to leave her side. My mate is furious. He's barely seen me in weeks because I'm too afraid to sleep too far away from her."

I wasn't sure what to say and how I could help when it was becoming apparent that this disastrous plan would not be for everyone's benefit. Especially not my mother's.

Yet I would see it through anyway, so I hugged Edwan tight and made him no promises. Then I watched him go.

Up the stairs, I entered the mending room, wove between the

stands of fabric to the large windows that overlooked a small portion of the front courtyard and one of the entrances to the city beyond.

People streamed in and out, more of those ribbons fluttering in the breeze. I watched two vendor carts crawl in behind the gathering masses, followed by horses carting a wagon of ale.

"You said private, Mother." I closed the drapes upon seeing a group of males laughing and drinking, tankards in the air, and turned to glare at her.

She stuck the handle of a small knife in her mouth, fussing with the beading on a lavender gown I hoped was for her, for I had no desire to wear it. "The ceremony, yes."

I unclenched my teeth, infusing calm I did not feel into my voice. "What point is there in having a private ceremony when everyone now knows?"

"Our people need faith, to believe this sacrifice is an end to the war. Celebrating grants them that reprieve."

Reprieve.

"You do not think he'll stay true to his word?" I asked what she'd already made clear. "He agreed to end the attacks, the bloodshed, only if I marry him." I made sure those last words registered, hit their mark.

They did, my mother's hands stilling over a flower made from ribbon. She swallowed, and the hairs upon my arms rose as I watched her busy herself with the baskets of tools by the wall.

"I know," I said, gentle and careful. "I know this must be hard."

"Hard," she said as though I knew nothing, and she would be right in assuming so. "You do not know the meaning."

"I have spent weeks away from here." I blinked at my own audacity, the firm tone I'd taken.

Linka appeared in the doorway, a large wad of lavender tulle in her arms, and paused. Her eyes gave away nothing, and she flitted to one of the two long desks, placing the fabric on a cleared space at the end.

I continued. "For countless days and nights, I have endured and survived and hoped to be the salvation you and father said I would be for this family. No, I haven't provided you with another heir, but I've still helped. I've made this happen. Do not let my efforts be in vain."

Linka made a noise, a snort perhaps.

I ignored her, kept my eyes trained on my mother's back as she drifted to the window, her fingers at her lips. "Do not speak of him."

"Father?"

Her entire body visibly coiled, and she hissed. "*Don't,* and do not stand there and try to make me feel guilty for all you have done while I've been here, doing nothing."

"You've been grieving," I said. "While also keeping this kingdom from the brink of collapse."

She turned from the window, her hand falling to her orange skirts, the sunlight catching the beading on her matching corset and sending orbs over the white walls. "Have you lain with him?"

Shocked, I stepped back. I could not answer.

She knew. She already knew. As did the female behind her, who pretended to be busy with tidying the desk.

They both knew. But they did not want to know. So I gave them what they wanted, what they needed, even though they were painfully aware it was nothing but a pretty rotten lie and shook my head.

"Right." My mother's chin rose. "Because to find yourself actually caring for the savage who destroyed our family would mean the end of the Gracewood line."

My blood curdled into poison that tainted each breath I tried to keep steady, but I held her gaze. I held it while two warring entities inside me threatened to send me to my knees—guilt for lying about Dade, therefore belittling and reducing all we'd become, and guilt for having done any of it at all.

Linka eyed me pointedly from across the room, and I eyed her back, unflinching. She tilted her nose toward the ceiling and turned away.

Back in my rooms, I found a king perched upon my window, seemingly flummoxed by the sights of the city. "Well, my beautiful

278 | ELLA FIELDS

swan, I don't know about you, but I'm beginning to think that mother of yours has spread the good word."

I placed the pitcher of freshly squeezed orange juice on the dressing table and poured us each a cupful. "I know."

"Everyone's together, their happiness brightening the fragile beauty of this land…"

The word fragile rankled, and I suspected there was more to what he was hedging at. I elected to put us both out of our misery rather than play. "And your thoughts on this are?"

He finally looked at me then, and that burn returned with a vengeance with one slow, deliberate sweep of those eyes. "That she wants us confused."

I offered him the glass of juice. Though I was inclined to agree, I still asked, "Why would you think that?"

"Because we are," he said softly, taking the beverage from my hand. "Thank you."

He drained half, then rose and set it down by the pitcher before collecting me into his arms. "I've missed you."

"It's been mere hours," I pointed out, yet I couldn't help but smile as I rubbed my face into his clean shirt. He must have warped back to his rooms. That or he purchased a new one. It reminded me of an important detail I hadn't overlooked. "There is a dress for me and no clothing for you."

"That makes perfect sense." He didn't elaborate when I looked up at him. Fingertips soft at my chin, he tilted it back for his mouth to ravage mine.

I broke away after a sweltering moment, my voice breathy. "Where did you go?"

"Where haven't I been?" Twirling a lock of my hair around his finger, he smiled at it. A crooked smile that didn't climb and popped just one dimple. "I went to visit a sorceress who stole your blood and handed you no fate."

His lashes lifted toward low brows, and my lips parted. *Of course.*

"You came here," I said, knowing it was true before I'd even pushed the words out. "You came here just to find out your fate?"

"You know what they say." He released my hair, the strands curling through his fingers and back against my chest. "Knowledge is power."

I didn't believe that was the sole reason, not entirely. "What made you visit her?"

Dade lifted a finger, tracing my brow with it, his eyes following his touch all the way down to the corner of my mouth. "Honest answer?"

I shivered. "Always."

A quick, satisfied grin as he noticed. "I wanted to know what most of us wish to," he said quietly. "If there was something else, I suppose."

"Something else?" I repeated, and that finger drifted from my chin to my chest. "Besides revenge, you mean?"

His eyes gleamed before dulling, and he withdrew a step before turning. "Yes." Cold washed in as I watched him walk over to the window, his large form nearly blocking out the sky. "It was that and wanting explanation for the intense attraction. I've heard of it, witnessed it countless times, yet to find myself mated to a Gracewood, a swan..."

"You didn't know that," I said, feeling my brow crinkle. "That I was a swan."

"No," he said, his back still to me. "But I suspected, scented that there was something more to you."

"You were hoping to also glean what that was."

"Indeed." He set something upon the windowsill. "I believe this belongs to you."

A strip of parchment. I hurried over, unraveling it and finding...

"Nothing," I said, then frowned up at him. "She gave you a blank piece of parchment?"

Dade's mouth curved. "Breathe over it."

Still frowning, I slowly peeled my eyes from his and did as he said.

Gold dust fluttered into the room, sprinkling over my fingers at the edges of the parchment and onto the floor. One golden line at a time, the words appeared in a cursive so thick, I could barely make out what was written.

Dade read the words, low and as though he'd memorized them already. "When feather meets fire, vengeance will expire."

"You received the same one?" I was about to ask him where it was when the parchment caught fire then disintegrated, falling in curls of black ash to the stone floor. "Did you know mine would say that?"

"No," he said, bending down to swipe his fingers over the ash. It danced into nothing at his touch, and he brushed his hand over his pants as he rose. "But I had a feeling it might."

His tunic sleeve slipped over his wrist as he straightened. I didn't miss the tinge of brown upon his skin, and grabbed him.

He didn't stop me as I folded the loose sleeve back and turned his hand, checking him for injury. I sniffed the air, no other signs of blood anywhere, then asked him, "What's this from?"

He smiled and gently took his limb back, the cotton falling. "I had to climb a trellis." He rolled his eyes. "Or ten, rather, as you lot seem so fond of the nuisance things. One of your feral flowers bit me."

I laughed, then cursed when I noticed the sun dimming to a golden orange.

Dade skimmed his fingers down my cheek, then released a heavy breath and walked by me to the dressing room. "Let's get you ready."

"But what are we going to do with you?" He could wed me wearing his cotton tunic and pants, I supposed, but I had a feeling that was not what he'd have preferred.

I smothered a snort, laughing again when he opened my dressing room door. A shimmering blood-red vest hung inside, a black shirt of rich silk underneath and matching colored dress pants. "My," I laughed out. "You have been busy."

He grinned, broad and smug. "Shall we dance, sunshine?"

My mind raced back to that cave, my heart trembling. Still, I answered, "I thought you'd never ask."

It finally sank in when the wide-open doors of the throne room loomed up ahead. That this was truly happening.

THE SAVAGE & THE SWAN | 281

Dade was already there. After dressing, he'd given me some privacy and time alone with my racing thoughts and heart, saying he'd be fine when wariness clutched at my vocal cords.

I'd already seen his attire, had seen him wearing it, but apprehension had kept me from absorbing it as wholly as I now could. Panic still swam inside my bloodstream, my heart a bell that rang deep and haunting in my ears, but all of it washed away when I saw him standing before the dais.

It wasn't his fitted pants, the vest that sat snug over his sculpted physique, that drew too much breath from me and refused to give it back.

It was his eyes. Radiant, they drank me in as though I were a prized jewel he'd spent his life hunting.

And now, he could officially lay claim to me.

That heated gaze floated from my slippered feet, the tiny bows upon the toes catching the lace of the matching cream gown I'd chosen over the ruffled mess my mother had selected for me. A tiny rebellion, maybe, but if I was really doing this, if this was actually happening, then it would happen in a dress I'd chosen for myself—one that made me feel more like myself.

Small, barely detectable until the light caught and revealed them, beads speckled the free-flowing skirts. The bodice was tight but not uncomfortable, silk ribbons crisscrossing over my chest and at my back, and lace belled sleeves cupping my shoulders.

Dade's eyes paused at my hands, which were clasped before me, fingers gently entwined around a cluster of black roses. They then crawled over my chest to my face.

I met his shocked stare, biting back a smile and then remembering I'd brushed red rouge over my lips.

"I did not expect the roses," he murmured in my ear when I reached him, fingers sliding over mine and stealing between them, linking as I stopped before him.

"I did not expect any of this," I surprised us both by saying.

Hesitant, he nodded, his mouth hovering over my cheek. "I will make you happy. This I vow over all else."

And the rough vehemence in those words, in his darkening blue eyes, made it impossible not to believe him.

Footsteps sounded, and I made to take a step back as my mother entered.

Dade's fingers tightened around mine, and I scowled at him, but he wasn't looking at me. Shoulders stiff and high, all affection and heat vanished from his eyes as he surveyed my mother, the closing doors behind her, then the rest of the shadowed room.

Daylight had faded, early evening throwing shades of orange and gold through the two arched windows on the far side of the room. Hydrangeas swayed outside them, their sweet scent unable to mask the tension brewing in the cavernous space.

Mother's eyes, narrowed with enough malice to burn down the sun, slid from Dade to me. "Are you sure you want to do this?" Noticing my gown, she hardened her expression, lips thinning. "Opal," she started, and I lifted my brows, awaiting her disapproval, but she sighed. "You look lovely."

Typically, we'd have someone draw a portrait of a royal couple upon their wedding day, and my heart sank when I realized that would not be the case for us. "Mother," I began, but a low hum entered the room.

The serpent sorceress arrived, tendrils of smoke slithering toward the rafters and a crimson smile brightening those red eyes. "Well, look what we have here."

My mother stayed in the center of the room, her apricot and lavender gown swaying with an unnatural breeze.

Dade's blank expression did not falter, nor his stance, as the sorceress's heeled slippers clicked over the white stone to the small carpet we were standing upon. "A beast and a bird."

"Thank you for coming, Silver."

I was still absorbing the fact that my mother obviously knew the sorceress on a first-name basis when Dade said, "You are to marry us." Not a question but a clipped acknowledgment of her presence.

Silver tore her attention from my mother, her lips curving as she stopped mere feet from us. Her two snakes uncoiled around her arms, writhing. "I did fail to mention that with your little visit earlier, yes." She forced a pout. "My apologies, king."

My mother's eyes flew to Dade, but he paid her no mind.

With a small wink at me, Silver whispered none too quietly, "Fates are funny things. Are they not, my bright flame?"

"You think this is funny?" My mother took a step closer and growled, "Let's get this done with. I want him out of my castle, my city, and our lives."

Silver gave me a feigned look of shock, then turned and spread her fingers toward me, her back to Dade. "Nikaya, darling, how your heart must bleed..." Moving back to face us all, she watched me and Dade, her snakes stilling. "Oh, my." Turning to the windows, she released a cackle that made all of us tense and gape at her back, her red gown scraping over the stone. "She doesn't know."

Dade's jaw clenched, his hand growing hot, too hot, in mine. With his other, he loosened the collar at his neck, and I could feel nearly every muscle straining. He wasn't just on edge, he was holding on to a fraying piece of nothing, and I had a feeling if it weren't for me, his mouth would not be closed.

He was behaving, had leashed himself, for me.

"What are you talking about?" Mother asked vacantly, and I noticed her eyes flick around the room. Indeed, she was impatient. So much so, she seemed to miss the fact that the sorceress was talking about our bond.

Surely, she knew by now. Surely, she was not merely pretending it did not exist.

Not all bonds could be sensed, but she was my mother, not to mention a queen with powers unlike many in our lands.

Silver tilted her head her way, then grinned. "Never mind. We are here to wed these two divine creatures." Sauntering back over, she snatched the roses from my hand, sniffed them, then tossed them to the floor. My eyes narrowed, then bulged as she climbed the dais and seated herself in my father's, now my mother's, throne.

Her red nails tapped over the golden whorled ends of the thick arms. Behind her, the spiraling curls of gold fashioned into sun rays rose as though a second crown to the snakes that circled and then stilled upon her head. "So let us proceed."

A golden priestess typically officiated at weddings, and I'd half expected one to be the witness to our pledge to one another. The serpent sorceress was reserved for nobility—should they request her over the priestess—too great a cost for most common folk to afford. Not to mention intimidating.

I wondered how much coin she'd take home with her after all this was said and done, or if she'd already received payment. The tapping of those nails said it was the latter as her own impatience sparked, her curiosity with this ordeal waning.

It was no wonder my mother was in a mood. It was already shameful enough that she'd agreed to marry her only child to the male who'd caused us such a great deal of suffering, made worse by the fact she'd had to spend good coin we likely did not have.

At last, Dade turned to me. His assessing gaze cooled marginally when I offered a small, tremulous smile, and he took my hands in his.

"Under the sun that is good and golden, under the watchful eye of the awakening stars, I bear witness and approval of a marital bond between King Daden Volkahn, and Princess Opal Gracewood." My heart couldn't keep up with the sudden words, and Dade pulled me a step closer. The sorceress needn't have bothered glancing around the throne room as she said, "If disapproval of this union exists, it must now make itself known or be swallowed by the tides of fate forevermore."

Silence, and then, the shifting of my mother's feet. I didn't look at her, could not bear to see what was surely horror stamped across her face. I kept my eyes on Dade's chest, my lip between my teeth, until the sorceress made us repeat after her.

Dade's voice did not waver, his heartbeat steady and slowing mine with his gentle vow. "For now and forever." Breath burned inside my throat as I allowed myself to meet his eyes—his damp, glistening eyes. "I pledge myself to thee, Opal Gracewood."

Everyone waited as I swallowed and found my voice, choked at first but firm in conviction I hadn't been aware I'd felt until those words passed over my tongue and his eyes held mine. "For now and forever, I pledge myself to thee, Daden Volkahn."

Dade's lashes lowered, creating shadows upon his cheeks as his hands trembled in mine.

The sorceress purred, "You may now seal your eternal promise."

He looked back at me, the water cleared from his eyes, but his delight unmistakable when our bodies closed the gap, joined, and his hands rose to swallow my cheeks.

My eyes slowly closed, anticipation brimming, then flared wide when he whispered over my lips, "I know you think me incapable, but I'm not, and I do." My fingers clenched the fabric of his vest, my eyes searching his as his mouth glossed over mine, his voice nothing but a barely audible breath. "I do love you, Opal Gracewood."

I heard every word, tasted their truth when he cupped the back of my head, tilting it for our mouths to join. They pressed, and they did not retreat, parting and gliding as we sealed our fates in earnest. His free hand roamed to my lower back and tucked me close. So close, but I couldn't get close enough, fisting his clothing and standing upon my toes to sink my fingers into his hair.

It had worked—far better than anything I could have dared hope for.

This king, this savage, wild monster of a king… he loved me. A whispered confession, yes, but it was merely confirmation of a truth I'd already suspected. A truth I'd run to and from for weeks now when I'd seen it growing within his eyes, thickening the air between us, and felt it within every searing touch.

Indeed, it had worked, and now I was thankful for those hands holding me so tight, his mouth bruising on mine, for otherwise, I'd have fallen.

I'd have fallen under the weight of everything I'd done.

I'd created a life with this king of wolves. Tentative, beguiling, aching, and wonderful, but I knew... I couldn't keep it. That we were playing with borrowed time.

But maybe this could work. Maybe I didn't need to forgive him the unforgivable in order to give in to all he made me feel. Maybe we could find a way to make this unforeseen piece of real we'd stumbled into a long-term reality.

I pulled back and sucked in a much-needed breath, my fingers running down his cheek and my forehead upon his. "Dade, we—"

Too late, I'd forgotten while lost in him as I had been countless times before, that my mother and the sorceress were still with us, still watching us...

Now separating us.

"*No,*" I screamed as soldiers poured in through the windows. Soldiers I'd known since before I could utter a word chained my husband in iron before he could drift into smoke and cedar.

The sorceress vanished, leaving my mother standing at the wall with her arms crossed over her chest. "Take it out to the square."

"Mother," I growled, hurrying to the soldiers. "Release him right now."

She ignored me when I repeated myself and ushered them to the doors. Dade laughed low, his head hung at the ground. "Nicely done, Nikaya."

Her teeth snapped. "I learned from the worst."

"Release him. You made a promise." I pushed and shoved at the group of soldiers, but I couldn't get through, and then strong hands pulled me away.

I kicked behind me, twirling to smack Elhn in the cheek. I didn't apologize, nor care for his shocked expression as I hissed, "Don't fucking touch me."

"You are married, are you not?" Mother drawled, nodding at Elhn. "You know where to take her."

"Take me?" I whirled toward her, but Elhn stole my arms from behind before I could shake some sense into her. "You're making a mistake, Mother. A grave mistake."

She paused at the door, Dade now gone, my heart dragging in his absence as the sound of struggle faded in the halls. He could shift. He could still shift and send them all flying, but...

But he was waiting until he was well away from me.

With her back to me, one golden eye peered at me over her shoulder, then she lifted her chin to the windows, the tapestry hanging high upon the walls between them still swaying. "You've accomplished all you set out to do. You saved yourself. You've saved your people. Now, you must ignore whatever guilt you might feel." She waded through the doorway. "Leave the rest to me."

"No, wait," I called, tugging to no avail as another soldier walked into the throne room and helped Elhn remove me from it and to the stairs outside.

My dress ripped under their brutal hold, beneath my frantic feet. I hissed and spat, about to shift when Elhn stopped and murmured, "Princess, please. We only wish to escort you upstairs safely while the savage is transported to the square."

Then they would guard me and ensure I could not escape. I refused, kicking and cursing, making to bite the young soldier's hand, and then the iron chains came out.

Halfway up the spiraling stairs, Elhn gave me a look that said he would use them if I did not comply. I didn't care. Let them tie me up and bound me. I would never forgive her if she killed him, and I would kill anyone who aided her with my bare hands.

My skin trembled with fury, with the shift I couldn't afford to make. Not yet. And if those chains wrapped around me... I wasn't as powerful as Dade nor was I of crimson blood. Even if I could still shift, I was a swan. I wasn't sure I'd be able to escape the shackles.

Inhaling deep through my nose, I forced myself to nod. To comply even though I longed to snatch the chains from his hand and swing them at both of their heads.

*In my rooms*, I told myself. Once I'd been locked within my rooms, I would shift and fly out the window.

Of course, they'd already thought of that, panic freezing every vein and breath as I was hauled higher up the stairs. Higher and higher we climbed until we'd reached the tallest tower in the castle.

My parents' rooms.

I was thrust inside, the door slamming closed behind me, and I knew it was spelled. I could sense it when I stumbled back into the impenetrable wood, so I didn't bother trying to open it.

Gulping in lungfuls of air, I scanned the giant room with its gold and cream furnishings, my father's scent already fading from his side of the bed and the clothes that still hung in the dressing room to my right.

I pushed away the guilt my mother knew I harbored but not for the reasons she assumed and hurried into the bathing room. The window was sealed, bars of iron burning beneath my fingers when I stepped into the tub and pushed with all my might.

Sinking inside the empty bathing pool, I knew the windows and doorway that led to the small balcony outside would be the same. With my gown clenched in my hands, I blinked at the salts and soaps.

She'd locked me away.

She'd taken the king.

My husband. My mate.

All along, I'd feared she'd have a plan. Weeks ago, I'd have even longed for it. For the female I once knew and admired to return from the grief that tried to drown her and take action so I did not have to.

For I was nothing but a naïve coward. A terrified little fool.

And although she had returned, she was not the same. She would never be the same.

Alarm shot through me as I realized I would never be the same if she went through with this. As I imagined Dade being hurled out onto the city streets to be made a violent example of. A fate handed to the worst of criminals.

He would pay for his crimes with a death slow enough to feel each and every one.

*No.* "No, no, no," I whispered, the sound breaking with every fractured breath. "No," I said louder, my hands slapping over my eyes. "I can't. He can't—"

A howl cleaved the air, ear-splitting enough to shake the foundation of the castle—and to shake me out of the suffocating fog of fear I'd let myself stay trapped within.

*Look at me, honey bee.*

I blinked back tears, my head lifting toward the bedroom.

Out. I needed out. Staring back at those salts, I studied them, the lavender and the citrus and the rose...

Tripping on my skirts, I clambered out of the large tub and hurried into the bedroom. There, under my mother's pillow where she'd kept it since the attacks began four years ago, was the dagger my father gave to her. A rare steel that came from an island across the Night Sea.

Supposedly enriched by the sweat and labor and resentment of its maker, a goblin slave, it would cut through anything.

But it would not break through iron.

That was fine. It didn't need to break.

Hurrying to the door, I lowered to the ground some feet away with the blade in my lap and spread my hands upon the stone. I wasn't sure if it would work, and if it did, how long it would last, but I had to try. I had to keep them from hearing what I was about to attempt.

Shouting and screaming echoed from outside, and I closed my eyes, begging, beseeching, coaxing...

*Grow.*

Vines snuck through and unfurled from the crevices in the stone, crawling with alarming speed and growing thicker, leafier, as they slithered up the walls and over the door. I blinked, marveling at the dense green wonder that twirled and danced and gathered. In near silence, the scratch of the occasional thorn the only sound, they curled around the cracks of the door and over every inch of the wood until they barely resembled vines at all, but a hedge. A giant, oblong hedge blocking entry.

Racing to the window, I sank below its edge so as not to be seen. I didn't know how long the barrier would hold if someone entered, perhaps only seconds. I needed longer than seconds, but I grabbed the blade, sawing with both hands and destroying the sharpened edge.

Sweat beaded along my nape, my hairline, and coated my palms, my panic a thrumming hum in my ears. My hand slipped when a crash sounded, loud enough to gather the attention of half the kingdom.

Slowly, I rose, knowing I shouldn't, that I was wasting precious time. That I would only panic more upon seeing Dade being thrown out of the castle gates and into the awaiting swarm of soldiers and citizens beyond.

He faltered, his clothing torn and blood smattering one side of his face, but he did not fall. He launched himself at the incoming weapons.

I closed my eyes and dropped to the floor. "Shit," I cried low. "Shit, shit, *shit.*" My fingers trembled, slid over the leather hilt of the dagger, but I lifted it and kept going.

I couldn't stop. There was nothing left to do but try. Nothing save for waiting and hoping for a fate I knew wouldn't come—a fate I'd never dared hope for.

Until now.

Infused with it, those calculated steps he took as he neared me, my every breath measured and timed, the predatory way he'd tilt his head and study my facial expressions, the movement of my mouth. Those eyes of stormy seas and sun-bright skies—a glimpse at two futures should I have the nerve and heart to decide.

I pushed the blade harder, metal shaving and curling beneath it. My arms ached as I pushed my entire body into each glide and foolishly gripped the bar with one hand while sawing with the other to try to weaken it quicker with magic—with warmth.

After mere moments, my fingers began to pucker. Dropping the dagger, I pulled away, blowing on the small red welts that appeared.

And when I looked at the bent metal in the lowest rung of a

square by the corner of the window, I smiled and pressed my fingers to it. Gritting my teeth against the immediate exposure to the iron, the cold ache that threatened, I willed my blood, my chaotic emotions, to obey and target.

With one shaken exhale, my power unspooled.

It unspooled and raced through every square, dark silver now a molten gold.

A wet laugh escaped, and I kicked at the corner, watched it crack, and kicked again.

Muffled questions at the door sounded, but I was already gone, pushing and kicking until the bolts in the moonstone came loose, and I could bend the metal open enough to squeeze through. My dress snagged and tore, as did my leg, but I didn't have time to pay it any notice when the door to my parents' rooms opened, and Elhn was cursing, slicing his way through the vines.

Behind me at the window within those correctly guessed seconds, he tried to shake the metal loose. He couldn't fit through the gap, and I couldn't wait around to see if he'd manage to haul the entire grate away from the window.

Upon the balcony, my blistered hands pressing into the moonstone wall, I tried to find Dade but could no longer see him amongst the herd moving in a slow line toward the market square.

My hair flew around my face, city-dwellers stopping with their daily business and closing up shop or following the commotion.

They'd known we were getting married.

Had they known my mother would try to kill my husband?

I supposed many of them had hoped for something like this, and I couldn't blame them. I'd once hoped for his demise too.

Dade roared, soldiers flying and landing on rooftops and awnings and the hard ground as the crowd moved back a step.

He was still chained, but the king was no longer there. In his place was a giant, white-winged wolf, horns flicking a sword skyward when a daring soldier leaped forward.

I wasn't sure what they were trying to do exactly. They were to capture and eventually kill him, I knew that much, but they were stalling, dodging deadly blows of his claws and teeth and those horns.

"Princess." Elhn grabbed at a piece of my dress, tugging hard back toward the window.

I ignored him while looking him dead in the eye, and then allowed my blood to boil beyond return. Beak first, I plummeted from the wall toward the gardens, the muscle in my still-healing wings stiff and sore as I lifted them and twisted toward the nearest rooftop.

A whistle pierced, followed by, "A black swan!"

I kept low, unsure what I'd do once I'd reached him, and wove between moss-shrouded rooftops, chimneys puffing merrily in many as though there wasn't a notorious wolf king within our midst.

I'd need to make a stand long enough for him to get away, but already, the eyes of those surrounding him were slowly turning toward the sky. I banked, sank low to fly around a half-emptied cart. A young boy seated upon the back waved a little gold and red flag while his father watched the commotion from the edge of the alleyway.

The male grunted and turned in a swift circle when my wings brushed him, the little boy laughing and pointing as I flew out into the street, rose over the many heads, and then squeaked as an arrow flew right at my chest.

I dropped, and it skimmed the feathers upon my back, soldiers torn between gazing at a nearing large black swan or the monstrous animal they'd surrounded to prod at like the wild beast he was.

Murmurings of, "Swan," and "Stars," and "Should we kill it?" came to me upon the breeze.

Before they could make a decision, the beast whirled, his large eyes pinned on me. A vicious snarl, an unmistakable warning for me to leave, ruptured the air.

He knew I would do no such thing. I flapped my wings, soaring high toward the nearest building where I could wait and scan the ground surrounding my wolf for a place to land while Elhn hurried downhill to inform them not to kill me.

He was fast—I'd give him that much—but not fast enough as

carriages ambled out of the chaos-strewn streets, seeking shelter, and people did, too. Dodging and circling and running again, Elhn grew larger the closer he came.

I wondered if he'd had time to inform Mother dearest.

A cry dragged my attention back to Dade, who had a male pinned underneath him. Twenty or more soldiers advanced, swords bared, some slicing. Horror struck me cold when one of them made contact and sank into his hind leg.

Dade whined then roared, spinning and throwing half of the soldiers to the ground with one swipe of his paw. Still, they came, the waiting game apparently over, weapons raised, arrows flying and skidding over his wings and fur when he ducked and lunged sideways.

I rose, wings rustling, spreading open either side of me, and waddled toward the edge of the roof. He wasn't fighting to kill.

Again and again, blades sliced pieces of fur from his side, sank into his flesh before he knocked them away, and he could have destroyed them. He might have died trying, but he'd kill a great many of our soldiers before that happened.

But it wouldn't happen. It couldn't.

*It would*, a nudge to my gut insisted.

It would because he was refusing to kill any who came at him.

Elhn closed in, hollering between cupped hands, "Princess, you must leave. Now."

I nearly laughed, but the edged tone of his voice stopped me. I looked at him, noticed his gaze swing from me to the sky, and then I looked down to the square at Dade.

His teeth were bared, a low growl rumbling as soldiers peeled themselves away, one being dragged by his comrade, his leg bent at a disturbing angle.

They were retreating. Why were they retreating?

I looked back at Elhn. He pushed through the throng, talking in a rush, and a few soldiers glanced up.

I did, too, and then I gasped and leaped.

I plummeted toward the square with everything in me at a speed

294 | ELLA FIELDS

I'd never flown before—fast enough that when I landed, I would break something. Likely many somethings.

Dade whined, shifting to take the brunt of my impact, and I bounced into him.

I shook my head, dizzy and fluttering against his side to my feet as a giant ball, clear enough to live in the sky and never be noticed, finished falling.

And engulfed us both.

# THIRTY

*Opal*

"**W**E'VE GOT HIM THIS TIME," CAME FROM ONE OF THE soldiers who spat at us.

His saliva hit the orb, sliding down it as though it were a sheet of clear glass. I knew without touching it that it wasn't. It hummed with a power I couldn't name or recognize.

*This time.*

The blood on Dade's wrist.

He'd said nothing had happened—hadn't wanted to alarm me by stating someone had tried something. I turned to look up at the beast beside me, who lowered onto his stomach, bleeding in varying places yet gazing at me as though he were worried I'd injured myself.

"You fucking moron," Elhn said, pushing to the front of the crowd and staring at the orb in evident dismay. His eyes closed, and he cursed, shoving at the male next to him. "Clean that filth off before her majesty arrives."

The soldier frowned, as did some of the others, shifting on their feet. A few were bleeding in places, others howling in pain beneath the awning of the most popular bakery in the city. I couldn't see them to gauge how injured they were, and I didn't care.

I stuck my beak in the air when the soldier said, "Are you a traitor, captain? I'll spit at the monster if I so please."

"In case you haven't noticed, *dipshit*," Elhn growled into his face
and stabbed a finger our way, "there is also a swan in there."

"So what?" the ignorant ass said. Meanwhile, various sets of eyes
widened around him. Perhaps they knew of our history enough to
know or remember that although one of my kind had not been seen
in a long time, every single one of us had been a Gracewood royal.

"The princess," Rodney, a soldier five years my senior who'd
sometimes brought me fresh seedlings when he visited the Spring
Forest, said upon a rushed breath. I stared at him, seeing no point in
doing otherwise. It wasn't like I could talk to refute it, and if I shifted
back, they'd know for certain. "It is her," he said, blinking.

The male who'd spat at us cursed, then raced forward, studying
me through the orb. "But it's just a swan." Giant dark brown eyes widened and blinked. "A huge fucking swan, but still a swan."

I honked, and he flinched, rousing laughter from the soldiers
who'd tried to hurt Dade just moments before.

The king grumbled behind me, then pawed me back closer to his
side even though no one could touch me if they dared. My webbed
feet tangled in the chains he'd snapped free from, and he flicked them
at the clear barrier. It hissed, and I stared as the iron began to melt.

There was a collection of curses as the soldiers noticed, and then
there was shrieking, the male quickly swiping away his saliva as my
mother arrived. The orb zapped him, and his hair rose high on his
head. He yelped, snatching his hand back and putting a healthy distance between us as he slunk between his brethren.

"Move," my mother shouted, the soldiers all parting as she raced
toward me, and her hand rose to her mouth. My heart sank with her
knees as she stopped before the orb…

And screamed.

The silence that followed her ear-shredding agony was nearly as
deafening. Dade grunted, tense next to me, and I felt my chest hollow
with dread at the fear shining in her eyes. I tried to shift back.

I couldn't.

Moving as close as she could get, the wind knocking her hon-eyed hair back from her shoulders to reveal the entirety of her stricken expression, my mother reached out as though she'd place her hand upon the orb.

It hummed with the approaching warmth as though calling to it, and she lowered her hand. "What have you done?" she cried. "Oh, stars, Opal, *what have you done?*"

Dade growled when Deandra approached, sword raised as though she'd slice through the orb. His feathered wing hauled me closer, nearly shielding all of me. I swung my neck around, but his gaze moved between the female soldier and the queen, muscles flexing and tensing behind me.

I couldn't answer her. I couldn't shift. I could only nudge the feathers of Dade's wings from shielding my view and stare back at her.

The soldiers at her back stayed quiet, watching, awaiting orders. Yet her attention stayed fixed on me and the wolf she'd trapped. It seemed to settle in her then, her face falling. Her mouth trembled as she released a resigned breath. "Fetch Silver," she said, then repeated herself, her voice raised. "Someone fetch the sorceress now."

As a small group peeled and raced away, we continued to stare. My heart thundered. The warmth of the bubble surrounding us seemed to increase with each passing minute.

Silver arrived, wreathed in snake-like shadows that evaporated right before the fifty-odd soldiers. The males and females eyed her as she neared, that serpentine smile in place.

Eyes glued themselves to the snakes twining around her upper arms, some daring enough to drift over her lithe, supple frame outlined by a tight long gown of glittering rubies.

She tutted. "Oh, Nikaya." A pleasure-roughened groan accompanied her next words. "This is too good." Her hands rubbed together, the glee in her voice evident in those red eyes. "My stars, just look at them." Stopping before the orb, she dragged a fingernail down it. Nothing happened. No charge. No recoil. "Aren't they quite the pair?"

The gown bent with her like water over a rock as she crouched, whispering, "Yes, quite the mated pair."

My mother's eyes shuttered, then reopened on the sorceress as she rose to her feet. "Fix it." Silver's eyes flashed, and my mother urged, "*Please.*"

"You asked me for an impenetrable cage for a beast." She sketched a hand our way. "So that is what I gave you."

"There has to be a way out."

Silver's smirk made Dade stiffen. "There's always a way out." Floating closer to my mother, she brushed some of her golden hair over her shoulder, her smirk falling while a long crimson nail traced my mother's cheek and jaw. Her voice melted into a softer tone I'd have never thought the overconfident sorceress capable of. "And as we already know, it will always cost you something priceless."

My mother's wet eyes flared wide when Silver said quietly, "I'm all out of favors now, my love."

Watching them, something murky began to clear, but then she was gone, my mother left snarling at fading dark air.

Her hands swept into her hair. "Shit." Elhn wisely told the soldiers to back up, allowing her a modicum of privacy. "That fucking female and her fucking riddles."

Dade huffed, and I swung a glare at him that said this wasn't funny. Not in the slightest. He merely yawned, and I felt my eyes grow huge at the sight of all those too long, too sharp teeth.

He licked his lips, then sniffed and smiled with his eyes.

I had no idea how he could remain so calm, how he could find any shred of humor in this situation. Then I remembered he'd been subjected to worse. He'd been on battlefield after battlefield. He'd been raised and conditioned for violence and brutality.

Which was why we were here, trapped and beholden to a riddle-loving sorceress and a queen out for revenge.

I shifted on my feet, swinging my neck downhill to where Silver's lair was.

*When feather meets fire, vengeance will expire.*

My mother called my name, and I turned back. "Listen to me carefully, okay?"

I had no place else to be. She knew I could understand her just fine from the many times she'd chased me around the castle when I'd accidentally shifted as a youngling and couldn't figure out how to shift back.

"Yes," she said, and a bead of water slid down her cheek as though she was remembering those times too. The times when my father would pretend I wasn't what I was, but my mother would scoop me up by my webbed feet, hang me upside down, and deliver me to my rooms where she'd read me stories until I'd settled enough to change back. "Just like then, we need to do this together."

I blinked. We couldn't do a thing together. Not only because I was in here and she was out there, but because we were now enemies.

She'd sought to kill my mate all the while knowing how it would kill me—for that same pain was clearly still far too fresh for her.

"Together," she whispered. "Don't be afraid."

I wasn't afraid of the orb. I was afraid of what she'd do to my husband once we were freed. And so I shook my head.

Dade huffed, nostrils wider than my head flaring as he curled into me and stared me down.

I glared. *No.*

*Yes.*

*You know what they'll do.*

He inclined his head as though it wasn't a big deal, eyes narrowing with impatience.

"Opal," my mother said. "Opal, look at me."

I did, reluctantly, and she smiled, silent tears dripping down her face. "I promise. He will be free to leave."

I stiffened, knowing she spoke true but still wary.

Dade's wing lifted as though he believed her, telling me I should too.

I stared at her, and she stared back with glistening eyes. Mine did the same when she said, "I'm sorry." Swiping beneath her nose, she whispered, "I didn't want to believe it. That you two had…" She shook her head, finally saying, "That you had bonded. If I didn't know, if I didn't believe it, then I could go through with what my aching soul hungers for." I waited as she peered at the king. "Vengeance."

I knew without looking that he held her gaze, for when she looked back at me, her eyes were no longer wet but determined, her jaw gritted. "But I can't do it. I thought I could, but I cannot put you through this pain, and though I had to try, Opal, *I had to*… I am sorry that I did."

I edged forward, and she placed her hand upon the orb, warmth sizzling from underneath it.

Her teeth clenched. Her hair began to rise. But I knew before she gestured with her free hand what I had to do.

I pressed the tip of my wing upon the orb, right over her palm, and I nodded. A crack echoed, slicing into my skull, my bones, as I flickered between forms. "I'm sorry," she said again, terror in her voice now. "Return to me, please."

It felt like pushing from the deepest depths of the ocean, crawling back into myself. My heart thrashed, and my sight dimmed and blackened. The orb cracked again. Dade's heat became firmer at my back as though he'd changed back already. Emboldened, I unraveled, each breath stuck and uncatchable until…

I panted on my knees. "Okay."

The ball fractured under our touch, rivers of gold striking through the clear orb in fast succession. We all gazed up, and Dade gathered me to his chest right as it exploded. As clear and sharp as glass, fragments rained over us, cutting and clinking as they hit the cobblestone.

When it ended, I twisted to inspect Dade, noting a cut at his mouth and eye, my hands patting down his stiff arms…

Then the screaming registered, my mother already on her feet as the war bell chimed from the castle.

A collection of howls, ferocious and haunting, was the only warning we had before beasts, some winged, all wolven, split through every alleyway.

The cavalry had arrived, and with it, another fracture large enough to slice me in two.

Only this time, it was not an orb but my heart.

Dade grabbed for me, a dagger in his hand he hadn't used earlier, and pushed me behind his back. "I'll call them off."

He'd... but they were already shedding blood. With claws and teeth and strength and numbers that were no match for our own, they attacked.

My mother stood frozen beside me, her wide eyes drinking it all in, then Elhn approached, barking orders for us to move, and she turned to grab my hand. "Inside the bakery."

I followed, floating upon the shock that seared its way through me, laying waste to every hushed word and bruising memory.

*He'd lied.*

He'd lied, he'd lied, he'd lied.

He'd looked me dead in the eye and lied through his razor-sharp teeth when he'd promised that he would come alone, when he'd promised that he would behave and that my people would be safe. When he'd promised the bloodshed would end.

I'd believed him. I'd believed in him. I'd believed that he'd changed, and that he'd finally begun to learn—to understand.

I'd been a fool to believe a wolf would ever be anything but a wolf.

When we reached the bakery, Elhn ushered us inside, and I slipped past him as he pulled the door closed. He reached for me, but I was already gone. A sword laid beside a fallen soldier, her eyes staring up at the sky as she bled from her mouth and a wound in her stomach.

I bent down, holding my hands over her stomach, warmth flooding and flowing through me, closing it but not fast enough. The female's red-brown eyes slid from the sky to mine, her mouth forming words I couldn't hear over the roaring and screaming and terror that had been unleashed upon my city. "Stop him."

Stop him. Don't save her. Stop him.

She was right. He'd said he'd call them off, but I'd made the mistake in believing he'd protect my heart once.

I refused to be so stupid ever again.

Gritting my teeth, I forced more of my energy inside that wound, and then I gathered her hands and pushed them over it. "Keep them there and don't move." She blinked, and I raised my brows. "That's an order."

I took her sword and slunk around two crimson and gold males, a battle axe meeting a broadsword and nearly cutting the steel in half by my head.

I didn't look to see if I recognized them. I couldn't. I kept moving, dodging running citizens, pushing by a cart that'd been deserted a little ways up the slow-sloping hill.

"Opal."

I stopped at the sound of his voice and looked up.

There, atop the rooftop nearest me, landed the king of wolves, the blood king, the murderous thief of my heart. He eyed my stolen sword, then said, "Duck," as a boulder sailed over my head, flying through the shop window behind me.

Glass crashed and tinkled, and then two males stumbled to the ground, weapons gone, fists and teeth bared. "Enough," Dade thundered.

The male halted, holding the gold soldier at bay as he swung blindly up at him from the ground.

Dade's gaze fell upon me, heavy and searching. I gave him nothing but ire in return. He stiffened.

He knew exactly what he'd done. But rather than waste time and piss me off more, he thrust his fingers between his lips, whistling four times. "Lower your weapons and retract your claws." He then hollered through cupped hands, "Fall in line to return home."

Elhn was marching up the street, heading straight for us. Confusion crumpled his features, and blood leaked from his nose as he gazed upon our soldiers. Some continued to lunge and strike at the crimson legions, while others stepped back, baffled and glancing around while the warriors slowly fell into two long, even lines.

Elhn ordered our soldiers who would not relent to cease fighting, barking their names as though he'd personally kill them himself if they disobeyed.

Dropping the sword, I fell back against the door as Dade landed before me and stalked forward. "Swan, you must understand—"

"That you lied to me?" I laughed, the sound cracking. "Oh, I understand that perfectly fine, asshole."

He grimaced, dragging a bloodied hand through his hair, red streaking the blond. Someone called him, and he threw a look at his gathered wolf packs over his shoulder, then stared back at me. "I'm sorry, okay? But I knew this would happen."

"So tell me that," I said, each word scalding, hissing through my teeth. "Tell me, talk to me rather than lie to me."

He stopped advancing three perilous steps from me. The breeze swept some of that soft hair over his forehead, his eyes a rival to the darkness that had invaded the sky. "Would you have listened?"

Stunned, I flattened the palms of my hands against the door at my back.

Would I have? I would've liked to think that yes, I would have, but this... what we had become multiplied daily, and I couldn't keep up. I'd humored him, fallen for him while doing so, while trying to make a difference, but I'd never wholly trusted him.

We both knew that.

His name was called once more, but he did not acknowledge whoever it was.

"I guess we'll never know." Eyes, too many, were upon us, but that didn't stop me from saying on a burning breath, "All I know is that I'll never listen to another word you say." The moans of the wounded, the shrieking of crows coming for the dead, slithered inside this new bubble of our own making.

His face fell and paled, his hand trembled as he took a step forward and reached out as though he'd touch me. "You don't truly mean that." He blinked as though suddenly unsure and stopped toe to toe with me. "Do you?"

"Don't," I warned. Knocking his hand away, I whispered, "Leave, and take with you the knowledge that I lied too, and that I *never* wanted this." I dragged my eyes from his mouth as it opened and met his narrowed gaze. "You needed to be stopped. Someone had to stop you." I lifted a shoulder as though I cared nothing for everything we'd been and all we could've been when I cared far too much. "So that's what I did."

Dade studied me, rage unfolding, sharpening and twisting each feature. It oozed from his pores and rolled off his skin. I'd witnessed him angered, though I'd never felt it quite that potently before, as though I were standing too close to a fire and starting to sweat.

The need to soothe and mollify itched at my clammy skin like a rash I wished I could scrape from my body, and I tucked my hands behind me, pulling back my shoulders.

As though sensing that, Dade's head tilted. He sniffed, a cruel smile lighting his eyes. "While that may be so, this"—those eyes wouldn't release mine as he pointed at my breasts—"that racing organ in your chest says you might have completed your mission but lost more than you'd bargained for, *sunshine.*"

"Leave," I gritted.

His smile slipped into a slight sneer. "Gladly."

Within minutes, they were clearing out of the city, our soldiers watching on in dismay.

I waited until he'd turned away before unleashing one loaded breath after another, my chest tight and aching no matter how much I tried to control each one.

I waited until his warriors had disappeared through the entrance to the city before falling back inside the empty store and to the glass-flecked ground.

# THIRTY-ONE

*Dade*

**V**ENOM COURSED THROUGH MY VEINS WITH EACH STEP AWAY from the moonstone fortress that held my crushed heart.

A game. I was but a leading piece in this game called war, and though my swan might have thought she'd played me well, it was I who'd decided I'd be used.

Her actions, her warring emotions, and those fucking eyes gave her away at every turn. I'd wanted her—a want so dire, so depthless and insatiable, that I'd accepted the role she'd thought she must play.

For I knew underneath that false bravado lurked my mate, a bond that suffocated all else. A tether of the soul that would outshine her ire and conflicted feelings until they were but a dim shadow I could erase with time.

She must have thought me no better than a brainless beast prone and often lost to baser desires, hungry for nothing more than her warm blood and body. At times, I was. Most certainly.

But not always.

That didn't stop her parting words from doing the damage she'd intended. The hatred brimming those golden eyes, the disgust, not wholly with me but with herself, weighing each breath and step and staining the imagery of rolling green hills, the fields of lavender cutting through them, with darkness.

All too soon, we entered the forest we'd marched through and flown above a handful of times before. All thanks to my swan showing me the last remaining bridge, the hidden hollowed tree, upon which we'd first met.

Legion three had flown ahead, now nothing but dark patches swallowed by the starlit clouds atop the woods across the ravine. I'd chosen to walk. There was little point in making a hasty arrival home when that home would now feel like the tomb it had always been.

Without her, it was just a Keep, just a palace to house ghosts and monsters.

Legion two chatted amongst themselves, quiet for the most part as they tried to make sense of all that had just happened, and Fang doubled back to walk beside me now and then. He knew when to keep his mouth shut and wisely did not open it as we meandered through the trees toward the low-lying cave.

Entering that cave, spying the space in which I'd laid over her and felt my soul connect with hers, was akin to taking a blade to my own chest and swallowing fire.

"Dade," Fang called, and I hadn't realized I'd stopped moving.

I hadn't realized everyone had left the cave, crossed through the aged trunk and over the ravine to Vordane.

Shaking my head, I prowled past him, deeper into the cave until the hollowed insides of the dead tree appeared.

Fang's boots crunched behind me over the dirt. "You, ah, do you want to talk—"

"No," I snapped, then stilled. Low, almost undetectable but growing in volume, howls entered the trunk.

We raced to the hole, climbed through, and while Fang took to the steep edge of the ravine to scale up the dirt and rock-packed wall, I shifted and shot into the air.

A myriad of violent curses flooded my head. Of course, they

would. While I was gone. When they'd discovered over half of my best warriors were absent, too.

More calls sounded from the south, and I flew over the ravine until it spread into a river, then veered west, the wind a roar that threatened to overpower the ones sailing from there. I soared straight up the cliffside to the trees and shifted as soon as my paws slammed into the earth. I'd barely drawn breath before I warped to the other side of the forest bordering the river.

The first village I saw upon welcoming back my beast was lit up—burning.

The winged legion were almost there, having heard the calls for help far before us, and I willed myself to fly harder, faster, my bones rattling with the force of the wind pushing back against me, tearing at my fur.

A snarl was swallowed by the night as I realized just how well I could be played after all.

And now, it was my people who would pay the price for my arrogance.

Fire raged from cottages and treetops, warriors clashing upon the ground. Up ahead, as though someone was merely lighting a collection of candles—fire followed fire, a burning trail heading straight for the city and all its hundreds of occupants.

On the ground, his smug demeanor unmistakable as he gave orders to his generals, to the men stealing females and children from their homes and tossing them toward what looked to be a pen used for livestock, stood the filthy human prince.

# THIRTY-TWO

## *Opal*

L INKA TAPPED ON THE BATHING ROOM DOOR. "PRINCESS, IS everything okay in there?"

I sank deeper into the cooling water and closed my eyes. No. Nothing was okay in here or anywhere. "Fine," I said and waited for her to enter, to offer me one of her feline smiles and a cloth to dry myself with.

There was only silence, and then the sound of her gentle retreating footsteps.

I could empathize with her anger toward me, but that didn't mean I would chase after her and try to force her into empathizing with me. I hadn't the energy nor the space in my bruised heart to fix anything when everything felt so irreparably... shattered.

This marriage was supposed to fix things. It was supposed to help us all come together. It was supposed to save and unite us—regardless of what it might have done to my heart.

But now he was gone.

My husband. My enemy. My unforeseen tragedy.

When I finally reentered my rooms, I eyed my wardrobe, the many gowns and nightgowns. Longing to create something more versatile, comfortable, I dressed in a pair of old leggings and a berry-colored shirt. In gentle pleats, the cotton fell from my breasts to my upper thighs, its capped satin sleeves puffy but not irritating when I turned my head over my shoulder upon hearing a creak.

My mother sat on the bed, her fingers clasped in her lap and her sharp eyes staring through the window.

The same window the king had sat by while studying the gardens and lost to his own thoughts.

The words left me without warning. "Why did you even bother allowing us to marry?"

Without averting her focus, as though she wasn't really looking at anything, she said in a quiet voice, "I did not intend for you to marry him." I walked closer, leaning against the bookshelves. "We just couldn't catch him unawares until then."

"So you admit to trying," I stated, then chewed my bottom lip when it wobbled. He never said anything. He did not warn me nor tell the truth when I'd discovered he'd been bleeding. I could add that lie to his list of atrocities, but I knew he hadn't done so out of malice or to protect himself.

He'd lied to protect me and the love I had for my mother.

"Your desire to see him punished was stronger than our family's fear of the stupid prophecy." I nearly laughed at the heartbreaking absurdity of it all. "So strong that I now carry his family name instead of ours."

She did not answer, there was no need, but she turned on the bed and patted the space beside her. "Come sit with me." I didn't move, and she looked up at me. "Please, we are running out of time."

"Time?" I moved then and hurried to take a seat beside her. "What do you mean? It's done."

She noticed the space I'd left between us, offering a sad smile as she gathered my hand in both of hers. "You must understand, Opal. We saw an opportunity, and we took it."

My mouth dried, giving bite to my voice. "An opportunity for what?"

"The human royals came through on their promise, though I do

not know if it is to help themselves or us. They've curated an army."
She nodded as my eyes widened. "They are already here."

"Here," I repeated, but there was no attack, none that I'd heard
of, save for that on the king…

My heart sank to my toes, launching me to my feet.

"They march on Vordane." Though her words shook, her chin
rose slightly. "The crimson king has been our enemy long enough that
it would make me a fool to believe he'd arrive without an entourage,
hidden or in plain sight."

A fool, she'd said. *Or in love*, her eyes said when mine closed, my
stupidity suffocating me once more.

Her voice softened. "We will gorge ourselves on lies to keep the
magic that is love."

*No.*

But my eyes reopened with a start. "Stars," I choked out. "What
have you done?" I raced to the window as if I could see the carnage,
but there was only star-painted dark skies, quiet city streets, and the
chatter of wildlife and flora upon the breeze.

But *there*, beneath it all, slight notes of ash could be detected.

I should've known. I should've known, yet I wouldn't have
thought she'd go this far. "You knew," I hissed, glaring at her over my
shoulder. "You knew he'd bring his legions, leaving the rest of Vordane
with little protection against an attack."

Tears glossed her eyes. "At the time, I wasn't aware that you two
had…" Again, her head shook. "I am still shocked, honestly, and I
won't say that I am happy." Looking me in the eye, she said with too
much calm, "I hate it for you, for us, for our entire family, but it cannot be changed, and so now I am torn between what is right for you
and what is right for our people."

"Our people?" I nearly shouted. "*We* started this. Your father
started this by killing his parents, and for what?" A crazed laugh left
me. "Because they were scared of those more powerful than them."

"Althon," she croaked out. "Your father slayed Dade's—he killed
Vern Volkahn." My head spun and spun as I tried to recall a time when

Dade had told me so. He never had. "Vern was wild with rage," she whispered, gaze unseeing as if she were back there amongst the start of it all. "My father." Her lips pressed tight, then released with a wet sigh. "My father had just killed his mate, and we knew he'd never stop. He'd never rest until every last one of us paid the price for what my father stole in a fit of anger."

My blood, my bones, chilled. "*Why?*"

"They were worried," she said, though her words were weak. "They were intimidated. My father more than anyone else, but it was his ego—bruised with embarrassment from Vern and Maya's refusal to submit to his terms—that ended Maya's life. He was never supposed to kill either of them." She spoke softer, lost to the past. "No one was supposed to die. He was a fool, and it cost him his life as well as that of my mother and my son."

"Vern Volkahn killed Joon?"

"No," my mother rasped. "Joon died from a fatal chest wound while in battle, and your grandfather while trying to protect him when he fell. I left your father's side and dragged Joon as far away from the carnage as possible to try to save him." She inhaled a shaken breath. "But Althon knew what must be done, that Vern had to be stopped, so he and our best soldiers cornered him so he could put the beast down. My mother," she exhaled, "she passed from grief not two months after."

"This is..." I shook my head. "All this heartbreak, and all because they were worried?"

"They were given information. That the king and queen's babe, Dade Volkahn, would be the end to the—"

"To the Gracewood line," I spoke over her, cutting her off. "Believe me, I know, but all these prophecies could mean anything." I released a flat, humorless laugh. "Such extremes, and it came to pass anyway."

She said nothing to that and sniffed, rising from the bed. "You love him." Not a question.

I was tempted to refute it, to say I did not harbor any such feelings, but this pit of fear that'd yawned open inside me, that threatened to pull me under and swallow me until nothing but bleak darkness remained said otherwise.

I averted my eyes and clambered onto the window sill. "I need to go."

"Opal," she cried when she realized what I was about to do. "It's probably too late."

"We don't know that." I refused to believe that.

Her scream followed me as I dropped from the window into a swan. My wings flared feet from the ground, and I swooped between the trees in the gardens below, then startled.

Hidden in the darkness of a maple tree, a flash of red burned through shadow.

Silver nodded when I turned and landed before her. "You should hurry," she said, her snakes still, so still, coiled around her shoulders as I shifted back. "I've got her."

My mother's sobs could be heard from my rooms, and I glanced back, knowing I'd have to leave her regardless, but... "You," I said, a little breathless. "You were before... her another."

Silver's eyes narrowed. "Another?" I nodded, knowing I wasn't making much sense but I was right. Her upper lip peeled back, but her eyes flicked up to the windows. "I am no one's *another*, and that was the problem."

No, I couldn't imagine this female being anything but someone's sole reason for breathing. Still, it remained. Whatever it was that her and my mother shared before my father came to Gracewood hadn't left the sorceress.

Perhaps not even for a moment, as she confirmed, "Why do you think I remain in this stars-forsaken place when everyone thinks me a fate dealer of darkness?" She scoffed. "My gifts would not only be appreciated but revered elsewhere."

"Yet you stay," I said softly.

Her shoulders fell, and she sighed, gazing back at me. A heavy breeze rolled in, gathering my hair and bringing with it the scent of smoke and uncertainty but leaving the sorceress untouched. "Fly, my bright flame. The winds of fate wait for no bird, no matter how rare."

Then she was gone, her words enough to have me shifting and shooting straight for the skies.

Hours crawled by while I wished for the ability to warp.

Treetops swayed, ash dancing above them, embers threatening to cross the river near the remnants of Old Bridge to create more carnage in Sinshell.

I continued southwest, spearing to the left to hide above the smoke-filled forest. My eyes watered miles from the first river village before it fully came into view. Black as night and red as deep as the setting summer sun, fire engulfed cottages and barns and small buildings.

I couldn't see Dade. I could hardly see anything through the haze of smoke. A roar came from the north, and I dipped lower toward the trees as varying colored dots soon grew into fast-flying beasts.

Help had arrived, but the legion without the ability to fly... it would take over a day for them to get here, and that was if they did not stop running.

Fury swept through me, pushing me harder as I followed the wolves in the sky. Half of them dropped to the ground at the village, immediately falling into battle with human soldiers, soldiers who appeared to be heavily armored in head-to-toe metal.

The other half followed the flames to the next village, to the farmland that resided just outside the city.

Livestock moaned and scattered, and I chanced a look behind me. Pens. They were herding the females and their young into livestock pens—much like the king of wolves and his warriors had done.

Only, they were not released nor given the chance to start a new life.

Arrow after arrow flew, slamming into heads and chests, mothers and grandmothers falling around their wailing offspring.

314 | ELLA FIELDS

I fell, in both horror and grief, turning and flying fast toward those pens.

I didn't know what I would do, only that I couldn't continue to look for Dade while innocents were killed.

He'd killed plenty of innocents—all of the warriors who clawed at metal-protected bodies, snapping necks and limbs, had killed innocent people. And I knew, no matter how different the circumstances, that none of it was right.

All of it was wrong.

He knew that now. He'd learned. I had to believe that much at least. I had to believe that no matter what, he would've continued to right those wrongs.

And now he was being made a fool for doing the right thing.

I dropped and spiraled into the arm of an archer, knocking the bow from his hands before he saw me coming, and tumbled over the next. "What the—"

We both fell to the ground, feathers splaying, my head ringing against a metal breastplate, but I forced myself up and back into the sky before the cursing soldier could curl his hand all the way around my foot.

Flying toward the flames, I banked and scooped up a burning branch. My eyes closed against the smoke and the heat traveling down toward my beak. An arrow whizzed, narrowly missing my wing. Screams sounded as more archers knocked their bows, the branch burning closer and closer, giving away my presence in the night sky.

A wolf howled and broke into a run, shifting and then snatching a tin of kerosene from a soldier's hand.

And tore it open with his bare hands, spilling it over the grass in a semi-circle around the pen, between the occupants and the soldiers.

I dropped the branch, fire spreading in a climbing arc, the trapped females and their young running for the woods as the wolves clashed with the soldiers and forced them back, giving them time to flee.

I followed the villagers as they dispersed into the trees, my wings spreading as I circled a tree and hit the ground with a jarring thump.

I shifted back, coughing as smoke filled my lungs, and raced after the escaping children.

I wasn't sure what I could do. I just knew I had to make sure the soldiers who were now entering the woods didn't reach them—

I rounded a thick cluster of trees, dirt spraying beneath my bare feet as I skidded to a stop.

One by one, villagers shoved children through a hole beneath a tree.

The elves.

Turning in a circle, I discovered more and more of them were climbing from their homes and taking the young, some of the mothers and elders running on if they could not fit through the tunnels in the ground nor the small doorways hidden in trees and under rocks.

"Climb them," I hissed, some hearing and gazing behind them before scrambling up trunks and into the dark foliage above. I repeated myself, urging the breeze to carry my whisper to those out of earshot.

"You should go, princess," a graying elf said, gesturing with her walking stick toward the deeper woods. "Queen now, no?" A sad smile tipped up her cheek. "Run, for they will hunt you too if they see you."

She was right. She was right, but... *queen.*

In all the chaos since the glowing early evening ceremony that now felt as though it had taken place days ago rather than mere hours, I'd forgotten. I was no longer a princess.

I was a traitor who'd been, and would continue to be, used as a pawn to bring Dade Volkahn to his knees.

Rustling sounded, men shouting over the thunder of approaching horse hooves, and so I ran.

And then I flew once more, escaping the cover of the trees. In the sky, I found it no easier to breathe as I followed the fire-lit trail for a few miles and chased that familiar roar. A roar so violent and agonized it shook the trees, my bones, and the stars themselves.

Beyond the farmland, a circle of fire raged around the river separating it from the city. I continued toward it, toward that sound, followed that incessant tug at the chains that would forever bind me to him.

The carnage was so complete, limbs ripped and shredded, the dead tossed toward the river or staring at nothing while fire licked and ate their broken corpses. Wolves whined and howled in both rage and injury, soldiers, hundreds of them, falling by the dozen but unrelenting as they tried to push through the line of beasts that blocked their attempts to get to the city beyond.

Arrows flew, some swatted aside by giant paws, others missing their marks, others sinking into furred hides. Swords and daggers and axes and even pitchforks clashed as males and females fought in their Fae form, and others arrived from the city.

And across the river, surrounded by those who'd managed to break through the line of beasts, was the king.

The king and Prince Bron.

Dade held him with a blade to his throat, barking orders at Bron's soldiers that I could not hear. A circle of his fire flared—its harsher glow and heat separating it from that of the manmade flames everywhere else—and surrounded them both, keeping the soldiers from their prince.

Then his eyes flicked up, and there was no mistaking the flash of fear in them when I circled lower.

An unearthly whine erupted, the ground shaking. The line of beasts broke, soldiers swarming around the river toward the city.

Toward the king.

I flapped my wings harder, shooting to the sky while scanning the ground for a way in, for a way to get in and get him out. He couldn't win. Not this time. But that didn't mean I would allow him to die.

I flew some yards away from the swarm to the ground and shifted.

The smoke was dense, crawling everywhere and making it hard to see. So I didn't see him coming until he was already before me with his sword raised. "Stop," I warned the helmeted soldier. "I am Princess Opal of Sinshell. We are not enemies."

The man smiled. "You are of faerie blood, Princess." The smile dropped. "We will always be enemies."

He swung, and I ducked, rolling to the ground and smacking my cheek on a rock. I grabbed the rock, blood pooling in my mouth from a cut, and rolled again when his sword came down near my head.

Again and again, he struck, ensuring I could not get to my feet. I shifted, losing the rock and then shifting back in time to use his shock against him. The rock rose from the ground before I could bend for it, smacking into my palm and then into his head.

Blood spurted from his nose, through his fingers as he stumbled back and dropped his sword. "You fucking faerie bitch." I snatched the fallen sword, then lifted the armor of the large man and buried it in his gut as one of his friends raced toward us.

He gaped at his fallen comrade, then charged for me. I didn't bother trying to use my title this time. Not when the hatred in his green gaze burned hotter than any understanding they'd all reached with my mother.

Her words came back to me as I dodged and ran, turning when he least expected it to send him to the ground with a kick in the leg. Perhaps this was not about Dade and his crusade of revenge any longer.

I didn't have time to contemplate that further after slicing through the soldier's neck. I had to hurry before anyone else decided to wade through the smoke to find out who I was and what I was doing. I back-tracked to steal a small knife from the man's holster, then raced into the smoke and into the throng.

I nearly stumbled over a log when I realized what I'd just done.

I'd murdered two people. Two men who were probably going to kill me, but even so, I'd killed them and without hesitation.

I gritted my teeth against the surge of guilt, remembering those females who were left in pools of blood inside those pens, their families forced to run and leave them behind.

The first soldier didn't see me, his blade dancing toward a wolf's head then falling with his severed hand. He screamed, blood spraying the wolf's face as he fought off another assailant, and I was gripped by the hair.

On the ground, I wheezed, the air rushing from me too fast and returning too slow. My scalp and lungs burned, and I lifted the dagger in time to avoid a sword to the face, pushing with strength I didn't know I possessed and then rolling to slice at my attacker's ankle.

I rose as he fell and left him to bleed out on the grass before slamming into a boulder of a man and thrusting my dagger into his stomach. It clanged over metal, unheard to regular ears, and I launched to the side as his fist slammed into my eyebrow, his axe following and skidding over my shoulder.

I bit back a moan, searing heat entering my skin.

Iron. Their weapons were not only steel but manufactured to slow our healing and any chance of survival should they strike a vital organ.

Hissing, I ducked as his next blow came, and then I ran at his chest.

*Close combat. You stab instantly.*

Dade's voice was everywhere and nowhere as I charged, somehow managing to throw the giant of a man to the ground.

*If they're armored, find the gaps and use them.*

Wheezing and shocked, his hands lifted, but they were too slow to stop the blade from inching between his breastplate and helmet— to keep it from sliding into his throat.

I released the blade and rolled when I felt an advancing soldier behind me and rose with the dead human's sword to meet his. Steel clashed, his teeth bared as he pushed, then retreated and swung at my legs. I jumped back, then forward, nearly slamming into a furred body.

A brown wolf tore into the soldier's throat, then raced onto the next while his blood still spurted.

I did the same, cutting and dodging and earning myself another slug to the head and a sliced stomach. Then he was there before I could reach him, furious and evidently frightened. "You shouldn't be here."

"Where else should I be?"

"Where's your armor?" He threw a knife, hitting a man in the eye, then met mine as he screamed and fell. "You're not even wearing shoes."

"Where is your armor?" I fired back and dodged an arrow.

His throat bobbed, his face bloodied and blackened with soot, and his wedding attire in shreds. Deep gashes could be seen in his abdomen, blood still racing from them. He wasn't healing fast enough to withstand an assault of this magnitude—and the chances of surviving and eliminating the numbers of this army were already slim.

"Dade," I warned, and he turned away, taking the shield from the advancing soldier and slamming it into his face three times. He went down, his four companions surrounding Dade before he could move.

I'd barely broken into a run to help him when a male's voice shouted, "Get down."

A ball of fire arced over my head, barreling toward Dade. He ducked as two soldiers launched over him with their blades raised.

Panic scorched my throat, but then a knife pressed into it, and a familiar voice crooned, "Princess." I swallowed, the blade nicking my skin as I did, and was turned to face Prince Bron. "Or should I say, queen?"

A bandage was wrapped around his neck, as though Dade had tried to kill him when his army had rounded the river and he'd been overwhelmed.

"Do you intend to kill me?" I asked coolly. "I saved your rotten soul, helped your equally as rotten family, so that would make perfect fucking sense."

Bron winced. "Yes, it is all so terribly convoluted, isn't it?" He waded closer, fingers tipping up my chin to meet those brown eyes I'd once dared to consider handsome. They flicked back and forth between mine, assessing, unblinking, then he stepped back. "No, I don't think I shall, but I will use you."

I didn't need to ask what for, though I was about to anyway to give myself time.

"Release her, Bron."

My mother and Silver warped into the little circle he and his soldiers had made, and the former walked straight to me. "If there is so much as a drop of blood on her skin, I will peel yours from your flesh."

The soldier's hold on me weakened, but that was all I needed. I shifted, then took flight, all of them save for my mother, who cut down two of Bron's men, gazed up at me. One dived at her from behind, but though I wanted to turn back, I had to trust she could take care of herself.

Wolves were everywhere, but they were no match for the number of soldiers who continued to overrun and push them back. In a valley beneath the city, fires raging on behind the hundreds in battle, the king and some of his warriors fought back to back, one of them falling and Dade roaring for him to get up.

A sword entered the wolf's eye, and though I knew he longed to, the king could not break free of the crowd surrounding him in order to help one of his friends—the only family he had left.

This was a bloodbath that would only cease with the king's defeat.

Not even my mother, I noticed while craning my neck, could reason with the prince as the two of them barked at one another back in the small clearing of dead bodies.

Dade knew this, but I hoped he knew that even if he surrendered, the carnage would continue. That they would not stop.

That he could not stop.

There was no safe place, nowhere to land that would help me get to him, nowhere to—

Tiny balls, golden and aflame, launched from the city sky. I tucked my wings enough to fall, swooping low and almost getting tangled in an old oak. Then I saw them.

More elves, this time on the rooftops of city buildings, with catapults three times the size of them, likely dragged up there by the crimson Fae who were standing upon balconies, launching catapults and arrows of their own.

The fireballs hit their marks and did not bounce off them, but rather stuck to their targets as though spelled to land and destroy.

I met the ground atop the valley, hope infusing each lurching step as I broke into a run toward Dade and his assailants, and nearly laughed with a relief so heavy and wild that I couldn't keep from smiling.

Fire smacked into two of the soldiers battling with Dade, taking them to the ground where they rolled and screamed. One clawed at his chest as the fire ate away at his skin, then fell silent when it incinerated his heart, while the other bashed his flaming face into the grass before falling still.

Dade collapsed to his knees, bleeding everywhere but still fighting—still managing to kill another with a weak bout of fire blazing from his hand to the human's face while two more advanced on him.

The fire went out when its task was complete, smoke sizzling from the bodies into the cool night air. It had to be nearing dawn, which meant more help would hopefully arrive soon.

Maybe we could do this, stop this, if we kept working together.

Snatching up another forgotten sword, I hurried to Dade, running, racing against time, the buoyancy of hope helping me to ignore the pain in my stomach and the ache in my skull to leap over body after body. A fallen soldier reached for me, trying to trip me…

"Get up." The words carried across the valley, but on his knees, he couldn't stop it, fire sailing through the air and hitting not the soldiers with their swords meeting Dade's but the group fighting a small ways behind them. "Get up, get up, *get up.*"

One of those swords met his side as he sliced the arm holding the other, and then he fell forward. The remaining soldier kicked him in the gut twice, then forced him to his back.

I was close enough now to see that Dade's eyes were closed, but his weapons still twitched in his hand, lifted slightly, then fell. Fear struck me cold, weighing each step as I screamed his name, screamed for him to shift, but of course, he couldn't.

He couldn't shift, which meant… "*Dade,*" I screeched at the top of my lungs as that sword came down, poised to pierce through his chest.

Then he grabbed it.

His hand wrapped around the steel, and with a swiftness no one could have predicted, he pulled it and the soldier to the side. The man cursed, lurched, and fell over the king. They rolled down a small slope, and I raced after them, dodging a man with a mace who ran past me, wailing, his other hand on fire.

They came to a violent stop before a giant rock, and then I was taken to the ground, a fist in my shirt and a blade aimed at my nose.

My dagger was lost within the grass, as was my sword, but I gripped the soldier's wrist before my face and sent a wave of heat into my hands. It startled him enough for me to plunge my heated fingers into his eyes. They bulged, then darkened. He screamed, black flowers exploding from where his eyes had once been.

A growl, and then a wolf launched at my attacker, tumbling with him into the ground behind me with earthshaking force. A one-eyed midnight black wolf tore at the soldier's face, then leaped toward the king as I climbed to my feet.

Scythe didn't make it, an arrow hitting his side. He rolled, shifting back into his Fae form to pluck it free before engaging in hand-to-hand combat with a bleeding soldier who sprang up from the grass.

I blinked, my vision blurring. *Dade.* I walked on, breaking into a run when I heard it.

A snarl vicious enough to tear down the moon as another blade sank into Dade's side. He'd shifted. His white fur soaked in red and brown, too much for me to know whether it was his or someone else's blood.

Both, I acknowledged with a rapidly sinking heart as he was forced back to his haunches, that same soldier now dead next to him, but another having taken his place.

Bron laughed, the sound spurring me faster, then lunged forward, too fast for Dade to dodge as he shifted back from his wolf form. He missed his heart but hit his shoulder, the sword pushing right through flesh and tendon.

Dade roared, the agony within heightening my rage as I snatched a sword from a fallen soldier's open palm and circled behind Bron's back.

Too lost to his attempt at another killing blow, the prince paid me no mind.

My blade hit home, sliding into the back of his neck...

At the same time, his sword cut through Dade's chest.

They both collapsed, and I screamed, shoving the dead prince from Dade and stabbing him again in rage, ensuring he was as dead as dead could get. And then, with shaking hands, I turned back to my king.

To my mate.

A crack flooded my ears, a ravine opening and yawning wide inside me, filling and overflowing with blistering pain.

No. *No, no, no.*

"Dade," I said, brushing his hair away from his face. "Savage." I pushed at the gushing wound at his chest. Blood oozed between my fingers, so warm. Still warm. "Hey." I leaned over him, nudging my forehead into his. "Hang on." I sniffed. "Wait, okay? I'll get help. I'll get a healer."

Twisting away, I looked for one while knowing I'd find none. None that weren't already tied up helping others or dead. Though it was fading, the elves and citizens' assistance having helped to gain more of an upper hand, the battle raged on.

No one was coming.

I didn't care. I called for help, shouted for it until my voice grew hoarse, then gave my attention back to the king. "Open your eyes," I demanded through gritted teeth. "Right now."

Silence. So much silence when I needed the solid thud of his heart against my blood-soaked hands. But he couldn't.

He couldn't because I hadn't, and *we* hadn't had the time to... My eyes burned then flooded, that chasm inside me too large, too overpowering, too much to bear.

It singed each breath, eroded my bones, and sliced at my skin.

"I forgive you," I sobbed, the words robbed from my soul, my heart, fracturing into the air warmed by his blood. It was all over me, slippery, so much of it, *shit...*

My fingers gripped the collar of his tunic, so wet with his blood, and I shook him with every ounce of strength I did not possess. "Please, Dade. Come back. Come back, come back, come back. I forgive you." I fell over his wounds as though I could stem them all if only I could cover them…

"I forgive you," I yelled, the words echoing into eternity, useless, meaningless now that he was no longer.

*No,* no. I grabbed at his cheeks, fingers desperate for his rumbling laughter beneath me, that smile. What I wouldn't give to see it, to hear it in his voice. The words trembled out of me, over and over until I couldn't breathe unless I said them to his mouth.

I kissed him. Gently, reverently, murmuring pleads trapped upon still lips. "I forgive you, okay? I forgive you, you vile, wonderful, merciless, incredible creature. I fucking forgive you." I sniffed. "Okay, Daden? I forgive you."

Footsteps crunched but never neared. I cared nothing for them, for whatever battle still raged around us. If he was gone, I wouldn't leave. I would stay.

I would stay wherever he was.

More wet washed over my cheeks, the salty taste of tears mingling with the coppery tang of blood.

"Opal," a male's voice said. Scythe maybe. I didn't know. It didn't matter. Nothing mattered.

He came closer, and I rose, hands slipping in the muddied and bloodied grass either side of Dade's head, to gnash my teeth.

He paused, then raised his hands, and though I warned him not to, the one-eyed warrior still pressed forward.

A stillness roared through me, so complete, so violent in its silence that he finally retreated—bounced back.

When he tried again, his mouth fell open, his hand hitting a wall he could not see. He wouldn't be coming any closer.

Relieved, I turned back to Dade, sniffing as I whispered, "I love you, too." I laughed then, brushing dirt and blood from his cheek. "Though I suspect you already knew that. But you," my lips wobbled, my body trembled with a regret so huge, I couldn't breathe as I pushed out, "you left before I could tell you that I forgive you. So come back."

"Stars," I heard someone say.

I smoothed his hair, insisting, "You have to come back."

"What the fuck?" came another.

"Opal," my mother called, breathless. "Opal, stop." Her rapid footsteps came closer, then halted as they reached that invisible barrier. She cursed, then softened her voice. I didn't look. I wouldn't move.

"Listen to me," she urged. "I know, believe me I know how much it hurts, how much it feels like the end, but you must stop."

*The stars made you just for me.*

I didn't know what she was talking about, and I didn't care. I was certain I would care about nothing for a long, long time.

*I do love you, Opal Gracewood.*

"She's burning, fuck. *Brim*," I heard Scythe roar. "Is Fang here yet? Someone get him and a damned healer."

"No," I heard Silver snap. "You will do nothing."

Then there was only light.

It surrounded me and my king—untouchable, impenetrable, and blinding. It tickled my skin, hummed in a comforting rhythm that matched my slow-beating heart.

Tears raced anew as I shielded Dade, leaking onto his face, dripping to the dirt. That ravine had finally broken, the roiling current too strong to be contained. It crashed through me.

It exploded.

"Not burning," my mother said, and it sounded as though she were talking inside a deep cave, her voice and others growing more and more muted. "She's glowing."

Strength evaded me with each ragged breath, and I curled over Dade, too weak to move even if I'd wanted to. I didn't. I knew I would eventually have to, but I couldn't fathom it. Not yet.

"Never," I croaked, my nose skimming over the stubble on his jaw, inhaling the faint cedar and smoky scent in his neck.

A thud sounded, something crawling beneath my arm.

I startled, rising but only to my elbow, everything too dark, too bright, too much effort—just a dream.

He groaned, and I dragged my eyes from his chest, from the blood that'd stopped flowing under my arm, from the skin that had begun to re-stitch. "Dade," I gasped, forcing heavy eyes to his face.

"Swan." His lips smacked together. He swallowed, groaned again, then cursed. "I heard you, and I . . ." he coughed out, voice hoarse, "I will hold you to that. To all of it."

I smiled, breath gone and long forgotten as relief slammed into me. I smiled, reaching for that face, my hand too heavy, flopping to his shoulder instead.

I smiled, and then everything went dark as I let myself fall inside the dream.

# THIRTY-THREE

*Opal*

**F**EATHERLIGHT, FINGERS DANCED ACROSS MY BROW, smoothing back my hair, gliding down and over my cheek.

I curled closer to that touch, knowing whose it was, wanting more—needing more.

Warmth engulfed me, a strong arm at my back pulling me into a firm chest. When I woke, he was still there, waiting, eyes bruised but faint, sleep lining his mouth and lingering upon his mussed hair.

My relief was instant, profound, as I reached for that face, that hair, then paused when my arm slid over something rough on his chest. A bandage. I blinked hard, bloodstained memories arising.

The battle.

Reading my panic, Dade cupped my cheek, his voice gentle but not reassuring. "It's over."

But for how long, I wondered, and knew he was aware by the dimming of his blue eyes. "We worry about that later."

Later. A bland word had never sounded so sweet. A promise I'd taken for granted my entire life.

Looking into those eyes, feeling his touch, so real, so warm, so blessedly *alive* upon my skin… "Dade—"

The doors crashed open, and I twisted to them with a wince.

328 | ELLA FIELDS

"Opal," my mother cried, hurrying into the king's chambers as though she had every right. "Stars." Stopping beside the bed, she lowered and reached for me, stole me from the king and hauled my body to hers. "It's been days," she whispered in strangled explanation.

"How many?" I mumbled against her sweet-scented shoulder.

Her hand rubbed down my back, fingers carefully untangling some of my hair. "Four. I thought, I feared..." She pushed me away and clutched my shoulders, tears cloaking her eyes. "You've never done that before."

The glowing. The ancient healing that, up until now, many had thought only a rumor spun into fiction with the black swan.

"It has been said that such a thing has ended your ancestor's existence," she whispered. "They would fall just like the honey bee after using all of themselves."

"One of them," Dade supplied curtly, as though annoyed she was scaring me. "One of them passed on."

*Father knew I could do that*, I didn't dare say, as it no doubt began to dawn for her too. The way he would evade me and make plans for me as though I were a waiting bomb, the nickname...

I swallowed thickly, not remembering much, but enough of the tingling desperation that had radiated from me, the flood from that broken organ inside me, to know I never wanted to do so again.

My mother eyed Dade distastefully. "And how would you know?"

I didn't need to look at the king to know he was smiling. That dry humor soaked his voice. "I know a great deal of things I'll wager you wish I did not."

Mother's eyes narrowed, then she looked back at me and brushed her hands down my cheeks. "Let's get you cleaned up." A quick glare at the king as she muttered, "You may leave."

He did no such thing as the last creature I expected to see entered the room with a small pile of cloths and a clean nightgown.

Linka. Gwenn followed with a smile and pail of warm, perfumed water.

"Is there something wrong with your hearing?" My mother stood and tugged the bedding from my body.

I wanted the warmth back but refrained from reaching for it when Dade said, "I'm sorry, what did you say?"

I snorted and turned to smack him, then remembered his wound and stopped.

He caught my hand on the bed, bringing it to his mouth. Endless turquoise stole my eyes, my breath, the beating of my heart as those silken lips glossed over each scratched knuckle.

My stomach flipped and heated, the sensation of wildfire spreading throughout each limb too fast to stop. Still, I mouthed to him, "Go, please."

His nostrils flared with displeasure, then his eyes grew and hooded as he no doubt scented something else.

I flushed and looked down at the crumpled bedding as he chuckled and rose. "Fine. I'll go." Rounding the huge bed, my mother chattering away with the pixies in hushed tones, he then smirked and readjusted the band of his low-hanging pants at his toned waist. "After I've washed my mate."

The pixies froze, stilling entirely.

My mother's spine turned to steel. "You will do no such thing."

"I'm sure it will boil your blood to know that I've done far wonderfully worse."

"Dade," I hissed, embarrassment scoring through me.

He ignored me as though he hadn't said anything incredibly untoward. I wondered if perhaps he wasn't aware it was. Until now, my glare said when he glanced my way.

He winced a little, but my mother's fuse had been lit, and she was three seconds away from blowing. "You repulsive beast, how dare you—"

Linka surprised us all by stepping between them and lifting her hands. "Both of you, out."

The king and my mother sent withering looks her way. I wanted to clap when she did not cower. "The princess has only just woken up. She does not need the stress of your bickering, nor does she need either of you present for a task I've been employed to do."

Dade's brows rose, his smile twitching with both anger and humor. "Queen. She is the queen of Vordane."

My mother opened her mouth, but Gwenn dipped low before her, and said, "Majesty, Merelda and I were wondering if you could assist us with the menu now that Opal is awake?" Linking her arm through hers, she began to lead my shocked mother out of the doors, her voice trailing after them.

Linka gave Dade an impatient look.

He squinted, eyeing her a moment, then moved back to the bed. I was torn between pulling him over me and reprimanding him for his disobedience, but then he kissed me. Soft and breathing me in, his lips lingered upon my forehead, and before I could reach for him, he was sauntering through the closing doors.

Linka busied herself with soaking some cloths, then gestured for my hand. Removing my unfocused gaze from the doors, I gave it to her, her touch cool and reassuring. "He worships you."

I wasn't sure what to say, so I said nothing as she squeezed out a cloth and laid it over the rim of the pail upon the floor. She helped me stand, and though my knees quaked, each step was a little easier as we headed to the table between the windows. The heavy black drapes were half-drawn, remnants of daylight splashing in slivers across the room.

I carefully lowered my stiff limbs to the chair and unbuttoned my nightgown. "Never," she said, as though worried someone might overhear. It would not surprise me if Dade was right outside the doors. "Never have I seen a male so frightened, so ready to claw at anyone who so much as neared these rooms."

I contained a snort. "I'm surprised he was a male and not his beast."

"Oh, he was," she laughed, gathering my hair from my neck to begin washing me. "For the first three days. After that, your mother demanded he shift back or she'd take you home." Another soft laugh, the warm cloth against my skin so welcomed that I nearly purred. "So, of course he shifted back in a rage just to argue with her."

A knot lodged in my throat as I imagined it, the two of them at odds, as they would be forevermore, yet... perhaps that would not be so bad.

"Then," Linka went on, offering the cloth for me to wipe my face. "Your breathing changed, as though you'd left the healing dark and had entered the realm of dreams, and I wondered if he would allow the tears in his eyes to fall."

I handed her back the cloth, gazing up at her own wet eyes in question.

"I'm sorry," she finally said, and lowered to her knees. "I didn't understand how..." her head shook, lips wobbling. "How anyone could love a creature, a monster like him, until I saw the way he loved you."

My heart softened, warmed, and I clasped her hand in mine over my knees. "It's okay. If it helps, I tried not to."

She laughed then, loud and wet, and I pulled her to me, hugging her tight. "He wouldn't like it," she whispered to my stomach. "Of course, he wouldn't. But he would love that you are happy."

A tear slipped down my cheek, and a buzzing drew my gaze to the window. "I know." A bee hovered and then continued on.

Some minutes later, Linka filling me in on how what remained of our army had come to help close out the battle—which did not officially end until an entire day after Dade and I had fallen and were taken to the Keep—there was a knock on the doors.

"Your king is likely to break down the doors."

Another followed Linka's words. A warning veiled as a request.

He was coming in any second now.

I smiled, shifting my arms into the straps of the clean blue nightgown. "Better let him in."

As though he'd heard, the doors opened, and Linka bowed before hurrying out with the pail and cloths in hand.

The doors closed after her, and I heard a click. "Did you just lock my mother out?"

"Of course," he said, prowling toward me with a grace that defied his injuries. Even with a bandage around his torso, his skin and muscles gleamed—radiant in the remaining sunlight that streaked across the room as though in search of him.

Taking my hands, he helped me to my feet, then lowered the nightgown with two careful tugs and shifted it into place. The brushing of his roughened fingers over my skin, the heat of him at my back, circling and caging me, had me nearly pleading for him to rip it off.

His mouth hovered over my shoulder, lips pressing soft. "Later."

"That word again," I said without meaning to.

He hummed as though understanding, then directed me back to the bed with a hand at my waist. As I slid onto the mattress, and he pulled the blankets over my bare legs, guilt overran me. "Dade, I need to apologize," I started, steady yet my breath quaked. "What I said to you outside that shop…"

"It was true, was it not?" He gestured for me to lie down.

I leaned back on my elbows instead, my neck cricking so I could read his tight expression. "Yes, but you need to understand that—"

"Stop," he said, and a rough exhale left him as he scrubbed his hands over his face, then carefully folded his large frame onto the bed beside my knees. "You think I wasn't aware that there were times you were toying with me?" I blinked, falling onto the pillows. "Your every deception was known and welcomed if it brought you closer to being where I needed you." His mouth curved. "Completely and irrevocably mine."

Torn between wanting to smother him with the pillow and with kisses, I just laid there, speechless.

"You love me." His lips curled higher, exposing a dimple and a flash of teeth.

I melted even while trying to resist doing so. "You forced my hand."

"You forgive me, and you love me."

"Again, you gave me no choice," I rasped, my smile shaking. "There was no other choice."

He sprawled himself beside me, head propped on his hand and that maddening grin still in place. "You love me."

I absorbed that face, the golden brows residing over eyes that contained an ocean reflected sky, and then that bandaged chest. A chest that contained a rapidly increasing heartbeat. A heart. A heart and soul that had been slow to warm, to learn, and to love. Absorbing everything, I declared vehemently, "Yes, I love you."

The king of wolves spread his lips into a smile so dazzling, so sincere, the largest I'd ever seen him wear, that I found myself saying so again just to keep it there. "I am in complete, utterly stupid love with you, Daden Volkahn."

That smile stretched, then fell a little with a breathy laugh. "I suppose I did force you." He frowned then, but it didn't detract from the magic in his gaze. Happiness.

Unfettered, undiluted, unprecedented happiness.

I gestured for him to move closer so I could smooth the creases from between his brows. His eyes shuttered. "You forced me, yes, but only by showing me who you truly are," I whispered, "who you could have always been, and who you are capable of becoming."

Taking my hand, he brought it to his mouth, lips brushing over my skin. "You showed me that." Another dazzling smile. "So I suppose it is *you* who forced *me*, my lovely swan."

I laughed, rolling into his arms. He caught me, held me close, fingers rubbing over my back, into my hair, and his mouth upon my forehead.

Within minutes, I drifted back to sleep, lulled by the comforting cadence of the beat within the unearthed heart of my sweet, savage king.

# EPILOGUE

*Three weeks later...*

## Dade

Fang's fist slammed onto the table, his annoyance arousing more of my own. "What part of not good enough don't you fucking comprehend?"

I wanted out of this fucking room and inside my mate. We'd made plans.

Well, I'd made plans for us, but I was certain she wouldn't mind.

Unperturbed by Fang's outburst, Scythe rubbed his chin and threw his knee over his leg. "I don't know what you want me to say. The captive won't talk."

We'd kept a collection of soldiers from the war waged by the humans. A war, we'd come to learn, that had indeed come about with the help of Sinshell. My brothers, though not thrilled about it, had agreed with me when I'd stated our time tormenting them was done—despite their duped plans of revenge.

For they had been duped, and in a huge way. Not only was my swan taken and forced to weave gold for the cretins under the guise of saving her family, but her mother was fooled into thinking those royal shits would actually lend them a helping hand in defeating me.

No. Their mission had been simple if planned right. A death sentence for all if not.

Now, they were curiously silent. What remained of their fleeing forces gone. Either they'd traveled back to Errin to heal and recoup before striking again, or they'd sailed across the Night Sea to return to their own countries.

Regardless, there was a good chance they'd be back.

Not only was that confirmed with the death of Prince Bron, and the volume of retreating numbers, but we'd also gleaned as much from our captives. A guard rotation was now enforced upon the Royal Cove, and more spies under my employ to keep tabs on the nobility, trade, and seas.

"Why?" Opal spoke up then, and Scythe seemed to startle as though remembering we now had a female in our presence. Neither he nor Fang were impressed when I'd decided to include my swan in our meetings as of last week, but the shock quickly wore off, and so did their reluctance to share important intel.

Especially after I'd threatened to kick them both out and leave the work of war and rebuilding to my mate and me.

My uncle was still alive. Unfortunately. He'd been given a promotion, too.

He now headed one of our new projects—the repair and restoration of Sinshell. I'd expected him to protest, but he'd simply nodded and vomited many thanks at mine and Opal's feet before Nikaya had swept in with a grim look of determination. The two had left a week ago, Sinshell's queen agreeing with what seemed a perverse pleasure to oversee the rebuilding of the fractured parts of her kingdom.

Stars, a fate worse than death if you asked me.

Yet I would soon be joining them. In a village far from where either of them would be working, thank you very much.

Opal had protested upon finding out, her worry over my presence so close to the border of Errin clipping each word as she'd suggested we both focus on rebuilding the ruined towns and villages here in Vordane.

It'd taken one ravishing kiss for her to remember who the fuck I was.

A creature not so easily bested—unless happened upon by a black swan.

So it took a night, but remember she most certainly did.

Scythe stared at my mate, and I bristled at the way he kept her waiting. Sighing, he drawled, "What do you mean, *why*? If I knew, I'd tell you," he added dryly, "my queen."

Opal smirked. "No, I'm referring to the humans overall. Why such large numbers? Why the sudden interest in ridding us from Nodoya?" Fang's head tilted as he watched her, listening carefully. "They've never tried such a thing before because they know they cannot eradicate us, kill enough of us to seize the continent."

"Swan, I'm certain that smug as fuck prince assumed he could but," I lifted a finger, feeling as though we were trying to catch something that kept evading us, "the armies from across the sea do not add up. More of our kind live on some of those continents…"

"Greed," supplied Scythe. "Gold is gold, and we've all been to battle for far less."

Opal's eyes narrowed, and I studied her, then sighed. "Ponder that. We'll reconvene in two mornings." I stood from the table before anyone could protest, and held my hand out for Opal's.

She eyed the map, the locations of places we'd brutalized in Sinshell now marked for different reasons, then looked at Scythe. "May I talk to her?" she asked, referring to a captive he'd taken upon himself to keep imprisoned in his home.

Scythe was halfway out the door when he grunted, "No, you may not." I snarled, and he halted, turning back with a sigh. "Why?"

Opal slid her hand in mine, saying softly but firmly, "Perhaps another female would encourage her to talk."

"A gentler approach, you mean?" He laughed through the words. "No, it does not care for such things as gentle." He sketched a half-hearted bow. "Trust and excuse me."

Fang watched him disappear into the dark hall, his lips rolling between his teeth, then followed.

"I'll speak to him later," I said between my teeth. The asshole was treading water with this captive situation, and it was beginning to really piss me off.

"No," Opal said, leading me out the door. "Don't meddle. I'll try again next time."

"You are a queen," I reminded her, something I so often had to do. "You may do as you wish, and he knows it." I gave her my best grin. "We'll go visit this captive tomorrow."

Opal smiled, her eyes laughing, and leaned into my side as we took the stairs that would lead us from the underbelly of the Keep. "No, you can't abuse his trust."

Prisoners moaned, cried, and shouted in the dungeon. It was spelled so no one could hear. No one save for the wolves.

She was right. A creature with a history such as Scythe's... it wouldn't matter that I was his king. His loyalty to me would be decimated if I disrespected him in that way.

Pushing thoughts of war, repairs, my shithead friends, and a myriad of other issues from my mind, I led Opal to my rooms. Well, our rooms. She'd been staying with me since she'd woken up after the attack on Vordane. I'd refused to let her leave my sight for days, and she seemed happiest when I did not stray from hers.

She passed me a confused glance when I tugged her from the doors and to the door of her old quarters.

I bit back a shit-eating grin as the wood swung open to reveal her new perfumery slash mending room slash library.

Upon one row of floor-to-ceiling white shelves, the titles I'd often seen her reread, and others I thought were of the same vein enough that she'd like them too, were tucked neatly. There were some empty rows for her to add to the collection as she saw fit. On the next shelf over sat glass bottles, vials, bowls filled with mismatched corks, ribbon, twine, differing oils, salts, and mixing pots.

In the corners of the room were rolls of fabrics upon stands, and on the shelves beside them, more materials folded and stacked. The afternoon sun splashed over them and Opal's roaming fingers as they swayed over it all with a reverence I grew hard and nearly jealous from.

And I would've been, if she didn't treat me in the same manner. She touched me as if I were the finest project she'd ever created, as if she couldn't believe I was tangible—that all of this was real.

I'd done plenty of hideous things in my life, yet I would never know it from the way she adored me. And though a better male might, I lost no time lamenting how undeserving I was. She was mine, and I would rather rot than waste time not enjoying all I'd been blessed with.

I stepped back against the closed door as she took everything in, heading from one shelf to another, fingers dancing but not touching, fluttering to her mouth and then to her chest. She twirled to the space where the bed used to be. Now, there was a large plush red and gold carpet beneath a long white desk.

Quills, inkpots, and parchment sat in tidy piles in the corners, and a large chair fashioned from a rich blue velvet with the help of Olivianna awaited her perfect backside. My swan didn't sit. She continued to float around the space, the beaded hem of her bronze dress knocking into the table legs and dragging over the carpet.

I couldn't wait to rid it from her body, knowing there'd be nothing but bare, wet flesh awaiting me beneath.

Restraining the need to take and bend her over that table, I left her to fuss and twirl about the room and plucked a bottle of rosemary oil from the shelf. I'd barely uncorked it before stuffing the cork back in place and crinkling my nose.

"Nicely done, savage."

I could do without her experimenting with that one. "Whatever do you mean?"

Opal drifted to me, taking the oil from my hand and putting it back upon its wooden holder on the shelf. "You know," she leaned into me, looping her arms behind my back and laying her chin upon my chest, "you could have just asked me."

I wiped my curious expression, feigned confusion with a tilt of my head. "Ask you what?"

"To share your rooms with you," she said flatly.

"Oh." I smacked my lips together and pushed out a rough breath. "Well, this is rather awkward. You see, I've had your things taken to a smaller room on the main floor."

Her arms slackened, as did the pointed expression upon her flushing face.

"My lovely, breathtaking swan," I purred, hands rising to cup her cheeks, "Will you miss being so close to me?"

She laughed, the sound a low, warm nectar bathed beneath the sunlight. "I suppose being closer to the kitchens, the library. . ."

I trapped a vibrating grumble behind my teeth, and she laughed harder, squeezing my hands over her cheeks and rising onto her bare toes. "Take me to these new rooms of mine."

Her heart hitched as I nipped the tip of her tiny nose, then collected her into my arms. "Gladly."

We'd barely made it through the adjoining door that entered that of our dressing room when she noticed her clothing taking up a good portion of the large space. With a laugh, she twisted in my arms for her legs to wind around me, arms tight around my neck. "Thank you," she breathed between kisses to my throat, my chin, and I stole her lips before they could reach my mouth.

She accepted my tongue with a greed that matched my own— rough, hot, and urgent. Her dress lifted from her body as I lowered her to the ground before the end of the bed, and I growled with approval at what stood before me.

Naked perfection.

After shedding my clothing, the scent of her desire permeating the air, her lips between her teeth as she watched me, I then picked her back up and fell over her on the bed. "I hope you're hungry because I've been starving all stars-damned day."

"We can go longer than six hours without fucking," Opal said, yet moaned and pressed into my fingers when they crawled between her legs.

"This says otherwise." I thrust a finger inside her, swallowed her mewl, and then demanded, "Say fucking again."

"Fucking," she echoed, a dancing gleam in her eyes.

I circled her clit as a reward, watched those lashes flutter and her arms fall to the bed as liquid heat sped through her. "Say I want you to fuck me morning, noon, and night."

A breathy laugh left her, followed by another moan. "I want you to fuck me right now."

I pursed my lips, even as my cock lurched and dug into her stomach. "That wasn't what I said." Trailing my fingers up her body, decorating her skin with her glistening want, I licked her essence from them and then rubbed her bottom lip. "Open."

She did, sucking herself from my fingers, those damned eyes never leaving mine. Her teeth gently scraped as they slowly left her mouth. I shivered violently. Before I could return them to her cunt, she stole my wrist and pushed one back in, writhing beneath me.

And I cracked.

She smiled when I cursed and readied myself to ram inside her. Our mouths fused, and we moaned together as I plunged deep and she hooked her thighs higher up my back. I circled my hips, my tongue in her mouth, then dragged her lip into mine with my teeth. "Wicked, disobedient bird."

She laughed through a moan and gripped my hips with her thighs. "Would you have me any other way?"

"Never," I grunted, thrusting deep and nibbling down her chin to her neck. Her body stiffened, then uncoiled beneath me, trembling when I hit that spot inside her. "There," I rasped, and bit the smooth curve between her shoulder and neck, moving with slow yet sharp precision. "Melt for me, swan."

Her nails scored into my back. I didn't let up, and she ruptured within seconds, her low cries and moans music to my fucking ears.

She squeezed me so tight, so good, I gritted my teeth and fought the urge to release with her and made myself wait.

I wasn't anywhere near being done with her yet.

Light as misted air, her fingers trailed up my arms, each muscle quivering, the fists by her head clenching harder. "Forevermore," she said to my shoulder, and I lifted my lips from her reddened skin.

Golden affection, the likes of which had taken me time to absorb, to realize what it was that shined in her eyes when she gazed at me like that, sank velvet talons inside my chest. "I want you at every meal, in the training yard, the woods, the kitchens, the bathing room, the gardens, annoying me while I'm reading..." she grinned when I scowled. "I don't want you morning, noon, and night. I want you"—a finger stroked down my cheek—"everywhere and always. All of you, forevermore."

A verbal promise unlike any she'd declared to me yet. A permanent embedment that clawed so deep, I nearly exploded inside her as a storm swarmed inside my chest and threatened to erupt from my eyes.

I lowered my head. "Fuck, sunshine."

She plucked it back up. "I mean it," she vowed, pressing my nose into hers, her eyes refusing to let go of mine. "I swear it."

I blinked back the warmth in my eyes and grew dizzy with all she was, all I'd found, all I now couldn't breathe without. "You were right," I said, and kissed her nose. "You were right to think I didn't have a heart. I didn't."

My queen's lips parted, but I kissed them and whispered, "It arrived when I found you. You are the beat within my chest, the heart I never knew I needed."

Tears glossed her eyes, and I kissed each one, then returned to her mouth. Our bodies moved, sliding and pushing. Our heartbeats thundered and crashed before we began anew with her climbing atop me.

And I vowed, with every caress and murmured affection, that no matter how many times the sun went down, I would never lose my light.

NEVER MISS A THING!

Follow on Instagram
www.instagram.com/ellafieldsauthor

Website
www.ellafields.net

# ALSO BY
# ELLA FIELDS

FANTASY:

*A King So Cold*

*The Stray Prince*

STANDALONES:

*Bloodstained Beauty*

*Serenading Heartbreak*

*Frayed Silk*

*Cyanide*

*Corrode*

*Evil Love*

GRAY SPRINGS UNIVERSITY:

*Suddenly Forbidden*

*Bittersweet Always*

*Pretty Venom*

MAGNOLIA COVE:

*Kiss and Break Up*

*Forever and Never*

*Hearts and Thorns*

Made in the USA
Monee, IL
20 July 2021

086cb972-b085-4b07-87ab-eede25a3a4ecR01